EXQUISITE DANGER

"Tai-ling," Harley said, "I want you. You know that. Please, we may have only a few hours together. I can't leave Shanghai without just once holding you in my arms."

This was the ride that he had dreamed of on their first day together. As the taxi honked its way through frenetic traffic, their hands clenched tight, sealed together with sweat. The furtive climbing of dark stairs and the rooms just as he had envisioned them. The smells of musk and incense and teak and fresh oranges. The thin chitter of glass bead upon glass bead.

She turned to him in the artificial twilight of the shuttered room and ripped away her cotton clothes with an awful intensity. She wanted him as much, he realized, as he desired her. Under their passion, he sensed the beginnings of an emotion far more profound. "I . . . I love you!"

Sweating, relaxed, physically happy, if emotionally still needy, he began to think of romantic words, of other, slower ways of making love; to plan the rest of the afternoon and how he would make *her* happy, when, with a clatter, the glass beads grated open. With a cowardice that until now he had not known he possessed, Harley buried his flushed face in the girl's neck.

"Who are you?" a terrible voice shouted. "What is this? By God, I'll . . ."

Harley rolled off the girl stark-naked and stood up to face . . .

"You!" his father exclaimed.

110 SHANGHAI ROAD

"A CRACKING GOOD STORY SET AGAINST THE TU-MULT OF 20TH-CENTURY CHINESE HISTORY."
—*Minneapolis Star and Tribune*

About the Author

MONICA HIGHLAND was born and raised in Shanghai. She is a Rhodes scholar, holds a Ph.D. from UCLA, and divides her time among the study of demotic Greek, Mexican dance, and the Cantos of Ezra Pound. She is a connoisseur of diamonds and champagne.

Monica Highland

110
SHANGHAI
ROAD

BANTAM BOOKS
TORONTO · NEW YORK · LONDON · SYDNEY · AUCKLAND

*This low-priced Bantam Book
has been completely reset in a type face
designed for easy reading, and was printed
from new plates. It contains the complete
text of the original hard-cover edition.*
NOT ONE WORD HAS BEEN OMITTED.

110 SHANGHAI ROAD

*A Bantam Book / published by arrangement with
McGraw-Hill Book Co.*

PRINTING HISTORY
*McGraw-Hill edition published July 1986
Bantam edition / August 1987*

ISBN 0-553-26572-5

Published simultaneously in the United States and Canada

PRINTED IN THE UNITED STATES OF AMERICA

O   0 9 8 7 6 5 4 3 2 1

For
Richard Becker Kendall
with affection, esteem, and love

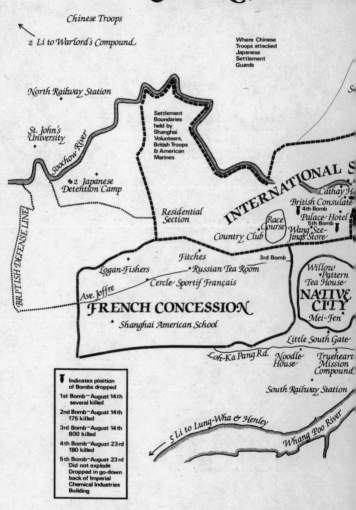

SHANGHAI U...

Chinese Troops

2 Li to Warlord's Compound

Where Chinese
Troops attacked
Japanese
Settlement
Guards

North Railway Station

Settlement
Boundaries
held by
Shanghai
Volunteers,
British Troops
& American
Marines

*St. John's
University*

Soochow River

*2 Japanese
Detention Camp*

INTERNATIONAL S

Cathay H...
British Consulate
4th Bomb
Palace Hotel
5th Bomb
Wang Sze-
Jing's Store

*Residential
Section*

Race
Course

Country Club

BRITISH DEFENSE LINE

Fitches
Russian Tea Room
Cercle Sportif Français

3rd Bomb

Willow
Pattern
Tea House

NATIVE
CITY

Mei-Fen

Logan-Fishers

Ave. Joffre

FRENCH CONCESSION

Shanghai American School

Little South Gate

Loh-Ka Pang Rd.

Noodle
House

Trueheart
Mission
Compound

South Railway Station

5 Li to Lung-Wha & Henley

Whang Poo River

Indicates position
of Bombs dropped

1st Bomb~August 14th
several killed

2nd Bomb~August 14th
175 killed

3rd Bomb~August 14th
800 killed

4th Bomb~August 23rd
180 killed

5th Bomb~August 23rd
Did not explode
Dropped in go-down
back of Imperial
Chemical Industries
Building

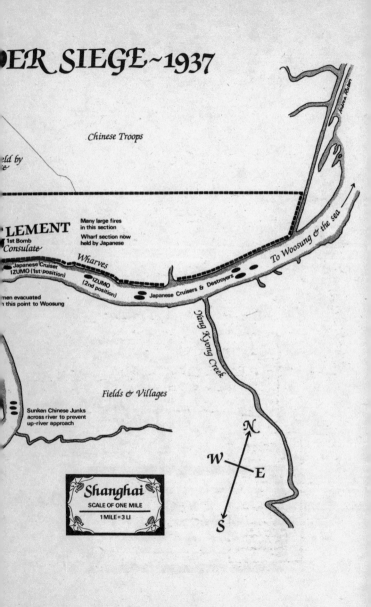

DER SIEGE ~ 1937

Chinese Troops

...eld by
...e

...LEMENT

1st Bomb
Consulate

Many large fires
in this section

Wharf section now
held by Japanese

Wharves

Japanese Cruiser
IZUMO (1st position)

IZUMO
(2nd position)

Japanese Cruisers & Destroyers

...men evacuated
...m this point to Woosung

To Woosung & the sea

Fields & Villages

Yang Kyong Creek

Sunken Chinese Junks
across river to prevent
up-river approach

N

W   E

S

Shanghai

SCALE OF ONE MILE

1 MILE = 3 LI

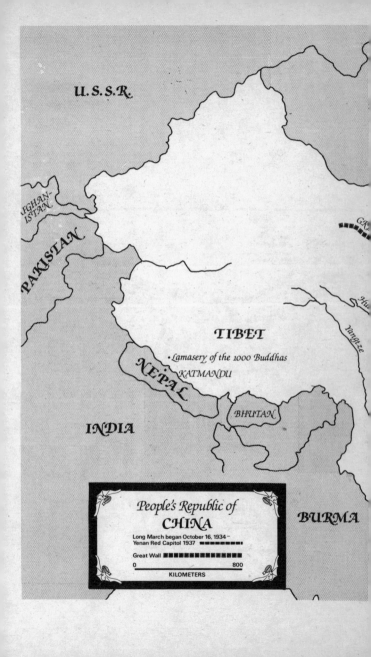

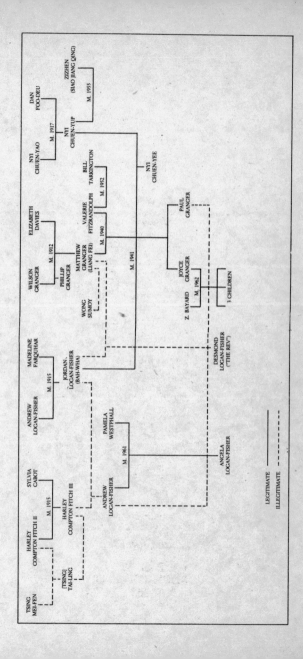

Contents

xi

110 SHANGHAI ROAD

Prologue

RANSOM
1926

"Little Master, we are honored to carry you, instead of that lump of white fat with the yellow hair."

Matthew Granger answered, doing his best to adapt to the local Chinese dialect, "Are you sure you aren't saying that just because I'm easier to carry?"

One of the coolies snickered, his breath steaming in the chill mountain air. "It is true, the Little Master weighs no more than a praying mantis. But his ready wit and his knowledge of our language give him the weight of a mandarin of high rank."

Harley Fitch III, in the chair behind Matthew's, called out, "What are you gabbling over, Granger, in that stupid language? Are these boys trying to cheat us? Tell them I won't stand for it!" The bombastic tone, coming from a ten-year-old, sounded ludicrous, and the coolies reacted intuitively to the arrogance.

"What is the white slug saying?"

The boy in the leading chair, his wiry frame bundled up against the cold, his spectacles catching the winter sunlight, clasped his gloved hands together and called out pleasantly, "He says that you smell. He says the smell is much like that of a rat smothered in straw matting and left for six weeks."

The coolies carrying Harley's chair, without missing a step, swung him, jerking him abruptly from side to side.

"Stop that! Stop that at once! My father is an important man! Granger, tell them right now!"

3

Matthew surrendered himself to the pleasure, the rhythmic motion, of being expertly carried. He felt weightless, suspended between two worlds. But he answered, using the sharp tongue that already had become his chief weapon, "Don't think your father runs everything, Harley! They wouldn't care even if they *had* heard about him. And don't think you can bully the coolies and get away with it. Remember, we're not in school anymore."

"Oh, shut up!"

"What does he say now?" one of the coolies asked.

"He says his father is important."

A coolie who had not spoken before snorted. "How could *that* be? His father must surely look as hideous as he, repulsive to gaze upon, just now emerging from the lower world, like all foreigners."

"Take care that you don't hurt my feelings," Matthew Granger said. "I, too, am a foreigner."

"Perhaps," the coolie said. "But you do speak our language, and you do not look too much like one."

"I have always wished," Matthew said, serious now, "that my hair was really black, like a true son of Han's."

"Well spoken."

It was ten o'clock in the morning. Matthrew Granger and Harley Compton Fitch III were on the first leg of their trip home from the Kuling American School—three days' journey up the Yangtze, high in the Lushan Mountains—to spend Christmas in Shanghai with their respective families.

At the moment, the bearers carried them up through the snow-covered slopes of the Kuling Valley to the small Chinese resort village where the trail started down the mountain. The summer cottages were closed, but the Fairy Glen Hotel was open year-round. Here, just two months earlier, Matthew's Boy Scout cub patrol had followed their scoutmaster to see if they could catch a glimpse of the new Chinese leader, Chiang Kai-shek, resting at the hotel for a few days during his northward march. Remembering this, Matthew shouted back to Harley, "You buggers didn't get to see the Generalissimo, did you?"

"So what! We were practicing for the soccer tournament. And who wants to see another shaved-head Chinaman anyway?"

The bearers may not have known English, but they knew

enough to react to some words. Harley's sedan chair rocked dangerously as his coolies muttered insults.

"So *what*? My father says that if any of us are going to succeed in this country, we're going to have to know who runs things. And our troop saw them all," Matthew gloated. "We saw Madame Sun Yatsen, Comrade Borodin from Russia, and everyone else."

"Well, *my* father says you missionaries are a bunch of cracked-brained nincompoops. Make your money and mind you own business is what *he* says. You can always buy what you need."

"What does the white slug say now?" one of Matthew's bearers asked.

"He says," Matthew answered, "that he and his family intend to work you and your countrymen until you and your parents and your unfortunate children, if you have any, shall die and be thrown to the winds. Then he will take his bags of money and go home."

"He is a wart! He is a tumor! He is an excrescence! He is a running sore!" went the muttered chorus back along the trail.

But from Harley came a final, fading thrust, as his coolies bounced him mercilessly. "I'll . . . bet . . . you've . . . never . . . heard . . . of . . . 110 . . . Shanghai . . . Road."

Matthew didn't deign to answer. He was already too far ahead anyway. That was the trouble with kids who lived in the International Settlement. They didn't know anything about the city. 110 Shanghai Road! Tsingtao had a Shanghai Road, but Shanghai didn't There was no such address.

Two hours later, the boys were more than halfway between Kuling and the point on the plains where they would take the bus—assuming that it was running—the next ten miles to Kiukiang. The trail, slippery with ice, took them through a thick bamboo grove. A heavy storm the previous night had frosted the stems and leaves in gleaming crystal. The slightest breeze produced a magic tinkling in the air that silenced both the chair-bearers and Matthew. As they passed through this enchanted, glittering aspect of nature, they scarcely heard the irate shouts of Harley, saying, "Hold up! Hold up!" But they did not hold up, and none of them spoke until they cleared the grove and saw the plain below them.

Luckily the bus was on time and not too crowded. They clattered through small villages, past frozen rice paddies, and

by early evening reached the outskirts of Kiukiang, stopping at
the open-air market at the center of the city, where most of the
passengers got off carrying armloads of foot-long radishes,
baskets of winter cabbage, and several loudly protesting ducks
tied together by their legs.

After the bus had started up again, the boys caught
glimpses of half-enclosed tea shops where old men gathered to
listen to local storytellers. The shops adjoined family residences—and every now and then a grim housewife thrust a
bamboo pole draped with laundry to hang out over the street
like a forlorn flag.

Slowing now, the bus took the cobbled streets cautiously
to the waterfront.

The *Tuk Wo*, one of the most comfortable river ships of
the Jardine, Matheson Shipping Company, lay alongside a
wooden wharf, the muddy waters of the Yangtze swirling about
her. The current here was especially turbulent, because it was
at Kiukiang that eight other streams flowed into the Yangtze
itself, giving the city its name—Nine Rivers. Now, in early
December, the *Tuk Wo* carried few passengers, at least as far as
the upper decks were concerned, though the steerage was
crowded with Chinese merchants and their families going
down to Nanking or Shanghai.

These passengers and the cargo of goods from upriver—
iron, coal, hides, and other Chinese products—made even the
winter passage profitable. Kiukiang was famous throughout
central China for its manufacturing of high-quality oiled-paper
umbrellas; wooden crates of these swung over the deck and
into the holds to complete the *Tuk Wo*'s full lading.

Local merchants checked the numbers on their records,
registering crates on the ship's invoice. A good bit of bickering
went on between them and Jardine, Matheson's Chinese
agent. This was sheer comic display, put on to satisfy not only
their taste for bargaining and commercial ritual, but also to
demonstrate to the English captain that the best interests of
the company were being protected. Money changed hands;
small bundles of opium disappeared into the long sleeves of
the merchants, who had presumably put on their best formal
dress to honor the generous company from across two oceans
that had so graciously brought them prosperity.

Captain Longsden stood at the top of the gangplank.
"How do you do, gentlemen?" he said formally. "We're
delighted to have you aboard as passengers. I hope you'll both

do me the honor of dining with me tonight once we've cast off. But for now, Matthew, you'd better rest in my quarters. Your mother has sent special instructions that you keep warm and not catch a chill."

Harley grinned maliciously. "Captain Longsden," he said, "would it be all right if I stayed out here with you?"

"I don't see why not." He put an arm across the blond boy's shoulders. "This trip promises to be something of an adventure. As you can see, we've had the crew put bales of straw and cotton along the railings of both decks to protect us from snipers. The warlords and the Nationalists have been taking target practice on us ever since we left Hankow. This civil war will give you both something to talk about to your grandchildren."

Alone in the captain's quarters, his slim shoulders covered by one of Mrs. Longsden's steamer rugs, Matthew clenched his thin wrists. At school, he'd fought battles and sometimes won. He was not even home yet, but already he had been pushed back into a role that he'd grown up with and that he'd learned to loathe. His mother had already lost one son out here in China, and she was determined that she would not lose another.

Catching sight of himself in the mirror above the washstand, he wished that he did not look quite so skinny. The women at the mission would soon be clucking about him with *blanc mange* and Baked Alaska. He wished that he didn't need spectacles, that his schoolmates didn't always call him "Four-Eyes," that his clothes would keep up with his growth. His father always took him to Shanghai's second-best tailor, saying, "Hai-kong charges so much that the investment won't be worth it till you get your full growth."

Matthew thought of seeing his mother and father again, but that did not make him feel much better. Still, the cook and the amah—the cook's gold-toothed wife, who took care of Matthew like a second mother—would be glad to have him. As Matthew consoled himself with thoughts of the warmth and comfort of his home kitchen, he felt the throb of the engines, heard commands from the bridge, and the answering shouts from the wharf as the ropes were cast off and the *Tuk Wo* swung out into the channel.

It was December of 1926, and it would be three days until they reached Shanghai. Although the extra threat of bandits promised some excitement, neither boy saw the journey down the Yangtze as anything extraordinary. At the age of ten they were already Old China Hands.

That night, as on every other winter night, dinner in the house of the Reverend Mr. Wilson Granger and his wife, Elizabeth, was announced by a small ceremonial procession. The table boy, in his freshly pressed, ankle-length blue gown, came first, bearing a glowing kerosene lamp, its light muted by an opalescent Tiffany shade. Following him, the cook, Da Sze Foo, similarly dressed, carried the large Haviland soup tureen. Tonight the table was set for two, an unusual circumstance in this household.

The Reverend Mr. Granger felt it was part of his wife's duty to entertain regularly. The missionary spinsters, euphemistically called "courtesy aunts," needed a place they could think of as home, and the two elderly childless couples who completed the staff also considered the Granger household a social center that reminded them of their American Midwest families.

They all lived within the Presbyterian compound, an area of about seven acres enclosed by a high brick wall, just outside the Little South Gate of Shanghai's old Native City. On the northern side, the wall curved, following the course of an old canal that by now had been filled in to make a wide road. Most of the eastern part of the compound was taken up with residences, the nearest to the Grangers' being a duplex for the half dozen single women. These buildings faced a large oval lawn which Wilson Granger hoped one day to convert into a tennis court. The western part of the compound was occupied by the True Heart School. In these four brick buildings two hundred and fifty Chinese children boarded and attended classes. Finally, there was a building that could have been a warehouse or an assembly hall—the austere Presbyterian place of worship, where the Reverend Wilson Granger often preached.

Here, in the midst of a Chinese city, the mission gave the impression of a completely Western institution of learning. Except for the Chinese servants and the fact that it was walled, it could have been duplicated in any one of several small American college towns. Even the food the Grangers would eat tonight—fried chicken and mashed potatoes—reflected their constant allegiance to their own country.

"It will be good to have the Young Master home from those barbarous northern regions," the cook said in Chinese.

Elizabeth Granger nodded. "It will indeed."

"I hope you will not be offended, but I have already planned to serve him his favorite foods for the next three days."

The table boy laughed and said, "That will mean plenty of turkey and venison for me to carry in." He bowed to Mr. Granger, who sat down with a somewhat abstracted air. "I have already sharpened the carving knives, sir."

The servants retired as Wilson Granger began to pronounce a longer than customary grace.

"Dear Lord," Mr. Granger intoned, "we give Thee thanks for this, our daily bread, but we thank Thee even more for the spiritual mission assigned to us. We are mindful of our son Matthew's gift of life, knowing that Thou art returning him to us in health and safety. We know, too, that when, in Thine own mysterious way, Thou didst gather to Thy bosom our own darling Philip, whatever pain was visited upon up was compensated by the purity of his early life. And, just as Thou hast, Dear Lord, carried us safely across the ocean from our American homes, we know that Thou hast spread Thy protective wings over Matthew in the danger-fraught passage from Kuling. Here, among these souls to whom we have been called to minister, in Thy name and in the name of Thine Only Son, we give Thee thanks. Amen."

The table boy returned and stood next to Mrs. Granger as she ladled out hot soup. He carried the serving to his master. The rest of the meal was eaten in silence. Before little Philip died, their evenings had been filled with cheerful conversation, sprinkled with occasional biblical puns and jokes. But since the child's tragic death from cholera, Wilson Granger had labored under the dark cloud of what he feared might be God's disapproval.

After they had finished their fruit compote, the Grangers made their way, routinely, into the sitting room, where they would spend the rest of the evening. An upright piano and a standing lamp filled one corner. A large Morris chair was placed in the bay window. Empire furniture, upholstered in green silk, blended in with the darker green Axminster carpet. A large coal-burning stove heated the room. It stood in front of a fireplace that, thanks to the ineptness of the local Chinese contractor, could never be made to draw correctly.

Back home in Iowa, Elizabeth Granger might have distracted herself by doing plain sewing, but here this would lower the dignity of the household. She could have played the Victrola, but she had heard her favorite Chopin prelude and the collection of arias sung by Madame Galli-Curci times beyond number. If Elizabeth had ever been able to reconcile her husband to the use of playing cards, they might have played double solitaire. After all these years he was still uncomfortable even shuffling the cards of a game called Rook, familiarly known as "missionary bridge." Since they had no guests to entertain, Elizabeth Granger settled herself in the Morris chair and went on with her rereading of *Henry Esmond*. Wilson Granger leafed through his Greek New Testament and worked on an original translation into Chinese of the passage from Revelations that he planned to use for his next assembly talk to the True Heart School. The only sounds for the next two hours were the ticking of the Seth Thomas mantelpiece clock and the rustle of turning pages.

At quarter of ten, Wilson Granger closed his Testament, looked up from his studies, and said, "If we are to be at our best tomorrow, we must be sure of our rest tonight."

In their upstairs bedroom, a small fire already burned and the counterpane on the four-poster had been turned down. Oil lamps on either side of the bed cast a rosy glow over the room. After each said a private, silent prayer, Wilson Granger settled himself against a mountain of pillows and once again opened the New Testament. It was his custom to read a few verses aloud each night.

"'Remember now thy Creator in the days of thy youth, while the evil days come not, nor the years draw nigh, when thou shalt say, "I have no pleasure in them."'" He paused in his reading to speak to his wife. "Sometimes it seems hard, but God has sent us to toil in these vineyards and we must do so without complaint."

"Six classes a day. Elementary English, elementary etiquette, Western history, arithmetic, religion, and girls' volleyball. I wonder if they understand any of it."

"We must remember the parable of the seeds—some of which fall on rock, some on sand, and some on fallow ground."

She sighed. "You're always so sure of things, Wilson."

Only after the lamps were put out and Elizabeth Granger, clad from neck to toe in white flannel, found the harsh winter night too chilling and clung to her husband for warmth, did Wilson Granger's assuredness falter. "No!" he cried out. "Closeness without procreation is forbidden by the Lord. He has already punished us by taking little Philip and I won't tempt His wrath again."

Close to midnight, the amah was roused from her slumber by a pale and trembling Elizabeth Granger. "I'm afraid I have one of my migraines again," she said in Chinese. "I'm sorry to wake you, but it has become almost unbearable."

The amah, after hurriedly putting on a padded robe, followed Elizabeth back upstairs to Matthew's bedroom. Her mistress lay down on the single bed.

At first the amah probed the base of Mrs. Granger's neck, feeling for centers of tautness. Once she had located them, she took two odd-fashioned engraved Chinese coins called *cash*— circles of brass with square holes in the center—and, fitting them on either side of the middle finger of her right hand, she used them as pincers to gather up the skin and torture the muscles beneath. Over and over the amah repeated her quick, primitive gestures. Then she spoke.

"Mistress, you must try now to think of happy times. Do not think about the tasks before you tomorrow. You should remember moments from your own childhood—the lucky chance that brought you to live in the Middle Kingdom, that place you Westerners call China."

The amah's rhythmic probings lulled Elizabeth to those old memories. For all her lack of learning, the Chinese woman was right. What was the point of thinking of a present or a future that offered nothing but the harsh call of duty?

Elizabeth came from northern Iowa. Her father, after homesteading what became a successful farm, bought other property, and later established himself as the banker of the nearest town. With prosperity came the expectation that Elizabeth and her sisters would attend finishing school, but she persuaded her family to let her go away to the University of Wisconsin. She recalled her dismay, after receiving her degree, on discovering that she was expected to wait passively in the tiny town for the "right man" to come along. She remembered bursting out in protest, "If I didn't find him in a big city like Madison, he's certainly not going to turn up here." But Elizabeth began to entertain the appalling prospect of spinsterhood.

By the merest chance, she noticed in a YWCA circular the advertisement for "a college graduate of good family qualified to teach the regular high school curriculum (Latin, English, Mathematics, and History), to English-speaking children."

What stunned her was the address to which applicants should apply: "Miss Jewell's School, Jinkee Road, International Settlement, Shanghai, China." For weeks she corresponded furtively with the school.

When the contract arrived, Elizabeth signed it that same afternoon and walked it down to the post office. She presented her father with a *fait accompli*, knowing that since she had given her word, he would have to go along with it.

Two months later, she boarded a train and, after two changes, arrived in San Francisco, ready to board the SS *Golden State*. The voyage had been pure joy; she had—at the captain's ball, on the last night out—won first prize for the most ingenious costume, designed to illustrate "any book with which everyone is familiar." Earlier, during the coaling stop at the Japanese port of Shimonoseki, she had gone ashore, and at a curio shop bargained for and bought two long strings of Chinese *cash*, the coins from the old regime with square holes in them. Dressed in her most elegant gown, she appeared at the ball with these strings of *cash* about her neck, the loose ends falling down to her waist. All the other titles—*Graustark, The Prisoner of Zenda, Little Women*—were quickly identified. But no one came close to guessing what Elizabeth represented. During the last waltz the captain had said, "Now, you simply must tell us."

Elizabeth, with a curtsy, announced, "I am a book that every one of you must carry to keep track of your daily accounts. I am your . . . *cash book!*" As she remembered the appreciative applause for this simple play on words, she smiled, for even now the amah was using *cash* to knead out her throbbing pain.

The amah giggled. "Ah, my mistress must indeed have found some old happiness. I can feel it through my fingers. But you must be quiet as I follow the tracks of your affliction."

It had not been pain, Elizabeth recalled, that overcame her the day of her landing in Shanghai, but acute embarrassment. She presented herself at Miss Jewell's after a rickshaw ride. She sent in her calling card. . . . Miss Jewell refused to receive her. They had not been "properly introduced." The young adventuress—unprepared for Victorian proprieties that prevailed in this outpost of Empire—dissolved into tears.

Within minutes, a young Chinese man bowed before her. "Miss Davies?" he asked, and handed her a handsomely bound black leather, silk-lined folder, which she was to learn later to call a chit book. Inside, she found a note written in a rounded, distinguished hand.

> My dear Miss Davies,
>   I understand that Miss Jewell has not yet received your identifying papers. Please put aside your worries and turn yourself over to the care of our messenger. If time had allowed, we would have sent our landau, but since it is a short distance, please walk with him to our home. Trusting to see you shortly,
>
> I remain,
Madeline Logan-Fisher (Mrs. Andrew)

The next thing Elizabeth knew she was being greeted by a slim, sophisticated, and elegant Englishwoman, wife of the British official in charge of distributing the Boxer Rebellion Reparation Fund in Shanghai, who said, "You mustn't mind that paper dragon, Miss Jewell. As soon as she gets your papers she'll crumple. What an introduction to port-city life! It's a good thing that everyone here in the International Settlement knows everything unusual that goes on, thanks to our network of servants. Here, have some tea—with a tot of rum in it. Our house is yours!" Elizabeth sank gratefully into a comfortable armchair, taking in her hostess's blond pompadour and marveling at her casual English drawl.

Her contract with Miss Jewell had been for only a year, and the waiting list of would-be teachers was such that she would have to go back to Iowa in early June. All around her Elizabeth saw young women like herself with the banked but still smoldering light of adventure in their eyes. They came out here for adventure and to find a husband. After a year they either found one or went home. It was a simple as that.

When the Reverend Mr. Granger, who often gave talks at Miss Jewell's School and sometimes stayed for Sunday dinner, appeared one afternoon with the announcement that he had come to call on Elizabeth, she became the envy of all the other teachers. It was easy for her to fall in love. Wilson was tall and well-built. He had played football in college and he loved his daily game of tennis. His sermons were rousing. Although he was handsome in a traditional way, he never overstepped the bounds of good manners or came even close to flirting. He was courteous to the ladies and liked by many of the other clergymen who came and went. She knew that he was in love with her too, and he offered her the chance of a life entirely different from anything she had ever known. She mentioned to him that perhaps her faith was not as strong as his, but with the natural ebullience of a man who knows he's chosen by God, he assured her that if he had chosen her in the first place, she, too, must be one of the "elect."

At first Wilson had been ardent and loving, their life full of simple joy. Wilson countered her natural shyness in the marriage bed by reminding her that Christ's first miracle had been the wedding at Cana. A man and woman who loved each other should be happy together, he assured her. She teased him for being a "muscular Christian," but loved the hard sinews of his body. Their two children had come quickly. Philip, pink and robust, everybody's darling, and a year later, Matthew, the "thoughtful one."

Neither one of them had been out of diapers that fateful summer when cholera struck the city. Elizabeth scalded everything that came in contact with the children; Wilson prayed for God's protection. In the end, neither method prevailed. Little Philip died in her arms. She wept inconsolably. Her husband sank to his knees and said in a tone she had not heard before but one that would become all too familiar, "We have sinned in God's eyes. Our union is not sanctified. He has taken little Philip away as punishment. If God intends for us not to have children, we must heed His warning and never touch each other again."

Elizabeth suffered a double loss during that terrible epidemic. She lost her beloved firstborn and she lost her happy, confident lover, who turned before her eyes into something close to a religious fanatic tormented cruelly by visions of God's displeasure.

If Elizabeth thought sometimes she would die of loneliness, she had, at least, the meager consolation that their life appeared abundant and leisurely. The Presbyterians at the Mission Board Office in New York had always insisted that their missonaries live in a way that was appropriate to the elect. She lived more richly now than any of her family ever had. She had the distractions of her work and she had her other son, whom she would see in three days. With that thought, she went to sleep.

Tsing Mei-fen's eyes were wide open and impassive. Her glance took in every corner of the small room. She traced the patterns of light that the flickering kerosene lamps of the vendors and the gamblers in the street below cast on her ceiling. Would he never finish?

It was not that she had no feeling for this man. He was generous and, in his own way, loyal. Tsing Mei-fen, former street girl of Shanghai, now the secure and even affluent mistress of a *yang-gwei-tse*, "foreign-devil" financier, clasped her arms, her legs, and the inner walls of her silken grotto about her lover and hissed into his ear. She knew just when to turn as, roughly, he heaved her onto her stomach. Ah, her neck was stiff! As he grunted above her, she surveyed her room. Expensive chests, low teak tables, heavy bronze pieces, and in the next room . . . All this was worth it, because of who was in the next room.

There is no help for it, she thought; we cannot choose how we live our lives.

He finished at last. The ravening beast turned into a man again.

"That was wonderful," he said. "You were wonderful, too, Mei-fen."

"You turn a simple woman," she said mechanically, "into a goddess of love."

His face was hidden in the shadows, but the lights from below caught glints in his hair. She stroked his curls absently. Her eyes fixed on her right hand and the enormous signet ring that he had given her. In heavy gold and rough-cut gems, it was a rendering of a bat eating a beetle—this man's own private "chop," the seal that he had told her he used as the trademark of his Western companies across the sea. Although he was married to another, he was generous with material things.

Seven years before, he had taken their baby in his own arms to a gold merchant and had a craftsman fit a bracelet with that same emblem around the infant's chubby wrist. He requested that the emblem face inward as their secret. Already, she thought, he began to withdraw from her in his mind, in his soul—if he had one. She would see to it, she thought cynically, that he would never leave the delights of her body.

As if reading her mind, he tweaked her playfully on the arm. "Mei-fen, you are a flame to my senses. You have given me everything and more, except"—and here he chuckled— "an evening in the famous baskets of Shanghai."

"Oh, you serpent, you devil," she breathed. "I should die

of pleasure, and then where would you spend your afternoons and evenings?"

He gave her a sharp look of jealousy and distrust. "How do you know about those baskets?"

"I have told you before," she said curtly. "I was a virgin when you ruined me. Every matter of lust I have learned from you and only you."

The glass beads that hung from the door of the other room of the tiny flat tinkled slightly. "Is it all right, my mother?" a childish voice murmured. "Is Uncle through? May I come in now?"

Quietly and respectfully, a slim girl moved up to their bed. With her chubby hands she wheeled a lacquer cart that held an ice bucket with Dom Perignon, a bottle of Angostura Bitters, and, in a small silver dish, sugar cubes. Carefully the child extracted chilled glasses from the bucket and then with tongs put one cube in Mei-fen's glass and two in the foreigner's. She doused them with bitters and watched as the man poured the champagne.

"May I have a sip, Uncle?"

As the couple drank, the little girl put her head on Mei-fen's breast and patted her hair with a babyish hand. This, thought the Chinese woman, who preferred not to remember the past and could not see far into a frightening future, was what it was all for—this precious life.

Three days later, in the second-floor study of the splendid mansion that overlooked the grounds of the Cercle Sportif Français—otherwise known as "The French Club"—Harley Compton Fitch II waved off a servant who had come in to turn on the electric light. "I'll ring if I need you," Fitch said, and the servant closed the door behind him.

Sitting in the half-dark, Fitch picked up a heavy brass paperweight, the principal object on his polished teakwood desk. The ornament weighed a good three pounds. Meticulously etched into one side of the solid metal oblong was the formalized representation of a bat eating a beetle, the official chop of Fitch Enterprises. This was what it came to, after fifteen years. This, as much as the girl he visited on so many sultry afternoons, represented his love affair, harsh as it may have been at times, with this country that had put him under a spell as soon as he had entered it.

His wife never understood this enchantment. Born in

Boston, initially more than happy to marry a merchant and an adventurer, she quickly fell out of love both with him and the life he'd promised her. Their honeymoon voyage on the *Empress of Russia* twelve years ago quickly turned into a nightmare. His shipboard embraces left her pregnant and resentful. Even during their first brief carriage ride from the dock to the Palace Hotel, she found it necessary to stop and be sick in the gutter. The smells of the land that to him were exotic and tempting were to her both a torture and a personal insult. For the next eleven years she refused to change her mind. Even here, in this handsome three-acre city estate, surrounded by well-tended lawns and formal garden borders, protected from the outside world by thick, neatly trimmed hedges, she kept the windows of her own rooms—stubbornly decorated in the fashion of the Boston she'd left—almost hermetically sealed.

Fitch had come home tonight to a seemingly deserted castle. The customary tray of champagne and bitters had been waiting for him in his study. His blunt fingers moved over the brass paperweight, the raised surfaces of the bat. Prosperity? Yes. Good luck? Perhaps there was a limit to what a man could expect in this or any world. He was a banker, a realtor, a speculator in stocks, but at home he was a pauper.

Tonight he would not be seeing Mei-fen. As the evening tide came in he would go down to the dock to pick up his son, Harley, whom he had not seen for four months. The decision to send the boy away to school had been an uneasy one. The harsh truth was that the boy's mother had, over the years, eased her despair with increasing doses of laudanum. He had decided to send the boy away for his own good.

What would the boy do through the long Christmas vacation or where would he go if the school did not reopen? No point in thinking about that now. Harley Fitch drained his glass, went downstairs, and called for his car.

At this magic hour all of Shanghai seemed enveloped in a lavender-silver twilight. Harley Fitch loved the sudden glow as they turned into Nanking Road, lit brightly on either side by multicolored neon signs. He knew that the Chinese characters advertised commonplace products, but, being unable to read them, he saw in the designs an expression of the infinite enticements of this world into which he had stumbled and from which he could not free himself.

At the end of Nanking Road his chauffeur skillfully maneuvered the new, sleek, low-slung Packard through the difficult right-hand turn that took them along the southern end of the International Bund and into the French Concession. Fitch glanced to his left and saw the impressive array of solidly Western business buildings that had sprung up over the years facing the Whangpoo River. Among them the Hong Kong and Shanghai Bank, the Shanghai Club, and the Customs House stood out. The Bund, which gave its name to this riverfront business section, was, in fact, a slanted levee controlling the flow of the river. Gardens separated the stone structure from the thoroughfare that faced the buildings. As the street continued to the south, it entered French territory, the completely French-controlled section of the city. Because it was removed from the original commerical center, many of the wealthy had built their homes there on two- and three-acre grounds.

These enclaves dated back to a China that was closed to all foreign powers near the opening of the last century. The East India Company had forced its trade on an unwilling nation. For many years its only port of entry had been Canton, where the foreign merchants were allowed to occupy a small island in the Pearl River. The trade grew out of all proportion to the restrictive confines allowed the "barbarians." With opium as their chief product, the East India Company built up an extravagantly profitable and unequal trade with China. They exchanged their "foreign mud" for tea, silk, porcelain, furs, and jade.

When the Emperor in Peking and his ministers tried to ban the importation of opium, the East India Company, fronting for the Imperial British Government, forced its continuance through a series of armed engagements. They used Western naval vessels to defeat the poorly armed Chinese junks and river forts in what were to be called the Opium Wars. As one price for peace, China was forced to open other ports, including Shanghai, and to grant total jurisdiction over the surrendered sections of land to the foreign powers. Shanghai's International Settlement—originally primarily British—came into being. Not long after, the French demanded their own concession as the new city rapidly grew into China's principal port of entry and exit. In times of social unrest, like the present, with Chiang Kai-shek's challenge to local warlords, these enclaves offered a measure of protection and security to the wealthy, regardless of nationality, and many of the newly rich Chinese families had joined their original exploiters in building mansions protected by British, American, and French armed forces as well as courts of law.

Immediately to the south, the inhabitants of the "real" Shanghai paid slight attention to the possible effects of political change. They were accustomed to repeated shifts in power. The old Native City had changed little during the years of the international city's growth. Crossed by narrow streets and alleys, it presented a characteristic combination of extreme wealth and severe poverty. Here, the compound of a rich merchant, containing at its center a formal garden, could stand next to a hovel or tenement that housed many hungry families. On the streets, men hunkered down near public urinals and gambled with their few coins as they dealt out hands from a worn pack of Bicycle cards. Foreigners entering this area were often confused by the sight of an expensive jewelry store next to a butcher shop selling dog and horse meat. This chaos, this inequality, this constant fear of pestilence, this filth next to inexpressible wealth was what drove the new leaders in China to promise change.

Fitch's chauffeur pulled into a break between a long row of buildings along the French Bund and parked. A series of storehouses—locally known as "godowns"—housed the enormous import and export trade that constituted the commercial life of Shanghai.

Lanterns and kerosene lamps outlined junks and sampans on the river. One or two of the more prosperous showed that they had their own electrical systems, proudly draping their decks in strings of Christmas lights in blue, yellow, magenta, and any other novelty color that had come into the electric stores in their last shipments. Once again, "China" was there for Harley Fitch in ways he could never foresee or hope to understand.

Fitch walked to the water's edge and, looking downriver, saw the running lights of the *Tuk Wo* as she came in to dock. Her power had been cut off. The pilot gauged the force of the tide accurately and brought the riverboat in for a perfect docking.

The dock was crowded now by Chinese coming to greet their relatives and coolies waiting for the late-night unloading. Customs officers held clipboards to check the cargo.

A meticulously polished Model T carrying two foreigners

pulled up and parked beside the Fitch Packard. Someone in the shipping office turned on a pair of arc lights that hissed and sizzled in the night air. The pilot of the *Tuk Wo* blew a series of triumphant toots on the ship's whistle.

The two Westerners from the Ford alighted and came over to stand by Fitch, near enough to be part of a foreign contingent, but not quite near enough to say hello. Fitch recognized a missonary couple from the compound out by the Little South Gate and irritably assumed that as a "corrupt businessman" he was about to be snubbed when an American voice said, "It's Harley Fitch, isn't it? I believe we've met before. You know my husband, Wilson. I presume you're here to meet your son." Fitch nodded his head. "I can see the boys up there on the deck."

The dockside coolies began to unload the cargo. Hemp, it was supposed to be, but each sturdy body bent almost double as it staggered under what looked like only medium-weight bales. Steerage passengers swirled about these straining workers and melted into the darkness beyond the docks and the godowns.

"Look, Wilson! Isn't there something odd about those loads?"

"I'm not sure what you mean," her husband said.

Fitch looked at the woman with frank appreciation. "There is some kind of metal in those bales, Mrs. Granger. Not everyone could see it."

"I consider myself so fortunate," she said, holding tight to her husband's arm, "to be able to see such things . . . not the smuggling! Don't misunderstand! But the adventure!" She extended her gloved hand in a salute to it all—and Fitch took it in with her.

The gangplank to the upper decks had been raised and made fast. Captain Longsden's head and shoulders could be seen above the bale of cotton that had to be pushed aside before that section of the railing could be removed. Harley Fitch recognized the stocky figure of his son and felt a momentary sensation of superiority when he saw his son push ahead of the others and start down the gangplank.

Matthew Granger wanted more than anything in the world to race down the gangplank and hurl himself into his mother's arms. But his pride wouldn't let him. For the sake of his parents, he stayed to make a correct farewell, holding his hand out to the captain, bowing from the waist, and waving, with easy camaraderie, to the engineer and mates who had come up behind them. For the sake of Da Sze Foo and the amah, he went up to the Chinese deckhands and, remembering his Chinese manners, put his fists together and thanked them for the safe voyage.

As the Fitch Packard sped away, Matthew stepped off the shifting foot of the gangplank onto the solid granite steps of the dock. He took just one step forward and the glaring arc lights illuminating fifty yards of the the dock went out.

In the first second of darkness, hands roughly seized Matthew and twisted his arms behind his back. Someone pushed a foul-smelling burlap bag down over his head, making it impossible for him to call out. His captors dragged as much as carried him through the crush of bodies. The first stunned silence on the dock was replaced by a rising roar of indignation and confusion.

As far as his abductors were concerned, there was no confusion. Gagging at the pressure of the hand over his mouth, Matthew deliberately relaxed. There was no way to escape.

He could tell when he had been dragged beyond the stone paving, between two godowns, and across the streetcar lines of the Quai de France. One of his captors, stumbling as his toe caught for a moment against the steel track of the tramway, swore quietly in the local dialect.

Now they were across the street, and after a brief jog to the left, Matthew knew he was being pulled into the area outside the East Gate of the old city. From the smell he knew they were not too far away from Fish Market Street. Then they halted. "You have him?" a muffled voice asked in Chinese.

"We have him," a voice from behind said.

The dock lights came on just as suddenly as they had been extinguished. All over the loading area, people checked those objects dearest to them: peasants counted their chickens; the ship's crew and local merchants quickly felt for the number of silver ingots in their straw disguise. Perhaps this had, after all, been nothing more than a failure of electricity. But the cautious return to normalcy was shattered by the foreigner beside the tall black car who shouted in his accented Chinese, "Where is my son? Someone has taken my son!"

The merchants stared at Wilson Granger with new respect. They had never suspected that one of these foreign "teachers" of their peculiar new god would be a man of sufficient wealth to be able to pay a ransom for a kidnapped child.

The British Assistant Head of Customs made his way over to the Grangers after first placing a quick emergency phone call to the French Commissioner of Police, who had jurisdiction over this area. Little by little the dockside emptied of Chinese. Families and businessmen cast glances of pity at these outlandish and barbaric foreigners.

In the purest Oxford tones, the English customs official introduced himself to Elizabeth and Wilson Granger. "I'm Peter Cave-Brown-Cave, sir," he said to Wilson, and automatically added with a self-deprecatory air, "with hyphens, you know." Then he went on, "There has, I'm sure, been some kind of mistake, and I've already put in a call to the French Police Commissioner—Monsieur Charles Dubois. He should be here shortly."

Elizabeth Granger let out a low moan. "Can it be," she asked, dazed, "that they have actually kidnapped our son?"

Wilson Granger clenched his fists and said, "My dear, we must trust in the Lord."

Elizabeth Granger burst out, "Matthew is in the hands of *Chinese* kidnappers, and they don't believe in the Lord! You know that when the Hawkes's boy up in Mukden was taken, and the Hawkeses were late with the ransom money . . ."

"We must pray. . . ."

". . . they sent the poor boy home in pieces, and you know it."

They heard the siren on the French commissioner's limousine, sounding louder and louder until it was cut off. The car skidded to a halt only steps from them.

Commissioner Dubois, summoned from a gala banquet at the Cercle Sportif Français, cast a jaundiced eye on this little group. Impatiently he heard out Mr. Cave-Brown-Cave's report. As he listened, his glance took in the high black Model T sedan. "*Un moment*," he said abruptly. "Was your son alone? Was there another foreigner here on the dock?"

"Yes, yes," the Reverend Mr. Granger stammered. "The Fitch boy, Harley Fitch of Fitch Enterprises. The boys traveled downriver together."

The Commissioner gave a snort. "There's no one more ignorant than an ignorant Chinese. I myself, *cher monsieur*, have seen the new low American vehicle Mr. Fitch rides in. I have seen it often at the club. Do you not see what has happened?" He shook with mirthless laughter. "*Your* car, though not luxurious, is *high*. To the Chinese, anyone riding in it would be a person superior in every sense. They have kidnapped—forgive me—the poor boy in the tall car, and let the rich boy they were doubtless sent for slip through their bungling fingers! *Salauds!*"

Elizabeth Granger stifled a scream.

"*Ma chère madame*," Dubois said to her, "kidnappings happen every day here. The word 'Shanghai' means to kidnap. This is a simple business matter. Neither Chiang Kai-shek nor the Communists would be involved. Each faction has enough problems of its own to solve. We must be dealing with the local warlord."

"What do you suggest we do?" Mrs. Granger struggled for control.

The Commissioner considered. "If I am right, they will be sending a ransom message to the Fitch residence, possible even as we speak of it. I suggest that we immediately repair to their estate."

It was unfortunate that this mother had been too ill to see him. Still, it was good to be home, and Harley swelled with pride as his dad took him into the drawing room and poured them each a glass of sherry as if they were friendly equals. Harley burst with stories: he'd been captain of the junior soccer team and had scored the winning goal against the team fielded by the Redcroft School, their notorious English rival. "I headed the ball just under the bar at one corner, completely out of the goalie's reach," he exulted and took another mouthful of wine.

"Good work!" his father said, refilling both their glasses. "I'll bet those bluenoses up there never gave you anything like this."

"You can say that again!"

"I knew you didn't want to go to begin with," his father said. "But with your mother's nerves . . ."

"Oh, it's great now," Harley said. "We hike on all-day picnics, and the first snowfall was really swell. We got a holiday and everyone went sledding down Morris Hill."

"Yes, you wrote about that," his father said, and grinned thinking of the latest model American Flexible Flier that was to be one of his Christmas presents to his son.

They were interrupted, first by the sound of sirens, then

by the high-pitched tones of the Fitch gatekeeper: "My masters are sleeping . . . you . . . !" Within seconds the French Commissioner of Police entered the room, flanked by assistants and followed by the Grangers, a British customs official, and an embarrassed houseboy, still buttoning the high collar of his gown.

It took only moments for the Commissioner to explain what had happened and to suggest his theory.

"The first place the kidnappers will come is here," the Commissioner said. "I have already given orders to have these grounds surrounded."

"Perhaps if we were to kneel down," Wilson Granger said, "and seek guidance."

Harley Fitch turned on the clergyman. "This is a time for action, not prayer! This is a matter of finances, a time to take a firm hand with the Chinese. Trust a missionary to fall back on crack-brained theology . . . !"

Wilson Granger's eyes glinted ominously. "If your kind hadn't, in its selfish, ignorant way, followed us missionaries out here to use all China to make a dollar, robbing the rich and gouging the poor—"

"*Please!*" Elizabeth Granger interrupted. "Can't we get to what's important? Can't we plan some way to save Matthew?"

"Don't expect either of them to fret over a little thing like that!" It was Mrs. Fitch, dramatically framed in the drawing-room doorway, her hair awry, her silk negligee falling away to reveal a rumpled nightgown. "A human life? That is nothing—to my husband! Unless you count the pleasure he takes when he destroys one." The disheveled woman continued directly to Elizabeth Granger, "Do you think it even matters to him whether it is your son or mine? No! If it were silver, if it were gold, he would leave no stone unturned, but—just a boy, a child whose only worth is that he makes his mother happy—"

"Sylvia!" Fitch, for all his usual aggression and decisiveness, seemed unable to move. The group stood in silence, until an ancient amah appeared and gently led her mistress away.

Several servants appeared carrying trays of sweetmeats and fragrant tea. Even though their master and mistress often seemed incapable of civilized behavior, they remained aware of the social obligations of a well-run household. Only minutes after that, the high whining tones of the gatekeeper once again penetrated the drawing room. "Am I never to get any sleep tonight?" he wailed. "Is this the house of a respected gentleman, as I have long believed, or is it a house of public assignation!"

His voice trailed off. Then the gatekeeper himself appeared, still grumbling into his sparse gray beard. "There are no manners any longer," he said. "This wretched piece of cheap paper was not even delivered in a chit book!" He handed it to one of the houseboys, who gave it to his master.

Suddenly, the french doors that opened onto the wide veranda were forced open by two Gallic officials who had been posted in the shrubbery. They held a Chinese man. He shook himself free and spat out, "My merciless master, who cracks children in his teeth like lichee nuts, is impatient for payment. He will stay his iron jaws only if you feed him fifty thousand Mexican dollars or twenty-five thousand in the green American paper. Those are the only currencies he will accept."

In a gesture that Elizabeth Granger would remember and admire for as long as she lived, the elder Fitch, without a word, moved suavely across the drawing room, slid aside an oil portrait of some grim Yankee ancestor, and began to work the combination of his private safe. If these Chinese had been mistaken in their victim, he would abet them in their mistake.

Wilson Granger shouted, "Back, son of Mammon! No tainted money shall ransom my son. A life redeemed by the fruits of sin is no life at all!"

Elizabeth would never forget the glance of incredulity and contempt with which Harley Fitch's face was stamped before he regained control. For the rest of her life she would burn with the horror of it.

"You damn idiot, this is your son's life we're talking about!"

"I will not offend my God any longer. I will not endanger my own immortal soul!"

"If you don't pay the ransom, you'll be as good as murdering your own son."

"Abraham was called to the same dreadful sacrifice and he did not shirk. I have given one son to God and I can give another."

Until the first light of dawn, the two men fought over the destiny of Matthew Granger. Harley Compton Fitch II saw the matter purely as a business deal—a few thousand dollars and the boy would be free. Wilson Granger knew to the depths of his melancholy soul that to use "tainted money" to buy his son's life was to commit an unforgivable sin. In vain did Elizabeth Granger weep. The French Commissioner threw up his arms and stormed out. In the end, it came down to a contest of wills between two strong, irrevocably opposed men.

In all the confusion, not one of them noticed that in a curtained alcove that overlooked the gardens, a young and sturdy figure bent over, shivered convulsively, biting his lower lip until it bled. It wasn't enough that if something happened to that snot-nosed, sissy-faced Matthew, he, Harley Compton Fitch III, would have it thrown up to him forever. But how could it have happened that that four-eyed gopher who couldn't even make the junior soccer team, and cried at night because he was homesick, could have been *kidnapped by bandits*! Harley groaned. He'd been cheated out of an adventure that would be the talk of Kuling and Shanghai for as long as there were people alive to remember the story.

Though Matthew's parents had no notion of his where-abouts, he knew exactly where he was—close to the Willow Pattern Tea House, set in its artificial lake. Its entrance required passing a group of permanent side shows. More than once, before he had been packed off to Kuling, Matthew had saved enough money from his allowance—by walking or riding third-class on the streetcar—to pay his way in to see the half-naked woman teasing a drugged python coiling slowly about her. Next to that stall he had often watched the bawdy parodies of the classical tales of the Chinese Empire. To the delight of the rest of the audience, he had laughed knowingly at the obscene travesties of the *Tales of the Three Kingdoms*.

They threw him unceremoniously into a windowless room, lit only by the dim glow coming from under two doors. He saw a cot, a simple stand with washbasin and a pitcher of water. Beside it, on the floor, stood a slop bucket, improvised from a ten-gallon Standard Oil can. Against one wall a small square table and a four-legged stool made up the remaining furniture.

His original captors disappeared as soon as the door behind him clicked shut. Now he heard voices approaching. The door opened slowly and an elderly woman, dressed in common clothes, carrying a small oil lamp in one hand and a cheap earthenware bowl in the other, entered. The door closed softly behind her. She smiled ingratiatingly and spoke in pidgin.

"No worry, no worry, Small Master. Your papa rich man. He pay many dollah for you." With a half-bow she placed the lamp and the bowl, with some wooden chopsticks, on the table before him.

Matthew laughed, saying in the Wu dialect, his tones faultless, "Old Mother, you are very funny. My father is not a rich man. He has given up his own family's riches to come to your country and to preach the saving of your souls."

The old woman looked at him with disbelief. This was not what she had been led to expect. "How can the son of a foreign devil speak like a scholar of the old Kingdom of Wu? Are you some kind of witch or sorcerer?"

The boy grimaced. "This is my country, as much as yours. I was born not many *li* from where we are now—close to the Willow Pattern Tea House, if my ears have not been deafened by the rude treatment I have received."

"*Ai-yah!*" the old woman wailed. "Those stupid toads! They're not even men. With only two round-eyed insects to choose from, they pick the scorpion! The only riches to be gathered from this big-nosed abomination are in the venom that falls from a disrespectful tongue!"

"Old Mother, whatever else is true, *your* tongue is as alive as mine!"

After she left, he was just a boy alone. He looked into the bowl and found cold though tasty noodles, which reminded him of his own cook's good home fare. That, in turn, reminded him of his parents, and he felt a cold wave of fear and homesickness. *Where were they*? What if they didn't pay the ransom?

That dumb ox Harley! This was all his fault! All money and no brains! The matron up at the Kuling American School thought they would like each other just because they came from the same city. But she didn't know beans.

His first night there, Matthew, homesick and exhausted, had crawled between icy sheets, hoping only for the lights-out call and the opportunity to shed a few silent tears. His legs had gone no more than eight inches into the bed when his roommate started laughing.

"Short-sheeted!" Harley jeered. "Don't you know enough to check and see if you've been short-sheeted?"

Matthew found himself using the weapon that would protect him and sometimes even give him the upper hand during the next few months.

"Gentlemen don't do those things. We were over that in kindergarten," he said haughtily. "Only little girls and children of businessmen . . ."

For the next four months, each boy had done everything he could to make the other miserable. Harley Fitch, muscular and stocky, bullied Matthew on the playing field, tackling him unnecessarily during football matches, punching him in the stomach, dabbing mud on his spectacles. Harley saw to it that Matthew was the last one chosen on any team.

If the raw fall afternoons belonged to Harley, the mornings in class were a continuing triumph for Matthew, who not only knew his lessons without ever studying, but could make his teachers and his classmates laugh. Most of the time he managed to have the laughter directed at Harley.

Matthew's latest triumph had come during the week of final examinations. He had plotted carefully, leaving out on his desk long and thoughtful answers to the American History Honors Test. "I'm going down to the post office," he had said cheerfully to his roommate. "Don't look at my exam!"

When he returned an hour later, he found his roommate deep in study. The next week, Harley was given an "F" for having written answers that were long, thoughtful, and absolutely wrong. Beyond that, he'd spent a dreadful afternoon in the headmaster's office. When he returned to the room, Matthew had been lying on his bed in the sleeping porch reading. He looked up and smiled. "That's what gentlemen do instead of short-sheeting."

But none of that counted now. Because of Harley, Matthew was stuck in a place that was even worse than boarding school. As he ate the cold noodles, he realized there was absolutely nothing he could do. There was no point even in crying. He finished his noodles, peed into the Standard Oil can, rinsed out his mouth with brackish water, rolled up in the rough blanket that covered the cot, and fell into a deep sleep.

That same night, in Shanghai's French Concession, a shiny limousine drove up to an ostentatious private mansion. Quickly the stranger knocked, and just as quickly he was let in.

"Our house is honored beyond words by the illustrious Nyi Chuen-yao," the Chinese majordomo said, and disappeared from the drawing room only to return with a tray of Veuve Clicquot, Beluga caviar, and a chilled dish of sliced abalone.

Nyi Chuen-yao sloshed champagne into his glass. The warlord greeted his host, a French official on the take, with a polite, enormous belch. "All the world knows that this home never fails in its obligations to the careworn traveler."

The official waved casually for another bottle. His careful eyes took in, yet seemed to ignore, the ornately carved ivory box that had appeared by sleight of hand on the frosted silver tray. In that box, the Frenchman knew, there were enough gold coins to feed a Chinese village for five years, or to buy up another set of buildings near the château in the Loire Valley he had recently purchased.

The two men sat together, drawing on *claros* from the latest shipment of Cuban cigars. Both knew that the political situation was dangerous, not to say explosive. Both thought of themselves as men of the world, although the worlds they knew were strikingly different. From arrogance, from unease, and from a gnawing need to know what was going on in these different spheres, the two men cautiously began, as the champagne lowered in the bottle, the careful exchange of information.

"I have every reason to believe," the warlord said, "that it is only a matter of weeks, perhaps a month or more, before Chiang Kai-shek will break with his left-wing radicals, who are led by a man called Mao Tse-tung, as well as his Russian advisers, headed by a certain Comrade Borodin."

The official gave no indication that his own sources had already informed him of this coming purge.

The warlord gestured impatiently. "Are you truly as calm over this as you would have me believe?"

"My fortune is in your hands," the official said smoothly, "and I have no doubt of your steadfastness."

"I pay you," Nyi Chuen-yao said crudely, "when opium and silver come in from the southern ports. If either side resolves this conflict, you may find your income cut off."

"It will be to everyone's interest to keep this old 'open port'—open!"

Nyi Chuen-yao sneered his disbelief.

The Frenchman went on, "Don't you see? China's real danger comes from across the sea. The Japanese want your land more than any Western foreigner!"

Chuen-yao reached for his box of gold. "So, should I take it back, and give it to the monkey people?"

The Frenchman, with a brutal grab, recovered the box. "I

tell you this because of kindness, and because we are both family men. You must look to your nest egg as I do to mine."

Both men breathed quickly. "My boy graduates from the *lycée* this spring," the official said with false calm. "And what of your boy? I trust he does well?"

The warlord eyed the foreigner, the room, the expensive refreshments. "*Kam pei!*" He took the Veuve Clicquot and, opening his throat, poured all that was left down his gullet. "Yes, I have a boy. I have allowed him to be educated at the mission outside the Little South Gate, in the hope that the barbaric language he learns there will be of use to him. If he picks up a few thieving ways, the time will not be lost."

The Frenchman chose to ignore the insults half buried in this speech. "Little South Gate?" he said, tossing off the rest of his glass. "Someone has kidnapped the son of those deluded heretics." He looked at the warlord inscrutably. "Too bad the hired thugs bungled the job, but I, in my duty, will do everything in my power to straighten this out. *Mais ces fanatiques!*" He shrugged. "You know as well as I—"

"I know nothing of this," the warlord said, scooping up cavier with a thick index finger. "Just make sure they know that the great Nyi Chuen-yao cares not whether the boy lives or dies, but I will call upon the forbearance of my ancestors, waiting for the ransom."

The French Commissioner of Police filled both their glasses. "À *nos santés!*"

On a Sunday close to Christmas, the congregation of the Community Church was larger than usual. The church, a nonsectarian Protestant organization, stood almost directly across from the Shanghai American School on the rural Avenue Pétain at the western end of the French Concession. At the individual missions—Episcopal, Presbyterian, Baptist, and Methodist—services were conducted in Chinese in a variety of emotions ranging from evangelical enthusiasm to disciplined reserve. Only here at the Community Church did these self-exiled visionaries and adventurers come together, creating an odd mixture of patriotism, echoes of regional traditions, and a sense of ongoing connection and nurture from their homelands.

Today, the Reverend Mr. Hulburt, in his black gown and starched white Geneva bands, stepped to the pulpit and said, "My good friends, as most of you know by now, two nights ago—it seems an eternity of suffering to this family dear to us all—the Grangers were visited by a tragedy that rent the very fabric of their life. Our dear brother, Wilson Granger, has asked us to join him in prayer for the safe restoration of his son."

The entire congregation stirred as Wilson Granger mounted the steps of the podium. His face showed the ravages of these two days. Behind his rimless glasses, his eyes seemed swollen.

He threw back his head, closed his eyes, and began, "Dear Lord, we come to Thee in humble petition for relief from our anguish. We know that this may indeed be a test put upon our own faith, yet we pray that the innocent lamb, our son, may be spared. For if there is guilt it is the guilt of the father. As didst Thou test Abraham, asking him to take the life of Isaac, his son, so let me, the father, offer myself. Strengthen me in my faith not to yield to the temptations of Mammon. . . ."

Those of the more evangelical faiths among the congregation were held rapt by this confession of sin and guilt. Others, though clearly sympathetic, were critical of this "abasement."

". . . Let us not forget the lesson which Thou hast vouchsafed to us so few years ago when one of our misguided sisters, in her zeal to collect funds for the buildings of this very edifice, approached citizens—I cannot state this strongly enough—whose wealth, whose inheritance, whose birthright was truly *filthy lucre,* their money, my friends, stained by nicotine and reeking of alcohol." Wilson Granger opened his eyes and addressed the congregation. "Dear friends, all of you remember what the right-thinking elders of this church were forced to do." His voice cracked with the strain. "We had to return it. To take it, to use it, even to obtain our dearest wish, would have been to make this not a holy sanctuary of the Lord, but one built upon sand. This is blood money and I cannot accept blood money now, even to redeem my child."

"The man's an idiot! He can't mean what he's saying." And, disregarding their usually strict conventions, the congregation began whispering excitedly.

Seven-year-old Jordan Logan-Fisher, daughter of Madeline and Andrew Logan-Fisher, one of the few British members of the congregation, ceased tugging on her golden curls, stopped admiring the lace on her brand-new little gloves, and stopped counting the black tufts in her tiny ermine muff or the diamond panes in the rainbow-hued stained-glass windows. Her sea-green eyes sparkled. For the first time in her short life, she paid attention to what was going on in church. What her amah said was true. People could come in the night and take you away. Had this Matthew Granger been a bad boy? When she was bad, her amah always told her that a fox spirit might come for her. When she had asked her amah what those spirits looked like, the old woman said, "Oh, they are beautiful. You see them as the images of your own desire, but once they have you in their grasp, their fox faces, their sharp teeth show themselves and they will nab you by the back of the neck and haul you away to their lair." Jordan shivered. When Peter Pan came for Wendy, they had wonderful adventures. Jordan glanced over to the adjoining pew where that big boy, Harley Fitch, sat. He looked so handsome and so strong. But the kidnappers hadn't taken him. What must the other boy be like? All the way home, as her parents discussed things like money, Jordan's mind was occupied with fox spirits. If they took you away, did you turn into one? Would that Matthew Granger carry a fox within him if he came back?

The warlord Nyi Chuen-yao, who controlled all the countryside surrounding the sprawling metropolis, lived just two *li* beyond the limits of the international city. Near the intersection of what the foreigners called Hungjao Road and Great Western Road, his compound was close enough to the Shanghai Ningpo Railway for him to commandeer its facilities when necessary. Seen from the outside, it looked like a typical large family compound, made up of a big front courtyard beyond which clustered several smaller units.

Nyi Chuen-yup, the warlord's ten-year-old son, looked around with both pleasure and distaste at the large and varied tapestry that had formed his life until he had been sent to school. His father's off-duty soldiers crouched down around charcoal braziers, warming their hands and exchanging rowdy jokes as they gambled. A man noisily blew his nose into his hand and carefully tossed the offending glob into the dust. Others coughed freely, spat, hawked phlegm into the hot coals. At the True Heart School, the teachers called such behavior "barbaric."

Chuen-yup knew that he went to the mission school only to learn English so that he could deal directly with the foreigners without fear of being swindled and to better pull tricks of his own against the odorous round-eye. Even so, he liked some of their strange ways. Their food was disgusting, but the women at the school had been kind and made jokes with him. The wife of the headmaster stayed up all one long night with Chuen-yup when the fever took him, bathing his forehead, singing barbarian songs, holding his hand, treating him—Chuen-yup felt—with greater concern than his own mother ever had.

Now Chuen-yup gazed upon his father with frank respect. He knew this man, so rough in his ways, was as brave as a dragon. He had fought other leaders up and down the China coast—always in the front of his army with his gun or his sword—and had brought order and decorum to almost all of this province. There was no one in the whole city and the country around it who was not afraid of Nyi Chuen-yao.

"Sit down, my son," the warlord said. "Tell me what it has been like to live among the foreigners, and how much of their language you have learned."

Chuen-yup did not mention the night of his sickness. Knowing that his father wished to laugh at the foreigners, and with only a slight feeling of disloyalty, he tried to be entertaining.

"For this great holiday of theirs—Christmas—they replaced their three-headed god with an evergreen tree, putting candles and strings of colored beads upon it."

His father looked at him suspiciously. "Do you joke with your father? You must tell the truth."

"I am telling you the truth, Father. One of their strangest customs when they pray to their unseen, three-headed god is to kneel facing their chairs, and call upon their god for help."

The warlord grunted. "Go on."

"They are so stupid and easy to fool. When our headmaster wished to make the first courtyard into a space for one of their games called 'tennis,' the oldest of the unmarried ladies had her gardener plant a flowering bush in the center of the vast field of grass. This was an insult to the headmaster. We all wondered what could be done to avenge this insult. This was our plan—every night, all the boys asked Cook to make us up a barbarian sweet to eat. They call it 'ice cream.' It is made of cow's milk and sugar—"

His father spat in disapproval.

"Yes, it is disgusting! It is made in a vat with water and salt. I cannot explain the process, but every night after we had eaten this sweet"—Chuen-yup could not admit that he had learned to like the texture and flavor of the concoction—"we took the salty water, waited until darkness came, and then two of us would run out with the bucket and pour it on the roots of the shrub."

The mighty warlord gazed at him blankly. "Why did you do that?"

"To kill the shrub, of course."

"Why?"

"Because of the insult to—"

His father scowled.

Chuen-yup felt an ebbing of confidence. For some reason—who knew why?—his father didn't like the story. All at once he longed for the safety of the mission. He had forgotten that it was always dangerous here. He fell silent and looked at the glowing coals and restless tongues of fire that licked up into the darkness.

On this night, his first night home, Chuen-yup was lucky. The awkward silence that had come between him and his father was broken as two henchmen dragged a cringing man and threw him on the ground.

"Just tonight we caught this pig with his snout in the rice barrel. We took him home and searched his hut. Between two mud walls we found enough rice to feed his family for a year."

Chuen-yao's soldiers stopped talking and looked over with keen interest. Some doors into the court opened. Chuen-yup shivered. His father, who had been gazing into the brazier and its tiny flames, did not change expression. His right arm drew out his sword. One flash of the metal in the firelight, one scream of agony, and the thief's hand lay in a pool of blood, clenching and opening, clenching and opening. . . .

"Take him away," the warlord said irritably, "and make him give back the rice if it hasn't been spoiled."

The men around the edges of the courtyard resumed their conversation. The warlord turned, smiling again, to his son.

"Good stories, Chuen-yup, and you tell them well. Now you must show me how well you have learned the language of the barbarian."

In only slightly accented English, Chuen-yup recited, *"Thou shalt love the Lord thy God with all thy heart, and with all thy soul, and with all thy mind. And thou shalt love thy neighbor as thyself."*

* * *

In this city given to trade, inevitable middlemen supplied the giants of export and import, the bandits of the East. Although most Shanghai Chinese disdained foreigners, a canny few turned to this calling and made their families rich by importing and selling strange and unsavory products for the round-eye. The most important of these "compradors" was Wang Sze-jing, a fleshy man of middle height who dealt shrewdly with his varied clientele. By now not only foreigners came to him, but those Chinese who had developed a taste for Western ways. Chuen-yao's men came here for cigars from Cuba; Madame Yiang's brothel was kept stocked with British gin and Russian vodka.

"Savages," Mrs. Wang grumbled to her husband from time to time. "You will bewitch us all with these foods from the Lower Kingdom. I am ashamed to go out in the streets. I, who came of good family, and was given to a merchant of shady credentials simply to redeem my father's gambling debts."

It was a familiar refrain, just as familiar as the ongoing chant which squadrons of filthy urchins sang outside Wang Sze-jing's store: "One, two, three, four, Wang Sze-jing is a comprador! Hoolung-za is a steamboat. . . . Americans are damn fools!"

This morning, Wang Sze-jing himself took care of the order of one his very best customers while his wife lamented, "The rich and evil merchant, Harley Fitch, steals girl infants from the baby tower—where girls from poor families are sent to die an honorable death. He uses them to satisfy his unspeakable lusts." The Fitches' cook, Ah-li, ordered tinned *babas au rhum* and imported *petit fours*. He also selected caviar, two cases of champagne, and a quantity of Angostura Bitters.

Mrs. Wang's temper turned to pure dismay when she realized that this morning she would have to wait upon Da Sze Foo, head cook to that missionary family whose patriarch had a worse reputation even than Fitch.

"It is well known," Mrs. Wang muttered to her husband, "that those purple-skinned foreigners must bribe starving men to go worship their devil."

"Swallow your tongue, old witch," he replied. "Money from the devil will swell your daughter's dowry."

Da Sze Foo, whose name meant simply "chief cook," was used to his icy welcome here and bowed formally as he placed the Grangers' order: New England water biscuits, two boxes of

soda crackers, Rose's lime juice, and (this was most unusual) a
bottle of spirits of wine, which, Mrs. Wang well knew, was far
stronger than foreign gin or vodka.

"Is this the honesty of your master?" she inquired,
showing a sardonic smile in which gold teeth glittered. "Has
he not taken pains to spread the story that he drinks nothing
stronger than Welch's grape juice? The entire city knows how
he humiliated the servants of Koon Hing-kee, who, on inviting
your master to a banquet, had provided the best red wines that
the foreigners make. And what did your master do? He took
one swallow, turned as red as the grape the wine was made
from, and ordered it taken away. Then he announced that he
had committed a sin in his own devil god's eyes so that disgrace
was heaped on a family of good quality. You may tell me, Da
Sze Foo," she said, thumping the bottle onto the counter, "that
you use this for disinfectant, but I know better."

"Swallow your tongue!" Wang Sze-jing repeated ominously.

But the Grangers' cook nodded his head in agreement.
"Your wife is right. This bottle is to be drunk and by my
mistress. It has been prescribed as a medicine to keep the
heart and soul from leaving her body. Strange as the foreigners
seem to us, they love their sons even as we do. My mistress
fears that her kidnapped son will never be returned alive."

"Why don't they pay the ransom?" asked the Fitches' cook
impatiently.

"Their god won't let them," Da Sze Foo said. "My master's
head is in the clouds instead of on his shoulders where it
should be, and they may lose their son."

The Fitches' cook exploded, "*Mei-kok-ngung sze dam-
folo*! Americans are damn fools!"

Only after the two men left did other servants crowd up to
the counter for their turns. Wing On, personal servant to the
warlord Nyi Chuen-yao, placed his usual order for Cuban
cigars, then, in uncertain tones, reading from a scribbled list,
"New England cold water biscuits and Irish oatmeal." The
servants behind Wing On exchanged glances. The next one,
stepping up, said, "My master, King of the British in this city,
requires . . ." And only after he had left did a slim Eurasian
girl of no more than seven approach the counter.

"So, Tsing Tai-ling, what evil errand has your mother sent
you on this morning when all the world knows you should be
home, learning the duties of a decent woman, or in your case,
the arts of a girl of the streets?" Mrs. Wang asked.

In a half-whisper, the girl put in her order. "I would like champagne, angostura bitters, and cocktail sugar cubes."

"Is that what the four-legged animal drinks at home?" Mrs. Wang queried.

And her husband repeated, in their tired ritual, "Swallow your tongue. The money from that animal pays for your daughter's dowry."

Out in the humid sunlight, Da Sze Foo, sitting in the back of the Grangers' Model T, surrounded by foreign groceries, felt sure that his errand had not been useless. If the foreigners he worked for were too incompetent to save their boy, at least now a muted cry for help had gone out along the lines of the Chinese servant network.

Midmorning of the following day, Andrew Logan-Fisher surveyed the crowded Bund from his seventh-floor office in the Sassoon Building—austere and cramped quarters for a not-too-distant cousin of the Duke of Dorset. He longed for his Oxfordshire family home, The Beeches, where even now his aged parents must be making ready for the holiday season. He remembered mistletoe and Christmas pudding and tramping along hedgerows turned silver with frost.

He cursed the tradition that sent younger sons of every upper-class British family out across the entire world to make their fortunes. A second cousin had founded his own hunt club in Southern California, making a fortune before he died; an eccentric uncle had bought up thousands of square miles of Australia's Gibson Desert, exploiting aborigines and forcing those acres of uninhabitable sand to yeild up another fortune of bauxite and zinc. His own younger brother was buying up farmland in Mexico.

Logan-Fisher lamented his own softheartedness, his inattention to profit and loss, his inability to store up sums of money and turn that profit into castles or factories. It was the enduring fate of the Logan-Fishers that their "poor" branch devoted itself to public service, to make up for the piratical excesses of its more savage relations. Andrew Logan-Fisher, fresh out of Peterhouse, Cambridge, had come to Shanghai with more ideals than money, and his loving wife, Madeline, who in her energy and boundless good nature, knew that they could surmount any difficulties that might come their way.

Logan-Fisher sighed. So far they had been lucky. His limited income stretched here in Shanghai so that he and

Madeline lived with a comfort and graciousness that were in some ways comparable to the sheltered beauty of The Beeches. Their only daughter, Jordan—and here his fingers unconsciously touched the wood of his old-fashioned roll-top desk—was strong, and so far had avoided the fevers and epidemics that periodically afflicted this enticing city. But to think of this kidnapping! What if kidnappings were to sweep the city, like the cholera that had killed Philip Granger nine years ago?

In the years since he'd come out, he had learned to love Shanghai. He had found a job that perfectly suited the Logan-Fisher idealism, becoming administrator to all China of the Boxer Indemnity Fund. In the past hundred years there had been a crazy tug of war between East and West. The British had forced opium on an unwilling China and then cried for reform. At the turn of the century, those young Chinese zealots who called themselves Boxers—devoted as they were to martial arts—had taken "reform" into their own hands and kept the entire foreign community of Peking under siege for fifty-four terrifying days. When Western soldiers relieved the beleaguered civilians, an outraged international community demanded reparations, but—and this was the characteristic that made Logan-Fisher proud to be an Englishman—the English had decided to pour those moneys back into the Chinese community to further the education of the youth of China, both at home and abroad. Andrew Logan-Fisher took inordinate pride in the fact that he'd seen more than a score of students he knew personally through either the University of Peking or St. John's University here in Shanghai. Above all else, Logan-Fisher cherished his own personal honesty. Citizens of Shanghai might sneer at the French for their corruption, but they could never say that Andrew Logan-Fisher in any way abused the privileges of his office.

Individual integrity counted for little in a political climate where the strongest man ruled. Again Andrew Logan-Fisher thought of his little girl. Jordan was so beautiful! Reason told him to return to England now before the authority of the British Empire was entirely undermined, but something stronger prevailed.

The Sunday after his last ill-fated appearance at the Community Church, and the tenth day after his son's kidnapping, Wilson Granger stayed home to deliver one of his monthly sermons in Chinese. Looking over the congregation of polite oriental faces, he felt despair. As was customary, the women sat on the left side of the church as he faced them, and the men on the right. The church was full, but he knew very well that many of them were what critics of the mission movement called "rice Christians."

The congregation stood to sing "Jesus Loves Me" in Chinese, and settled itself for the hour-long discussion on the mysterious nature of the One God in Three Parts. Wilson Granger—dressed in the gray silk Chinese gown he wore for these services—appeared to be at a loss. Even his quite fluent Wu dialect deserted him. Instead of the usual sermon, he asked simply that God should forgive him his sins.

Small children began to cross the aisle from one parent to the other. In his early years, Wilson Granger had found this distracting. Today, however, he saw it as a special reminder from the Lord that no child of his was here to gladden his heart.

Usually aware of each member of the congregation, he failed to notice a plainly dressed Chinese woman and her Eurasian child sitting in the back pew on the women's side. The mother was in the full flower of womanhood. To anyone with an eye for such things, and there were many of those across the aisle, she exuded an animal attractiveness. While the other children skipped back and forth, her daughter sat quietly by her mother's side.

At the end of his faltering remarks, Wilson Granger preceded the congregation down the aisle and out onto the church steps. It was his custom to greet all members as they filed out. Most of them responded with formal phrases.

"You have indeed brought us the message of the true god," they would say. But this morning, more than one parent said, "We, too, know what it is to suffer for our children."

The Chinese woman with the Eurasian child held back until all the others had left. Then she approached, pushing her daughter to one side, telling her to wait with the other children.

"I have some information concerning your son," she said tentatively.

Wilson Granger looked at her for a few seconds before he recognized her. She was far from being a regular churchgoer, but he knew that Elizabeth had taken a special interest in the child.

"When the adulteress was taken out to be stoned," he began, "our Lord himself stepped forward when all the people of the village stood ready to be part of that slaughter. He said, 'Let he who is without sin cast the first stone.' None of us is without sin. You must know that only last week I refused tainted money. How then can I take information from a woman living in sin? It is not too late for you to repent."

Mei-fen flushed. She walked away, her head held high. As she approached the nearby group of children, she saw that her daughter, Tai-ling, was the center of it, a target for teasing insults.

Seeing her mother, Tai-ling broke away. She took Mei-fen's hand, and together they left the mission compound.

Later that same afternoon, Mei-fen, still smarting from the minister's harsh words, considered that at least he had been right about one thing. She was not yet ready to give up her life of "sin." Languid, she gazed at the body of her contented lover. Surely he was more handsome than the crucified Christ. She thought she could discern behind the swaying beaded curtain the somber figure of their little girl. How cruel they had been to her today!

"To give up your child for something you cannot see. What stupidity!" she said out loud.

Harley Fitch brought the palm of her hand to his lips. "What is it, my darling?"

"Our daughter came home from the comprador's. . . ." For a moment shame stopped her speech, but then she blurted out every particular, including her humiliating morning. "Don't misunderstand. I can bear the thorns of the missionary's remarks although they make me bleed. But when I think that Nyi Chuen-yao will kill an innocent child—a boy that could have been your son Harley. . . ."

Her lover looked at her in the dying light. "What do you want me to do?"

"Rescue that boy. I know you have the power to do it. That way, you reward a mother and you punish the man who insulted me."

As soon as Harley Fitch returned home that evening he sent a messenger to the warlord's compound out by the Hungjao Road announcing his intention to call upon him within the hour.

Young Harley, who had passed a boring afternoon banging

tennis balls against the brick wall of the garden, followed and watched in awe as the older man drew down a half dozen pistols always kept in a locked cabinet in his study, loaded them, and distributed them to a ragtag entourage of Fitch servants.

"Dad, what is it? Where are you going? Can I go along?"

"I'm sorry, son. This could be dangerous. But if everything goes the way it should, your little missionary friend will be home by midnight."

"I can shoot a gun. . . ."

But already his father was clattering down the stairs. "When a man crosses you, destroy him."

Young Harley watched in mounting fury as the Fitch town car skidded down the gravel driveway and turned north out of the gate. The rescue as well as the abduction had eluded him.

The members of Nyi Chuen-yao's heavily defended compound reacted hurriedly to the announcement of the notorious foreigner's imperious message. Chuen-yao walked through the courtyards ordering his lounging soldiers to snap to attention, commanding the servants to build great bonfires. The women prepared as great a feast as possible under these curtailed circumstances. The guards at the outer gate were tripled. Chuen-yao, once he saw that his orders were being carried out, quickly returned to his quarters, shucked his bulky military uniform, and donned a mandarin's robe: dark gray and emblazoned with an embroidered phoenix both front and back—a gift from an actual mandarin who had hoped in this way to be spared the warlord's wrath. He dipped a small towel in water scented with jasmine and buried his face in its steaming, fragrant folds. He scrutinized every inch of his inner courtyard. Something—someone—was missing.

"Where is my son?" he bellowed. "I need him to speak the barbarian tongue, and I wish to see him in barbarian clothes."

A few minutes later, a door opened. Chuen-yup was thrust out, his hair hastily combed, his face fearful and anxious. Father and son waited in silence until the Fitch town car arrived at the gate.

Fitch—no more honest in his business dealings than Nyi himself—had an eye for the dramatic. He stopped the Packard a quarter mile away and arranged his bodyguard, three to a running board, pistols drawn, fedoras pulled down to conceal their features. Traveling at no more than twelve miles an hour, the town car made its progress. Harley Fitch knew that all the members of the Nyi compound would recognize this display from the imported Hollywood gangster movies so popular in the city. If all went well in these negotiations, Nyi Chuen-yao could become an important business partner.

In a matter of minutes the two men confronted each other, with a ten-year-old boy standing nervously between them. Nyi Chuen-yao grinned savagely at the American businessman. The warlord spoke to his son. "Tell our visitor in his own language that we are happy to see him and we hope that his family prospers."

Chuen-yup began to do his best to speak this message in the English that he had learned, but he was cut short by Fitch, who said, "*My* family prospers, but we have no time for this politeness. Please tell your father that we must do business."

The warlord grunted.

Fitch rapidly continued. "My family prospers because last week some hired thugs made a foolish mistake. I'm sure that your father," he said, nodding at the boy, "knows what it is to deal with stupid underlings."

As Chuen-yup, trembling, whispered out these words, Fitch went on arrogantly, "As the most powerful man in Shanghai, I was the one chosen to have his son stolen by thieves in the night. Since these thugs, whose stupidity knows no bounds, took the wrong child, it falls to me to repair this embarrassing mistake, not just for myself but for the honor of the natives who took the boy, since everyone laughs at thieves who are sent to steal a chicken and come home merely with one rotten egg."

The warlord said something in Chinese, which his son knew should not be translated.

"Tell your father," Fitch said to the boy, "that I come to him because he is a powerful man, at least among his own people, and perhaps he can help me in this matter."

"May your genitals shrivel and turn as bitter as the dried plum," the warlord remarked.

And his son translated, his voice steady, "My father suggests that you refresh yourself with a few of the sweetmeats which the women of the compound are even now bringing."

Fitch coughed. The warlord spat. "What about the ransom?" he said.

Fitch answered immediately, without waiting for Chuen-yup. "Half now and half when the boy is home in his mother's arms. It occurs to me that the course of civil order might be best served if your father, the renowed Nyi Chuen-yao, were to mount this 'rescue' himself, returning the child to the missionary compound. That way his honor in the city will be heightened and the peculiar beliefs of the missionary will not be challenged."

The men's eyes locked. Then the warlord bent double with laughter. "I get the ransom. I do the rescue. I get the credit. And you may tell that barbarian," he said to his son, "that I will be sure those bungling thugs get the punishment they deserve."

Fitch barely waited to hear the boy out. "Very well, my work here is done." He bowed formally and said, "Perhaps your father will be good enough to send you with me until his work in the city is completed. When it is, I shall send you home with the other half of the ransom and with, of course, my most profound thanks."

This time it was the warlord who cut his son short. "A street dog afflicted with ringworm has more dignity than our visitor. You will go with him while I go with my men to dredge up the sea slug they set such value on and return him to his mother."

"Your father is the very emblem of courtesy in this part of the world and, of course, that is no more than I expected." It was Fitch's turn to laugh.

For the first time in Matthew's life the manners that both his mother and the cook had taught him seemed important. He realized that the men who stayed with him during the long days—precisely because they were so insignificant—needed every scrap of respect that he could give them. The better they knew him the more apt they might be in an emergency to spare his life.

Twice a day when the ancient woman brought him meals, he protested, saying, "This is too much food for a worthless boy. You will spoil me so that I won't want to return to my family when the time comes." And even though his stomach growled in protest, he insisted on giving half of each bowl of gray noodles to the old woman for her grandchildren.

Matthew had been delighted when some of the men taught him their gambling games. First because it took his mind off his fear, and second for the sheer pleasure of the intellectual exertion it took to master these fairly simple rituals. The men, for their part, were gratified and amused by the submissiveness with which the young foreign devil gave himself up to their instruction. By the middle of the third day, Matthew was able to win, but he knew by the grumbling among the grown-ups that he had made a serious mistake. From then on he took care to lose almost every game, protesting all the while that he would never learn, and running up a debt of millions of dollars which he insisted, since he had no money on earth, that his father would pay them in heaven. This joke appealed to them enormously. They made a great ceremony of keeping the accounts. But even the novelty of gambling with his captors on a Sunday was not enough to relieve the tedium of his days.

Tonight, as on the last ten nights, his guard laughed triumphantly and slapped his cards on the table. "*Ai-yah!*" Matthew howled and smote his forehead with the palm of his hand, repeating the joke. "It's a good thing my father will be a millionaire in heaven!"

Was it his imagination or did they laugh less loudly? His answer came to him more quickly than he could have guessed, because by the end of the next hand the street noises below had increased to pandemonium. He saw the guards exchanging knowing glances, and he heard one of them whisper, "Here they are."

Down in the street, a voice of brass shouted, "We've come to rescue the small white devil in the name of our warlord, the most honorable Nyi Chuen-yao, who desires nothing more than order and decorum, and is willing to risk life to make justice."

The invaders beat on the door with clubs. Quickly, Matthew's caretakers let them in. With mock energy, they attempted to protect their charge. They shook their fists at the rescuers, one of them saying, "You cannot have him. You're taking our wealth. This boy is worth fifty thousand dollars."

"Fifty thousand for such a small boy?"

"Yes, fifty thousand, but seeing there's so many of you, we bow to your superior force."

Matthew felt gentle hands on his arms as he was taken to a waiting car. He climbed into the backseat. A man in full military regalia turned to look at him. Matthew knew that it must be Nyi Chuen-yao.

Soon, Matthew stood at his own front door, conscious of
the heavy hand on his shoulder. The Grangers' servant opened
to the warlord's harsh knocking, and Matthew heard the voice
just behind him boom out, "Yes, it is I. Your eyes do not
deceive you. It is I, Nyi Chuen-yao, whose concern for
community order extends to all our citizens hereabout, even
the intrusive foreigner. Go, young man," he said, "make your
parents happy and tell them that the vigilant armies of the
mighty Nyi Chuen-yao are ever mindful of their safety."

Then Matthew felt his mother's arms around him and her
tears upon his upturned face. The warlord did an about-face.
As they heard him departing, Matthew's father came out from
his study, which opened into the large front hall. Seeing his
son, Wilson Granger cried out, "Our prayers have been
answered! The lost sheep has been returned to the flock. We
must give thanks to our Lord for his mercy."

Wilson Granger fell to his knees. Some few of the servants
followed suit; others withdrew. Before Matthew and his
mother could kneel, Matthew said in a clear voice, "But it
wasn't the Lord at all, Father! Harley Fitch's dad paid off the
warlord. That's what they were saying on the stairs. . . . "

In the awkward silence that followed, Matthew realized
that he had said the wrong thing. His mother's arms were still
tight about him, but Matthew saw that her eyes were on her
husband. Then he heard his father's voice take up his prayer.

"Even as Abraham was ready to sacriface Isaac, the Lord
in his infinite mercy intervened. . . . " His father's voice
faltered and his anguished eyes scanned the small group
assembled in the entry hall. Without another word he rose and
stumbled to his study.

Matthew's mother gave her son one last convulsive hug,
hesitated for a moment, and followed her husband into his
sanctuary, shutting the door.

Almost before Matthew could think that this was an odd
welcome, the servants closed in around him and spirited him
away to the kitchen. With high-pitched screams of rejoicing,
one after another hugged him, pinched his cheeks, told him
how much he'd grown—though he needed feeding.

"You must be as poisonous and hard to digest as the
scropion, Little Master, since the ferocious sea serpent, Nyi
Chuen-yao, tried to swallow you and was forced to cough you
up."

"With the power of his words alone the Little Master has

set himself free," another said. "His wit must be as dangerous as ten thousand knives."

Then Da Sze Foo's wife, Matthew's amah, came out, and began to cry. "These old eyes never thought they would see you again. Come sit on my lap and let me feed you a little something."

Matthew perched on the stout woman's knee and felt his head being drawn to her shoulder. Even though he knew himself to be too old for the comforts of his amah's lap, he yielded to this welcome, knowing at last that he had finally come home.

Before the time came for the spring semester to begin, the Kuling American School closed indefinitely. Chiang Kai-shek's northward sweep to unify China encircled the Lushan Mountains. Anti-foreign feeling had intensified and even provoked riots in some of the interior cities. *China for the Chinese!*—a cry that had been heard intermittently since the death of the Empress Dowager in 1908—once again swept the land.

The children of foreigners, for so many years packed off to boarding schools, found themselves in the not unpleasant predicament of having to attend a handy urban substitute, the Shanghai American School. Matthew knew only too well that the beginning weeks at a new school were a period of proving oneself. On his first day at the Shanghai American School, he felt part of the shyness of a new student until Maud Brown, whom he'd known forever, came right up to him and said, "Well, if it isn't Matthew Granger! We thought you were never going to escape from those awful kidnappers!"

Matthew felt a surge of relief. This time the proving had been done for him. He felt no uncertainty until his third-period Latin class when, looking guardedly around the room, he saw staring at him the half-hostile, half-friendly face of Harley Compton Fitch III. As the lunch bell rang and the other students ran pell-mell out into the yard, Harley held back and so did Matthew.

"You don't really want to hang around here," Harley said. "Let's go down to Avenue Joffre to the pastry shop. I'll treat. We can pretend we're going to 110 Shanghai Road."

"Isn't it against the rules to leave the school yard?" Matthew asked. But as the other boy waited, he said, "Sure,

I'll go along, but what's this junk about 110 Shanghai Road? You ought to know there's no street in the city named that!"

They had sneaked out of the back gate beside the bull pen of Culty's Dairy and gone down a narrow path to Avenue Joffre, where they turned left.

Harley strutted. "That's what you think. Of course there *really* isn't. But that's what men say when they're going off to do dirty things to girls . . . or, well, gamble . . . or, well, you know. . . ."

At the pastry shop, Harley took the initiative and pushed his way to the front of the case. "I'll have one of those," he said pointing, "and one of those."

When the girl behind the counter looked puzzled, Matthew stepped forward. "*Il voudrait un napoléon, et un éclair, et pour moi, un napoléon, et une mille-feuille.*"

"You still think you're smart, don't you?"

"Well, I still am, and it may not be too late for you to learn decent French. It always comes in handy."

Harley thought to himself, Oh, you stuck-up little bugger. But he was enough of his father's son to recognize the main chance and take advantage of it.

"Tell you what, Matt, I'll make sure you get on my soccer team when we choose up sides this afternoon if you help me with my homework tonight."

As the boys took the pastries to a tiny table, the proprietor hastened over with a big pot of chocolate and two extra desserts. "For our returning hero," he said in French, "and please give our regards to your family." Without speaking, both boys crunched into the delicate crusts.

Inside this little shop the world seemed cozy, intimate, and safe. Outside, all of Shanghai, all of China, and the rest of the world seethed with unrest.

Book I

ROMANCE
1937

With heavy whimsy the board of the American Shipping Company had named its most important freighters after the great ships of history. The SS *Golden Hind*, one day out of San Francisco on its way to Yokohama, Shanghai, Macao and Singapore, carried a valuable cargo of auto parts. But Captain Wylie Cochran—bluff, hardy and a seaman of the old school—gave thanks for his second cargo of two human beings. By nature a gregarious man, Cochran cherished the fleeting friendships that he struck up on the all too monotonous trans-Pacific run. After twenty years of seafaring in this part of the world he could truly say that he had friends—as well as women—in each of his ports of call.

Surveying his guests at dinner the first night out, Captain Cochran's genial face lit up as he surveyed the two young Americans returning to Shanghai from college—both of them Stanford graduates. The captain was experienced enough, through his Shanghai connections, to know that the names of Fitch and Granger had standing in that international community. Cochran also knew that each had represented a different aspect of Shanghai society. More than anything else, Captain Cochran loved the company of beautiful young women. Failing that, he delighted in the presence of youths whose lives lay before them. It brought out his philosophical turn of mind, and after dinner, the captain introduced as a conversational topic the evanescence of life.

"Well, boys," he began heartily, "it may surprise you to

51

know that I've heard much about your families. Old China Hands, the lot of them. But haven't you both been to Stanford?" He found himself almost speechless as he struggled to put his notion into words. "At the university, I remember, life stretched out. It seemed as if I had all the time in the world. But you're going back to a country torn by war."

"We won't be there for long, sir," Harley said. "After the summer, we'll be going to school in England."

"That's right!" the captain said. He looked straight at Harley. "Didn't I read, while we were laid up in San Francisco, that you've won a Rhodes Scholarship?"

Harley shrugged. His broad shoulders tensed under his Brooks Brothers Palm Beach suit.

"I am going on to Oxford, but I'm not the Rhodes man. My friend here is the scholar."

"I go to class, if that's what you mean."

Although Matthew was dressed as correctly as his friend, his dark brown hair and long-lashed brown eyes gave him a slightly foreign look. Prominent cheek bones, hollow cheeks, an almost frail wrist barely showing under his perfectly shot cuffs, all this—together with his tall, lean frame—gave him the air of someone with a touch of the tar brush. In this light, he looked almost oriental.

"That's the problem with Matt, Captain. He wouldn't know fun if it punched him in the nose."

Several rounds of brandy later, the young men's bickering ceased and the conversation grew markedly more frank.

"No, no, no," the captain insisted. "I allow myself beautiful women as a tantalizing dessert, but I knew I'd be destroyed if I saw them on a daily basis. There is pain in love! Even in sex, there is often as much anguish as ecstasy."

"In *my* experience, women have been all too eager to seize pleasure. Isn't their whole life a search to find a man who can fulfill them? Why, I know a place, at 110 Shanghai Road . . ." Here Harley winked conspiratorially at Matthew.

But the captain was used to the braggadocio of youth. "Some of us haven't been as lucky as you've been, Fitch. What about you, Granger? Seriously, what do you think on this subject?"

Matthew stared into his brandy. "I have no experience at all. But I would imagine that the captain is right. Whatever the pleasure between men and women, isn't there always the possibility of rejection, or separation, or domination, or even cruelty? And wouldn't it be true that the more you love somebody, the more those things would hurt?"

A somewhat morose silence settled over the small party. The captain rose. "We'll have twenty more nights to ponder these questions. Luckily, we don't have to settle them all this evening."

Later that night, Harley and Matthew lay stretched out on their bunks, reading. Matthew, though he turned the pages steadily, concentrated most of his thought on his cabinmate. Just two weeks before, Matthew had received an unusually long letter from his mother. Among other things, she had said that she regretted not being able to send him anything beyond his regular allowance.

"It hasn't been a month," she wrote, "since the American and Far East Bank closed its doors, and yesterday Harley Fitch was arraigned in the American Court on charges of embezzlement and misuse of funds for his own personal investments. I need hardly say that your father has reminded me more than once of his disapproval when I made that investment of my own family money. But, of course, I considered that I had a lifelong debt of gratitude to Mr. Fitch for saving your life eleven years ago. And it always seemed to me that since Mr. Fitch was the president of the bank, nothing could go wrong. Your father—and I suppose we should be thankful for it—has never had any confidence except in the Hong Kong and Shanghai Bank, with its imperial stone lions staring out across the Bund. . . ."

Matthew had tried to think of a tactful way to broach the subject with Harley. But how do you ask your friend if his father's a crook? Matthew had been surprised tonight when Harley announced his plan of going to Oxford—something he had never mentioned before. For years in Shanghai, the rumor had been that Old Fitch made daring investments abroad, depositing the profits in his wife's private Swiss account. In effect, Harley would be going to Oxford—at least in part—on Matthew's mother's money. But if Harley preferred to keep his family scandal a secret, at least until the *Golden Hind* put in at Shanghai, that was his own business.

Matthew allowed his eyes to flick over toward his friend, whose book had fallen on his chest. Asleep, Harley looked almost as sexually innocent as he had when they were boarders together in Kuling. And, Matthew suspected, he really was.

What a performer! All that bawdy boasting at dinner, when it was probably nothing more than his own fevered wishes.

Matthew thought about his own life. He smiled when he thought of what "Shanghai" meant to the outside world: that old daydream of 110 Shanghai Road; opium dens, brothels, beautiful women beyond count who would acquiesce to your most bizarre desires for a few silver dollars. Matthew thought of the tea parties, the "courtesy aunts," the gallons of lemonade, the Boy Scout encampment, the father-and-son tennis tournaments that made up *his* Shanghai. How could a young man go about losing his virginity in the midst of all that? The mere thought of pushing Maud Brown up against a hedge and ravishing her while everyone else munched French finger sandwiches and exchanged pleasantries made him grin. Whatever his anxieties about this matter, at least he had the satisfaction of knowing—almost for sure—that Harley shared them.

Lights upon lights upon lights. Whole cities of twinkling lights whirled past her as mirror upon mirror returned the reflections of the huge chandelier in the great ballroom of the Shanghai French Club. The band played a Strauss waltz and, reflected in those glittering mirrors, one sole couple danced. He was tall and courtly and in full dress uniform. A red sash crossed his chest and he wore his medals just for her. Nestled into his shoulder, she could see, caught in the mirrors, a head full of dazzling golden curls. Her amah had labored over them all day and told her that tonight she would be a foreign witch, a Silver Princess, a Queen of Lights.

If she glanced down from the mirrors, she saw herself dancing in a sea of silver-gray chiffon flecked with marquisette florets and a light spray of silver sequins. How she had fought! What tantrums she went through to get this dress! Her mother pleaded with her to choose the powder blue—or even worse, pale pink taffeta—but she said no! She was eighteen now. An adult, a woman of the world, and living in a metropolis that valued, above all else, sophistication. After the dress, the entire effect would have been ruined if she'd not had the high-heeled silver sandals. Only this afternoon had she remembered that those sandals, which set off her almost perfect ankles, would make her the same height as her escort for tonight.

But she didn't have to worry about that now. Because

now she danced with the Honorable Andrew Logan-Fisher, M.B.E., the handsomest man in Shanghai, her father. And she knew without a doubt that she, Jordan Logan-Fisher, just now celebrating her eighteenth birthday, was the most exquisite girl in Shanghai and perhaps all of China.

Her blond curls, her deep green eyes, her perfect teeth, the cheeks that her amah said took their color from the peony blossom, everything attested to this fact. Tomorrow every teenage foreign girl in the city would be crying her eyes out for a dress of silver-gray chiffon.

If, on some other occasions, working with her father in his office translating in five languages—Russian, Wu, Cantonese, Mandarin, and her schoolgirl French—the stories of refugees who literally were willing to give anything to get out of this country, she questioned the whole fabric of this life where she was so pampered and safe, let her not think of these things tonight. She was eighteen, she was loved, and her party was just beginning.

The waltz ended with a flurry of applause. Flushed, her head held high, Jordan left the floor with her father. Just as he turned to his wife for the second dance, Jordan gave her mother a kiss and said clearly enough to be heard by the circle of chaperones in the background, "Thank you for everything, Mama, you've made my life so wonderful!" As her mother danced off, Jordan went straight to her childhood amah, sitting shyly against the wall with a few other favorite family servants. "*Doo zia*, Amah. Thank you for everything, Amah. You've made my life so beautiful." She knelt for an instant and placed her head—not without an idea of what a pretty picture it would make—in the black satin lap of the ancient Chinese lady.

"Truly that girl is a pearl of the Orient," she heard her amah say as she turned back to the party and had the satisfaction of hearing other approving voices in Chinese: "She was trained well enough to be a daughter-in-law in one of *our* finest families."

Now, Jordan stood on the west side of the room near the table that held the alcoholic punch. She dispensed kisses to her father's many business friends, exchanging small talk with them in a variety of languages. In the background she saw the impatient face of Harley Fitch III—her escort for tonight— waiting for the next dance, his blond hair carefully slicked back, his broad shoulders hulking in a well-cut dinner jacket.

"In a minute, Harley." She waved at him. "I just need to say hello to a few people first. Do go dance with Maud. There's a good boy. Don't you see she's over there talking to that *stick*, Matthew, and he'll never ask her to dance?"

With satisfaction she looked over the shoulders of Colonel Le Poirrie and his wife and watched as Harley, unwillingly, crossed the floor and asked Maud Brown to dance. Jordan waited for and received Matthew Granger's look of sadonic resentment. She shrugged and turned away, as did he. In the previous February, within the same week, she had received two letters from Stanford undergraduates, both asking to be her escort at her eighteenth birthday. What did it matter whom you really cared about in high school? Harley had been the popular one, the rich one, the smooth dancer. Matthew had been tall, shy, and the son of a missionary. She had sent off two charming notes saying that she had asked her amah to gamble over the letters, and Harley had come out the winner.

Then, in April, Harley's father had been indicted; there had been the scandal of the arraignment. In late May, the news of Matthew's Rhodes Scholarship made all the Shanghai papers. And at the first summer tea party that the three of them attended she saw a tall, lean, elegant young man in a dazzling white linen suit bending attentively over that stodgy Maud Brown, whose organdy blouse pulled taut over her vulgarly large breasts. The young man was Matthew Granger. And he didn't even wear glasses anymore! Drat!

There was nothing she could do about it now. Surely it would have been silly to ask Matthew to take her to tonight's dance, because his *father* wouldn't dance, his *mother* wouldn't dance; it was against their *silly* religion! The rumor was that Matthew's father thought it could get you pregnant . . . and his parents hadn't accepted tonight's invitation. *Her* father had said it was because they were worried about a possible Japanese skirmish, but that was foolish! There had always been unrest in Shanghai and there always would be!

And anyway, *veh yeu fah tse*, "there was no help for it." That was what the amah said. The third dance started. Harley waited impatiently to take her in his arms. They danced to "Those Little White Lies"—"The moon was all aglow, and heaven was in your eyes. . . ." Harley's right hand grasped her back up under her shoulder blades and found its way under several layers of chiffon to her bare skin. His breath, as he half sang, half whispered the words into her ear, made the hairs on her neck stand up, and sent gooseflesh along her arms. And she could feel—oh, my—she remembered that her mother and her amah had told her to step away if that ever happened, but she just didn't want to because it felt so delicious.

Then she could feel, literally feel, between her shoulder blades, a glance as chill as Harley's hand was warm. As she was whirled about in the languid movements of a dance that somehow even she knew would be unique in all her experience, she saw across the room those dark resentful eyes of the boy she should have come with. Goddamnit! Well, if you're just going to stand there like a stick, she told him silently. If you're just going to serve lemonade to spinsters, if you're just going to stay there on the religious side of the room and look superior to everyone who's having a good time, why then you deserve everything you get, Matthew Granger!

Harley stumbled badly. The high heel of her sandal ground into his instep. This sort of thing never happened, and she had begun to apologize when she realized that both his arms tightened around her now with a kind of desperation. The floor shook beneath her and the chandeliers set up a dissonant clatter.

"It's the Nips!" someone shouted.

"Are they coming over here?"

"No," another voice called out from the balcony. "Don't worry. It's no more than half a dozen planes and they're just bombing the old Native City."

"Oh, do come out and look!" Sonja Biberman, the sloe-eyed daughter of a Russian jeweler, called. "It's really quite spectacular. Much better than Bastille Day or the American Fourth of July!"

Trapped in an ever-growing sense of unreality, Jordan, hardly conscious of Harley's arm around her, hurried out to the balcony. The Russian girl was right. At least a hundred grotesque fire flowers blossomed out there in the crowded streets of Shanghai, and the entire sky above them had turned the color of a ripe persimmon.

"What do you think they're aiming at?" she heard one person ask.

"They're missing Hungjao Airport by a mile."

And another: "They'd do best to take out the railroad. Trains are everything in this country."

And finally someone's careless "Oh, it's just the Native City, Philip. Let's go back in!"

Jordan would reflect in later years that her early life had been a series of blindnesses and visions. She would remember her utter blindness until that instant, when suddenly for just a moment she was allowed to take it all in—the wide veranda, the spoiled festivities of the night, the uncaring women in their silken frocks, that arm still around her, which represented nothing but a physical imperative (and she saw, as well, her own wish to lose herself in that physical imperative). What she would never forget was her tiny amah, who had made her way on bound feet out to the balcony railing and stretched out both her hands, crying over the distant smoking city, "My parents, my children, my life. What have you done to them?" Just beyond her, his face contorted, the missionary's son looking out over the scene in agony.

"It's all right, Matthew," she heard Harley call out. "They're nowhere near the Little South Gate. We can go on in." She felt his arm tighten about her.

She turned on Harley with a frenzy of disdain. "Oh, *why* don't you go dance with Maud? And then take her out for a drive in your brand-new car. Perhaps you can go down and see the ruins for a lark."

She saw the hurt come over his face like a dog who's been kicked but is too stupid to know the reason for it. But then she turned, blocked him out of her sight, and ran down the veranda in her precariously high heels. She knew where she wanted to go and whom she wanted to comfort, but she couldn't, so she knelt again beside her amah and put the weeping face against her neck. She said in the language that she had grown up with since she was a baby, "We will blow those filthy monkey people out of the sky, Little Mother. You shall live to see grandchildren, great-grandchildren, and great-great-grandchildren."

Later she would wonder if Matthew had looked at her at that moment, but she would also remember with a rueful inward laugh that it was the first time in her life that for a few seconds she hadn't been conscious of herself, and if she had gained a glance of approval from that strange and tormented boy, she would never know it.

The red sky lit up the courtyard of the mission compound. Elizabeth Granger looked around her at the children clothed in matching mission nightgowns, their faces tinged a strange burnt sienna by the flickering horror from above, each contributing to a fragmented chorus of wails. Their voices came to her from across the courtyard: "Is it the end of the world you've told us about, missionary lady?" "Will the devil come and take us away?" "Has hell started?"

Elizabeth Granger knew better than to curse, but curse she did those maiden missionaries who had so frivolously left their responsibilities to watch worldly people dance. Now she and her husband alone were responsible for over fifty Chinese charges. Thank God it was summertime. Thank God most of the Chinese families had had the sense to anticipate the coming attack and take their summer pupils home. But other families were evidently too far away, or too poor, or too fatalistic to think of saving their children.

Elizabeth experienced a feeling of total helplessness. She made several forays out into the quadrangle, reaching for this child or that one. Suddenly she felt a moment of un-Christian fury as she thought of her husband, who was meeting this Jap attack in his study on his knees under the sublimely egotistical assumption that the Japanese had mounted a second attack on Shanghai, as agents of the Presbyterian God, to show the Reverend Wilson Granger the error of his ways.

"Children, please!" Elizabeth called out and fought the quaver in her voice. "Remember that Jesus loves you and there's nothing to be afraid of. He wants you to come inside with me right now." She could have easily been speaking to a barnyard full of chicks, so distracted were their movements, so mindless and pitiable their squawks.

Then her worst fears were realized. A lone biplane, its Japanese markings—the dreaded rising sun—plainly visible against its ghostly white fuselage, swooped like a great bird above the mission compound. Slowly, slowly it dipped, made one pass across the grounds, then circled and came in again over the Reverend Mr. Granger's prospective tennis court. Slowly, slowly as in an interminable dream, the plane laid down two parallel lines of machine-gun bullets. Then the twin lines left the court and came across the bare earth of the compound, leaving in their wake little puffs of harmless-seeming dust. Mrs. Granger simply stood and watched, and all the children—silent now—did the same, as if mesmerized by the bright and deadly pattern of tracer bullets. Only as the plane banked once again did Elizabeth Granger find her voice. "Children!" she shouted.

But against that, a sharper, higher, more metallic voice

rang out: "*Siao nyoen!* Children! Boys and girls, form a double line like the fiery bullets and quick-march in with me this minute like little soldiers."

Once inside the first floor of the dormitory, Elizabeth Granger gazed admiringly on the only one of all her pupils she could be sure she had succeeded with. Tsing Tai-ling had survived a hell on earth as a child in this mission—scorned by both Chinese and Caucasians because of her mixed blood, the target of taunts from her schoolmates. The little girl had grown up hard as flint, impervious as steel. By now her position in the mission was absolutely secure, as the favorite teacher of the youngest children, because, forlorn and homesick as they so often were, they saw an invincible quality in the Eurasian girl that nothing and no one could touch. Elizabeth Granger loved the young outcast as she might have her own daughter, and she knew that beneath her icy facade Tai-ling cherished her. Sometimes Elizabeth Granger worried. This reciprocal emotion burning so hot beneath the ice was against all laws of blood and religion. Tai-ling did not believe in God. Indeed, Elizabeth wondered in some dark moments if she herself did anymore. Tai-ling owed her own mother, poor unfortunate creature, the debt of filial piety. But Tai-ling consistently defaulted on that debt. Her life centered on this school.

"You've saved them," Elizabeth said to Tai-ling. "You saved them when I lost my courage, dear."

Tai-ling acknowledged this with a nod and a flashing smile. Then, without appearing to raise her voice, she spoke in tones that filled the entire room and, Elizabeth felt, might have carried as far as the banks of the Whangpoo if there hadn't been an air raid in progress: "Now then, Little Soldiers, the older ones are officers. They go to the Lady General Granger for further instructions. You enlisted boys and girls will stay with me."

Mrs. Granger looked down at a circle of expectant faces, some of them still tear-stained. "Good and evil have had many wars," she said to the children, taking her cue from the brave Eurasian. "Little David fought against the strong Goliath and he won. And when Joshua led his army . . ."

She was drowned out by Tai-ling, who sat her tiny charges in a triple circle and led them in a spirited version of a hymn that would have swept the Reverend Mr. Granger away to his reward on the spot had he been there to hear it. "Rock of ages cleft for me, monkey people don't bother me! From the mountains to the sea, all the monkey people do is pee. . . ."

Elizabeth looked down at the older children and saw that their attention was wandering. "Officers," she said sternly, "go and join your troops, and that's an order." Then she went to the kitchen and ordered the terrified servants to make some hot chocolate. Tai-ling had not only saved the pupils, but taken away their fears. What a pity that the church had not seen fit to ordain women. With that girl in the pulpit there wouldn't be an empty seat in the congregation.

Elizabeth did not often pray, but she implored a distant Western god to intercede in this oriental war, if at all possible, and to let it go no further than this terrifying skirmish. She knew that, thanks to the dedicated efforts of Andrew Logan-Fisher, she and her husband held steamer tickets that were good up until an actual Japanese invasion. But what if the Japanese really did enter Shanghai? What would happen to Tai-ling?

It seemed to Tai-ling that she had aged a century in the last twenty hours. The night before in the courtyard of the compound, she had been a child playing games. She had wondered at Mrs. Granger's terror, her strange vulnerability. It seemed to her that those tracer bullets—and last night she had not even known their name—were no more than fireworks. Since when had a Chinese been afraid of loud noise? Certainly the plane and its little show was nothing to what she saw in the Native City during any Chinese New Year.

Mrs. Granger admonished her to go up into the city early this morning, to see if her mother was all right. Wondering, Tai-ling went, inwardly shrugging just a little. She thought to go as usual by tram, and then her education began. Just at the stop where she ordinarily waited, she saw that the street had become an enormous crater. The steel tracks of the tram line curled up carelessly to the sky like the stalks of steel flowers. She decided to walk into town, and before she had gone a block she saw the body of a child stretched out on its back, but without an arm. Was the child alive? Were its lips moving? She began to run. It could have been one of her students.

Until this morning she'd thought she knew the city of Shanghai as well as her own little room in the mission compound, but now, repeatedly, she lost her sense of direction. Where there had been a business building, now there was rubble. Where there had been a series of tiny gardens, now mud spattered everywhere over shacks and streets, and uprooted plants were undergoing private deaths of their own.

As she reached the block of her mother's apartment, she slowed down, relieved beyond words that no ruin awaited her. Pray God, her mother had stayed in the night before.

Her mother's rooms were darkened as always against the morning's harsh light. Mei-fen stood in her bedroom door clutching an expensive wrapper about her body, slender almost to the point of emaciation. Her tired eyes lit up at the sight of her daughter.

The two women did not embrace. They rarely saw each other. The elder projected a self-abnegation about her life that was almost palpable; her daughter felt the natural scorn of the young and chaste for one who yielded so obsessively to the pleasures of the flesh. Tai-ling's life now lay with the mission. They scarcely spoke the same language.

"Mrs. Granger sent me. She said to give you her best regards."

"Please tell the missionary lady that I am glad you had a safe shelter last night. The monkey people threw many handfuls of trash down out of the sky."

The awkwardness between then broke. Mei-fen poured tea. They relived their experiences of the night before: Tai-ling's coolness under strafing, Mei-fen's horrors seen and heard from this room—the bomb that crushed the house of Lo Mien-yuk, the local gossip. "*Ai-yah!* I will never have to listen to the evil sayings of that turtle head again!"

"I saw a child on the way here," Tai-ling said. "Her arm had been torn away as carelessly as if she had been a doll."

So they went on for hours. Tai-ling began to fall into a kind of dream of what it might mean to belong to a family. In a little while she and her mother might go out. They would walk the city streets and perhaps window-shop together. Perhaps they would stop at The Chocolate Shop and order sodas or a malted milk. Her mother would sit with her knees together and her lips pursed over a straw.

Then Mei-fen broke into her daughter's reverie. She stood up, cleared away the tea things, and brushed back her hair with a practiced gesture. "He will be coming soon. I must bathe and dress. Again, please convey my thanks to Mrs. Granger and tell her I wish her nothing but good fortune." Mei-fen disappeared through the beaded doorway into the dim recesses of her bedroom.

Tai-ling, who had not hesitated as a child to follow her mother through that wall of shimmering beads, stood up now ramrod-straight and heard her own voice as she said, "Oh well, I shall be going now. They will need me at the school. Health and long life to those who live in this building." She slammed the door behind her.

Fifteen minutes later Tai-ling stood in heavy traffic at the corner of Fong Pang and Chung Wha roads. She looked at the people around her—her own people—with rage and contempt. "Fools, fools, fools!" she said out loud. "How could you let the monkey people get the better of you? What have you been *doing* for thousands of years? *You* invented gunpowder! Where is it now?"

A few people looked at the schoolgirl who talked out loud, but without great curiosity. The city was full of people whose minds had split into pieces today. Was this not the very street corner where, in past days, young wives who had been treated mercilessly by their husbands' families came to shout out the injustices that had befallen them, until messengers came to beg their pardon and take them home? But nobody came for this girl as she stood vilifying her countrymen.

She began to walk toward the International Settlement. She had no idea how far she had gone when her attention was caught by a rickshaw boy pulling an obese foreigner. A Sikh, one of the fierce Indian natives whom the English had imported to serve as policemen, self-importantly directed traffic through the crowded intersection, pointing this way and that with his white-gloved hands, flourishing a billy club to badger already compliant people into submission.

"Hold up for the load of cantaloupes," he barked out at the rickshaw boy. "Let the load of jute come through."

But Tai-ling recognized the "boy," already in his forties and perhaps six months from the grave, as one of the many Cantonese who had lately swarmed into the city in the pathetic hope of eking out a living, and she knew he could not understand the Sikh's badly accented Wu dialect. The rickshaw puller struggled into the intersection as the foreigner, seeing what was going on, began to hurl imprecations upon his human beast of burden in what Tai-ling thought must be German. Tai-ling watched it all. The cantaloupes spilled. Passers-by lunged for them. The jute teetered. The German stood up, continuing to shout. The Sikh, obviously happy at a chance to put his billy club to some real use, swung again and again at the rickshaw boy, whose blood spilled easily, so easily, onto the rough road.

"Enough," Tai-ling's voice rang out, and she put her hand up in a gesture that all the world knew meant *halt*. "Hairy foreigner! Turbaned pig! Go home to your own impoverished mudhole. Beat up you own kind or"—she paused, conscious of the small crowd beginning to gather—"beat up this swollen foreign leech, who is as tight as a tick with the blood of our people."

She stepped out into the street, no more than an arm's length from the Sikh, who looked down at her in amazement. The top of her head came no higher than the last of his ribs and she felt a tremor of rationality. *What have I done?* The Sikh drew back his arm. A smile cracked his coarse brown face. Tai-ling saw the sweating German grin in anticipation.

"Hold up there!" It was the voice of Western authority, perhaps the only one the Sikh would have answered to, and as he hesitated, Tai-ling saw his arm brought down by another foreigner as easily as if the Sikh had been the rickshaw boy himself.

"Hitting women now," a voice said almost jocularly. "Is that what the British pay you for? What is the name of your chief? I shall report you before this business day is out." He bowed to the girl he had saved and spoke, carefully pronouncing each syllable, hoping she might understand his thought if not his words, "He won't hurt you."

"It takes a brave man to stand up to a Sikh," she said in perfect English. "I thank you not only for myself but for the rickshaw man who was suffering. I think God sent me a lesson just now that not all foreigners are evil."

Even in the stress of the moment, she enjoyed his look of blank astonishment. "But you," he said, "you speak English."

The crowd, who had gaped slack-jawed at this tiny drama, began to break up. The cantaloupe man wailed over his lost wares as if those fleshy globes had been his wife and children. The jute cart lurched and moved creakily out of the intersection. The Sikh straightened his turban and went back to directing traffic in the obvious hope that the young sahib would forget his threat. The German swore, stepped out of the rickshaw. The stranger who had saved Tai-ling reached into his pocket, pulled out a wallet thick with currency, peeled off several bills, and folded them into the hand of the sweating rickshaw man.

"Tell him to spend the afternoon in a teahouse," he said to Tai-ling. "To buy a present for his children so his bloody head won't frighten them when he comes home."

Then they were alone in the teeming streets.

"I . . ." he said, looking down at her, "I have just lately returned to this city. I find myself free this afternoon and I wonder . . ."

She watched him closely to see how he would cross the social abyss that separated them. Did he see her Western blood? Surely he knew that there were at most three respectable places where a mixed couple might be seen in public: the Cercle Sportif Français, the Russian Tea Room on Avenue Joffre, and The Chocolate Shop.

"I have just returned from the States," he said. "This hot weather makes me long for an ice-cream soda. Would you care to join me at The Chocolate Shop, assuming, of course, that it's still there?"

"Yes," she said demurely. "I am not expected back, and I'm sure that if my mother knew you she would give me permission."

The tram line split into shards at the Little South Gate. The ancient streetcar spewed out peasants and workers frantic with exhaustion and fear. The last voyager out, his arms full of books, heaved a heavy sigh. Nyi Chuen-yup was all too familiar with this part of town and he loathed the obsequious compliments he knew he was about to receive.

"Your father is as strong and fierce as the great black bear of Mongolia," the driver said. But he knew the driver's mind as well as everyone else's here was locked in the past. Last night's bombing proved once and for all what his professors, his classmates, and his new friends at the noodle shop on Loh Ka Pang Road had been saying for months. The day of the warlord was over. Feudalism—overnight—had been consigned to history, and his poor country, as uncomplaining as a farmer's wife, was to be ravished repeatedly by the weapons of who knew how any industrial conquerors.

Only the night before, as bombs fell near them, the men at the restaurant talked of a possible coalition between two great leaders of the past and future: Chiang Kai-shek, with his Christian education, his worldly wife, could deal with the West, and Mao Tse-tung, the poet-soldier, who rallied the peasants behind him. But they were too greedy. Each wanted China for himself.

Nyi Chuen-yup thought hopelessly, as he looked at the crater before him, that while those two undeniably powerful leaders fought over who would possess the compliant body of this country, the vicious Japanese despoiler had already begun his unending rapine.

Nyi Chuen-yup thought of his present destination with distaste. His father, "Renowned Warlord of the South," no doubt still labored under the delusion that he controlled a good part of his old territory. In reality, Chuen-yup knew, his father—with his elite guards, his armored cars, and his fortified compound—writhed as helplessly as a nightworm in sunlight.

His father, Chuen-yup learned once again to his chagrin, was all too well known in this quarter. It took him the better part of three hours to find a taxi driver who was willing to take him out to the fortifications of Nyi Chuen-yao. The man who finally drove him braked to a stop a full quarter mile away from the great chained gates of his father's outpost and refused for any sum of money to go farther.

"That place is a temple of evil," the driver said. "I beg you, no matter how much they have paid you or what they have told you, don't go in there. Boys who go in never come out."

Chuen-yup carried his books (he had sent the rest of his gear on from the university) up the dusty incline that led to his home. What had his father been doing in the last five months since he'd seen him? At least in the old days he'd been respected as well as feared.

In the old days, his father, for all his brutality, had been a soldier, a warrior, a man of the outdoors. Now Chuen-yup was taken by frightened servants to a windowless room in one of the farthest buildings of the inner courtyard. Chuen-yup stumbled into an almost completely darkened chamber.

"Who's there?" a thin, querulous voice wheezed. "Chuen-yup, is that you?"

Chuen-yup instinctively put a handkerchief up to his nose. The air was thick with the smells of perfume, incense, opium, and human excrement.

"Come here, my boy, and give your father a kiss."

Shuddering, Chuen-yup moved to do as he was told, but then drew back with a stifled gasp. His father's eyes, hooded with drugs, had been heavily lined with kohl, his nails lacquered. The pile of yellow silk, which Chuen-yup supposed was pillows and bedding, twitched suddenly, revealing a boy no more than eight years old.

"Come closer, my son, do not be afraid. Did my little toy startle you?"

Chuen-yup nodded cautiously. It was true then. His father, in dealing with opium and selling it to Chiang's soldiers, had fallen victim to his own merchandise.

Though opium had been officially outlawed since the founding of the republic—Chuen-yup could remember going to a great public burning of the confiscated drug when he was seven years old and knew even then that this was all for show—a profitable trade continued, scarcely underground, outside the limits of the International Settlement. Within those boundaries one needed to be careful and to have the right connections.

But this other thing . . .

His father, as if reading his thoughts, smirked and drew his long fingers lightly across the neck of the drugged child. "He is my medicine," Chuen-yao leered. "Of late I have been much troubled by constipation. I have required constant . . . lubrication from some of my strongest men and that, of course, arouses feelings that only this little boy, my other son, can slake." He kicked at the child petulantly. "But they wear out so fast and they whimper so. I tell this one if he cannot learn"—and here Chuen-yao, to his son's horror, began to stroke his own phallus—"to contain his cries during these 'treatments,' I shall throw him back into the canal from whence my soldiers dragged him." He fixed his son with a rictus grin. "Chuen-yup, may I offer you a pipe? No? Then sit down and tell me what you have been studying."

Harley took one last look at himself in the mirror, gave a slight tap to his straw boater to cock it at a rakish angle, and left his room to say good-bye to his parents. Today he faced—as he had continually since returning from the States—another ticklish situation. The invitation for the Empire Day Picnic, which Andrew Logan-Fisher planned as an annual affair for the elite members of the International Settlement, was addressed solely to Harley Compton Fitch III. This year, the only part of the celebration that was to be discarded, as a precaution against a possible Japanese air attack, was the regatta. Otherwise, the celebration would go on as it had for years at the Lungwha Pagoda to the west of the city, near the stretch of

the Whangpoo named Henley-in-China in salute to England's
Henley-on-Thames.

As an eligible bachelor and a Stanford graduate, Harley
was—as always—invited. Since his father was under suspicion,
Harley's parents were passed over by Logan-Fisher.

Harley took a deep breath before entering his father's
study. Although it was early morning, the curtains were drawn
and the smell of brandy hung in the air—rank and stale.

"Dad, I'll be late for the party. I've got to go."

His father merely nodded and poured himself another
drink. Since his arraignment, the elder Fitch had steadily
deteriorated. "Just be sure you get something for yourself.
Find the right kind of girl and she'll be your ticket to
respectability." Then the alcohol took over.

The sun was still low in the sky as Harley and his driver
made their way through the clogged roads of Shanghai and out
onto the country lane that led to the Lungwha Pagoda.

He never thought of himself as a sentimentalist, much
less a Kiplingesque patriot. But today Andrew Logan-Fisher—
whose civil service duties now included the safe repatriation of
every British national—was determined to "show the flag," to
go on with tradition in the face of the Japanese threat. Again
and again, as he saw to the last-minute preparations, the hoary
cliché played through his mind—"The sun never sets on the
British Empire."

In the old days, it had taken an hour by carriage, then just
twenty minutes by motorcar. Now, the potholed roads were
jammed with slow-moving clusters of refugees either entering
Shanghai seeking the refuge of the international metropolis or
peasants leaving the city—going back to what they supposed to
be the safety of home villages. Perhaps, Logan-Fisher
thought, as the caravan of cars inched along the highway, perhaps everything will be fine. Perhaps the servants have made
it to the pagoda and have the picnic completely set up. Perhaps none of the guests will notice what is so apparent—that
these days of Empire are almost over.

Andrew Logan-Fisher's fears were temporarily laid to
rest. The guests—mostly businessmen and diplomats with
their families, as well as a number of his daughter's friends—
strolled about the grounds tasting the delicacies that the
Logan-Fisher servants had spent a full week preparing—
salmon in aspic, pork pies, local strawberries, canapés,

cucumber-and-watercress sandwiches. Men quaffed Pimm's Cup, and the ladies took tea. Logan-Fisher hoped that everyone, except for the most rock-ribbed missionaries, would be persuaded to drink the monarch's toast in champagne.

How natural it seemed then in this temporary pastoral haven that Matthew Granger should approach Jordan Logan-Fisher and, after complimenting her on the sumptuousness of her picnic, casually ask if she'd care to stroll through the ancient ruins. How natural that she should say yes.

He was conscious of her small body walking next to his. How perfect she looked! Beautiful. Innocent. Angelic. Golden. Would she think him too forward if he offered her his arm? Just as he thought this, she stumbled—or did she just pretend to?—curling her slender fingers confidingly into the crook of his arm. Her green eyes looked up at him and his chest constricted.

"Daddy says this is the last picnic we'll have here at Lungwha."

"The Japs have to invade soon."

"We'll be leaving China anyway, at least *you* will," she said lightly. "Tell me, Matthew, will you miss . . . China?"

He knew she was flirting with him, but elected to take her at her literal word. "China! I've lived here all my life, and I don't really know it at all. *Yes*. I'll miss it more than . . ."

"Matthew," she said demurely, "wasn't it just around here that we used to play tag when we were little?"

"It scandalized the servants, I remember." But before the sentence was complete, she had kicked off her sandals, hiked up the folds of her wide organza skirt, and dodged around a crumbling gravestone.

He could only gawk at her as she half crouched, stuck her tongue out at him, and said, "Bet you can't catch me, Matthew Granger. You never could! You're *it*!"

She was right. He caught her finally only because she let him, her face flushed, her curls in a tangle, her breath coming hard. She held on to him as he caught her and put her ear against his chest.

"Oh, I'm so out of breath," she said, "my heart is pounding. Is yours?" She stepped back and gave him a look. "I'm not flirting, Matthew. I'm not, I'm not!"

But he looked at her soberly. "Someone as beautiful as you could hurt a person like me. I'm afraid of getting hurt."

"I could never hurt you in a million years, Matthew. I've thought about you ever since I was a little girl."

Quietly, he said, "If the world ends tomorrow, I don't care. At least I will have had this day with you. I love you, Jordan. I always have."

They walked back to the picnic. This time, they kept their arms down at their sides and a good foot of distance between them. Each time their eyes met during the festivities, Jordan's cheeks flushed as pink as an English briar rose. By the end of the afternoon, the members of the party were agog over the new romance. And if one surly young man skulked about and blasphemously kicked over a few Chinese grave markers, nobody thought it worth mentioning.

Reality closed in soon enough for Andrew Logan-Fisher. If on Empire Day he had shown the Union Jack, in the next week he was charged with the much more dismal task of folding that flag and slipping it unobtrusively away. Not only the British, he vowed privately, but every Westerner who needed it must be given safe passage out of this besieged city.

This morning, the Japanese consul bowed and hissed and slithered and gave him repeated assurances that every citizen in Shanghai, regardless of race, would be perfectly safe in the event of possible Japanese occupation. Then the consul spoke at length of British and American holdings, by his very knowledge showing that he saw them already as part of a new and emerging Japanese empire.

Later, in yet another interview, Logan-Fisher had the unpleasant duty of explaining to a White Russian, who had already fled from another revolution and held nothing but a League of Nations certificate, that only passports of "free" nations could be honored. The Russian, like so many of his nationality who crowded into Shanghai after fleeing from the north, was already half crazed by what he had been through.

"I have no rubles," he said desperately. "You will have to find bribes from someone else. I and my family shall die here in the streets while you and your family are safe on the high seas."

"I'm sorry."

The Russian had been right about one thing. He and his family would almost certainly die here after the Japanese came. Shanghai, which had been a truly international metropolis for three-quarters of a century, was shaking itself like a terrier. Who could say whether civil war or the Japanese menace was the larger looming catastrophe? Whatever the cause, the city's foreigners frantically prepared to evacuate.

But the Russian was wrong about the other. Andrew Logan-Fisher, because of his conscience, because of the faltering empire that he pledged to serve, and simply because he was who he was, would be the last representative of the "Western world" to leave the city.

Although it was part of his personal code "never to bring his work home with him," in these last days of British hegemony Andrew Logan-Fisher did his most important work at night. In the continued calm of his drawing room, he drew upon all the solace his family was able to give him as he played a frightening game with lists of people wanting to leave the city and an ever-shrinking list of steamship tickets.

At least he knew his own family would be safe. Only a fortnight before he had received word that his bachelor elder brother, Harold, had died after a hunting accident. As next in the family line, Andrew stood to inherit two thousand acres of prime farmland and forest in Oxfordshire as well as The Beeches, the stately home of the Logan-Fishers that dated from the sixteenth century. Its customs had sustained him through his years of exile. No matter what happened to him, Madeline and Jordan would be entitled to live out their lives there. If there was no male issue, a great-nephew would then succeed.

How he admired the women in his family! They went about their evening pastimes with as much serenity as if they had a lifetime ahead of them here. Madeline worked her needlepoint. And Jordan, whom Andrew had always thought of as a delightful flibbertigibbet, showed herself made of Logan-Fisher steel. Always an accomplished young lady, Jordan in these past days allowed her talent for sketching to become something close to an obsession. She was never without her block of drawing paper. Andrew thought he could guess something of her feelings. He knew—as she must—that they were caught in the vortex of history. Tonight she sketched this room with pastels, recording a life that would soon no longer be theirs. The only sound came from the scratchy notes of Schumann's *Lieder* on the gramophone.

Then the calm was shattered. Andrew looked up to see that the double doors to the drawing room had been flung open. At least a dozen Chinese stormed in.

"Stand up, foreign vermin," one of them barked out in broken English. "Stand up for the ever-glorious Nyi Chuen-yao!"

Madeline and Jordan froze at their work, then with iron self-control, began again.

"I say," Logan-Fisher said, exasperated. "Couldn't you boys have stopped in at the office?"

"The vermin shall be ex . . . ex . . . ex . . ."—and as another interloper whispered into his ear—"exterminated! The foreigner shall be expelled from our soil."

"Come to the point," Andrew Logan-Fisher snapped. "Who are you and what do you want?"

The intruders formed a double line—the more ferocious near the front, the more timid ranged up against the wall. From this second ranking, Chuen-yup, first son of the "Renowned Warlord," had the satisfaction of watching his father cope with the humiliation of learning that he was not renowned at all, but was, in fact, genuinely unknown to this member of the ruling classes.

"Tell these dung heaps I need a ship for my personal use. I need it before the monkey people come."

Haltingly, the translator relayed the warlord's demands. The whole world knew that Nyi Chuen-yao was invincible, the very size and complexity of his wealth and chattels made it inconvenient for him to oversee it all at this time. It was imperative that a vast shipment of his gold be taken away from Shanghai, either down to Singapore or to Port Moresby.

"The helplessness and stupidity of this representative of the round-eye empire is known throughout this city, but he has some small reputation for being honest. It is for this reason that Nyi Chuen-yao demands from him the use of one or several ships. His payment will be generous. He will allow your wife and daughter to continue living. He will not chop them up into bones to sell as necklaces to the Port Moresby natives."

Chuen-yup listened to this ill-rehearsed speech, so clearly meant to be terrifying, and watched the Logan-Fisher women to see how they would take it. The mother went on with her barbarian needlework. The young woman, who had hair the color of flax, continued with her painting. Cautiously, Chuen-yup moved around behind her to see the picture. He saw the room they were standing in, and he saw that she had added, in stark contrast to the pale pinks and greens of the

room, a harsh blue slash where the intruders stood. Picking
one soldier, she rapidly filled in his features. He cursed this
girl who with a few careless strokes of a brush might see into
their souls.

"The gold," the spokesman said, "is in the Number
Seventeen godown on the French Bund. You will deliver the
ship and we will spare your family."

"You are speaking to the wrong person," the foreigner said
gently. "An Englishman does not respond to . . . intimidation." That was all he said, but the unspoken word—
"Chinese"—hung in the air. A moment of intense awkwardness followed. The barbarian family continued with its activities. The room could have been empty for all the attention
they paid to his father.

Uncertainly, the translator turned to leave. "You will be
sorry when your women drown in the muddy waters of the
Whangpoo."

Nyi Chuen-yao said, "Yes, that is true."

"May the ferocious snapping eel, which makes its home in
the rocks of the harbor, bite out the entrails of the soft white
dog and his two bitches," an aide taunted. There came a
mumble of assent, but Chuen-yup sensed the petulance
beneath. These were not even threats, but the whinings of
small boys accustomed to having their way. Chuen-yup took
one last glance at the gold-and-silver girl. Then the little troop
of militiamen filed out, and he melted into their ranks.

Leaving the question of parentage aside, to ally oneself
with an opium addict and a sodomizer would be unwise. Now
that Chuen-yup knew about the gold, he could arrange to
leave with it, assuming he found a ship. But the thought of
leaving the boundaries of the Middle Kingdom made his heart
shrivel. He knew that if there were people like Andrew Logan-
Fisher "out there," he wanted no part of it. He hated them all
too much by now for what they had done to his country. The
men at the restaurant said that the Japanese were not the final
threat. China—his world—had been split in two like a
succulent fruit. Two men fought over that fruit and neither
would settle for half. Should Chuen-yup cast his lot with
Chiang Kai-shek? It was the intelligent move, one his father
might approve. Chiang had the money, the power, a Christian
education, and factions backing him beyond China's borders.

During the past decade, Chiang Kai-shek had, with his huge army, swept the country and had done in actuality what Chuen-yup's father only pretended to do. Chiang brought some measure of order to a country reeling with poverty, divided by hundreds of dialects and ethnic groups, and plundered by avaricious Westerners. But at what a price! Production here in the city went up, but last year twenty-nine thousand bodies floated in the waters of the Yangtze and the dark and narrow alleys of the Native City. Opium importation—thanks to his own father in part—almost doubled. The factories of Shanghai were filled with children who had been sold to them by families starving to death. These children labored sixteen-hour days and dropped where they stood each night onto matting just below their machines. Certainly none of this was new. Drought, famine, pestilence, and oppression had always plagued his country. They said that even now, in one of the drought-stricken inner provinces, peasants sold their wives for two days' worth of rice.

At the True Heart School they taught that the poor were "blessed," but that didn't change their condition. The old Christian missionary himself chided his wife when she wanted to help the Chinese outside their gates during a flood: "The poor you have with you always." That came from the barbarian book that was supposed to be "good."

In all his years as a child, Chuen-yup thought his feelings were his alone, that he was the only one on this vast earth who was made miserable by the sight or sound of another person in pain. Only in these past few months had Chuen-yup met human beings who shared his thoughts, who dared to question why one man should lie in a silken bed and own a thousand pigs while a thousand men slept in mud hovels and let their children go hungry so that they might pay tribute to swell the estates of greedy landowners.

These revolutionaries had their own vision of a unified China. Their leader, a man named Mao Tse-tung, in asking these questions frightened the spiteful Chiang Kai-shek to such an extent that he ignored what little good he might have done for his own country. Chiang abandoned all reform for a headlong chase, pushing Mao eighteen thousand *li* to the farthest outposts of the parched and barren cliffs of the northwest. Chiang preferred to fight his fellow Chinese—even as the ferocious monkey people attacked his vulnerable borders.

Mao's people loved to say that they lived on the land as fish swim in water. Chuen-yup heard stories of peasants offering the Communist troops food and giving them shelter. In "payment" the Red cadres set up schools to teach the illiterate population. Chuen-yup knew also that even as the two armies engaged in their prolonged struggle, Mao's ideas bred new fish in the aquariums of the great port cities of China.

The only trouble was that Mao's followers loathed Chuen-yup. They felt about him much as he felt about his own father. Night after night a man from the army of the Long March came back to inspect the new Red recruits in Shanghai. Night after night, in the bare little restaurant, "Mr. Iron"—obviously taking great pride in his new revolutionary name—quizzed young men as he pointed at Chuen-yup. "What would you do with the son of a parasite like that?"

Chuen-yup was the constant target of their barbs. They repeatedly told him that his prick would be lost in anything wider than the tiniest asshole, that his testicles were the size of pecans. When he tried to defend himself, they shut him up with the devastating command "Be silent, woman!"

And still, he went back to take more abuse, partly in the forlorn hope that someday they might accept him, and partly because no matter how they tormented him, in their presence he was not alone.

"Behold the eunuch!" The greeting was all too familiar. This time Chuen-yup shrugged it off.

"Where is Mr. Iron?" he said. "I have an important message for him."

The restaurant was almost deserted. Only a handful of Mao's followers clustered at a bare table at the back, their dishes empty.

"Mr. Iron sends you all his kisses, but he says he cannot play tonight. He is off doing man's work. He has gone to join our leader."

"You say too much to this dog," another man snarled. "I have said to you all along he is part of the White Terror, the fascist forces that are bleeding China. This dog's father is a warlord and Chiang, too, is a warlord. Curs sleep in the same kennel."

Chuen-yup found his voice. "For many nights I have come here."

"Silence, woman!" the familiar refrain rang out.

"I have endured humiliation," his voice rose, "because I wanted to know the truth."

One of the men puckered his lips in a kissing motion.

"You are right," Chuen-yup rang out, shouting now so that even the proprietor looked up in mild alarm, "my father is a dog! I have come to join you now."

"Get out, traitor!" one of them snarled.

"And since you see me as a woman, I bring you a dowry—a warehouse full of gold. My father extorted it from the masses and I am returning it to you."

Five men gaped at him. Finally, one of them said, "If you were indeed in possession of that gold, you could be a warlord yourself."

"You betray your own ideas, comrade," Chuen-yup sneered. "It is you who thought that, not I."

Another man spoke. "We know for a fact that Chiang Kai-shek is rounding up our people, especially in Shanghai. If you do indeed have this gold and we go to pick it up, the police will have five more prisoners in their jails."

Chuen-yup called to the proprietor, "Honored sir, bring me a cleaver." And then to the Reds he shouted, "If by chance your Mr. Iron has returned from his travels, please request him to come out."

The proprietor brought a cleaver, put it down, and turned to go back to his pots. But Chuen-yup stopped him. "Wait a moment, Old Father. I am the son of Nyi Chuen-yao, defiler of children and predator of this neighborhood. Eleven years ago I watched as that bandit chopped off the hand of an unfortunate such as you." Chuen-yup put his left hand, which he was happy to see was trembling only slightly, in the air for all of them to see. "I beg you, Old Father, to even the score." He placed his hand, fingers spread, on the soft wood of the table.

The proprietor looked at him in amazement, then turned and ran. Chuen-yup saw Mr. Iron come into the room and appraise him with an expression in which caution, cynicism, and curiosity blended.

"Very well, then, I must do it myself," Chuen-yup said, and before anyone could stop him, he brought down the cleaver. His index finger rolled and twitched across the table. The restaurant went black before Chuen-yup's eyes. With his right hand he held strongly to the table until his vision cleared. "You are right, Mr. Iron. I am a coward. I could only take off one finger. But I have between my legs another finger that, should you wish it, I will give up as a sign of my good faith. You have called me a woman often enough, and if it takes that to be part of your band, I shall make that sacrifice."

"Where is the gold?" Mr. Iron demanded. "And when do we get it?"

"I will tell you, but first I need a bandage."

What fascinated him most was her mouth. As she spoke—and her voice had a range that went from the huskiest whisper to a rich contralto—she rested the rim of her glass against her lower lip. She had perfect almond eyes, the lustrous black bangs of an unmarried Chinese girl, but her lips were wide and full, betraying her European heritage. Like a child, she delighted in making her Ramos Fizz last as long as possible. He loved to watch the silver foam disappear into the mouth he had touched only in his dreams. He loved to watch her tongue as it made a slow trail through the foam on her upper lip. She insisted on drinking outside on the terrace, even though he tried to persuade her to go indoors to the other bar, where in the cool darkness he might have had a chance to hold her hand.

"In the sun," she had said to him often, "I am safe from you." But he knew and she knew that she was no more safe than a rabbit from a python. He watched her with cruel fascination; it was only a matter of time.

"*Garçon, encore deux Ramos, s'il vous plaît. Mademoiselle a grand soif.*"

They were at the Cercle Sportif Français, generous in its hospitality to mixed couples. But she wasn't Chinese, that was the hell of it. On that first afternoon when they walked to The Chocolate Shop, he was so full of himself and his victory over the Sikh that he didn't notice. But when they sat in the ice-cream parlor with the familiar gray facade, suddenly he was overwhelmed by awkwardness. He saw the two people behind the counter whisper to each other before one of them—with obvious reluctance—came over to take their order. He was aware of the large plate-glass windows through which passers-by could see in, and he remembered with bitterness that his father was a convicted criminal in this town.

"I am something of an outlaw," he began to say to Tai-ling with all the bravado he could muster. But then her tiny hands clenched into fists.

"You mustn't be surprised at their reactions. I am Eurasian. Of mixed blood. This happens all the time. I have grown accustomed to it and I forget." She laughed and spoke in a voice that could be heard in every corner of the room. "I am neither Chinese nor Western. No one likes me very much."

He knew by now that a part of her gloried in it, delighted in the racial fear and prurient thoughts that gave rise to this hatred. She took that hatred and threw it back at them with her low, exciting laugh. He had been taken in by that net of desire himself on that first day, and after their soda, he asked if he might see her home. She used all of her tricks—ran her tongue over that sensuous mouth, cast down her eyes, put her frail hand to her delicate breast.

"Could we take a taxi, not just a rickshaw?" she asked.

His throat engorged with blood. He could hardly speak. Would today be the day he would cease to be a virgin? Would the lies he had told in college begin to be the truth? God knows what melodramatic fantasy he expected: the home of a glamorous Chinese woman of the world with the smell of incense, the textures of silk, beaded curtains, and the inviting, sedutive sense of a household where the worst had already happened. This girl, Tai-ling, simply by her existence, was the living proof of sin. Her mother—used by some Westerner. What could prevent it from happening again—with him as the seducer?

His hopes were dashed when, as soon as they climbed into the taxi, she gave directions to the driver. He recognized the address even in Chinese. It led to the True Heart School. They drove in silence until the cab pulled up by the Little South Gate. She asked him, with a mischievous smile, if he wanted to come in and meet the maiden ladies that she worked with. He declined the invitation, but found that he couldn't bear to see her leave.

"When will I see you?" he called out, and his throat tightened once again.

"Tomorrow maybe?"

"But this time for a drink. Do you go to the French Club?"

"I never have, but I would like to very much."

In the next weeks they met each afternoon and he taught her at least one vice. She learned to drink. If Harley felt sometimes that there was much more to this than simple lust—that they began sentences with the same words, spoke sometimes with the same inflection, laughed at exactly the same moments—if he felt sometimes with a sinking sense that he had indeed met a soulmate, but that she was the wrong color, he tried to erase it from his thoughts and remember the electrifying physical attraction she had for him. It was only a matter of time, and for now he could content himself with looking.

"*Garçon*," he said thickly, "*encore de Ramos. Mademoiselle a grand soif.*"

Jordan and Matthew were at the Memorial Temple erected to Frederick Townsend Ward in Songjing. It was Ward who, in the middle of the nineteenth century, led what the Empress Dowager dignified by the title of "Ever Victorious Army"—actually a troop of mercenaries—against the Taiping Rebels. Ward had been an American adventurer from Massachusetts who went on to serve China with such honor that the country built him this shrine.

"I suppose I like this place so much because when I was a kid, I wanted to serve China, to save it in some way."

"You were so cute when you were little, Matthew."

"No, seriously, Jordan. There's something out here underneath the poverty and the everyday life that pulls me. Harley and I never got along very well, and when we were both kids he'd tease me about 110 Shanghai Road. I think to him it meant a big red-light district. But to me it meant the Empress alone in the Forbidden City, or the jade that you see in museums sometimes—"

She broke in eagerly. "What about the land beyond the Great Wall—the desert and the nomads . . . ?"

"That's right, that's it exactly. That place in all of us that we can never find."

How easily she understood everything he told her. Ah, he wanted to tell her everything he knew, and the miracle of it was that she wanted to listen. Her sweet face, as she painted, reflected pure delight. They had sat together under trees and recited *The Waste Land* line by line from memory, trying to catch each other out. After they talked of Eliot and Pound, they went back to the beginnings. Eliot said that the finest poets in English lived in the seventeenth century; Matthew and Jordan discovered them together. Lord Herbert of Cherbury, on the one hand, Andrew Marvell on the other—and

how she'd feigned composure when he had daringly read her
"To His Coy Mistress." But the poet they returned to again
and again was John Donne, and it was Jordan who put it into
words.

"What I love best about him, Matthew, is that he could
put his faith in God and still be so enamored of the ladies. And
they say he could preach a fine sermon. Your father would
appreciate that."

I wonder by my troth what thou and I didst till we loved.
What had Matthew done? He had been precocious, a scholar,
and even a flirt. But now that he was with Jordan, he was
happy, happy, happy.

Every morning he woke with a jolt of excitement. He
spent each day with Jordan. They played tennis at the British
Country Club and were almost perfectly matched. They went
out with groups of young people and he forgot his newfound
college dignity enough to pull taffy. For the first time in his life,
he didn't dread Sundays, since they gave him the chance to
sing from the same hymn book as Jordan Logan-Fisher.
Jordan. Oh, he was happy.

She came from a good family, an old family. But he could
trace his family, he had told her more than once, back to the
Huguenots. Not bad for an upstart American. Their mothers
had much in common. Both were warm and charming women.
Jordan pointed out that their fathers, despite differences of
behavior and culture, were extraordinarily alike. Both shared a
ferocious dedication to the service of other people. Both
shared a strict sense of right and wrong. How she laughed
when Matthew suggested that both their fathers could never
admit to being wrong. He truly understood now what it might
mean to be married, to be part of a family. In the drawing room
of the Logan-Fishers, he felt himself at home, and when he
took Jordan out to the mission, he knew by the way she
embraced his mother and the maiden ladies that she, too, felt
at home.

"'If ever there was a dream I had and lost, it was a dream
of you. . . . ' You, Jordan." She looked up from her painting
and he knew that she was waiting for him to ask it. "I have
three years as a Rhodes Scholar, and we can't marry. Do you
believe in long engagements?"

For a moment she considered and his heart sank.

"Matthew, I have three things to say. I'll be living at The
Beeches while you're at Oxford. So our engagement, even

though it's long, won't be a lonely one. But you must promise me that when we marry, we'll come back to China, because I love it as much as you." Then she took a deep breath. "And, can our engagement be a secret just for a little while, just a few weeks I mean? I've always wanted a secret engagement. Matthew," she said finally, "I think I understand what that poet was doing. He was trying to put into words something that can't be expressed. Matthew Granger, I am *inexpressibly* happy."

Chuen-yup, hiding in the stifling godown, felt time take on a new dimension. He counted the seconds and fractions of seconds. The bales of raw silk that surrounded him on all sides generated moist heat. Chuen-yup listened to the rhythm of his own breathing. Behind him, six feet away, through air that seemed as thick and oppressive as gruel, he heard the rasping exhalations of Mr. Iron's men. It was close to two in the morning.

There was another way of measuring time—the regular, painful thud of blood as it pulsed against the stump of his index finger. *Will* he come? *Will* he come? *Will* he?

By now, it was not a question of the gold. Of course Mr. Iron's men all acted as if it were, but the gold was already in their possession, in this very godown. They had been here for more than four hours, but still they delayed at the order of Mr. Iron. Chuen-yup knew why. He could only hope that his father would come. He knew that without his father, the plan, such as it was, would be fruitless. Mr. Iron would have a fortune in gold ingots, and he, Chuen-yup, would be the one greeting the dawn floating facedown in the waters of the Whangpoo.

He knew his life hung by threads as sore and painful as the scraps of raw flesh that trailed from the stump of his amputated finger. Earlier that day he had sent a message to his father. He didn't trust himself to give it in person. Even befuddled by drugs, his father spotted lies as easily as a beggar might find glittering coins in the dust. "Beloved warrior, I fear for that cargo which you would send beyond our borders," he had written. "I have heard that tonight there might be a . . ." He had hesitated over the last words and finally left them unwritten. Let his father fill in his own fears where Chuen-yup's imagination ended.

But perhaps he'd underestimated the old animal. Perhaps Chuen-yup's life might nearly be over. Mr. Iron could not afford to wait beyond summer's false dawn.

Chuen-yup was too hot, too miserable, too depleted to care. However it ends, he said silently, let it end quickly.

Suddenly tires squealed, doors protested, sticking in the salty damp night, ritual grumbling sounded from familiar voices, powerful flashlights zigzagged across the cobwebbed rafters of the godown's interior. Chuen-yup knew by the voices that it was the same twelve hand-picked men that his father had hauled out to the home of the British barbarian a month before.

Chuen-yup felt a stab of pity that had nothing to do with what was about to happen in the next minutes. That his father should have fallen on such hard times! That his father's army should have melted to a dozen incompetent ruffians! That his death would be so ignominious!

He could hear his father's voice now, thin and querulous, so different from the old days.

"Is this a trap, Bao-lop? I suspect it might be a trap. No one knows of this gold, except for you men and my son. And it is well known that my son sniffs at me. What do you think, Bao-lop?"

Perhaps the Communists were right. Perhaps there was a larger destiny that ground individual human beings into the rough flour that would make the bread of the revolution. How else could his father have been so stupid? Only many, many years later, when Chuen-yup had a son of his own, would he allow himself the excruciatingly "Christian" thought that perhaps his own father had done it all on purpose—had given up his life for his son.

At any rate, the plan proceeded with ease. The foolish henchmen with their flashlights made perfect targets, ripped up the back by the knives of Mr. Iron's men as uncomplainingly and with the same strange sound as a child being dressed with a zipper. Within seconds the flashlights pinned Nyi Chuen-yao, whose eyes peered uncertainly past the irregular circle of flickering light.

"Is that you, Chuen-yup?" he asked.

Before his son had a chance to answer, two men grabbed the flaccid body from behind. The drugged warlord stood impassive as Mr. Iron disemboweled him. His guts fell, slithering on the wooden floor. Nyi Chuen-yao did not cry out, and the quiet was broken only by sounds best not heard by any human. Chuen-yup knew that all eyes were upon him and he stepped forward heavily, conscious of the crunch of his military boots.

"Die, foul dog!" he said to the man he had loved and hated for all these years. "Die, traitor to your country, exploiter!"

It was possible that Mr. Iron had some bourgeois feelings left. He did not require Chuen-yup to help in the awful task of picking up the almost dead man, whose ruptured bowels gave off the dreadful stink of a confirmed opium addict; he was not required to help these strangers toss his father—still-living sewage—into the muddy waters beneath the Number 17 godown.

He followed and looked for some last clue in his father's face, a clue to all the years behind them, to both their lives. Did he imagine it? Could his father still see? His eyes opened wide, his mouth spread, a harsh gurgle came from his throat. Then he was gone, tossed away into the water, his shredded intestines strung out like a kite's tail behind him.

Mr. Iron wasted no time. He came back to Chuen-yup and announced brusquely, "You will supervise the loading of the gold and then you will go into hiding until I send for you."

The summer drew to a close. Harley would soon be leaving. In a little less than twenty-four hours he would be bound southward on the SS *Conte Rosso* to Ceylon, through the Indian Ocean, the Suez Canal, the Mediterranean, and then north to England—to Oxford, where Harley knew he would be an outsider, a philistine, there only on sufferance because of his money. But that would be true almost anywhere. In Oxford, at least, he would have a friend. It was almost not to be borne. He was a virgin, and when he left, he would still be a virgin.

It was four o'clock in the afternoon. It was their fifty-seventh day together. God knows how many Ramos Fizzes he had poured down Tai-ling, and still she had not let him touch her. How he had laughed at college men who bragged about their conquests and had come home with nothing more than a vagrant smell on their unwashed fingers; his fatuous roommate who returned once with a pair of torn panties and waved them about the dorm, imploring his fraternity brothers to sniff, to touch, to feel, to rip.

Now he began to understand the fury behind the foolishness, the mania that could grip you. When everything you wanted was less than a yard away but still untouchable . . . She was talking about something now. He could barely listen. The races and some horse, a favorite of hers. He had taught her about that too.

No! It wasn't a horse. It was the mysterious man she thought of as her father—the Westerner who had supported her mother for as long as she could remember.

"He was strong," she said. "His legs were finely muscled. He was kind. I haven't seen him in—oh, for years. My mother keeps him from me. But I remember when I was very young, they would let me come into their room. I was just tall enough to lean across the bed and put my head on his chest. He would hold me, Harley. And then . . ."

"Tai-ling," he said, "I want you. You know that. I know that you want me. Please, we may have only a few hours together. I can't leave Shanghai without just once holding you in my arms."

This, then, was the ride that he had dreamed of on their first day together. As the taxi honked its way through frenetic traffic, their hands clenched tight, sealed together with sweat. The quick alighting. The furtive climbing of dark stairs and the rooms just as he had envisioned them. The smells of musk and incense and teak and fresh oranges. The thin chitter of glass bead upon glass bead. He thought he could hear breathing in the room beyond, but he would not allow himself to think of it, because as soon as the door had closed behind them, she turned to him in the artificial twilight of the shuttered room and ripped away her cotton missionary clothes with an awful intensity. She wanted him as much, he realized, as he desired her. Under their passion, he sensed the beginnings of an emotion far more profound. "I . . . I love you!"

There was a low couch with yielding cushions. And in minutes it was over. He saw, just under his face, her own, her eyes wide, asking the silent question "Is this it? Is it over and so soon?" Sweating, relaxed, physically happy, if emotionally still needy, he began to think of romantic words, of other, slower ways of making love; to plan the rest of the afternoon and how he would make *her* happy, when, with a clatter, the glass beads grated open. With a cowardice that until now he had not known he possessed, Harley buried his flushed face in the girl's neck.

"Who are you?" a terrible voice shouted. "What is this? By God, I'll . . ."

Harley rolled off the girl stark-naked and stood up to face . . .

"You!" his father exclaimed.

Afterward, Harley could remember only the incredible nightmare of simply finding his clothes, putting them on, making his way downstairs, out again into the hellish streets where he walked, it seemed, for hours. He then returned to the relative cool and quiet of his own room, but not before he opened the door to his mother's bed-sitting room and took one last, finally comprehending, look at the drugged and worthless creature who was, in fact, his mother.

How familiar his mother's look of dumb suffering. He thought of his father's pompous injunction to "find a proper girl" to pull the family out of disgrace. His father had cheated in more than one way. He had stripped his business clients of their funds, but he had also used two women and robbed them both, though he had given them money enough. Harley's mother had been a proper girl; now she was a laudanum addict. Tai-ling's mother . . . It was intolerable. Now Harley, too, as his father before him, had stamped that expression of sufferance on the face of a girl—his own sister, who until this afternoon had been impervious to pain. This was life and it was shit.

Just two short months ago, she'd been the center of attention, and Jordan Logan-Fisher knew that by the end of this evening she'd be the center of attention again. How she'd changed in these last two months! Gone were her silly girlish ways! She hadn't fought with her mother over her gown for this evening, choosing a blue-and-white polka-dot georgette with a Peter Pan collar. Her amah twisted her hair into a neat but sophisticated chignon held in place by a modest pair of silver clips—her mother's, a gift in honor of the secret that was to be revealed tonight.

On the surface, this evening's party looked like any one of a hundred late-summer receptions her father had given over the years. French doors opened out on every side of the house to the wide veranda to catch the breezes that wafted in from the peaceful Whangpoo River. Tonight the Japanese menace was put aside. This was a farewell party for two of Shanghai's finest young citizens, two boys born and raised in the shadow of pagodas, leaving the very next day to pursue their careers at the finest university in the Western world.

But Jordan knew tonight was no ordinary celebration. The

paper lanterns strung all about through the garden seemed to glow with a special light. The same old punch bowls on either side of the drawing room shimmered with a special luster. Because of the secret.

Jordan shivered in spite of the balmy air. A new inward voice she had only lately begun to hear cautioned her. It will be a long time, it said to her. Rhodes Scholars are not allowed to marry. Any number of things can happen to ruin a long engagement. Remember that even though you'll be living in England at The Beeches, an Oxford Scholar lives like a monk. You'll be able to see him only on weekends and rare weekends at that. You'll always be chaperoned. Still, the girlish part of her answered back, Yes, but there will be dances and parties on the River Isis and the regatta at Henley. And Matthew and I will go punting on the Char. And we won't be chaperoned all the time!

All this she thought as she greeted guests, gave them punch, gaily chastised them for talking about the war. "Not tonight," she said over and over. "Tonight is a celebration."

Across the room a pair of eyes watched her every move. Matthew, usually so aloof, was animated tonight. He wore his happiness like an invisible shining cloak. Only an hour more and then everyone will know. The secret will be out.

Standing at the door beside her mother, Jordan shook hands with members of almost every part of the International Settlement, except of course the Japanese. She greeted missionaries, schoolmates, bankers, and businessmen. "But," her mother remarked, "I do wonder where young Harley Fitch is." A flicker of concern crossed her face. "I do hope nothing serious has happened. That family has suffered so much already. Harley is such a nice young man."

Then there he was, careening in his yellow convertible up the driveway, slamming the door without a word for the Chinese car coolie, taking the stairs with just a trace of a lurch. "My goodness, Jordan!" her mother said to her under her breath. "Has that boy been drinking?"

But Harley, as he gave a half-bow and raised Madeline Logan-Fisher's hand to his lips, seemed adequately in control. "A slight family emergency," he remarked. "Nothing serious, but we thought it best that Mother should stay home."

Jordan's eyes followed Harley as he headed straight for the champagne punch, but then she gave an inward shrug. After all, it was none of her concern.

Matthew hovered about the maiden ladies of the mission, circulated around the room with the ease of the perfect host. He even helped arrange chairs for the Italian quintet that would play dance music in the latter part of the evening.

Then the Logan-Fisher staff passed among the party with fresh glasses of champagne. The Italians struck up an exuberant, if ragged, fanfare. Andrew Logan-Fisher tapped for silence. He thanked all their friends for coming. He said a few words about the glorious years that all of them had spent in this brave and exciting city.

Then he said, "Our missionary friends have told us often that God is infinite in His generosity, and if He takes one thing away from us, it is only to give us something better. Tonight, my own personal happiness knows no bounds. . . ."

Jordan felt Matthew's body behind her, touching her as delicately as her amah's caress. Roguishly, he brought his chin down on top of her head. She leaned lightly into him.

"Tonight I have the honor to announce the engagement of my daughter, Jordan, to Matthew Granger."

In the round of applause and happy little cries that floated up around her, Jordan saw Harley Fitch redden, the veins standing out in his neck. He was holding one of her mother's crystal goblets in his beefy hand, and for a moment she was afraid that he would crush it.

But then his face cleared and he carefully put down the glass. The new inner voice reminded her, Isn't it enough that you have one man in love with you?

The dancing began. She waltzed first with her father and then, awkwardly, with Matthew. They'd practiced for weeks. "You can hold me closer," she said, giggling. "I won't bite. And remember, your father was wrong about what he told you. I won't get pregnant."

He laughed, but didn't hold her any closer. He couldn't. "When we're alone," he whispered.

Harley cut in. "Congratulations, Matt. I guess the better man won. But you'll give me this dance with the prettiest girl in Shanghai." Harley held her close, and to her shame she felt a prickle of that old enjoyment.

"Harley," she said, putting her small hand against his collarbone and leaning back so she could gaze into his face. "Forgive me. Please forgive us both. Matthew said we should have told you, but I wanted it to be a secret."

His expression told her nothing. "It's true, I like you, Jordan, but then I've always liked you. We used to play tag out in those gardens and hide-and-seek all through the house. I'll be sorry to be leaving all of this, won't you?" His strong arms almost released her. He held her now with a propriety that even a Presbyterian might almost approve. "Do you remember all those nights we played upstairs in our nurseries? Maud's amah was no fun. And Mrs. Granger would bore us all with Bible stories." He looked at her intently now. "I always enjoyed coming here the most. Your amah would let us play keep-away indoors. You had a drum and xylophone, I remember. Do you think"—he hesitated—"we might . . . do you think you might let me say good-bye to it all for the last time?"

Whispering like naughty children, they ducked out through the kitchen and up the back stairs. "Of course, I don't sleep here anymore," she said. "But I believe the nursery is much as it once was."

Upstairs, in a long and narrow screened-off porch, she saw her old single bed neatly made up, a collection of teddy bears long undisturbed in a dusty pile, some stacks of games in the semidarkness, and along the narrow end of the room, under the eaves, an elaborate dollhouse that had taken shape over a period of at least five years, a product of her father's and mother's loving handicraft. It was a miniature English country house, a replica of The Beeches, a full four feet high.

"The care that my parents took with this," she said, and bending slightly she turned a switch that set the tiny mansion ablaze with miniature electric lights. "I suppose just as Matthew's parents always told him he was an American, Mummy and Daddy made this to let me know what my future might be like—"

There was no answer. She had been stooping, looking down into this miniature enchanted home that soon would be her own, when she felt one fleshy hand slide up her thigh and inside her panties. As she took a breath to scream, another hand closed over her mouth.

"You bitch, you slut, you teasing whore! You want it as much as I do, as much as any dog in the streets, and that's how you're going to get it, like a dog!"

The more she struggled, the more he appeared to love it. Whimpering, grunting, groaning, fastening his teeth into the back of her neck, he released one hand, once he had penetrated her, to fondle her breasts, which swung free and

helpless under their loose covering of flimsy georgette. It
lasted an eternity, and when it was over, he said to her, "Did
you like it, slut? I fucked someone else this afternoon and *she*
liked it." As he got up, he threw her away from him. She fell
heavily on her side, her hands picking futilely at her ripped
dress and torn stockings. She watched in horror as his heavy
boot smashed at the frail house until its little lights went out
and left them both in darkness.

The next morning was overcast and sultry. The SS *Conte
Rosso* swayed gently in its berth. At the far end of the dock a
party of relatives and friends surrounded Matthew Granger as
he was interviewed by a reporter from the *Shanghai Press*.

"Yes, I'll be at Oxford for at least two years. I'll be taking
political science, philosophy, and economics, and I hope to
continue my study of Chinese dialects on a private basis.
Naturally, I'm very happy, since my fiancée, Jordan Logan-
Fisher, will be following me to England in a few weeks. I want
to say how much I owe this good fortune to my parents, who
have done so much to give me a good education and"—here he
faltered—"how much I owe to this land where I was brought
up. I owe the Chinese people so much. I only hope that
someday I can repay that debt." He blushed furiously. "I'm
talking like the mayor. I'm just a kid going away to school."

Over the reporters' shoulders Matthew could see his
parents and courtesy aunts gathered in a customary circle.
"I'm afraid you'll have to excuse me," he said to the reporter.
"The ship will be leaving quite soon and my parents still have
to pray over me. I suppose some people might find it
embarrassing, but our family has been separated from each
other over and over and in some pretty risky situations. I must
say, none of us has come to any harm yet."

As he bowed his head and submitted himself to the
sonorous and undeniably embarrassing requests from his
father and even his mother to the Eternal God to keep their
son "well, temperate, chaste, safe from car accidents, and give
him good study habits," Matthew reflected that this was one
time that he actually didn't mind those prayers. His father
pined after God the way some men might pine after a woman.
His prayers were primitive love letters to the universe, and if
prayers were any incentive to the Divine Intelligence, surely
nothing but good would be heaped upon any of them until the
day his parents died.

Matthew looked up from under his lowered lashes and sought out his own, earthly beloved, his beautiful Jordan. She wore a severe gray suit. Her face was pale. She held tight to her mother's arm. She had been crying. How lucky he was to be missed like this, when their parting would be for only a few weeks. He remembered with a pang how last night at their engagement party an obstreperous guest had gotten sick on Jordan's dress, and she'd excused herself. It had taken her almost an hour to rejoin the reception. When she came back her eyes were reddened then too. When he'd asked her what was wrong, she'd said, "It's just that I won't be seeing you for so long. I don't think I can stand it." When, later, in a secluded corner of the veranda, he bent to kiss her good night, she turned her face from him and buried it in his chest, saying again, "No! I can't stand it." He was so lucky.

All too soon it was time for him to board. Again she avoided his kiss, but held on to him until it was he who had to break the embrace. His mother hugged him and whispered, "She's a wonderful girl. We love her very much." His father shook his hand with what seemed like genuine emotion. Matthew was the last one up the gangplank.

Almost immediately the boat weighed anchor. Jordan's eyes searched among the little crowd of passengers who had gathered by the ship's railing and were waving their final farewells. She found Matthew and felt a momentary peace. There was an elemental comfort simply in seeing him, as well as an intense relief in knowing that they would not have to be together for the next few weeks. She needed time more than anything else. Time to put the nightmare, which already in some ways seemed little more than a hideous dream, safely in the past.

As Jordan had listened to Matthew's parents with their well-meaning prayers, she, too, prayed an intense and heart-felt thank you to the kind God that had given her not one mother but two—the blond mother who had bought her dresses and taught her manners, and the wizened amah who had heard her despairing cries the night before—just as she always had when Jordan was a child—and appeared, carrying an oil lamp like a wraith, in the darkened nursery. Her canny eyes took in the situation immediately.

"Matt-hiu? Matt-hiu do this to you?"

When Jordan sobbed no, the amah's eyes narrowed into slits. She took Jordan down the back stairs, past a few curious

servants, and into her own tiny room. There she bathed the
girl and submitted her injured parts to a stinging poultice of
herbs that she said would minimize the danger of Jordan
becoming a mother and bearing a child forever cursed. Then,
by lamplight, she sat Jordan on her lap, held her as if she were
still a child, and let her cry until there were no more tears in
her. Miraculously, there were more herbs for her eyes,
cooling, refreshing. Under the amah's sharp directions, a
frightened servant brought fresh clothes for the ravaged girl.

"You are a strong woman," the amah had said. "Misfor-
tune is a flea bite, but you are a scorpion. You will have
revenge on this monster and your revenge will be the deadly
sting of happiness." Then she returned Jordan to the party
armed with the perfectly plausible story about a vomiting
guest. Not once had her amah asked who had done this to "her
little girl," although Jordan knew dully that she must have
guessed who it was. . . .

Harley made his way through the crowd on the afterdeck,
muscling just this side of rudeness through families and
couples, until he found a place beside Matthew Granger. He
put an arm heavily across his friend's shoulders and waved to
the little group below. "You're a lucky man, Matthew," he said
jovially, "and you've got a great family. Now that mine is pretty
much *persona non grata*, do you think your folks would adopt
me?"

He watched a stricken look come over the face of the girl
below, and a surge of hilarity almost inundated him. What
fools they all were. *Harley* knew what it meant to have a
family. His father this morning, bawling like a disgraced
schoolboy, imploring his son for forgiveness for taking Tai-ling's
mother as a mistress in one breath, then speculating in the
next that if the Japanese invaded soon he might not have to go
to jail. His mother was sitting up, for once fully dressed,
smiling amost gaily as she chattered to her son about the
reports that her servants had brought her this morning.

"So you've finally found out that you have a sister," she'd
said. "Isn't that charming? I'd hoped you two might meet
someday. Harley, your father has placed all of his considerable
funds in my name in Switzerland, so that he will have
something to live on when he finishes his presumed sojourn in
prison. I have this morning already seen my lawyer—you
mustn't think I'm a fool as well as an addict—and signed my
power of attorney over to you. That way at least one of your

surprises will be pleasant. You have never been an introverted boy and you must not waste time worrying about your poor mother." She gave him a smile so twisted with hate that Harley's heart quailed. "You have always seemed to me very much like your father, and I see now that you have begun to carry out his destiny. You must use his money as you see fit. I have no doubt that you will have an interesting life."

"But," he blundered, "you don't intend to stay here, do you?"

"There is nothing for me anywhere," she had said. "Your father, and now you with your Eurasian whore, have seen to that." When he'd bent to kiss her, she'd turned her head.

Why did my mother give me the money? To pay back Dad. Why did I fuck Jordan? To take away Matthew's sweet little virgin. Harley couldn't explain it, but he knew how it worked. He would get those bastards. He tightened his grip on Matthew. He had the rest of his life for vengeance and it would be sweet.

The American and British and French governments had strongly advised the evacuation of women, children, and invalids. There were the usual die-hards, who said they had been through this kind of thing before. The Japanese would never dare attack Shanghai. But Andrew Logan-Fisher, having traveled through the outlying areas, having seen the devastation of the old Native City and the surrounding area of Nantao, knew that this time they were wrong. The country was already at war. China had been invaded by Japan. Chiang Kai-shek and Mao Tse-tung temporarily put aside their civil war to join forces against the common enemy, for there would be no country for either of them to rule if the Japanese took over.

On July 7, 1937, Japanese troops on night patrol clashed with the Chinese at the Marco Polo Bridge just outside Peking. The fighting spread rapidly and led to the Japanese seizure of Peking and Tientsin within three weeks. Every day from then on brought news of the Japanese advance in the north, as they took Kalgan early in September, and the fall of Paoting was expected daily. Since August 8 the Chinese areas of Shanghai had been under attack.

If Logan-Fisher had thought before that he operated under pressure, if he thought himself inured to tales of woe and disaster, he realized in these last days that before he had seen only the fringes of a vast and filthy oriental rug whose patterns were almost too hideous to look upon. Still, within this new world, he was bound by the grinding responsibilities of having to say yes or no.

In the end it was Jordan who saw him through these awful days. Every day since Matthew left, Andrew had gone downstairs in the morning thinking he was leaving early, only to find Jordan already dressed and set to accompany him to the office. She made herself busy filling out forms for distraught families. Each afternoon she made tea for him while the work went on. On Sundays, Andrew tried to persuade her to get the rest she so obviously needed, but she obstinately refused.

In her own mind Jordan knew that this concentrated work kept her sane. It had been two weeks since her period should have come. There was simply no getting around it. Jordan thanked God that her mother was the trusting type. She had gone to school with girls whose mothers kept strict track of such things. Here again it had been her other mother, her amah, who had approached her within twenty-four hours of when her period should have started and suggested with an enigmatic smile that she might want to drink this cup of strong tea as a "fall tonic." Innocently, naively, Jordan had done so, and had spent a night and a day doubled up with agonizing cramps. Her amah stayed with her during the ordeal, wiping her head with steaming hot towels, rubbing her back, and as the potion had worn off, shrugged her shoulders and said, "There is no help for it. The baby who holds on through the tortures of ergot is destined either for great evil or great good."

Jordan knew that her condition was no secret from any of the servants. Each day she was touched almost to tears by their many simple kindnesses, their concern, and most of all, their lack of censure. She understood at last the old saying "In China we have no bastards."

She shuddered at what her parents would say when they found out. She ground her teeth at the disgrace—inevitable in its consequences—which would come upon all of them. When she tried to think of Matthew, her mind went blank.

At the end of this day, her father handed her exit visas and tickets for herself and her mother.

"Does this mean that you are staying?" she asked.

"Certainly. I must not desert my post."

"Let me stay with you."

He put his arms around her. "You know that's impossible.

All women are under orders to leave. Not only that, but think of how lost Mother would be without you."

"Still . . ."

"Jordan, dear, I need to know that your mother will be safe, and I can trust you to see that that will happen."

It was then, with the tickets in hand, that she'd made her decision. She knew her mother would be on board the SS *Princess Louise,* but she would not. In England, a country where she had never set foot, in a new home that to her had been only a child's dollhouse, she could bring only opprobrium. Here in China, the servants would not condemn her. One final thing convinced her that this was the right decision. It was her only chance to see this ordeal through without Matthew ever knowing.

In the mission compound of the True Heart School, the children had their bedding rolls ready in the event of an evacuation. The compound had already suffered some damage. In the first few weeks the Japanese had concentrated their fire on the South Station of the railroad, knowing that the Ningpo-Shanghai-Peking line was China's chief artery for transport and communication. The North Station had already been seized after heavy fighting, and now the old arsenal became their chief target. The mission stood in the direct line of fire between the arsenal and the Japanese gunboats in the Whangpoo.

The mission could no longer be a sanctuary. The children gathered in the storehouse behind the mission residences, close to a back gate. When Elizabeth suggested that Wilson, too, take shelter, her husband just retreated to the safety of his beliefs. "Prayer is our only salvation." Feeling that this was no time to rely on prayer alone, Elizabeth rallied the women to help her, knowing that by doing this she would at least diminish their own fears.

She chose the storehouse because it had a small rear door that led to a seldom-used gate in the compound wall. In an emergency, the children had a means of escape. As she was busy directing these activities, her eyes hit upon Tai-ling. The girl, usually so vivacious and helpful, was pale and apathetic, as she had been for the last six weeks.

Elizabeth was worried for the children, but the thought of what might happen to Tai-ling when the Japanese actually entered the city horrified her. Stories were already circulating of the atrocities committed by troops. Andrew Logan-Fisher had already supplied the Grangers with tickets and exit visas. She kept these documents, together with travel money, in a pocket always in her purse, but what of Tai-ling?

Elizabeth heard shots, screams, and the terrifying din of a population in flight. She slipped out of the front entrance of the storehouse and looked across the courtyard. The gatekeeper ran the double bar across the main gate, but it proved pathetic protection. With shouts of "Banzai!" the invaders easily forced it open. Bursting into the compound, three Japanese soldiers, led by an officer flourishing his sword, stepped through the gaping hole. The gatekeeper put his hands together in the traditional greeting and bowed. Elizabeth saw the flash of the sword, and the next thing she knew, the old gatekeeper's head rolled in the gravel. A great spurt of blood came from his neck as his body pitched forward.

Elizabeth ran back into the storehouse. Opening her purse, she took her precious packet and thrust it into Tai-ling's hand. "You must go! This should help your escape."

Tai-ling looked at her with dull eyes. "Death means nothing to me."

"Don't be foolish! You are young. Go with the others. I will do what I can to delay the Japs. It's only a small patrol."

Hurrying back toward the gate, Elizabeth looked around the compound that had been home for a quarter of a century and gave a last thought to her husband, who was still in the house at prayer.

The small cluster of invaders halted in confusion on the lawn. They seemed puzzled by the deserted space, the silence.

Elizabeth Granger walked slowly toward the Japanese, calling out, "There is no one here." They began to shout and bicker among themselves. She walked on, knowing that every moment of time gained might save another child's life. She halted at a distance of twenty feet from them and said, once again, "There is no one here." The officer's sword glittered in the sunlight. As they advanced upon her, Elizabeth Granger closed her eyes and prayed silently, "May God protect the little ones. . . ." The sword slashed again.

The only two foreigners in all of Shanghai not clamoring for tickets out were the Harley Compton Fitches. The only thing Fitch—who had been under informal house arrest in the

International Settlement—had to look forward to Stateside was a long jail sentence. He now stood on the upper balcony of his study looking toward the Native City. He could see smoke rising and hear steady shelling and gunfire.

The door opened behind him. Thinking it must be one of the servants, he called over his shoulder, "Leave the brandy on the table. If there's any ice left, bring it to me."

"Still thinking of yourself and your own comforts," Sylvia Fitch taunted him. He whirled to face her.

He crossed the room, picked up the decanter, poured himself the last of the brandy, gulped it down in one long swallow, and, bleary-eyed, looked at her.

"But don't forget, my money kept you in your fake Beacon Street rooms all these years."

"I wasn't the only kept woman! I've known for years about everything you've been up to."

With the acumen of a weak person who now knows that her prey is finally weaker than herself, Sylvia Fitch began to tread into a final, forbidden zone. "Your son," she laughed, "he's just like you. Sleeping with—no!—I mean fucking—"

Her sentence was cut off by the first bomb the Japanese forces aimed at the Hungjao Airport. It fell short. Fitch saw the far corner of the room collapse, a wall toppling onto his wife even as she spoke. He took two steps forward, then heard the crunch as the central beam fell. He watched, helpless, while the rest of the ceiling seemed almost to drift down. He could feel plaster in his eyes, filling his mouth, drowning out his calls for help.

This was how his grand adventure would end, he thought, in this seductive land.

Tai-ling veered to the north, stumbling along with no plan, no hope. Her body alone carried her toward her mother's house. She saw looting, groups of Japanese soldiers breaking into shops, guzzling down wine and spirits, jeering at anyone who challenged them. She saw shopgirls caught in the arms of invaders. But Tai-ling had no fear. She was invisible. Those who looked at her drew away, for they saw she was a woman possessed, possibly even a fox spirit passing among them.

She wandered in this way until she halted in front of the wreckage of the building in which her mother once lived. Two women approached her. One of them said, "Daughter, the monkey people have made you an orphan. They have made us all orphans. If you have anywhere to turn, let your footsteps guide you to what we ourselves can never find."

"Old Mother, you are kind. It may be that there is a way for me." As the women returned to their traditional mourning wails, Tai-ling turned her back on her past and began to make her way east.

Tai-ling arrived at the waterfront of the Whangpoo, the old French Bund, dazed and uncertain. Refugees of all nationalities crowded together, pushing, trying to find the right tenders to take them downriver to where the few remaining steamers lay at anchor, ready to take them to the safety of the high seas. Unscrupulous men took bids for their tickets, scalping them for astronomical sums. Here and there a child separated from its mother called out desperately.

She pushed her way to the entrance of the jetty. At the gate, the inspector looked first at her ticket and than at Tai-ling. "There's nothing wrong with this," he said, "though you must have some kind of pull to get it."

Minutes later the tender veered out into the current of the Whangpoo. The evening tide turned. From a bend in the river, Japanese warships kept up a steady bombardment of the territory surrounding the airport. Caught in the cross fire, the passengers in the tender crouched low—all the passengers but one. Tai-ling sat motionless, upright, disdainful, not knowing that she was creating a legend that would surround her like a nimbus for years to come.

Already on board the SS *Princess Louise*, Jordan, standing on the lower deck, watched the tender tie up to the ship and its eager passengers climb aboard. Forcing her way to the head of the short plank, she called down to the tender's Chinese pilot, "I am going back with you."

The pilot looked up at her. "Are you crazy?"

"No," she said, starting down the plank. "But even if I am crazy, perhaps this will persuade you." She opened her hand and the pilot's eyes widened as he saw five gold coins.

"It is obvious that the lady has some greater wisdom than mine."

As the tender swung away from the side of the ship, Jordan crouched below the level of the deck. While the pilot and crew busied themselves handling the boat, turning on more power to fight the outgoing tide, Jordan began to weigh the possible consequences of her rash act. She fought back tears thinking how she had deceived her mother, saying that she was going to the cabin to change her clothes, when she knew all the time that her trunk was waiting back on the dock in her amah's care.

Their boat was one of scores, each with its flickering lamps in the prow, but every one of them, except Jordan's, headed out to the comparative safety of the open sea. The pilot of the boat hunched his shoulders as they approached the shore. Jordan's eyes picked out her amah sitting on the trunk, waiting.

Once she was on the dock, her amah stood up stiffly. "*Ai-yah! Ai-yah!* A headstrong girl is more tenacious than an octopus."

Jordan embraced the tiny shivering woman. "My own family is gone and now you must be my real mother. Take me to your home village, the way you used to when I was a little girl."

"You can't mean Nan-ziang," the amah said. "It is many *li* from here. The roads are dangerous. You told me you would go home to your father. Your place is with him."

At that moment a Japanese shell burst somewhere in the city, lighting up everything with a violet glow. Jordan put her arms around her amah's shoulders, stooping so that she looked directly into the older woman's eyes.

"Surely, mother of my heart," she said matter-of-factly, "you know better than anyone that my condition would make me an outcast among my own people now. You must take me home with you until my child is born." She grinned. "I will work very hard and be your servant. That will be a nice change for both of us."

Jordan's amah dragged her into an alley between the godowns. With speed that came from long practice, she shucked off Jordan's clothes and flung them away. Just as quickly, she dressed her in the standard blue trousers and jacket of an ordinary peasant woman. For her feet there were soft, worn slippers of black cloth. The amah opened a small canvas pouch, took a handful of a substance Jordan didn't recognize, and smeared it on Jordan's face, hair, and neck.

"Goose grease and ashes. No one will know you now."

Jordan had thought she'd known China, but already she inhabited another world. She fell in behind her amah, shuffling, keeping her eyes modestly downcast, and realized with an extraordinary sense of freedom that no one even gave her a passing glance. She was one of the millions now.

In the failing light, Jordan saw that they were at the head of a flight of stone steps. A sampan glided into view. Jordan felt hands reaching out to help her aboard the low, dark boat. She felt herself gently pushed down to sit on a bedding roll as the sampan pulled away from the Bund and headed upriver. The oarsman rowed steadily but swiftly, taking care that his blade made no splash.

Her amah whispered in Jordan's ear, "We must be quiet until we pass the ships of the monkey people."

In the shadows, the sampan passed under Japanese guns, and, still clinging to the shore, went far beyond the Chinese section of the city until nothing but a faint glow in the distance showed the place that was Shanghai.

A hectic air of hilarity prevailed in the grand salon of the SS *Princess Louise*. For this first night, the captain set out an informal buffet, plundering his own stores of champagne for these refugees whose elation at escape still kept them from the inevitable sadness of enforced exile.

For now, all was delight. A quintet of exuberant Italians played for hours without a break. A few couples went out on the dance floor. At first no one noticed when a well-dressed Englishwoman appeared in the salon and asked for the purser.

"My daughter should be on this ship and I cannot find her. Even her luggage is not in the cabin."

An hour later, the missing girl still had not been found. In order to calm Madeline Logan-Fisher, the purser offered to send a cable to her husband and took down every word of a largely incoherent message.

"Please return to your cabin now, Mrs. Logan-Fisher, and leave everything to me." The officer waited until the woman was out of sight, then went into the radio room and tore the paper he held into bits. It was imperative that the ship maintain radio silence until they were out of range of both China and Japan.

Since she was the youngest in the house, it was she who rose before dawn, coaxing a few twigs into a fire hot enough to brew the morning tea, waking each member of the house with soft respectful words. This had been a home without a daughter-in-law, but the pregnant round-eye filled that position as best she could, eagerly taking on the most difficult tasks.

The old woman who had raised her received many compliments, which she passed off with a prideful shrug. "She is clumsy and not beautiful, but she knows how to work."

The girl, who took the name of Bah-wha—"White Flower"—combined modesty with industry. She worked hard all day, and at night sought the advice of village women.

"He who is conceived in hatred will live a life of hatred. It is best to take him from you now. He will give you nothing but pain. All the world knows this."

"Killing is easy," another woman said. "Any *man* knows how to do that. Only women give life. Would you take this power from her so easily?"

"Her own family would not accept this child. All the world knows that foreigners are as low as the sea slug and as malicious as the serpent."

Jordan listened to all of it. In the end, nature made the decision for her. She was meant to be pregnant. She was meant to have this baby. She was meant to live, for a while at least, in the pretty town of Nan-ziang. And her handful of gold coins amounted to a fortune here.

After only a month or two, she felt her personality change once again. She was no longer an artificially modest "Chinese daughter-in-law." Her ease with the language. Her exhilaration at being "free," and her natural stamina transformed her into a new "Bah-wha." When village toughs questioned her virtue, she said with a merry smile, "The mangy dog longs to lie down on the silken pillow." The beauty of it was that she could make them laugh, but she was learning more than the colorful language of the countryside.

She hadn't known that the land could be so lush. The neighboring rice paddies shimmered with a life of their own; the ancient burial mounds, in their grass coating, seemed to pulsate with untold tales of past lives. All around her, people devoted their attention to the soil. She learned to anticipate its changes, always so varied, so entrancing, and in her mind all this was forever associated with the picnic grounds of the Lungwha Pagoda and the magic afternoons she had spent with Matthew.

Because of her ready wit and because she had money, Bah-wha was soon the one in the household who did the shopping. Every morning farmers brought in carts heaped with string beans so fresh they seemed to breathe, and mountains of eggplant that gleamed purple in the sun. There she stood in the central market, shoulder to shoulder with other women and men, heaping insults upon the produce that they intended to buy.

One morning she heard a rough voice, in the strong Wu dialect of urban Shanghai, rap out, "You are no village woman and you are no Chinese. Have you come to collect material for your paintings?"

Astounded, she looked at the speaker, then said pertly, "The ruffian from the city comes to the village begging for a wife, but he will have no luck."

The villagers laughed and the stranger colored. Recovering, he said in a loud voice, "What do I need a foreign wife for? I go to fight the people's war in the faraway cliffs of Yenan. We'll build a China for *our* people, not the foreign devils."

"This girl," a grizzled farmer said, "could have been born in our own village. She knows our customs and has shunned Western ways."

"I bow to your knowledge, Old Father," the man from the city said in Chinese. But in English he said to Bah-wha, "It isn't safe for you here. The Japanese advance daily. You must leave this place at once. You should come with me. In Yenan, you will be safe."

"The mangy dog," she said automatically, "longs to lie down on the silken pillow. . . ."

"I do not long for your body, pale clumsy cow, but I . . . I care for your safety." He flushed. "I admire your bravery, but you must come with me. You have no idea of the danger."

"If I was worried about safety, I certainly wouldn't go with you," she said, switching back to Chinese. The villagers chuckled.

Bah-wha remained in Nan-ziang, but what the stranger had said sent her back to a pad of paper and a block of Chinese ink. In the long afternoons, when her belly grew too large to let her work in the fields, she sketched the village, her new family, and sometimes the harsh strong features of the stranger who had invited her to leave for unknown mountains. Again and again, she drew him—his arm thrust up in the gesture that symbolized the new revolution.

In the months to come, Nyi Chuen-yup endured many privations. He ate millet instead of rice. His teeth grew loose in his head from scurvy. His body froze in the harsh northern winter while his mind burned with new ideas of the Revolution. If he thought from time to time of Shanghai, it was a strange and unattainable dream. He had walked thousands of miles away from his own city by now, and the Japanese had overrun most of China. Still, Chuen-yup thought, more often than he should have, of the foolhardy foreigner who had elected of her own free will to live the backbreaking life of a Chinese peasant.

Book II

ROVING
1937

The rickety bus lurched dangerously, and twenty bamboo cages housing hundreds of noisy chickens came loose from jerry-built luggage racks. Children catapulted from their mothers' arms as the rattletrap vehicle slid from the mud embankment, plunged into the flood-swollen river, and drifted downstream until it beached itself on a sandbar. The wheels struggled for purchase.

Jordan—Bah-wha—enough of a cunning peasant by now to insinuate herself into a space on the hard bench next to a window, watched with detachment as the river whirled about her: the harsh rain-drenched cliffs they had just descended, then a green glimpse of young bamboo bordering the riverbank, then a vision of yellow boiling hell. A chicken squawked and her arms automatically tightened around her bundle and her year-old son. She felt beneath her feet the roll of sketches that she took with her always.

Little Andrew screamed and struggled against her with his chubby fists. The baby, named after her father, proved to be everything that her amah and the old women of the home village predicted. He was a devil child. Jordan barely survived the long and torturous birth. The baby greeted the world with a wild howl, and now the blond fuzz on his head seemed to bristle in indignation as he fought against Bah-wha's protective hold.

As the men descended from the bus to push it from the sandbar into the waist-high river, Jordan wondered for the hundredth time if she was doing the right thing. She couldn't go back to Shanghai because it was already in Japanese hands. (Had her father gotten out? She had no idea.) She couldn't stay in Nan-ziang, her amah's home village, because the Japanese tightened their grip on the rural regions. The Japanese ran detention camps in the cities for those Caucasians foolish enough to stay behind, but there were no camps in the countryside. To be caught by the monkey people would mean sure death.

She could have journeyed toward Chungking and Chiang's Nationalist stronghold, but her months in the village had only confirmed her own feelings that the new government was a gang of thugs. Jordan knew that these were not the people who would save China or feed her multitudes.

The idealistic words of the brash young stranger came back to her: "In Yenan, you will be safe," he'd said to her. She'd chanted these words to herself during her long labor and survived. She chanted them now as the bus lurched sickeningly, finally pulling up on a wide, low embankment to continue its journey north.

Matthew knocked on the door to Harley's suite of rooms in Longwall Street. How typical that Harley settled so easily into his own luxurious flat—entrenched in comfort and already at home with a group of newly made friends. Harley was only a member of Oxford's St. Catherine's Society, not really a college at all, but a mixed bag of graduates and undergraduates either earnestly pursuing degrees or generously spending their families' fortunes. Certainly St. Catherine's didn't have the glorious traditions of Matthew's own college, Merton, one of the most ancient academic foundations in the history of Western civilization. Nevertheless, Harley—in terms of appearance—seemed to be the typical Oxonian, whereas Matthew was still shy.

Harley opened the door himself. "Come on in."

Harley took Matthew by the elbow and led him into his study, where a coal fire was burning.

Without any preliminary small talk, he blurted, "What are you going to do in the war?"

"I can't think about that now," Matthew said, taken by surprise. "I have my degree exams coming up, and like an idiot I'm trying to take a diploma in Chinese at the same time."

Harley gestured impatiently. "You think you have a

handle on things, but the war's coming here to Europe whether you like it or not. I guess what I'm asking is, what are you going to do with your life?"

"Well," Matthew said, "ultimately I imagine that China is going to be my life. Don't worry, I don't mean the way my father tried to make it *his*." He shrugged uncomfortably. "I have inherited something from him, though. I don't want to save souls, but it's obvious that China's a country crying for help. It's a question of debts, don't you see?"

"Debts! China killed you mother. It sentenced us to years in boarding school away from our families. God knows where your father is. My parents, well, I know what happened to them! And Jordan . . ."

"That's not what I mean. . . ."

"Listen," Harley said. "This is not going to be a glorious war. Let the others take their commissions with their family regiments. I want to make some money out of all this." As Matthew took a breath to speak, Harley cut him off. "Hold on. You have your talents, Matthew, your economics, your philosophy, your languages, but I have mine! Mine is making money. The English think this will be just a European war, but you and I know better." His breath came fast as he tried to put his vision into words. "This isn't a war about heroism. This is a war about tungsten, zinc, copper, rubber, gold, and oil. Don't you see! This is New Guinea, Malaysia, the Philippines, Singapore, Macao. This is *our* war, Matt! I've got the bankroll and you've got the brains. What I'm asking you to do—after your exams, of course—is to come back home with me. I mean America, Washington, D.C. We'll see what we can do to make things run our way."

Matthew held out his glass for a refill, and looked into the dying embers of the coal fire. "I had considered the Foreign Service."

"Bugger that, Matthew, you're too smart to be caught up in red tape. I'm asking you to come back to the States and *do* something. That way you *can* help the Orient—if that's what you really want."

The apartment was painted a bright kelly green throughout. Mirrors lined one wall and half the ceiling. A bowl of wilting gardenias filled the room with a sickening aroma. Though the wood shutters were still closed tight, Tai-ling sensed the midmorning Hollywood sun. As she woke, she instinctively pushed the stale satin sheets from her face and turned on her side to see a white, thick neck, balding head, and a broad, fat back matted with moist black hair. He sweated as he slept and breathed with an adenoidal wheeze. Quietly Tai-ling slipped from the bed, made her way through the stuffy living room, into the kitchen, opened the refrigerator. A half stick of butter—Tai-ling's stomach recoiled—an opened carton of milk, and some cookies in wax paper. She went to the cupboard and, by luck, found some tea.

She stood by the window, looking down on the tar-paper roofs of the apartments that lined Rampart Avenue. Nothing in her old life remotely prepared her for this.

Then she heard him on the phone in the other room and curled her lip as she thought of him damp and naked in his dirty bed, holding the phone to his ear as he scribbled on a little yellow pad.

"I tell you, Sid, it's just a matter of time. The war's already started over there, and as soon as we get into it, you'll be crying, you'll be crying to me for this girl." He laughed. "I didn't say she's *got* the cutest slit in town. I said she *is* the cutest slit in town."

A few more muffled snickers, and from the silence, then the grunts, Tai-ling knew he had left the bed and was coming out here. She turned to him; something in her bearing made him shiver.

"The part's in the bag, baby. It's just a matter of a week or so. They want you to change your name to plain Tai-ling. Listen, babe," he said, running a clammy hand across the clean lines of her ivory-smooth body, "I've been good to you, haven't I? I took you in when you didn't have a dime. Now, look at you! You're going someplace. So you be good to me. You know what I like—especially in the morning."

Tai-ling set her teacup carefully on the table and, managing not to touch his body in any way except the essential one, knelt and efficiently performed her part of the bargain.

Matthew knew that to some, these days might appear dull, but to him, life at Oxford offered a series of distractions that—by their very diversity—kept him from brooding about his parents and his fiancée. He enjoyed his classes. Though he had studied Chinese haphazardly at home, Matthew Granger looked forward to his Friday afternoon sessions with Ernest Lowther, the University Reader in Chinese, with mixed feelings. As Matthew rode his bicycle up into North Oxford to the Lowther residence, he reflected that he was taking advantage of his parents' acquaintance with this former English missionary who yearned to revive his early ambitions as an oriental scholar. One reason Lowther accepted Matthew as a student for the diploma in Chinese, while he was still reading for his degree, was to bolster his own claims for promotion. Merton was, after all, one of the oldest foundations, and Matthew knew that Lowther had already ingratiated himself with the warden and dean of the college.

Matthew got off his bicycle and leaned it against the steps leading to the front door. The Lowthers' parlor maid stood at the top of the steps. "There you are, Mr. Granger. Mr. Lowther is waiting for you in his library."

"Thanks," Matthew said. "You don't need to announce me."

"It's my pleasure." She preceded him through the hallway and opened the door to a private retreat.

Lowther greeted him almost too eagerly. "Matthew, do come in. What do you say to a spot of sherry?"

"Delighted."

"I thought you would be." Then: "Damnit! Where are the clean glasses? Ah, here they are after all."

Matthew wondered what his own father would make of this scene, the Reverand Mr. Ernest Lowther swearing self-consciously while drinking the best Spanish sherry he could buy. For the next hour Matthew carefully avoided correcting Lowther's slightly inaccurate tones as they shifted into Mandarin.

If Harley's Oxford passion was rugger, Matthew had developed considerable skill at riding, and had agreed to take Harley along this Saturday to the Stanton-Harcourt estate for the Oxfordshire Hunt's last meet of the season. Harley was to drive them both in his Humber sports car. As soon as Matthew saw his old friend, he had second thoughts.

Harley wore full hunting pinks, in contrast to his own sober hacking-length tweed jacket. He even sported a derby. But Harley's rig was just the first of a series of embarrassments. This was Matthew's fifth hunt with the Oxfordshire, and he knew it was up to him as they pulled into the courtyard of the country house to introduce his gaudy friend. The Master of the Hunt, in pinks so faded that they were almost orange, came up to them.

"Sir Oliver," Matthew said, "allow me to present Harley Compton Fitch."

"We have a couple of old Burton's hunters for you gentlemen. Burton says they haven't been out enough. They may be a touch rambunctious."

"All the more fun," Matthew said.

They were joined by a mixed group, some of whom Matthew had come to know. Among them was Vanessa Richardson, the Master's daughter. Harley leaned in and spoke familiarly to the fresh-faced young woman. "I hope you'll let me ride with you. You know, I don't know this countryside, and I badly need a guide. . . ."

"I'll be delighted, if you think you can stay the course." Her voice held a note of challenge.

"Just try me!"

As soon as Matthew was up, he understood what Sir Oliver had meant. The groom said, "This here's Rex, sir. Mr. Burton hasn't had him out in three months. If you don't mind my saying so, sir, you need to hold him in on the runs, but when it comes to a jump, just give him his head."

Turning to Harley, already up on a big gray, the groom went on, "This is Quicksilver. You've got to gather him in and hold him steady going over the hedges." Harley and Vanessa had already turned away.

Then came the seeming disorder of whipping in the hounds, of riding down the avenue of the estate into the open fields. Matthew, holding Rex in near the rear of the group, saw that Harley had his hands full keeping Quicksilver from breaking ahead of the Master and the whippers-in.

They had ridden no more than a hundred yards when the leading hounds picked up a scent and the pack was off, belling loudly. Sir Oliver gave the cry, "View halloo!"

The first sharp yelps came from far to the left. The hunt spread and went up a short rise. As he reached the top, Matthew saw a large field ahead of them and some kind of fence or hedge at the opposite end. The leaders had reached the midpoint of the field when their quarry veered slightly to the left—the hounds following.

They were making for a break in what Matthew could see now was a high fence that had partly fallen into decay. He turned Rex along with the rest of the hunt. But two of the riders held to the old line. No one could mistake the farther rider for anyone but Harley Compton Fitch in his flaming getup. Even if Harley's mount had wanted to turn, Vanessa gave him no chance. The young woman, gathering her mount, took the fence in a clean jump. Quicksilver, with no help from Harley, started his jump too late, failed to clear, and crashed on the far side.

Matthew put Rex through the gap and turned him along the fence. Sir Oliver came up with him, and they saw that Quicksilver, thrashing helplessly on the ground, had not only broken a foreleg, but had been ripped open. Looking up at the fence, Matthew saw that it was topped by a strand of rusted barbed wire.

Vanessa dismounted. As Harley, his gorgeous coat muddied and grass-stained, limped toward them, she flashed an innocent smile and said, "I'm dreadfully sorry for Quicksilver, Papa."

Her father took the pistol from the groom. "I don't look forward to calling on Burton."

At the sound of the shot, Matthew flinched. He watched the convulsive movement of the horse. Harley, for once, could find nothing to say.

"Sir Oliver . . ." Matthew started.

"It's quite all right, Granger," Sir Oliver said. "Perhaps it would be best if you cared for your friend." Then he lost control for a moment and turned to Harley. "Young man, I don't mind you hoping to seduce my daughter, but I can't have you ripping open the horses of my old friend."

A groom rode up leading a spare mount. The two Americans exited in disgrace. Later, as they drove through the narrow streets of the closest village, Harley insisted they stop at a wine merchant's, and limped out with a bottle of Old Sporran Scotch. When Matthew took the wheel, his passenger swilled the whisky as an anesthetic.

"Matt, you've got to understand it wasn't my fault. It was that slut. She wouldn't let me turn. She's the one who made me take the fence." A quarter of an hour later, Harley blurted, "Stop the car. Stop it now!"

Scarcely had Matthew braked before Harley lurched from the Humber. On hands and knees, he puked into the hedgerow. "Believe me," he said, wiping his chin on the torn sleeve of his pinks, "it was the woman, Matt. They'll do anything they can to make you look the fool. . . ."

* * *

Matthew took special pleasure in observing the Sabbath in his own way. He put a jaunty swing tune on the gramophone and let it play over and over while he read Ronald Firbank's *Prancing Nigger* and smoked cigarettes. He stayed in his dressing gown in front of his fire, and still before noon, shook himself a generous martini. What more could he do to make this day different from the endless and dreary Sundays he had spent in the mission? He smiled as he anticipated the final fillip in the face of Presbyterian tradition.

Late this afternoon he was due to take the train into London with H. H. Fong—the son of an old Chinese family—shunted off to Oxford to keep him away from the war. Despite all his years in the Orient, Matthew had had to come to Oxford to meet someone like Fong, whose family riches probably amounted to more than all the wealth of all the warlords in the provinces surrounding Shanghai. Fong's father had moved all his liquid assets safely to Hong Kong, Switzerland, South America, and the United States. Fong's family had no political affiliations, and built their own power base. China's adversities had been a windfall for them.

After a long, self-indulgent afternoon, and two more martinis, Matthew unsteadily dressed in his evening clothes. H.H. waited for him with a taxi. At the railway station they went through their standard charade of who paid for whom and who preceded whom. They both knew that H.H. would be footing the bill. It was typical that H.H. had already bought first-class tickets. They had the compartment to themselves as the express rattled on down to Paddington Station.

H.H. had heard from his London cronies of a new club in the West End. In the taxi he nudged Matthew and said, "My friends tell me the hostesses are very generous, especially if you are generous with them."

Each table of the Paradise Club sported its own pink telephone. Across a postage-stamp-size dance floor where a few couples writhed in sexual languor, dance-hall girls sat, one or two at a table, waving at whoever came in, all too ready to pick up their phones.

"Shall we have company now," H.H. asked, "or wait for later?"

"Let's have dinner first."

"That's right. We've got to give our jade spears a little strength."

But after a *Vol au vent* with asparagus, followed by a

lemon soufflé, H.H. put in a phone call and hung up, indignant. "Because I'm Chinese, they want to charge me double. Tell me, Matthew, do you think that's fair?"

"Give me that phone!" Matthew demanded. "Which girl do you want?" Shielding the mouthpiece from H.H., Matthew whispered into the phone urgently. Across the room, the joke spread from table to table. Some girls hid their faces behind spread fingers, others boldly waved.

"What is it?" H.H. asked. "You're speaking too fast. I can't understand what you're saying."

"I'm saying that they should pay *you* for the privilege of learning the centuries-old arts of lovemaking. I'm telling them of your smooth, golden, almost hairless skin, of your agility, and of your jade spear that remains rock-hard for all eternity."

H.H. lit a cigarette and smiled mysteriously. A bargain was soon struck with a lissome girl in gleaming emerald silk. "But tell me, Matthew, which one do you want?"

"You go ahead," Matthew said. "I don't think this is my night. I'll meet you at Paddington in time for the last train— you know, the one they call 'The Fornicator.'"

Before H.H. could say anything, Matthew was out on the London street. All around him it seemed that the city was taken up in pleasure, companionship, fun. Yes, he loved Oxford, and his rooms, and his studies, and his new friends. But the laughter of one of the girls had brought back a stabbing memory. What was the point of joking—no matter how good-humoredly—about jade spears when the girl that he loved was missing in enemy territory?

"Turn your partner, a grand right and left, California twirl."

If Bah-wha, as that rocking bus swept down the muddy stream of the waterway, had conjured up the future rather than review the past, never in her most farfetched dreams could she have thought it would come to this.

"Bow to your partner, do-si-do, and walk your pretty little honey back home."

The words were English—Californian with a strong twist of Cantonese. The enthusiast who bawled them through the microphone had spent years in Los Angeles, where he had taken square dance classes to meet Western girls. He had worked as a bus boy, then as maître d', at L.A.'s most stylish Chinese restaurant, the Dragon's Den in Old Chinatown.

Now, eight thousand miles away, he proved by his presence that Communism was indeed a worldwide movement by bringing the American West to an even farther, dustier frontier in the forbidding cliffs and valleys filled with the choking dust of Yenan.

Bah-wha survived this as she did everything else—by remembering her upbringing, her poise, her natural grace, her sense that as a daughter of the English raj she was equal to any social occasion. And, of course, at children's parties she had grown up dancing the Lancers. Now she bowed to her partner, a pudgy-faced, toothless newcomer hopelessly out of step, clamped his right hand to her waist, grabbed his left, and determinedly promenaded him back home.

The gramophone music blared. The footsteps of a hundred clumsy dancers kicked up clouds of dirt. A few kerosene lamps hanging from the scrawny leafless trees shed an eerie glow upon them all. It could have been a scene from hell, except that everyone was laughing.

Besides the usual callow recruits, every day brought a new wave of lovely young women who had flocked to Mao Tse-tung's rural outpost in these last months—women faced with the same choices as Bah-wha herself—death at the hands of the Japs, exploitation (and boredom) in the grim and corrupt eastern bastion of Chungking, where the devious Chiang Kai-shek held sway, or—fun, relative safety, and the promise of new beginnings here in Yenan.

Every day brought newcomers, and one of the most prominent—a Shanghai movie starlet, Jiang Qing—had successfully cast her net for Mao, fighting his revolutionary wife for him. Bah-wha heard that earlier, the great leader, drunk with love, visited the cave of Agnes Smedley, one of several Western journalists there to chronicle the revolution, only to flirt with Smedley's interpreter. His irate wife had followed him, and beaten him mercilessly with a king-sized flashlight. That night, as he would on many others, the great leader demonstrated his ability to keep cool in the face of warring factions. "You are not helping the Revolution" was all he said as she had rained blows down upon his majestic pate. But within weeks he switched allegiance to Jiang Qing, the young Shanghai film actress.

The other women in the camp, the old guard, complained bitterly. Some had not bathed since they'd arrived. They still cut their hair with a cleaver. But men in the cliffs, they said,

are the same as men anywhere—all too ready to leave their
careworn comrades of the Revolution for these flashy new
camp followers.

How easy it all seemed and, at the same time, how
different from anything Bah-wha ever dreamed. The vain
young Jordan, with the crimped curls and silken dresses, had,
for all her seeming freedom, only two romantic alternatives:
the withdrawn, sardonic Matthew, and his brutish, sodden
counterpart, Harley. Here there were hundreds of men,
hundreds. Some of them ugly, it's true. But many of them
handsome, with the sweetness that only joy and hope can
bring. And as surely (now that they capered through the paces
of "The Beer-Barrel Polka") as she'd known it in the upstairs
ballroom of the French Club in Shanghai, she knew that—
except for Jiang Qing—she, the strong and courageous Bah-
wha, "White Flower," was the center of attention. Then, just
as surely as in that Shanghai ballroom, she felt she was being
watched. She scanned the male wallflowers, those shy bachelors not lucky enough to have found themselves a female companion.

After the dancing stopped and the assembled group
settled down to their nightly campfire sing—"My Darling
Clementine," "I've Been Working on the Railroad," "She'll Be
Comin' Round the Mountain When She Comes," and verse
after verse of "Jingle Bells," as well as all the new revolutionary favorites—Bah-wha heard, as someone huskily
breathed into the crook of her neck from the row behind her,
"The mangy dog waits and watches, and yes, he does long to
lie down on the silken pillow!"

She turned around to confront the upstart, and recognized the impudent stranger who had passed through the
home village. Just as she began to frame a suitably flippant
reply, the sonorous strains of "The East Is Red" began.
Subdued but strong in their faith, the campers rose to sing.
From the cliffs all around them, peasants appeared in the
mouths of caves that stretched as far as Bah-wha's eyes could
see. The stranger's voice rose behind her:

> "The east is red from the rising sun,
> In China appears Mao Tse-tung.
> He is our guide,
> He leads us onward to build a new China."

Mothers called to wandering children. The older men and women began the arduous climb, each to a cliff dwelling.

Bah-wha hesitated, made sure that her baby son still slept comfortably under the wooden platform where the square dance caller had stood, then turned again to address the stranger. She extended her hand and spoke in a manner more appropriate to a drawing room than a Chinese army encampment. "I don't believe we've been properly introduced. My name is Bah-wha and"—gesturing in the Chinese manner with her chin—"there is my son, Andrew."

"Bah-wha," he answered, matching her Chinese with his missionary English. "White Flower. You're right, we have not been properly introduced, but we have met more than once." As she blinked her disbelief, he said, "We met once before in your father's house. You were painting. Your mother was doing needlework. And my father, as I recall, had great need of a ship."

"Do you mean . . ." she began.

"I remember you, but it's natural that you would not remember me, because you never once looked up from your sketching pad."

"But if you were part of Chuen-yao's gang . . ."

"Not part of his gang, White Flower, but his son, his firstborn."

"What are you doing here?"

"Your memory is as faulty as your grasp of reality was when we first spoke in the village of Nan-ziang."

The open-air dance floor emptied. The dust settled. In an easy motion Chuen-yup reached for one of the last kerosene lamps that swung from a bare tree branch. "Come. Let us go out awhile and exchange stories of our journeys here." As Bah-wha cast a nervous glance at her sleeping son, Chuen-yup smoothly guided her away. "We won't go far. We'll hear him if he cries. I will share a revolutionary of secret with you. I have half a bottle of rice wine tucked away in my knapsack."

Two years later, everything and nothing had changed for Matthew. Again, he walked, to give his soul comfort. But how drastically the scene had changed. Instead of the cramped, quaint quarters of the Old World, his eyes took in the vast greensward that swept from the Washington Monument to the Ellipse of the Capitol.

A year before, Matthew had taken a First, plus his

diploma, at Oxford. Then there remained the problem of what to do with his glowing academic achievement. Everything that he had done so far pointed to a career in the academic establishment, but he disliked the sheer drudgery of day-to-day scholarship.

Henry Luce, because of his own missionary background in China, had heard about the young scholar and sent an emissary to Oxford to feel out Matthew on the subject of a career in journalism.

"The chief's gone bonkers on China," the emissary said. "You'd be our correspondent in Peking."

But Time-Life was backing Chiang Kai-shek. Just because the Generalissimo and his wife were self-declared Methodists did not prevent them from running a corrupt regime.

In the end the persistent proddings of Harley prevailed. Matthew arrived in Washington as chief liaison officer between the newly organized Compton Fitch Enterprises—a budding corporation that promised to become a worldwide conglomerate—and the United States Government. Harley formulated policies; Matthew—his trusted confidant—sold them to a Congress in desperate need of new raw materials.

His official title at CFE, or Compton Fitch Enterprises, was Executive Vice-President in charge of International Relations. Matthew entered this position with only one caveat. He knew he couldn't be a full partner, but he refused in any sense to be Harley's inferior. He assumed that Harley labored under the delusion that he was "using" Matthew's brains, but Matthew saw it as a symbiotic relationship. He planned to use Harley to at least the same degree. When he thought of Harley's money, he remembered always that at least a fraction of it had come from his own mother's life savings. He would reclaim that financial backing and use it for his own goals.

This morning he was attending a meeting of a group of powerful senators at a prayer brunch given by the International Institute of Christian Endeavor. A private dining room of the Shoreham Hotel had been set up for a breakfast for no more than twenty of the most powerful names in Washington, members of both the Foreign Relations and Armed Services committees. Matthew thought he recognized one or two influential clergymen and, as counterpoint, some of his own ilk—high-level executives from international finance. Under the veneer of prayer, he guessed that a good part of the upcoming discussion would concern the war; if there was to be one, and how America would conduct itself in it.

The Reverend Dr. Alexander MacFarland Lewis was not aware that his prayer was to be no more than an opening act.

"My text is from the prophet Micah. 'Nation shall not lift up sword against nation. Neither shall they learn war anymore. But they shall sit every man under his vine and his fig tree and none shall make them afraid. . . .'"

And so on and so forth. A discreet clatter of heavy pewter at the doors to the dining room signaled that the waiters were ready to wheel in plates of eggs Benedict. Still the voice droned on, advising the Lord to keep America to a path of strict isolationism. Matthew, reverting to the practice of his mission boyhood, his head bowed and motionless, opened his eyes and peered both right and left. On his right hand he saw that the junior senator from Nevada still kept his pretense of devoutness. On his left, his eyes caught the half-amused gaze of Senator FitzRandolph of Virginia, whose eyebrows slowly raised. Matthew responded in the same way, and knew that he had already found an ally—to his astonishment, a powerful one.

It took a series of coughs amounting to what sounded like a miniature bronchitis epidemic before the clergyman concluded with a reluctant "Amen." The guests raised their heads in visible relief.

During brunch the discussion took a direction by now all too familiar to Matthew. The Orient was torn by strife, and Europe at war. One faction of these people wanted America to be prepared.

Matthew noticed that Senator FitzRandolph kept his own counsel this morning, allowing himself to say only, noncommittally, "Time tends to solve most problems." Turning to Matthew, he gave a self-deprecating shrug. "On a beautiful morning like this, I'm afraid I'd rather be out riding than brooding over the international scene."

Matthew eagerly took him up on it. "I hunted a bit during my years at Oxford. But since I've been here, all I've been able to do is rent a broken hack from a public stable and use the bridle paths of Rock Creek Park. My only comfort has been that Henry Adams used to do the same thing—though not, surely, on a rented nag."

"By God, I suspected you were a horseman. You must come out to Halcyon Hill. I'd be obliged if you could lend me a hand with my stable. No matter how many people there are, there's always a mount that doesn't get the exercise it should."

Matthew answered with real pleasure, "Nothing would delight me more."

"We're having some guests out this evening, just a few people for a drink. It's under an hour's drive from here. If you can get away early, we could squeeze in a short canter."

With a few words, Matthew's life changed utterly. That night, after riding through country almost as lushly green as anything he'd ever seen in England, he and a handful of the senator's friends—after freshening up—trooped into the neo-classical drawing room of the former plantation house.

There, standing by the crackling log fire—her high color accentuated by the flames, her thick brown hair done up in a severe chignon that cried out to be disheveled—was the senator's daughter, Valerie FitzRandolph. Beautiful, well-educated, and rich. A jewel of aristocratic Virginia. Where Jordan had been all blond blandishments, Valerie strode forward and took Matthew's hand in a strong grip.

"So you rode," she cried out instead of waiting for a formal introduction, "while I had to stay in like a lady and hand 'round refreshments. But you won't get away with it again! I ride every Wednesday and Saturday morning without fail and I pine for company."

Matthew felt the senator's eyes upon him. "You know now why I brought you out here, young man. What Valerie wants, she usually gets. You may as well stay for dinner."

Of course that directness was all a brand of indirect Southern good manners. In the following weeks Matthew would never be sure whether he was being chased, courted, or merely being made fun of. All he knew was that he rushed through the days so that his evenings might be spent at Halcyon Hill and he looked forward to the long weekends spent with the FitzRandolphs.

This was the second year that the great cliffs and valleys of Yenan had gone without water. Each day sullen clouds gathered at midmorning. Peasants looked up to the sky with eyes grown dull and disbelieving. "The old man of the heavens is so thirsty he swallows his own spit." "A raindrop would hiss on this ground like peanut oil on a skillet." The cadres took a fierce pride in not ransacking the villages that lay about them. They knew now, even more than before, that it fell to them to grow their own grain. They still spent the grindingly hot middays in the cool shelter of the caves discussing the new thoughts and sayings of Mao, but there were no more barn dances, no more sing-alongs. Every morning at three o'clock lads put bugles to their parched lips and blew a rousing reveille. Cadre members trod along dusty cliffside paths, swinging lanterns, poking their heads into each cave. "Plant grain, reap revolution!" "The enterprising farmer uses the morning dew!"

Every morning, without complaint, the members of each household became water bearers. Forgoing their morning tea, they dipped calloused fingers into muddy river water to moisten their lips and tongues, then began the hour-long walk to the millet fields, which trip they completed three times before the burning, merciless sun came up over the forbidding eastern hills.

Daily, Bah-wha fell in behind her husband, part of a seemingly eternal procession. In the old days she might have seen it all through sophisticated eyes, noticing that she was finally part of what seemed to be a medieval "field of folk," or stopping to take in the pure abstraction of the design— hundreds of yellow lanterns zigzagging down blue-black rocky cliffs. Now she simply kept her eyes on her husband's cracked heels, and if she walked behind him, it was not in deference to old Chinese customs, but simply to follow his footing on the treacherous paths.

The mornings were not so bad, and midday, with its relative coolness and the single meal they all shared before their political classes, seemed like heaven. The late afternoons were given to heavy slumber, and then the nightmare began again. Already a few debated the subject in the discussions: "If we rise before dawn and work until the sun is directly overhead, why should we work after the sun goes to its own rest? Not even the peasant in the surrounding villages work as hard as we do!"

The cadres, exhausted themselves, would labor to explain: "How will the peasants learn proper conduct unless we show them? There may be days in the future when we will rest and sing, but now that future depends on our own muscles."

Work. Dimly Bah-wha might let her mind drift back to a past that seemed like a dream—a dream where her fingernails were not split to the quick, where the cloth against her skin was silk and not cotton, where people danced instead of toiling across dangerous cliffsides. In the dim light of their cave, she might steal a glance at Chuen-yup. He, too, had memories, but he never spoke of them. She was more thankful than she could ever express that he had taken her in. She was thankful that although he hated her young foreign son, he had not insisted that she give him away to a farmer's family, the way Mao himself had divested his several wives of their children. Chuen-yup was generous with what he had, although he had almost nothing. And for that other matter that women spoke of wearily as they took their turns preparing the communal meal, he was not unduly demanding.

Bah-wha gave an inward shrug. What dreams she'd had as a child of what pleasures there were to be had between a man and a woman! That was the point of dressing up, of flirting, of curling your hair into absurd ringlets! What did it all come to?

"Lwan-ong forced his way into his wife not ten hours after she had given him the son he'd asked for," said one sorrowful woman as she shook clothes free of dust.

"Can we not bring it up at a meeting?" asked another. "Do they not say we are equal here?"

"True, there are no more rulers and peasants," said another, "but there will always be men and women, as long as the sun makes its way across the sky."

"As the jade girls come in from the big cities," a young girl said, "our men cast away their revolutionary wives for the pleasures of new soft flesh."

An older woman interrupted with raucous laughter, which Bah-wha could tell concealed a deep resentment. "Their skin has seen water in the past six months. Soon we will become like the peasants of this region who as it is well known—"

The women joined in the ritual joke: "—take only three baths—when they are born, when they die, and on their wedding night."

Even a few months earlier Bah-wha might have felt threatened by this talk, but now she knew herself to be safe. She was as unkempt as any of them. Would a little soap and water, some oil, some perfume make any difference in the nightly fifteen minutes when Chuen-yup thrashed and grunted above her? She thought not. Sex was simply another form of bourgeois exploitation, a way to trap women—and even men—into the eternal round of reproduction to manufacture labor for the ruling classes. She knew Chuen-yup respected her, and at least their coupling was as nothing to the horror she had experienced while in Harley's disgusting grip. Carefully, she kept her head down and nodded at everything the women said.

This afternoon she was the first woman out on the path, with her two buckets and her bamboo carrying pole balanced across her aching shoulders. Grimy hair fell across her eyes; she misstepped and spilled a cup of precious water across a rock, which steamed as the liquid hit it. *"Tsah!"* she muttered. "Fuck!" Stepping lightly in straw sandals without missing a stride, she reached for the knife that hung at her side and hacked away handfuls of her hair. At least she could see now.

The reception line had formed in the vestibule of the National Cathedral. Valerie had toyed with the possibility of being married at Halcyon Hill, but her father, surprisingly, vetoed that idea. "We can't really bring all of Washington down there," he had said. "And it will be *all* of Washington. Even though for you and Matthew this is a personal milestone, nothing you can do can keep it from being a national political event as well." Her father kept as a surprise, until the rehearsal supper, his decision to deed over to his daughter and son-in-law the family estate as his wedding gift. "The old place needs young blood like yours," he said. "I know I can trust you with it. As for me, I can settle into my town house without any worries about what will happen to Halcyon Hill."

Indeed, all Washington attended the wedding. Eleanor Roosevelt, accompanied by her Secret Service guards, led the formal procession of well-wishers. "Well, Senator," she said, shaking FitzRandolph's hand, "I know what it is to marry off a daughter in this world." Moving on to Valerie, she said, "My dear, Franklin has asked me in particular to wish you all good fortune. And as for you, young man," she said, looking at Matthew, "we've heard fine things about you."

After the Vice-President and his wife, Cabinet members, followed by representatives of the diplomatic corps, expressed their felicitations. Washington society itself, led by Alice Roosevelt Longworth, in an extravagant broad-brimmed hat, made stately progress. "I always say, Valerie, that if you can't be married out of the White House, God's little hovel here is the next best thing."

"Who could hope to equal you—still our one princess?" Valerie said.

Obviously delighted and flattered, Mrs. Longworth said

in a confidential tone, "I hope my poor cousin Eleanor didn't depress you too much with that dowdy gown. It's the third time I've seen the poor dear in it."

Matthew kissed her hand. "May you be our guest when *our* daughter is married out of the Rose Garden."

"Oh, you rascal!" Princess Alice laughed. "I can see that you'll go far."

"But not without you," he said gallantly before he turned to greet the Mellon contingent.

Five hours later, the nuptial couple collapsed in the backseat of the FitzRandolph limousine. Harley had done his duty as best man, keeping crowds away from the car and providing a bottle of Dom Perignon and two crystal glasses.

"I'm prepared to do anything for your political career, my darling, but from now on *you'll* have to dance with Senator Hickenlooper."

"But he loved you," Matthew said. "He danced with you . . ."

"Twenty-seven times!"

Matthew opened the bottle, filled their glasses, and they settled back into the leather seats. As the car sped through the outskirts of Arlington and entered the Fairfax County countryside, an unseasonable storm began to gust about them. Squalls of heavy rain pelted the windows. Flashes of lightning lit up the highway. Secure in their moving shelter, Matthew and Valerie lapsed into companionable silence.

Dizzy with champagne, Matthew reviewed the events of the past hours. The whirlwind of dancing couples. The warmth and beauty of the ballroom. The almost avuncular pride that Harley had shown in his duties as best man, leaving behind—if just for one day—the competition in which they'd engaged since childhood. The vision of his wife—stately, dignified, and just a little shy—as she cut into the ten-tiered wedding cake and then tilted her face up for the photographer. The knowledge—and so many had confirmed it for him this day— that he had married not simply one of the most beautiful, or even the most eligible, but one of the finest girls in all Washington society.

His thoughts were interrupted by a tightening of Valerie's hand about his. He looked over at her. She had put away her veil, but still wore her wedding dress—an ivory satin, beaded heirloom from her grandmother. Her face against the seat was suddenly pale.

"Matthew," she said, "I have something to tell you. I've never been so frightened in my entire life." Then she stopped and considered. "Except for the time when Bronco ran away with me when I was eleven and I fell and broke my arm in three places."

Matthew answered carefully. "I suppose if you got through that, you'll get through this. I won't bite you, Val, and I won't run away with you."

"No?" she asked.

The silence that fell on them then was a complex one.

A welcome fire burned in the upstairs suite that would be their master bedroom and sitting room. Matthew, in gray silk pajamas—a stag-party present from Harley—stared into the flames, trying to unravel the mysteries of what would occur next. In vain did he try to put together what the Chinese servants had told him in his youth, the vague injunctions of his own father, and every book that he'd read on the subject since he'd become engaged.

Then the door to Valerie's dressing room opened. She had chosen a nightgown of layered and ruffled peach batiste that concealed as much as it revealed. She came across the room to him and put her arms around his neck. "When you fall off a horse, the only thing to do is to get back on. Now, you must tell me if I do anything awful. Do you like this? Do you like this? Do you like this?" He liked everything she did.

The night's storm had left Halcyon Hill gleaming in the morning sunlight. As he opened his eyes, Matthew caught sight of the sleeping figure beside him. Feeling a tender wave of affection, he reached out to touch her but stopped his hand, not wishing to break into her sleep. Unable to lie still, he carefully pushed back the rumpled bedclothes and swung his legs to the floor. He went naked to the nearest window and looked out over the glistening fields. In a matter of moments he had crossed to his own dressing room, tossed his wedding finery aside, pulled on a pair of chinos and a sweatshirt.

After slipping his feet into his tennis sneakers, he went back into the bedroom and after embarrassing himself by throwing Valerie a silent, sentimental kiss, carefully closed the door behind him. He descended the steps of the sweeping staircase two at a time. So this, he thought to himself, was what it meant to be a married man.

Once outside the door, he inhaled deeply and stretched

his muscles. For all too long, his flesh, like the fields of this old plantation, had lain fallow. For a moment he considered going to the stables, but rejected that idea. This morning he wanted to be close to the earth. This was his land now. He could not believe in his luck. The lost years were over.

Home, here, was at the very center of a man's values, an echo of the Confucian order that had been so much a part of his heritage. Here, old values prevailed. The servants served. The husband supported. And the woman . . . He allowed himself to think for a moment of children, and all that they might mean. He paused in his walk and leaned his elbows on an old timber railing. All around him, the earth was blanketed in new rye grass. His feet sank into green. He waited, with an unquiet expectancy. Something was missing. It was . . . He laughed out loud. Who'd ever have thought of a water buffalo on a Virginia estate? And yet, strangely, he realized that at the very deepest level, this was one of the reasons why he felt so at home. He had not seen such earth since he'd left China. England was cultivated to the last hedgerow. In America there were traces of wilderness still to be tamed.

Then, through the morning silence, Matthew heard the unmistakable sound of a spade slicing into wet earth. He walked around one of the outbuildings next to the stables. As he turned the corner, he saw an old man in overalls, obviously a caretaker.

"Morning, Mr. Granger!"

"Morning . . ."

"Chet's the name, sir."

"You're up early."

"Morning's the best time for planting. If I'm going to save anything, it's gotta be now."

Furrows creased plowed fields of seedlings that had been almost totally washed away by last night's downpour.

"I didn't know anyone gardened out here."

"It's the coming thing, they say. Who's that friend of the Senator? Mr. Ickes? Harry Ickes? I heard him say more than once that when the war starts—*if* the war starts—every American citizen will have to pitch in and give a hand. He's gonna call them victory gardens, so that everybody will feel like they're helping. I don't know, though. Once you get past radishes and carrots, it's not so easy."

"What you have there doesn't look like carrots and radishes to me."

"I thought I'd . . . we're not going to win this war with radishes. We can't expect the average citizen to plant his whole backyard with wheat or oats. Countries live by starchy foods. So these are tubers, sir. Potatoes. Yams. Things people can live on for a long time when things get rough. Looks like these are washed out though."

Matthew leaned over and scooped up a dying sprout in his palm. Beneath the wilting sprig of green, he thought he could feel the swelling root. There had to be a way that life like this could survive. He would put his mind to it.

Book III

REPRISE
1944

On the afternoon of the fourth day of the epidemic, Andrew Logan-Fisher came down with the typhus that had begun to sweep the Number Two Japanese Detention Camp for Foreigners just outside of Shanghai. Logan-Fisher protested that he was "fine, fine, old man, topping, in fact." The marks of the fever etched his face. He lost weight rapidly as dehydration set in. He couldn't stand or walk to the latrine and defecated helplessly on the rotting slats of his narrow bunk. "Sorry, sorry," he mumbled repeatedly. "Stay away from me. There's a good chap. Do."

But the Reverend Wilson Granger was faithful in his attendance. In the final hours, when Logan-Fisher began to babble helplessly of The Beeches, Granger felt a dreadful pang. By now he knew by heart the stories of the Logan-Fisher estate that hovered always in the corners of the Englishman's mind—a paradise both tangible and inaccessible.

The two men had grown close over these long months. After the lights were turned out, they had crouched together whispering so as not to be heard by the Japanese guards, who imposed discipline to the point of fiendishness. Granger told his story: the young minister fresh from the Middle West burdened with a belief in God that was to make all joy suspect. He confided to Logan-Fisher about the night he read over the Articles of Faith just before he was to be ordained, and found to his horror that in fact he was lucky if he believed half of them. He'd stormed across the tiny Presbyterian seminary

129

campus and wakened his spiritual adviser, poured out his heart, confided his doubts, only to have this superior say to him, with thoughtless smugness, "After God has touched you and after you have gone out into the field, you will never have a doubt again." From then on, especially after little Philip's death, Granger's spiritual life had been a contest between his will to faith and his equally powerful mind, which could not help but see the gaping rents torn in the fabric of Christianity. Since then he had felt, he often confessed to Logan-Fisher, like Adam cast out of Eden for a sin he could not remember committing. An Adam now, since his beloved Elizabeth had died, without an Eve.

Logan-Fisher's memories were at least as disturbing. "An American can never understand what it is to be a younger son of a great family in England. I was pushed out, Granger. Pushed out like the worst remittance man. The Beeches should have been mine. I loved every acre. But Harold came first. When he died, I inherited it, but now I'll never see it. China's been good to me, I admit. We made a good life here before the Japs came. But it just wasn't home."

On another night, Logan-Fisher told a story of his fabled Uncle Percy. He, too, had been a younger son, but had made a fortunate marriage, traveled to Southern California, where he amassed vast holdings, only to be struck down at the height of his success. Who, in the twentieth century, could believe that Southern California would be afflicted by an epidemic—no matter how small—of the bubonic plague?

So in the last night that Andrew Logan-Fisher spent alive—separated from his wife, his daughter, his ancestral home, and everything else in the world he held dear—his barely audible words turned again to The Beeches: "Remember to tell them they meant everything to me." His eyes widened and, with bony fingers, he pulled Granger's face down to his. "A knife, a knife beneath my bed. Take it."

It remained for Granger, with a numbness the others about him saw as rare courage, to lift the pitifully thin corpse in his arms and stagger with it across the yellow mud that the Japanese insisted on calling a recreation area. Granger whispered a prayer as he slid the body of his dead friend into a common grave where decaying corpses were covered by layers of lime.

Granger stood swaying under a sepia sky. He had no way of knowing if the half-light in which he found himself was dawn or dusk or the dark moment before a tropical storm. He thought, oddly, of Herman Melville. The vision of the Encantadas—that gray place where all spirit, all joy were forever banished—had stayed with Granger since he had first read it, and was with him now.

Then he saw the two redheaded boys, almost naked, covered with sores, squatting on their haunches, looking out into space. For months, he knew, they'd had nothing to eat but rice gruel. Their stomachs were distended from malnutrition.

Stepping over to them, he said gently, "Boys, boys, it can't do you any good to just be sitting there! Jesus wouldn't want you to be sitting like that. We have to . . . we all have to . . ." Wilson Granger fell silent, as he fought his own disbelief.

Though Wilson Granger was unaware of it, his soul was already redeemed. The chill, the emotional coldness with which he had approached the task of "saving the heathen," that same chill with which he had kept his own family at arm's length for so many years, melted forever with his wife's selfless death at the hands of the invaders. She had died so that he might live, and in doing so, made a Christian of him.

The camps themselves had provided the kind of suffering that cleansed. Granger was forced to steal, to fight for scraps of food. He witnessed the murder of a fellow prisoner and saw the murderer go free. He came to the full realization, in all its sadness, of what it meant to be a human at this point in history. But even here, God had been good and given him a friend for the first time in his life. In this hellish pit he had not been lonely.

The two youngsters, their faces like those of shrunken old men, looked at him blankly.

"Soon the Allies will send a ship. They'll take us away to America. They say there'll be an exchange of prisoners soon. I remember the last ship. Oh, she was beautiful, boys. Her lights twinkled on the water. She glided through the waves so easily."

Seized with inspiration, Granger picked up a piece of splintered wood that, miraculously, had been overlooked in the constant search for fuel. He set it skimming across a stagnant, sewage-laced puddle.

"See, Robert, I'm sending it sailing over to you. Now you send it sailing back to Johnny. Keep it going, boys, just like that. And Jesus—because he was once a boy your age—will know that we're all praying for Him to send a boat soon. He saved the fishermen from storms, and I know He'll save us."

Once he saw that the boys had forgotten their hunger in this new game, Wilson Granger laboriously got to his feet. He had been living on short rations, giving at least half of his food to women and children in the camp. As he unsteadily made his way back, Granger began to pray. *Let this cup pass from me, oh Lord.* He dreaded the night, when maddened Jap guards sometimes ran amok through the barracks, raping women, bayoneting children, and Granger—answerable as always to God and to his beloved Elizabeth—deliberately taunted the guards so that it would be he that they would beat and sometimes ravage rather than some innocent woman or child. He prayed for many things: that Logan-Fisher's knife might not have been discovered in his absence, that he might find a moment to speak privately from his tormented mind to his dear Elizabeth. And that he might be—in what remained of his life—worthy of her, so that in death they might be rejoined and he could tell her, as he had been unable to in life, how much he loved her.

"Come on, Joyce. You can see Daddy now. Don't you want to see how his plants are growing?"

Joyce's answer, though unintelligible, was evidently negative, for the next thing that Matthew and Chet heard was Valerie's determined voice insisting, "Darling, you know you love to see the plants grow, and besides, if we don't see Daddy this morning, you won't be able to see him until tomorrow."

Another silence. "Joyce, you know perfectly well why. It's because Daddy's helping America win the war. Why, I'm not at all sure that we could win without what Daddy's doing."

Chet grinned. "That woman is a wonder, Matthew. Always has been, always will be. Even when she was a girl she made heroes out of all her men."

Matthew picked up a cherry tomato—he had been experimenting extensively with hydroponics these last months—and hurled the red bullet with deadly accuracy at his assistant.

The early morning sun slanted into this laboratory which doubled as a greenhouse. Outside, a light dusting of snow covered the ground. Inside, thanks to various ingenious gadgets devised by the two men, the temperature was a pleasant seventy-eight degrees.

Matthew's first glimpse of good Virginia dirt four years

before evolved into a hobby, an obsession, and then—as a sop to his friends and family—a profit-making enterprise. All across the country in American backyards, from Bangor to San Diego, Victory Corn, impervious to drought or flooding, grew, was harvested, and consumed by patriotic members of the home front. The corn was Matthew's most practical accomplishment. The picture on the seed packets—a perky, wholesome girl in shorts holding generous shocks of corn in one hand while she held up the fingers of the other in a V-for-victory salute—had been Valerie's contribution. They had put the corn money into a separate trust fund for little Joyce and the baby on the way.

Valrie and Joyce came in for their cermonial morning visit. Matthew chatted, making the husbandly conversation he knew was required of him, even as with another part of his mind he kept tabs on a batch of millet seed drying out in a slow oven. He reflected, as he did every day at this time, on what a lucky man he was.

It was true that he had lost his mother and hadn't heard from his father in some years, but compared to others, he was fortunate. He had a daughter and another child due at any second. He had a home he loved. A beautiful wife who loved him. And his work.

Looking around this sunny lab, he saw himself at the center of a group of people who lived, in a sense, to make his life productive. Chet was a valuable friend; Valerie lived for him. She left nothing undone that might further his career or advance his happiness. If she was disappointed that so far he hadn't run for office as her father had, she concealed it well. If she felt that his obsession with the science of farming had grown out of proportion, she was patient. In their many long talks, they agreed that any serious career plans should be put off until the end of the war.

True, they had their disagreements. She never argued openly when he tried to enlist, but he had strong suspicions that he was turned down by the Army, Air Force, Navy, and Marines because she asked her father to pull strings. He knew that Valerie's perfect good manners hid an iron will. Sometimes he wondered uneasily what she really wanted from him.

The timer on the oven sounded. He took out his tray of millet. Only two out of five hundred seeds had popped.

"This means we can put these straight into the ground!" Chet said, jubilant.

"Not until we've written up the results," Matthew answered, "but we can do that by noon."

"You promised Joyce you'd spend the morning with her," Valerie interrupted. Matthew focused his attention on the toddler. "Joyce, let me talk to you like a big person. I have a lunch today with the Governor-General of Borneo, and then I have meetings after that with Uncle Harley that will last until five. You know how important it is that seeds get planted on time."

Joyce stared at him suspiciously.

"Tomorrow night your Mommy and I are having dinner with the President, and you know what *that* means. I'll have to work all day, so that if he asks me a question, I'll know how to answer it. But listen, Joyce, if you let me go to lunch today, I'll come home early for dinner tonight, and I promise I'll take you sledding."

After a long moment, the girl nodded her head. Valerie concealed whatever irritation she felt. The men waited until the mother and child had gone.

"Now, Chet," Matthew said, hoping the relief didn't show in his voice, "let's get to those seeds."

Harley checked in at the main entrance of the White House on Pennsylvania Avenue where he would attend a so-called family supper with the President and Mrs. Roosevelt. He felt keen resentment at the fact that he was here not because he was a major supplier to the government of essential material, but because of Matthew's rise in power.

As far as Harley was concerned, Matthew was just a lucky fortune hunter whose success loosened Harley's control over him. Matthew was such a bore, with his "spread," his dutiful wife with her chintzes and her money.

"Welcome to the scrambled eggs and tuxedo circle," Matthew greeted him.

"I guess you're an old hand at this," Harley said. "It's the first time for me."

"You'll love it," Matthew said. "It'll remind you of those old Sunday-night leftovers they used to give us to chow down in Kuling."

By now they'd reached Senator FitzRandolph and his daughter.

"Well, Fitch," the senator said, "everything I hear indicates that you're being a real patriot."

"Thank you, Senator," Harley answered, not certain that the senator's remark was necessarily praise. Compton Fitch Enterprises was making a bundle out of this war. When Valerie joined them, he thought she looked a little tense. She was grotesquely pregnant, but she smiled automatically when he said, "I guess the next generation is just around the corner. Pop or drop!"

"You sound just like my doctor!"

A frumpily dressed woman came up to them and said, "You must let me introduce you to the rest of the party before Eleanor and Franklin come down. I'm Lorena Hickok."

As Lorena introduced them to the others, Harley recognized name after name of important Washington figures. Matthew really *had* arrived, and, as for Lorena, the way she carried herself make him think that the stories going around town about her and the First Lady were more than just gossip. Then the Roosevelts came in, the President in a wheelchair, attended by Harry Hopkins, the First Lady greeting them in her high nasal tones.

"It's so good of you all to come to our family entertainment tonight. I know Lorena has made you feel at home. Let's go into the Red Room and enjoy a Roosevelt family evening."

It was true. They actually were going to be served by the First Lady herself. Three large chafing dishes were arranged on a table beside the fireplace, where a log fire crackled. The President, with his hearty laugh, waved to them all and said, as he raised his martini glass, "Just make yourselves comfortable. We can pretend we're up at the old homestead in Hyde Park. Sit on the floor if it makes you feel better."

National leaders and their wives in formal dress obediently slouched down into the overstuffed furniture or sprawled out on the carpeted floor.

"That's right," came Eleanor's voice, high and approving. "And now I'm going to start working for you. It really is just plain old American scrambled eggs. The only thing fancy is this onion curry that Lorena has prepared. The recipe came into our family during the days of the clippers when the Delanos took part in the China trade."

Eleanor's voice fluted out again as she stirred the eggs in the chafing dishes. "I'll never forget, when Franklin and I moved into the Governor's Mansion in Albany, how shocked the staff were by the simple way we lived. Al Smith had imported a French chef and stored the best vintages even in those years before Franklin abolished Prohibition. The Smiths entertained in—well, I wouldn't want to call it pretentious—style. But when you consider, after all, who the Smiths were and where they came from—"

The President's voice sounded out with hearty command, cutting off his wife, "All I can say," he said firmly, "is that good old Al really was a happy warrior. . . ."

Harley watched as Matthew maneuvered his way to the President's side. His old friend, still his employee, engaged the President in his typical intellectual elitist small talk. What would it be this time—a new strain of popcorn to go with the curried onions?

Under the pretext of getting a second helping, Harley joined them. "I hope, Mr. President," he said, "that my schoolmate and, I'm happy to say, my vice-president, isn't trying to sell you on his hobby."

"Fitch!" the President said, fitting a cigarette into his long ivory holder. "I don't know much about his current farming experiments, but my political savvy—and that's really all we Roosevelts work from—tells me that Granger here will be able to give me a hand one day."

The two men looked at Matthew expectantly, but his attention was focused on Valerie, across the room. Harley took advantage of this lapse and soon had the President deeply involved in a conversation about government contracts. If Matthew wanted to act the cooing husband, let him.

Within two hours the evening's festivities had drawn to a close and the guests waited under the portico for their cars. As they stood there, Valerie choked back a cry of pain and clutched Matthew's shoulder.

"Dear, can't you hurry them up?" she asked. "The contractions have been coming faster and faster all evening."

So Valerie's labor was the cause of Matthew's earlier abstraction! At that moment Harley's chauffeured car drew up. "Here, why don't you two get in the back? I'll sit with Felix. What hospital do you want?"

Once in the car, Matthew said, "I told you, Val, that it was risky for us to go."

"Matthew," Valerie said impatiently, "it wouldn't have been wise for either one of us not to have gone. You know as well as I do that only the happy few are invited to share Eleanor's awful scrambled eggs."

Harley and Matthew spent the next few hours together in

the waiting room. When the nurse announced the birth of a healthy baby boy, Harley pumped Matthew's hand. "Congratulations, old man," Harley said, "you don't know how much I envy you having a son." To himself, he thought, What a pile of shit.

The tarpaulin had been spread as a makeshift tent on the dust of the valley floor beneath the cliffs of Yenan. There were no gods to be thanked anymore, but in a spirit of thanksgiving to the Revolution and to its leaders, this Harvest Banquet had been arranged, and—as in the old days—after the dinner and the speeches, there was dancing. Chou En-lai was present, and Lin Piao, and Mao himself. Jiang Qing, Mao's new wife, put aside both her Shanghai ways and her revolutionary fervor and roamed among the tables, pouring hot *cha* like any good Chinese wife.

After years of hardship, victory permeated the air. Mao's men knew that even though their leader was a Communist, he still followed the teachings of the ancient zodiac. Mao was born in 4590, the Year of the Snake, while the odious Chiang Kai-shek was born in 4587, the Year of the Boar. Traditionally the Boar eats the Snake. But the Snake could always wriggle away. And what had the Long March been, if not a great wriggling across eighteen thousand *li*? Chiang-the-Boar just could not touch Mao-the-Snake, protected on both sides by two "Dogs": Chou En-lai, who performed as the civil officer on the left flank, and General Chu-tek.

The next year would be the Year of the Rooster, the dawn of a new era. Astrologers predicted the end of the war with Japan. In no more than four years, they said, Mao would rule all of China.

When victory came, there should be a plan for it. Already, as part of the Autumn Harvest festivities, they invented titles—if only in jest. One of these they gave to a man who had cast off his despicable warlord father, mended his ways, and come over to the side of the oppressed peoples—Nyi Chuen-yup.

"To Nyi Chuen-yup, who sprang from the loins of corrupt Old China, to become a force for the New!" This toast came from Chou himself as he raised an earthenware cup filled with fiery *mao tai*. "To our next Sub-Minister of Land Reform, for the People's Repossession of the Earth!"

The cadres raised their cups in salute before the *kam*

pei—the full tilt of liquor down an open throat. Bah-wha smiled, but kept her eyes suitably downcast. She was proud of him. But it was not appropriate to show it.

Only two short years ago she had fallen in love with Chuen-yup, her revolutionary husband. In the beginning there had only been resignation, hard work, and a sense of fear kept in check. Bah-wha was not the only white devil in Yenan, but she was the only white woman who'd come here with a baby, and who spread her legs for a soldier. If the People's Army held their tongues before foreign journalists Edgar Snow and Agnes Smedley, they made up for it with Bah-wha.

"Bah-wha is no white flower! Her private parts are as dark and smelly as an overripe loquat!"

"Anyone can bite into it, but the taste is disgusting!"

But after her skin roughened; after she greased her fair hair to keep it a dull brown; when they saw she worked as hard as any of them, they shifted their attack to her son, who, they sensed, she loved as little as they did:

"Surely an albino scorpion would be more prepossessing than this crawling insect!"

"Take my advice," said a palsied grandmother. "It's not too late to leave this spawn from your old life with a worthy peasant family. Our own great leader has given his sons away to farmers in the countryside, and his wives were happy to make this contribution."

To all this her son listened. To all of their cruel epithets about her she simply bowed her head silently. But one day when they began on Andrew—whom they had perversely refused to give a Chinese name—and whom they addressed, sometimes with a mocking joy, as "Ahndlooh," Bah-wha knew suddenly that she'd had enough.

"Ignorant witch!" she hissed at the same old grandmother. "My son comes from an empire where the sun never sets. His father was from a ruling family that spits on peasants like you. Touch him at your peril! I will hear no more words of disrespect for my firstborn."

A low chorus of *ai-yahs* answered this remark, and the women settled into an ominous silence.

That night Chuen-yup had reproached her sternly. "I have fed your white slug. I have sheltered him in my cave. I, too, have endured a thousand insults. And this is how you repay me."

"Only a barbarian would take pleasure in taunting a child."

Chuen-yup did not speak the rest of the evening, and the next morning he left the cave before she kindled the fire. She resigned herself to the possibility that before the day was over, she and Andrew would be turned out of the camp. That might mean that she had less than a month to live. Even though she was fluent in the language, this was wartime. She was a foreign devil, and her son, with his white-blond hair and watery blue eyes, would be cast out as an evil omen by any Chinese village, no matter what its politics.

Silently she cursed her temper: the haughtiness that could make her not only show disrespect to an old woman—a serious breach of Chinese manners—but also her inborn assumption of British superiority, which had turned her rudeness into treason, a repudiation of the future government of China. Agnes Smedley had spoken to her of this more than once. "*I* only write and observe," Smedley said. "Yes, I know, you do the 'people's work,' but I am here by choice. They trust me. . . ." Her voice had trailed off. Jordan redoubled her efforts in the fields, and confined her drawing to the simplest charcoal sketches by the light of a single kerosene lamp, but she had never fully gained the trust of Mao Tse-tung's Yenan outpost.

She had finished her chores in the cave. At her insistence, Andrew slunk off to the community school. She refused to think what this was doing to him, because she was powerless to help. With a sigh, she pulled out the sack given to her by her amah so many years before—a sack that, properly packed, could carry all her worldly belongings.

The rough-hewn door creaked open on its leather hinges. In his calloused hands, Chuen-yup carried a roll of papers, which in her fear Bah-wha thought might be some kind of formal certificate of exorcism, even execution. He tossed them down on the deal table. She recognized her own drawings.

"Complaints have been made about you more than once," Chuen-yup said. "This morning I decided to go to Mao himself, since he is a man of the world and might understand your situation!"

For once, she knew enough to keep silent.

"The Helmsman asked me, why should we keep a woman who sows dissension, and does not even understand our Revolution? The Helmsman told me what all the world knows, that foreign women are as cold as yesterday's gruel. That is why your countrymen hunger after our warm Chinese women. He laughed at me for a fool."

Chuen-yup turned his back to her. "What could I do but agree? I said yes, Bah-wha's brain is a woman's brain, tainted irrevocably with the values of the bourgeoise. I could not deny what he said about your coldness. But I showed him your drawings. I told him fearlessly that what your brain did not know was understood by your eyes and your fingers. Now, Bah-wha, you have been designated by Mao himself as the Official Pictorial Historian of the Great Deeds of the People's Revolution. You have nothing to fear anymore."

Bah-wha stepped forward and laid her head on his back. When he turned to her, she saw passion that she realized now had been there all along. When her lips sought his, she felt a quickening in her own body. Their peasant's pallet seemed as soft as the bed of an empress. Not one month later she was pregnant with Chuen-yup's child. And in another ten, the bouncing and winsome Nyi Chuen-yee smiled up at her.

Days went by when no English word entered her mind, when she felt no trace of that self-consciousness which plagued Western artists. She did her work. She was mother to her children and wife to her man.

Now, dizzy with *mao tai* and good feelings, she adroitly used her chopsticks to pick a duck foot out of the common bowl. Chuen-yee could chew on it for the rest of the evening and it would make him strong. Chuen-yup stayed her hand.

"Do you not see that all the men have not taken their fill? Is it my fate to be forever married to a woman who thinks herself a foreign princess?"

But Chou En-lai himself, seated at the place of honor, reached forward with his own chopsticks and, picking up two of the succulent pieces of gristle, dropped them into Bah-wha's rice bowl.

"The world will see our war through the works of this 'princess,'" he said, laughing. "We must keep her strong for the future."

At that moment Bah-wha felt a tug on her arm from the toddler, Chuen-yee, mischievously confident of his welcome. She swept him up into her lap and coaxed him to chew on the claw. Out of the corner of her eye, far out under the trees just where the light stopped, she saw the glint of white-blond hair. Her other son sulked in the shadow, but she would not let herself think of him tonight.

Four silver heads leaned forward intently. The Maryland Club—one of the most popular in Washington—was kept even darker by day than by night. Senators took their mistresses there. Foreign agents of every stamp conferred over food that was rumored to have come from the black market.

But today Harley stoutly insisted to his four distinguished guests, each at least twenty years older than he, that this food—two-inch-thick aged steaks and hefty tumblers of Old Sporran Scotch—was not from the black market but simply a present from some people who could not be here today and wanted to send their best wishes: rubber planters from Malaysia, occupied Singapore, Borneo, and Yap.

"I don't know, Harley, some of these people you want us to do business with aren't even on our side! It just doesn't seem patriotic to me."

The others nodded their agreement.

"Boys," Harley said convivially, "we all know that trade goes on whether there's a war or not. Why, Jeb, I know for a fact that your firm was selling scrap iron to the Japanese right up until December 7. And, Mr. Byrne, over there, may look like Abraham Lincoln behind that beard, but the Japs couldn't have seen their way up the Yangtze without his kerosene. Here's the way to make it up, don't you see? The Malay Peninsula is bursting with rubber, and the Japs can't take it off their hands. I've made a deal with the provisional government-in-exile. With your ships, Norman, and Barry's pull with the customs officials, we can sneak those raw materials right out from under the Japs' nose!"

"I don't now, Harley," Jeb said. "If word ever got out that we'd been trading with the enemy during wartime . . ."

Harley Fitch put both his hands down on the table. "That's why I set up this lunch," he said firmly. "I'm willing to take the risk for you. I'll be the front man. You put up the funds. I'll buy the materiel direct from the planter through CFE, and sell it back to you."

They listened as Harley continued, taking as his own the tragedy that had happened to Matthew.

"Some of you boys don't know this, but my parents were missionaries in China. My mother gave up her life to the Japanese soldiers so that my dad might live to go on preaching." His voice broke. "He's rotting in a Japanese prison camp. I haven't heard from him in years."

They sealed the deal with a round of handshakes. Harley accepted their words of sympathy and saw them to the door of the club. "You all go back to the hotel," he said. "I've planned a little party there for you. I'll meet you later."

He stood under the porte cochere until the limousines had pulled away. Then, whistling jauntily, he went back into the club to the men's room and asked the boy who worked there for a double shoe shine.

The boy snapped his rag intently for fifteen minutes. "That will be fifty cents, sir."

Harley pulled out five dimes and counted them out one by one into the boy's hand. In answer to the kid's incredulous gaze, Harley, grinning from ear to ear, said, "I don't believe in tips. There's a lesson for you, sonny. Always get your money up front and be sure who you're working for. You'll thank me for that someday."

As he turned to leave, he felt the dimes pelt him. He turned and faced the boy with a smile. "Kid," he said, "you're a slow learner!" Nimbly he bent down, snatched up two of the dimes, and took the stairs two at a time.

Not until two or three weeks later did the Messrs. Byrne, Krost, Rosebrook, and Stephens, dulled by daily cases of Old Sporran and the expert ministries of the most expensive call girls in the country, realize that they had been suckered. Fitch doubled the original selling price of all the rubber he brokered. Not only that, he pulled the same act with many other industrialists, and made agreements with the governments of Bolivia, Peru, Argentina, South Africa, and Chile. From now on hardly a scrap of metal or an ounce of fuel could be sold by anyone to anyone on the entire surface of the globe without first going through the office of Compton Fitch Enterprises.

The glossy facades of Los Angeles's New Chinatown caught the vivid light of the setting sun. Thousands of glass panes glittered like mirrors. The turned-up eaves of the fake pagodas at the corners of Broadway and Spring displayed fresh gold leaf and these, too, caught the sun, transforming for a few precious instants a tourist trap into a fairy land. Miles of red bunting hung from the windows of business buildings and tenements alike. Red cardboard letters and Chinese characters broadcast a message in two languages: "Special Benefit Performance—Tonight Our Own Tai-ling Stars in the New Hollywood Hit *Bombs Over Hangchow*—Proceeds to Go to the Fund for Free China."

A crowd of at least a thousand people gathered in the streets of Chinatown. Many of these people would never find their way into the auditorium. Chinese families, some of them in this country only a matter of months, milled about, clutching toothless grandmothers in black satin slippers, American housedresses, and a few pitiable jade pieces that represented a lifetime of saving and toil. Patiently they waited, hoping merely for a glimpse of their idol.

Outside the steps of the Chinese Benevolent Association, which also housed the Los Angeles branch of the Kuomintang, a series of cars began to line up. Drivers pounded on their horns and shouted excitedly as, one after another, families alighted. Members of the Chinese upper-middle class were dressed in Western clothes. The women wore hats with veils and gardenia corsages pinned to the lapels of their woolen suits.

Carefully muted ohs and ahs swept over the onlookers as at least a score of Chinese actors—each surrounded by a half-drunk snappily dressed entourage—drew up in limousines and mounted the steps of the hall. A chorus of hisses as well as cheers followed these men, because they made big Hollywood money by playing the parts of the odious Japanese invaders. One of them turned and faced the crowd. "You surlplrised I sprleak yourl ranguage?" he said broadly. "Crass of Harlvarld, '32." The crowd clapped and groaned.

A white limousine glided into the court and stopped just at the base of the steps of the Benevolent Association hall. Hundreds of people fell silent as a wiry Chinese chauffeur, barely out of his teens, hurried around the front of the car and opened the door with a low bow. The people gasped as an ineffably slim, almost supernaturally luminous young woman emerged, and stood motionless for their appraisal.

Either the gods or perfect timing had contrived to envelop Tai-ling in the last rays of the sun. Her gown, which in ordinary light looked like simple white satin, was embroidered with thin metallic threads. Gold decorated the ancient bindings that held her hair, and elaborate jade earrings hung almost to her shoulders. It was not a movie star but a goddess who had condescended to come here, and who stepped lightly, clinging to her chauffeur for support, almost as though she still tottered on bound feet, and walked up the stairs to the auditorium.

The lights dimmed and *Bombs Over Hangchow* began. Tai-ling had made at least six of these war films in the last four years and they all followed the same pattern. Only the location and the character of Tai-ling herself changed from film to film.

She played dutiful daughter, beautiful wife, brave war orphan, and intrepid spy. But this time, the Hollywood hacks, never any closer to the war than Universal's back lot, inadvertently struck home.

The scene was a small mission compound outside Hang-chow. Chinese peasants, all of them with good intentions, but an appealing ignorance about everything from plumbing to balanced meals to the rising threat, were patiently taught the rudiments of civilization by Alan Ladd and Geraldine Fitz-gerald, selfless American missionaries. Then without reason or warning, the Japs attacked! Japanese Zeros covered the sky, strafing hundreds of peasant children who had come to the mission for shelter. However many children were gunned down, their tiny bodies stayed together in one piece and no blood spattered the dusty earth of the mission courtyard. Then the camera zoomed in on a lovely Eurasian Christian girl dressed all in white, standing dramatically in an open door with a nunlike veil about her head and a Red Cross band on her upper arm.

Tai-ling's lips twisted in a bitter smile as she watched the rest of the preposterous story. Aftr the planes came, the lecherous Japanese commander, a Zero pilot with enormous goggles, demanded Tai-ling's virginity, in return for which he said (lying in his oversized teeth) he would spare those of the children who were left. In a gripping scene, Tai-ling persuaded Alan Ladd to take the children away to a "better place." The real Tai-ling grimaced with distaste as she realized that to American audiences it would seem no more than reasonable that the Americans should escape, leaving a Eurasian to be slaughtered.

And slaughtered she was. Key Luke—also in the au-ditorium tonight—gunned her down in a rage when he saw that his plot had been foiled. But the cameraman, James Wong Howe, also a Chinese and the most talented one among the oriental expatriate community, had filmed this unbelievable story so expertly that most of the audience was weeping. After the brave missionary girl was shot and lay dead—again with no blood, no feces, no hideous twisting of the corpse—a double exposure showed her still standing, still "alive."

"Yes," the apparition said to the terrified Japanese sol-diers, "you may murder a poor Chinese girl. You may take your tanks and guns and rip to pieces the defenseless children of China. You may burn our homes and raze our churches, but *you cannot kill our spirit. Because the spirit of Free China lives."* Here the apparition faded and pictures of Chiang Kai-shek and Soong Mei-ling filled the screen, to be followed by scores of marching Americans, hundreds of enormous B-52s, and the flags of China, England, Russia, and the United States. *"You may kill me,"* the lovely voice declaimed, *"but you will never, never kill the spirit of China."*

The lights went up to an extravagant burst of applause. Sylvia Sidney shook Tai-ling's hand and rasped hoarsely, "Great job, honey, but I still liked you best in *Shanghai Lily.*"

The Los Angeles head of the Kuomintang took the stage and gave a speech in which he explained that Chiang and his beautiful wife, bravely withstanding the Jap in the wartime capital of Chungking, needed their help more than ever. Chinese Boy and Girl Scouts romped down the aisles, each carrying milk bottles with pictures of Chiang, his wife, and Tai-ling.

Suddenly it was over. The Chinese tended to come in groups of twenty or thirty, and most of them had providently made dinner reservations. The Dragon's Den was closed for the duration, but the Golden Pagoda, Men Hung Lao, and the Grand View Gardens were open and waiting. A group of actors left for a stag party. In a matter of minutes, Tai-ling and her chauffeur were left alone. Once again, Tai-ling had been used—not for sex this time, but for money.

"Esteemed mistress," her chauffeur shouted out in ringing tones, "we must hurry or we'll be late. Gary Cooper waits for us at his special table at Romanoff's."

Her heart went out to Lee-on. He had prepared this speech in advance. She inclined her head and allowed herself to be helped out and into the limo. In silence they drove home to the Malibu Colony.

She was beyond tears and even anger, but she saw that when he opened the door for her, Lee-on had been crying. "That those misshapen animals should do that to you constricts my heart," he choked out. "If I could, I would kill them."

"There are too many," she said, smiling. "And it is too difficult a task, but you may find some champagne if you like, and bring it to my room. We will look across the ocean together and see if we can find China."

Matthew paced the floor for what seemed like an eternity. His young son, Paul, barely three weeks old, did not believe in sleeping during the dark hours. Valerie relinquished these late-night vigils to her husband, saying, more than once, "You're the one who wanted a son, dear."

The baby had just—after crying, eating, burping, gurgling—given a last gasp and dropped his head onto his father's shoulder when, at 3:18 this Wednesday morning, the telephone rang. Matthew's body jerked. Little Paul stiffened and let out a shriek.

Matthew held the receiver to his ear and tried to cover the mouthpiece as Paul howled on.

"Mr. Granger, is that you? This is the White House calling. Please hold for the President."

A half hour later, Matthew eased himself into a threadbare Morris chair in Harry Hopkins's office.

"I don't need to explain the China situation to a man like you, Granger." Hopkins's eyes were red-rimmed from hours of constant meetings and nights without sleep. "A Japanese defeat is inevitable. It's only a matter of time. We've been backing Chiang Kai-shek all along, and the support here in America for the Soong family is high. But Mao's forces in the north are gathering strength. I'll be honest with you. Some of the people around here think we've picked the wrong side. I don't think Chiang has fired one shot at the Japanese during this war. But we've already given the Generalissimo a loan of a half billion dollars. That financial wizard of his, T. V. Soong, persuaded the tightfisted British to match it with another five hundred million. *Now*, Chiang claims he's lost face, and the only thing that will restore it is a completely *new* loan of a billion American dollars! Some of us feel that a postwar Chiang-Mao coalition would be in the best interest of the United States, but we can't go ahead with that strategy without a full report from both fronts. We need an objective evaluation. We were talking about it tonight and your name came up."

"My name?"

Hopkins snorted. "Get serious, Granger! How many men in this city do you know who can speak Cantonese, the Wu dialect, and Mandarin fluently? With your background at Compton Fitch Enterprises, and your interest in the soil, you'll be able to give us an accurate sense of the big picture—the economy, agriculture, morale."

"How do I get in?"

"Two weeks from now you'll be part of a convoy on the

Burma Road. We'll fly you the rest of the way. You'll need a parachute. You go into training tomorrow. What do you say, Granger? You'll be going to Chungking. Then you'll be on your own to go cross-country to Yenan."

"I have a wife and two small children."

"Your Valerie is a senator's daughter. She'll go along with this, I'm sure."

That morning, as baby Paul slept contentedly, now that the sun had come up, Matthew warmed his hands around a cup of coffee at the big kitchen table and told his wife what Hopkins had said. "I could be gone for months."

"Matthew, this could be the adventure that you've wanted so much. I know that when you tried to enlist—"

"I'm not sure I want to go up. I'm not sure I should. After all, there's you, there's Joyce and the baby. It's hard for a foreigner to go undetected in China. When I said 'months,' what I really meant was, I might not come back."

"We both know that's not it, Matthew! Years ago you had another life in China. But that life is gone now. We can't have 'what might have been' hanging over our lives. I don't know if it's the memory of your parents or that poor dead girl, but . . ."

"I don't know what will happen when I go back. I don't know what I'll find."

"You must think of what this will mean to us, for our family, for your career. You'll be carrying out a special mission for the President!"

And just as easily as she had seen through him, he saw through her. "With you behind me, Val, I'll be a senator yet."

She looked at him steadfastly. "I'd always thought of the Cabinet, dearest."

Three weeks later, Matthew floated in thick, humid air, gliding down in velvet darkness. *Keep moving as you land. Keep your knees bent. Expect rice paddies. Fold your chute and bury it. Remember your compass. Remember your food. You are not protected under the Geneva Conventions.* As his brain reiterated the facts, his heart thumped against his ribs. He took in this adrenaline rush, but under the excitement, the adventure, he became conscious of another sensation. He could only compare it to the combined sense of peace and contentment that he'd felt as a child when the riverboat from

Kiukiang chugged the last few *li* up to the docks in Shanghai. In the profoundest possible way, he knew himself to be coming home.

He landed in a flooded rice paddy, pungent with the scent of night soil. He folded his chute, but kept it with him. With instincts he'd had since he was a boy playing in Da Sze Foo's home village, he found the paddy's border and trod along the raised dirt path until he reached a cluster of a dozen dwellings. Again, on instinct, he went to the one that must belong to the headman, knocked once, and waited with his head bowed until the door opened.

"I know this will be hard to believe, Estimable Old One," he said, and his mouth loved shaping the words. "I have come from out of the sky to visit you. I need to go to Chungking, the eastern capital. To make up for this intrusion, please accept this poor gift from those of us who live in the clouds." Still keeping his head down, he thrust forward his chute and heard whispers as several pairs of chapped hands stroked a fabric softer than any they had ever touched.

Again he was in a plane, this time a sputtering one-engine job. Matthew cleared a place in the condensation on his window to get his bearings. He couldn't see anything. He knew from studying maps of the terrain that cliffs rose on either side of them, much higher than the plane was now. The turbid Yangtze flowed below, dotted with sandbars. The engine coughed like a sick old man, and the plane lurched as unsteadily as the British pilot had when they were still on the ground.

With an alarming *thunk*, the wheels of the plane hit the ground. The plane bounced and shuddered and finally settled. Matthew unlatched the dome of the cockpit and gratefully breathed in the foggy air.

"I don't know how you do it," he said, barely keeping the tremor out of his voice. "It's a hell of a way to make a living."

They both swung down onto the packed-sand runway. Matthew thrust out his hand.

"Thanks, Mr. . . ."

But the pilot, after checking a nick in the propeller blade, immediately climbed back into his seat. "Got to get out of here while there's still some light," he shouted out over the wheezing motor. "And do yourself a favor, old man. Don't ask any white man what his name is when you're in Chungking. Nobody comes to Chungking under his own name."

A pale green, battered Willys-Knight waited by the hangar and wind socks, the only signs that this sand bar was the airport of a world capital. Matthew gave the password. The driver of the vehicle, answering with a sloppy salute, opened the door and waved for Matthew to get in. They left the airfield and began climbing a narrow dirt path that cut across the face of the cliff.

Matthew spoke in Mandarin. "You're a brave man to drive a car up this road."

The driver turned his head and stared in amazement at his passenger. "*Ai-yah!*" he exclaimed. "The round-eye speaks our language like one of us."

The car headed directly for the cliff. Matthew leaned over and grabbed the wheel, steering them back to safety.

"Confucius taught us that the true guide keeps his eye on the path of the future!"

The driver said courteously into the hundred-foot drop they were skirting, "The round-eye even quotes the Great Sage in a perfect accent."

"Listen, *Siao Dee Dee*, Little Brother," Matthew gasped, "let's just keep our minds on getting our asses up this bloody hill in one piece."

The driver snickered.

Only the presence of two armed sentinels, pistols drawn, at a modest gate, showed that this might be Chiang Kai-shek's headquarters. At a word from one of the militia, the gate clanked open. A servant took Matthew's pack and ushered him in.

Matthew saw that this, like all other Chinese compounds, began with apparent poverty. Each successive courtyard increased in luxury. As he was shown into the fourth, he entered an imperial palace. His feet walked on thick Peking rugs. The walls of this waiting room were hung with priceless scrolls from the Sung Dynasty, and though the formal furnishings were the stiff, hard-backed teakwood chairs that he remembered from his boyhood, the upholstered sofa that the servant showed him to was as yielding as an eiderdown quilt.

As soon as he was seated, an attendant came in with a tray that held a full fifth of Johnny Walker Black Label and hors d'oeuvres that might have come direct from Maxime's. As the attendant poured him two fingers of whiskey in a rice-pattern teacup, he said, "This was a gift to the Generalissimo from your American warrior—General Joseph Stilwell. Please make yourself comfortable."

Matthew crunched anchovy and mushroom puffs and sipped slowly at his drink. He knew he must be careful. After the fatigue and strain of the last few days, he could not let down his guard. He did not doubt that all this was a part of his host's plan.

The pounding of military boots sounded the Generalissimo's arrival. As the trim figure came through the door, Matthew rose, put his fists together, and bowed formally. Chiang smiled as he returned the courtesy.

"We are honored that you have come this far." A retainer in a blue satin gown poured drinks for them both and carried in a fresh tray holding tiny shrimp and pigeon's eggs before he withdrew.

Matthew understood the challenge. Taking up a pair of ivory chopsticks, he expertly picked up one of the slippery, slightly soft eggs and put it in his mouth. The general sucked in his breath with an audible hiss.

"We have not been misled," he said in Mandarin. Shifting to his native Cantonese, he added, "If I could not see your face, I would think we had been brought up in the same family."

"You flatter me," Matthew said. "There is no reason for you to recall it, but I remember well our first meeting of many years ago."

"Can we indeed have met? Surely I would remember such an occasion."

"The occasion, yes. The person, no. It was at the Fairy Glen Hotel in Kuling, in the Lushan Mountains, when Comrade Borodin and Madame Sun were still with you. I was a Boy Scout, a member of the Pine Tree Patrol. You waved to us. We always pretended at school that it was a salute and not a gesture of dismissal. It gave us great face."

The Generalissimo threw his head back and laughed. "I remember that day," he said, "and my bodyguards remember it. They were severely punished for allowing you and your friends to break the security of my temporary headquarters."

Behind this amiable voice, Matthew heard a note of cruelty. Perhaps it had been a mistake to mention the incident. He had caught the General off guard, but it gave Matthew the clue to the conversation that followed. No matter how flattering Chiang was in expressing his thanks to the Americans for their aid, Matthew heard the undertone of resentment over having to depend on the foreigner. It was fine for the

Generalissimo to speak of his "Methodist Christian brothers across the sea," but he was driving as fast and directly as custom allowed to what really interested him—the new American loan. Looking around him, Matthew could see where most of the other money had been spent.

When Chiang almost directly demanded the new loan as a minimum condition for continuing as a member of the Allies, Matthew retreated diplomatically. "You must understand, President Chiang, that I am in no way an official member of the American Government."

Chiang grunted, "I am telling you to go back to your government and let them know that I must have the money to continue the struggle against the Japanese."

"I shall certainly deliver your message," Matthew replied, holding his voice even, but thinking to himself that this man was not called General "Cash-my-check" for nothing.

Soon Chiang's wife, Mei-ling, joined them, "How happy I am to meet one, who like myself, is part of two countries. I know that you will do your best to help the stricken land we both love." She wavered delicately in pink silk lounging pajamas, her small feet on platform shoes; the buckles of the straps were jeweled butterflies. He could not think of nothing else but a jade girl.

Later that afternoon, Matthew stood in the compound's entry. His battered car drove up and he got in. He did not know quite what he expected. He supposed that he would be taken to the nearest hotel and enjoy the luxury of a good meal, a bath, and a long night's sleep. But as the Willys clattered noisily through streets barely wide enough to take the car, and an unhealthful miasma began once again to seep up through the alleys from the river, he discerned that of course there was no hotel—no bath, no night's sleep.

The car sputtered up to a nondescript building.

"This is the Foreign Press Club," his driver said. "You'll find good times here. Don't worry."

"When will you . . ."

"I'll find you tomorrow. Everyone in Chungking will know where you are."

The Chungking Press Club consisted of a bar and four or five tables at which clustered perhaps a dozen depressed newsmen. The captial's only "stories" were the daily bombings. If the fog came, as it did today, there was no bombing—

and no story. There was nothing for them to do but nurse the respiratory diseases that plagued them all, and whack at rats with their shoes as the rodents ran through the game room. When the sun shone, their bronchitis had a chance to clear up, but the sun drew the Japs like flies to sugar. Every afternoon planes came over by the dozens to drop their loads. The journalists could either join the Chinese of Chungking in their caves—in which case they stood a fine chance of being suffocated or trampled to death—or they could stay in the press club and drink.

Two men were arguing as Matthew came in. A man dressed in a bathrobe introduced himself simply as Yardley. He said he was a cryptographer and insisted he was part of the Chinese Black Chamber. A fresh-faced kid named Teddy White nodded to him. As Matthew inquired if this place had any beds, or a place to wash up, or at least a drink, they jeered at him.

"Too late, bud. There's not a drop left in the place. My name's Yardley," he repeated, "and I crack codes." This struck him as funny. "That's when I can't find any other cracks," he said, and almost choked to death from his own mirth.

"Come on," said Teddy White, leaning back in his chair to get a good look at the sullen Chinese bartender. "Are you telling me there's nothing more to drink in this hole?" When the bartender didn't answer, Yardley put his head down on the table and began to sob. "Why couldn't they have sent me north? I had a career at home. I had a wife and kids. I'll die before I ever see the States again. Oh, why couldn't they have sent me north?"

"You need a good stiff drink," White said. "Let's call a car."

Yardley laid his head on Matthew's shoulder.

"Disease," he confided. "They've got things out here nothing can cure. I can never face my wife again."

After a short bumpy ride, the three of them were dropped off at Yardley's house on the muddy banks of the Yangtze.

The main room was cluttered with dirty laundry, furnished with contraband antiques, and dotted here and there with king-size cans of Cock-of-the-Walk canned peas. Yardley swayed vaguely for just a minute.

"Have patience," he mumbled. "What did you say your name was? Granger? You go to the crapper, you'll find a gallon of rubbing alcohol. Teddy, roust out Ah-long and tell him to bring in the bread I ordered."

Ah-long came in with a loaf and a kerosene lamp. The three men pulled up chairs around a wooden table. Matthew, in spite of himself, was hypnotized by the painstaking process, as Yardley distilled drinks for each of them by dipping rubbing alcohol through thick chunks of white bread.

"Not yet, Ted. I'll tell you when. It's one for all and all for one. If we're going to go blind, we'll do it together."

Within fifteen minutes, three thick glasses stood filled to the brim with clear liquid.

"*Kam-pei,*" Yardley said. "*Ting-hao.* All that. Plenty of snatch and a free China."

Matthew opened his throat, closed his eyes, and tossed it back in one gulp. It hit him like an express train. He doubled over and crumpled to the floor. He had found his good night's sleep.

For the next eight days, Matthew spent drunken nights, anxious early morning seizures of nausea and anxiety brought on by the denatured alcohol (which Yardley insisted kept away the clap), and long, gray afternoons in which, racked by his endless hangover, he drifted about this unattractive inland capital.

Was this the new world, the "Free Democracy" that Chiang Kai-shek offered? At the University of Chungking starving professors told Matthew that their tiny salaries wouldn't let them eat and buy paper at the same time. Another visiting foreigner, Professor Fairbank, had all but stopped his work for the government and spent every waking hour simply trying to keep his young scholars alive. If intellectuals starved, the plight of the common man seemed a thousand times worse. Small children labored at heavy machinery making bomb casings in day-long shifts, with only a single cup of rice gruel to sustain them. This was not the new China but the old. Here in Chungking, Matthew saw the same system he had lived in as a child: the very poor slaved and died, a few middlemen put money by, taking advantage of the squeeze, and at the top of this pyramid a handful of the very rich stored up wealth with callous disregard for those whom they supposedly governed. But Shanghai in the old days lived by ebullience and stamina and the sheer joy of being alive. Here, all was illness, hopelessness, and a smell of defeat as foul as the daily afternoon fogs.

On the day before he left, Matthew was granted a second

appointment with the Generalissimo. This time there was no Scotch and no hors d'oeuvres. Matthew knew that Chiang had objected strenuously to his aides when he learned that Matthew was conducting genuine research to put together a genuine report.

This morning, the beaky Asian bestowed a face-splitting grimace on his guest and said, "You have seen our children giving their very souls for what you call 'the war effort.' Luckily, since many of them are Christian, they will go straight to heaven to live with Jesus. But remember, Mr. Granger, war is an expensive enterprise. We here on the earth still need our billion dollars." As Matthew hesitated, the General hissed, "Thousands of us die every day so that you Americans can prosper and grow fat."

"Sir," Matthew said, and he knew that this lack of a title enraged Chiang, "you know that I'm on my way to Yenan. You know that America wants a coalition. May I relay a message from you to General Mao Tse-tung?"

"I have no message for that toad. One flaw I find with the government of your vast United States is that you deal with a man who has so low an intelligence. He is a peasant, really, whose mother used to carry the family night soil to someone else's fields. But because he is a 'Red,' a Communist, you fear him. I tell you that in Yenan they are no more than babies playing in what you call a kindergarten. They hold hands and sing songs and make pretty pictures and they think that can make a great nation!"

Chiang waved a languid hand. The dim light caught the sheen of his manicured fingernails. "All this," he hissed, "the heritage of centuries, the treasures of the past, this is what China has to give to the world. A peasant would defecate in this room and build a bonfire out of our finest carved objects." He shrugged, then, pulling open a drawer, drew out a sheaf of yellowed rice paper. He shook it at Matthew. "I am to unite with people who call *this* art? They say that archaeologists have found cave paintings from ancient tribes, almost apes, who lived thousands of years ago. This is what the apes of Mao send me from their caves. Look at these drawings and tell me they are the work of civilized human beings."

The style was simple, but obviously that had been the artist's conscious choice.

Here, against stark cliffs rendered in black and white, an old woman fed bits of bamboo to a fire pot. A bride received the gift of earrings from her grandmother. A brigade of young soldiers piled their rifles neatly. People danced, smiled, except for one. . . . A child lurked in the background. His hair, did it curl? Matthew shivered.

The General snatched the drawings from his grasp. "Let me ask you this, Mr. Granger. Do you see anyone in these pictures going about the business of running a great nation? No, they are babies. They have the minds of babies. They cry out in their ignorance for a great leader and I am that leader."

Matthew turned to the door, scarcely able to say good-bye. The General's light, unpleasant voice followed Matthew out: "A leader rules with money and power. Your country will see that I have enough of both."

Some days it was hard to remember that there was a war. As he traveled through the rural countryside, he saw less poverty, less anguish, less despair. He passed villages that had endured for thousands of years. He saw children tending buffalo and women who were not afraid to go outside the compound walls to draw water from their common well. Men tilled the earth, still secure in a perishable ignorance. No aerial barrages had hit this area. Matthew's guides made every effort to find him motorized transport. But there were many times when he rode astride a donkey, bumped along in a cart, walked.

With a rush of excitement, he felt each day his grasp of colloquial dialects coming back to him. Every day he felt closer to the land, stronger and happier than he had ever been before. When he tried to focus his mind on Washington, it seemed even further away than those evenings spent in hard drinking and banal conversation with Yardley on the banks of the Yangtze. Images. Washington was only images.

He loved his wife, his children. But, now that he was back in China, he walked to another rhythm, barely discernible under the flow of his blood and the beat of his heart.

A hundred miles southeast of Yenan, he was put on a bus with perhaps half a hundred soldiers who traveled to a different rhythm than Matthew's.

"How shall we kill the running dogs of capitalism?" they sang. "How? With a pitchfork! How? With a plow! How? With a bayonet! How? With our clenched fists of indignation! How? With our words of sturdy truth! How? With our right sayings and right deeds! How? With common work and common play!"

After twenty-four hours of this—as the bus's radiator broke and was patched up; as tires went flat and were repaired; as they waited from midnight until dawn on the floor of a dusty gorge for more cans of gasoline carried across country on bamboo poles by coolies—Matthew began to have a pretty good idea both of the enthusiasm of these recruits and how they aimed to destroy the running dogs of capitalism. Touchingly, these boys showed little surprise that Matthew was able to pick up their dialect and even sing along with them. Did not the whole world know that a new world was coming to China? Did not the whole world speak with one tongue? And was not everyone under the great sky of China engaged in the struggle to beat the last remaining right-wing counterrevolutionist scoundrels into the dust with the rest of the vermin of the earth?

When the bus took the grade into Mao's mountain stronghold, silence fell over the boys, and Matthew marveled. He saw, with an unaccustomed melting of the heart, that each boy carried with him a dampened square of rag or paper. Each recruit used this on his own face, scrubbing away the dust of the journey until his youthful cheeks turned pink. They slicked back their hair, and a cheap smell of brilliantine filled the vehicle. Matthew lent out his comb and a young cub punched him in the arm.

"Lucky foreigner, to be able to see with your own eyes, as we soon will, the man who brings with him a new dawn for our country."

They slowed to no more than five miles an hour. The bus passed a few nondescript outbuildings, and then, incredibly, an officer stood and pulled out a pitch pipe. The boys stood in the still-moving bus and sweetly, with a sense of newness as if they'd never sung before, began the first lines of "The East Is Red." Matthew stood too. He bowed his head as he had when he was a boy in church. Let this be true for them, he prayed silently, let this be real for them.

The bus came to a halt beside a large wooden platform jammed with women, children, and old men clapping and waving red handkerchiefs. As Matthew descended, two young Chinese greeted him, shook hands, and looked deep into his eyes, projecting an optimism almost as overpowering as the singing of the soldiers on the bus. He found that his legs were a little shaky.

"A lifetime of being carried in sedan chairs has made you as soft as those missionaries they used to send us."

"We'll put him to work in the fields," the other one said. "He'll learn how a man of the people spends his days."

Then a woman came up with tea and a bowl of millet gruel.

"Sit down," the first man said, not unkindly, "under this tree. Let your strength come back to you, but keep your eyes open. What you will see is the new China."

Matthew spooned the gruel to his lips with the vague sense that he was a child being punished. The men were right. All around him human beings stood, but they seemed from another planet. They walked in step, they marched, really. They cocked their heads at forty-five degree angles, and when they waved, they held their arms in a stylized three-quarter salute. Most of the adults were filthy beyond words, tanned and stained with dirt almost to the point of negritude; but the children, who attended an outdoor class taught by a woman with steel-rimmed glasses, had been tidied. Some of them wore red scarves around their necks.

Matthew caught phrases of the song of "The Running Dogs of Capitalism," but mercifully it ended after less than twenty stanzas. The boys and girls bent studiously over slates held in their laps. Matthew felt drowsiness sweep over him. His two guides must have watched and waited for him to shut his eyes, for the instant he did, he was shaken awake and chided with words that he had not heard since his amah and Da Sze Foo had let him nap in the kitchen.

"Oh, sleepyhead, the world will run away while you have your eyes closed."

Matthew knew the next line was "And the dwarfs of the underworld will take you."

He said shortly, "It was a long trip."

"The People's Council will see you now."

The men took him by each arm and the three marched to a door that opened into a sheer wall of stone and dirt. Finally, he was here in the fabled caves of Yenan. And though he tried, he could not keep from gagging at the stench.

"I told you he was soft," the first man shouted out to the assembled council. "He spends his day on a pallet where young women dab him with soap and water."

Matthew found his tongue and shouted out, "You are speaking of a traveler who has not bathed in two weeks, and who relishes every grain of Chinese soil he finds in the crevices of his body and between his toes."

A voice from the back said, "We must marry him to one of our village girls."

"And why is that?" Matthew asked, playing the straight man. He used the extra time to let his eyes grow used to the darkness, searching what faces he could see for signs of discontent, malice, or greed.

But all he saw were smiles and confidence as the men, perhaps thirty of them, answered almost in chorus, "The peasants in our region take baths only three times in their lives—when they're born, when they marry, and when they die. A revolutionary must never hold himself above a peasant."

He realized soon enough that this was not an important council, far from it. Rather, it was one of several screenings that he would go through before—or even if—he was to be allowed to see the leaders here, Chou En-lai or Mao himself.

"We have many visitors these days," a person across the table from him said. "They come from all over the world, now that we are winning. Should we kill our ducks for you and make a banquet? Are we to be delighted at your visit?"

"I come from a long way," Matthew said. "I have even sacrificed fourteen days out of my life to spend time with the baldheaded gopher of Chungking so that I might report to your leader what he says. *Now* tell me that I am just one of many visitors."

The conversation went on more soberly about conditions in Chungking until Matthew's eyes, against his will, began to close. "Your soldiers sing well, but it is not music to sleep by."

"Let him rest," one of the men said. And then to Matthew: "To be truthful, you have conducted yourself well. You will spend tonight in the cave of the Sub-Minister of Agriculture, and tomorrow at dawn he will take you out to inspect our fields."

Matthew held on to the jacket of the man in front of him, and they climbed what seemed hundreds of yards up the face of a cliff, on a switchback, to another door that opened into earth. His two guides pounded loudly on the door, opened it, calling out, "Here's your foreigner!" Peering into the gloom, Matthew saw that another Chinese cadre waited for him against the wall. Matthew kept silent, knowing that it would not be polite to make the first move. If the game was to continue throughout the evening—throughout his entire stay here in Mao's camp—then he was ready to play.

The figure stepped forward. "Welcome to my home."

"Greetings, Sub-Minister . . ."

But at the sound of Matthew's voice, the figure halted. "Can it be? Do I know you?" the man inquired. "Are you originally from Shanghai?"

"Shanghainese walk faster," Matthew answered, switching to the Wu dialect to give the traditional response. "They think faster. That is why our city is a pearl."

"You're Matthew Granger, the mission boy," the voice rasped out.

"Have we met?"

"They told me it would be a man by the name of Granger," the voice continued coldly, "but I discounted it."

Matthew felt memories flood through him. "Chuen-yup? You're Nyi Chuen-yup? It can't be! But this is marvelous, to see you again after all these years!"

Something was terribly wrong. Is it because I knew him when he was the warlord's son? Matthew thought, his mind racing to find the answer to the awkwardness. Is it the Red Army, testing both of us? Do they know about the mission? Or the kidnapping? Or do they seek to test or compromise or embarrass one of their own?

"We've both changed so much," Matthew began tactfully. He was interrupted by the arrival of a young tot who raced into the room, yelped for attention, and hurled himself up into Chuen-yup's arms.

"My son, Chuen-yee," he said forcefully, even tauntingly.

"You are most blessed," Matthew answered, bewildered.

"Doubly blessed," the strained voice continued. "My revolutionary wife came to me already with a son of her own."

Chuen-yup cocked his head toward a carved-out alcove in the walls of the damp cave. It was only then that Matthew saw the boy. The stickiness he'd felt from his arrival here turned into rivulets of sweat that ran down from his armpits, stuck to the back of his shirt, dripped from the backs of his knees. Matthew was transported back, far back, to the riverboat taking him from Kiukiang to Shanghai, looking with envy through the porthole at Harley, the strong boy who could do anything. But this boy was so sad, he . . .

Matthew took in the boy, the vaguely Western ambience of the cave, the drawings that decorated the rock walls, so similar to those he'd seen days ago in the Generalissimo's office. He heard the crystal windchime of a voice—a voice that by now he knew he expected—calling out in perfectly accented tones, "Honored guest, our dark cave is made bright by your visit." Jordan stepped into the room with a tray of tea and cakes.

Matthew saw a nightmarish vision. His Jordan—pure, beautiful, blond, always so carefully groomed—his Jordan ravaged—her golden hair chopped into an uneven, dirty mess, her peach complexion hardened now to rough leather, her trim little body toughened and cloaked in peasant dress. He watched as she paled and staggered, and then saw her old control return as she continued into the room and set the tray down on the makeshift table.

Chuen-yup watched all this. "Ah, mission boy, perhaps you remember Bah-wha? And you, respected revolutionary wife, the gods smile on you today, for you have at long last found the father of your child. My congratulations!"

"Oh, Matthew," she whispered. "I thought I'd never see you again."

"Yes," Matthew said numbly. "We all thought you were dead."

"I didn't take the ship."

"I was at Southampton on the dock. I waited. . . . We all waited for some word of you. . . ."

Chuen-yup snorted. "What lovebirds!" He gave a loud theatrical laugh. "Luck has always followed the mission boy. Today you will go home with a son. I grant you permission to take this albino beetle off my hands. Food is short for those who serve the people."

The three adults stared at the trembling boy, who still lurked in the shadows. Wordless, Matthew forced himself to look again at Jordan.

"It happened at the engagement party," she stammered. "Our engagement party. I didn't know how to tell you."

"And that's why you disappeared."

"My amah . . ." But Jordan couldn't continue.

The silence was palpable between them now. Matthew reached within himself for the voice of his father and drew himself up stiffly.

"Perhaps, Mr. Sub-Minister," he said coldly to Chuen-yup, "it would be better if we conducted our interview in the morning."

Without waiting for an answer, Matthew left the cave. He was aware that Jordan attempted to follow him, an attempt that was halted by her husband's arm, his hand closing over her shoulder, holding her back.

* * *

The next day at the People's Cabinet Meeting held to sum up Mao's progress to the foreigner, Matthew was struck by the confidence with which Madame Mao—whom all referred to as Jiang Qing—expressed herself, giving her opinions freely to this otherwise all-male group.

"Everything that is happening now," she said, "is just as I predicted. I told you that it would be a waste of time to try any kind of cooperation with Chiang Kai-shek, that impotent captive of the whore Mei-ling!"

No Chinese man liked to be lectured this way by a woman, especially when she was right. But Jiang Qing, carried along by the pleasure of hearing her own actress's voice fill the room, scarcely paused.

"No matter what the corrupt Kuomintang does now, no matter how badly they fight the Japanese, they will appear to be winning. But it is not they who are winning. It is their foolish pawns, the Americans, who will squeeze out the monkey people. Then China will belong to us."

The men sipped their tea noisily with obvious satisfaction, as the Vice-President agreed with almost fawning approval.

"The wife of our great leader speaks the truth. The people are already with us. In the areas that we have held from the beginning, we have thrown out the evil landlords and redistributed the fields. Already surplus crops are available for feeding the newer territories."

The Minister of Transportation chimed in, "That is true, and we have built roads, a thousand new *li*. We can even think now, instead of just dreaming, of a great bridge over the Yangtze, joining the north and south."

One of the secretaries asked, "Is this true? The foreign devils have always said it was impossible."

Seizing this opening, Jiang Qing exclaimed theatrically, "Ah, those foreigners! They may still throw sand in the eyes of our rice Christians, but we who follow the Red Star have learned our own strength. Even if they *had* been able to build such a bridge, they probably would have collected toll fees from us for the privilege of using it."

"And we have planted trees," said a man whom Matthew assumed was connected with the Ministry of Agriculture. "Millions of trees are changing the landscape of *our* territories while the rapacious armies of that rodent Chiang still devastate *their* land, cutting anything that grows over three feet for firewood."

Matthew drove his mind the way one drives a car, shifting, slowing, speeding, sifting the relevant from the irrelevant. As he took notes, images of the land coincided and overlapped with the young Jordan Logan-Fisher. A land of soft hills like breasts, which were to have been his, but had been invaded by another. *How?* How could it have happened? Unbidden, another image came to his memory. Jordan on her eighteenth birthday, dancing close to Harley Compton Fitch.

He took note, automatically, of the Minister of Education. "Now we have the village day schools. In our own lifetime we may see all our country speaking one language. The many tribes of China will soon become one people."

The meeting went on for more than eight hours. Every representative there had something to say. There were arguments still—should the farms be collectivized? Should Buddhism and Confucianism be allowed to flourish, or were they tools of the old regime? What about the temples, should they be razed? What about merchants in the cities? And what about those Chinese who had worked for foreigners? Must they all be executed? Matthew thought, with a pang, of Da Sze Foo. But even through his distress, Matthew was dazzled by the sheer amount of work that the Reds had done. They had taken de facto control of the country, but—far more important—their energy appeared to be equal to their vision. The old dragon of China that had slept so many years was finally wakening.

As the meeting broke up, Matthew's "responsible person" drew him aside. "At dawn, you are scheduled to meet with your old friend, Bah-wha." When Matthew flinched, his guide coldly went on. "The great leader says that personal emotions cannot be allowed to interfere with the thrust of the revolution, and the neighborhood watch agrees that this must be talked out in a full meeting."

"So many meetings!"

"You have no choice in this if you wish to stay here."

At five-thirty the next morning, in the same room that had housed yesterday's political discussion, a much smaller committee filed in and took their places. Their faces were expressionless.

Chuen-yup came in followed by Jordan and her son, who carried many of Harley's features in his tormented face. A middle-aged Caucasian woman came up and sat between Jordan and Chuen-yup. Matthew's "responsible person" whis-

pered into his ear, "You are lucky that Miss Smedley is here to
act as your interpreter."

Immediately Matthew's resolves about diplomatic calm
melted away like ice on a hot day. "I speak the language," he
snapped. "I speak it as well as a person educated in your best
schools, better than—"

His guide looked shocked. "You foreigners are slow to
understand how tired we are of your arrogance. Today we
search not for education but for truth. Our Chinese committee
will record the findings, and Miss Smedley, a personal friend of
the Great Helmsman himself, will record for the rest of the
world how our new justice prevails." He tapped Matthew's
arm to make it perfectly clear. "Your bourgeois learning and
you, yourself, mean absolutely nothing to us. This is a matter
between a revolutionary husband and wife, and it is to be
solved in a way that most benefits the revolution."

Cheun-yup stood up. "You all know me," he began. He
held up his mutilated hand. "You know what I did in the old
days in that city that was a brothel to foreigners—Shanghai. I
chopped away my own flesh to become one of you. And you
know as well what I did voluntarily to the man who gave me
life, my own father. I cut him from me. I threw him away so
that I might be one of you. And yet I criticize myself now that
some of the craven love of foreigners and of the ancient regime
must have remained with me. With all of the good and honest
women who have made the Long March alongside our
soldiers, why didn't I listen to your advice, old women, when
you told me to pick a Chinese wife? But no. I had to wallow in
the bed of a yellow-haired foreigner who has been full of
trouble as a water buffalo with bloat. You know how I met her.
I saw her in her own house when I was with my father's
hooligans, and she"—here he coughed and spat noisily—"was
painting. I used to think it was courage, honored neighbors,
that kept her from any fear of my father's thugs. But in truth, it
was her own conceit, her delusions of aristocracy, that made
her indifferent to the threats or the suffering of our great
people."

A wooden chair fell over. The dirt floor raised dust as the
harridan on the other side of Miss Smedley jumped to her feet,
dug both her hands into her husband's hair, and pulled as hard
as she could.

"Sea cow! Green, wart-filled toad! My father paid off his
country's debts to your people. You gouged the poor and try to

take credit for it now." She whirled to the assembly, ignoring Matthew completely, and shouted out, "My husband says he gave up a finger for your cause, as if he had ever done any work with his hands!"

Jordan raised both her arms high and her voice filled the room. "He gave up a finger as a snake sheds a skin. But I, oh, my companions, who have so often been unfeeling to me, I have given up everything to be part of your revolution. There are things to be said today that I have never said before. Although *you* think me ugly, to my own people I was once a great beauty. Although my own parents were not rich, my father's family owned the equivalent of three of your villages! But unlike your old landowners, my father worked for the good of all your people, happily sacrificing his own comfort to bring a better life to all around him! I did not ask to be born in this country. When the monkey people came, most of you had already run away—"

A rumble of hoots and hisses interrupted this statement, but Jordan, perhaps taking a cue from the shrillness of Jiang Qing, merely waited them out and then pitched her voice higher. "You are only releasing your own guilt. Who of you were still there as the bombs fell on Shanghai?"

She paused, her lip curled, and waited. Matthew, his head in his hands, listening to the accusing tirade in colloquial Chinese coming forth like lizards from her once beautiful mouth, remembered those same lips gently reciting lines of John Donne or whispering to him, "I'm so happy!"

Jordan continued. "Not one of you dares to answer! Not one of you was there! My father was there, striving to help your people as the bombs rained down about him. And I! I saw the city of Shanghai in flames. I stayed until the monkey people were at the very gates of the city!"

It was Chuen-yup's turn to stand and shout. "She stayed because already she had this abomination in her belly!" He pointed with his chin at the young Andrew, who shrank in his seat under his stepfather's gaze. "Who knows how many others like *him*"—pointing now at Matthew—"she had put her feet over her head for."

Agnes Smedley translated, in a manner both laconic and sympathetic, to the official recorder, who bent studiously over his notes. Then as Smedley looked up, she caught Matthew's eye. His hands clenched under the table, and he directed his remarks only to her.

"I belive that my estimable acquaintance Nyi Chuen-yup is laboring under a misunderstanding. It is true that in Shanghai I knew Jordan Logan-Fisher. And it is also true that, as she says, her family endeavored to carry out what they saw as their duty to the citizens of Shanghai. It is true as well"—and he struggled with a tremor in his voice—"that Miss Logan-Fisher and I were once engaged. But we kept the unwritten rules of our class and our religion. So far as I knew, my fiancée was a virgin, and as far as I was concerned, she remained one."

Now the tone of the chorus changed. Chuen-yup's face showed confusion.

Buoyed by the energy in the room, Matthew stood. "It is clear to me that Nyi Chuen-yup is not satisfied with his wife or prepared to be a father to her child. Of course I will be more than happy to escort this unfortunate woman and her son back to the United States. But I must have it recorded here that I can take no responsibility for them once we have landed in New York. I myself have a wife and children." As he felt the indignity of his position, his voice rose. "I will, of course, be happy to put her and her son in touch with the man I once thought was my best friend, the boy's father, Harley Compton Fitch."

Only the table kept Bah-wha from attacking him. "How very kind of you, Matthew. What a demonstration of your undying love! You'll put me in touch with my rapist. How very, very kind of you!"

Agnes Smedley's eyebrows raised, but her voice remained low and noncommittal as she relayed these words to the recorder. A skeptical murmur traveled around the room.

"Is there an unmarried girl on this earth who does not say, when she finds herself with child, that it was forced upon her?"

Jordan faced Chuen-yup. "You are responsible for this slander! You wanted me in your house and in your bed. You take your pleasure with me and crave my companionship, but outside of our cave you never defend me. You have always let those women—"

Chuen-yup shouted back, "I went to the Great Helmsman himself with your drawings. . . ."

She answered, her voice low and direct, "Do you think I'm a total fool, Chuen-yup? Do you think I don't know you've used me and my talents all these years? The old women have been right about one thing. I have been a ornament to your household and as useful to your career as any rich wife of the old days."

Bah-wha had hit a nerve. Her husband's skin became blotchy before a truth he had never admitted even to himself.

"Harlot!" he breathed. "Whore! Slut! Western girl of the streets!" He stammered, and in a desperate attempt to take attention off himself, pointed once again at Matthew. "He denies having intercourse with this woman, but what else can he do? Would you expect him to *admit* it?"

But his wife laughed in his face, and then addressed the old women. "Some of you have memories of the old missions. Some of you were rice Christians before you turned to the learning of Mao Tse-tung. The stupidest among you must realize that if I were half the jade girl my husband thinks me, I would not go to a missionary's son for pleasure."

"You bitch! You narcissistic little bitch!" Matthew burst out. "Have you ever for one moment in your life thought about anybody but yourself? It's always been you, you, you, and how much attention you can get. You may be right that I couldn't give you the pleasure you wanted. I saw you dancing with Harley. If you want to call what happened rape, be my guest. If you want to pass yourself off here as some kind of sacrificial maiden of the people, that's all right with me, but, Jordan, I know more about pleasure than you ever will, no matter how many men you sleep with. . . ."

"*Ai-yah,*" the old women crooned, but Jordan was silent.

"Yes, I am a missionary's son, and some of what my family said was true. Find a good and beautiful woman and stay with her always."

"Beautiful?"

"Yes, beautiful. Very much as you used to be before you went native." He shouted to everyone in the room, almost out of his mind with rage and loss. "She's right about one thing. She was the most beautiful girl in Shanghai." He reached across the table and grabbed her rough jacket. "Do you know what Harley's father, that financier, used to say? A man's capital is his beauty; a woman's beauty is her capital. You've spent yours, Jordan. You're bankrupt now. Look what you've done to yourself. You've been as careless with yourself as you've been with everyone else. You haven't asked once about your parents, let alone about me. You've thrown yourself away. You're covered with filth. Look at what the sun has done to your face. You look like a woman of fifty. And your hair! What do you cut it with—a butcher knife?"

Tears came to her eyes and spilled down her cheeks, but

she didn't pull away from him. "Yes, what you say is true. I live as my sisters here. And I suggest that you return home to your beautiful wife who adorns herself in a way you find pleasing."

The tide in the meeting turned. The old ladies nodded. A jumble of comments came from them: "Yes, it is true. Bah-wha lives as we do." "There's no vanity in her." "She is a good mother and wife." "She works from dawn to dark in the fields and with her paints."

Then there was profound stillness. Emotions had been spent and the crowd was satisfied. Matthew Granger found himself still holding on to the jacket of a Chinese peasant.

"Jordan," he said, but as in a bad dream he could hardly hear his own voice, "you don't belong here. Please, let's get out of here. I'll take you home."

"My name is Bah-wha and I *am* home. I'm sorry, Matthew. You've always been smart, and in a way that's your trouble. You can't see what's right in front of you. I have a life and I'm useful here. And history is more important than either of us."

Chuen-yup said, "You must take the boy."

Once again, everyone looked at the unfortunate child slumped in his chair. Jordan wavered, then said, "No. He's my son. He doesn't belong to either one of you or to any man. I'll stay here only if you treat both me and my son with the respect we deserve." Her arms spread out, once again, into the larger-than-life style of her own revolutionary drawings. "Mao himself has said, 'We are all human beings under the sun.'"

"Jordan!" Matthew cried out. "Please!"

The woman's lips drew back in a sneer. With both hands she twisted her hair into a mass of unruly knots. "My name is Bah-wha, mission worm, and don't you ever forget it!"

"Meeting adjourned."

Both old politeness and new rules dictated that honest men and women never touched in public, but Bah-wha put out her hand and Chuen-yup took it. Their agreement was sealed.

On the second day out from Manchouli, where he had boarded the Trans-Siberian Express, Matthew looked at the darkening forest through which the tracks cut a straight line. The safest way out of China had been north to Harbin and then west across Siberia on his way to Moscow. He had learned by now the routine each time the long train pulled into a brake-squealing halt. The compartment doors were thrown open and the passengers—army officers, traveling officals, a few peasants—each carrying some kind of container, rushed for the huge samovar standing in the waiting room. After haggling for their other supplies, they returned while the water was still hot to brew endless glasses of tea.

That was one thing that his Chinese guides had failed to tell him about. He'd been able to pick up some packages of crackers that were more like hardtack. Salt fish in cans were also available. But no amount of money could buy him anything like a kettle or the simplest tin container. He had solved this problem by laying in a supply of double-quart bottles of Stolichnaya vodka, which was known here as "the poor man's" brand.

Tonight he waited forty-five minutes before being seated in the dining car, and found himself in the company of high-ranking Russian officials. Glumly, he ate his way through a czarist feast: caviar and biscuits with vodka, filet of sole with a dry sauterne, braised venison accompanied by a silted burgundy, finally coming full circle with triangles of toast covered with braised mushrooms, and the smoothest vodka he had ever yet tasted sliding down his throat.

The general across from him first loosened his belt, then unbuttoned the collar of his tunic. The other two men at his table were in civilian dress, one of them wearing a vaguely familiar necktie. At the end of the meal, they talked. The general looked directly at Matthew. Raising his glass of vodka, he said, *"Tovarich!"* Matthew responded, knowing that his accent would betray him. All three men, startled, looked at him. The man beside the general smiled and said, questioningly, *"Vous êtes français, monsieur?"*

"Mais non," Matthew replied. *"Je suis américain."* Like a trio in a comic opera, the men exclaimed, *"Amerikanski!"* and jumped to their feet. After the general refilled their shot glasses, they clinked them and said, "America, rah!" and downed their vodka in one gulp.

Matthew knew he must rise to the occasion. Raising his glass, he said, "All health to our common victory!" The entire car roared, and drunken shouts ricocheted from table to table. The man beside the general, continuing in French, asked him what his position in government was. Matthew replied according to his instructions.

"C'est ici la guerre, et vous êtes un touriste?"

In a perfect English accent, one of the men in civilian

dress—and now Matthew looked again at his necktie—said, "You must carry a very interesting passport, old man!"

Thrown back to his past, Matthew said, "I'm an Old Mertonian myself. You were clearly at Balliol."

"You've hit it right on the nose—I don't know how. I *was* at Balliol."

Matthew said, "Your tie, sir."

His fellow Oxonian let out a stream of Slavic syllables: "*Amerikanski, Englandski, Oxfordski!*" At the sound of the last of these, the other two men repeated, "*Da, da! Oxfordski!*" And another round of the smoothest vodka in the world disappeared.

Matthew reached for his money clip, only to have his arm taken hold of across the table with shouts of "*Nyet, nyet!*" No money ever appeared. Group after group came up to him and drank toast after toast to Comrade Stalin, to Comrade Roosevelt, to the Soviet Union, and to the death of Hitler. One late joiner, holding a full tumbler of vodka in his hand, shouted, "I drink to Chicago!"

Back in his soft-class compartment, Matthew stretched himself out on his bunk with a groan. He poured another drink and reflected upon the events that had led him to this luxurious wagonette on the Trans-Siberian Railway. Hearts might break, and a twelve-course meal, the finest vodka, a round of drunken jokes might numb the pain for an hour or two. But now his despair returned. His alcoholic bonhomie soured.

After that disastrous meeting in the caves of Yenan he had not seen Jordan again, although in the room where the children sang, her drawings formed a bright fringe around the walls.

Matthew had not had time either to collect himself or to feel his grief. He had simply been fed more bowls of millet, escorted to another meeting about the use of pig dung as fuel, and then to a concert of Young Pioneers, who had sung about the future.

He stayed four more days in Yenan before traveling to Harbin, where, after negotiating for passage with the Russian consul general, he was received as something of a visiting celebrity. Four days filled with the agony of loss.

Going home, going home, going home, the train clacked out now. He was going home to a life that many would kill for. He knew that. Two wonderful kids. A beautiful home. And not one but two jobs that he loved. He thought of Valerie. The train obligingly ticked out beautiful, dutiful, beautiful, dutiful.

But all the vodka in the world, and all the work, could not numb the overwhelming feelings that had reached Matthew in these past days. He wanted to rip Harley to pieces, literally rip him to bits. To castrate him, to disembowel him, to hear him howl in pain. And in turn he thought that—if Jordan was telling the truth—Harley must have made *her* whimper in pain. He, Matthew, would never taste her flesh. Now he saw clearly that the activity, the money, the "achievement," his ambition, his children, and even Valerie were at some level inadequate, even pitiable, substitutes for that woman who had come into his life however briefly and touched his soul. No one before had ever hurt him as Jordan had in that meeting. No one had ever touched him as she had. "And no one ever will," he muttered out loud. He thought of the magical 110 Shanghai Road that he and Jordan—yes, even Harley—had so longed for when they were young. There was no Shanghai Road. He had known that all along. There was only rectitude, and the glum satisfaction that came from doing the right thing.

He would live out his days in a charade of success. He would . . . run for office. He would give Valerie at least that much, since he could not give her his full love. And he would never tell her. He would lose himself in his work. He poured another glass of the soft liquid fire, rolled up his sleeves, and began to write his report. The government would want to hear a glowing account of Chiang Kai-shek, and Chungking described as a kind of Methodist heaven. If Matthew told the truth—that Mao Tse-tung, the egomaniacal, charismatic Great Helmsman himself, had managed in a few short years to encompass the vast vision of China in his mind and begun to do something about it—Matthew's own political future would be finished before it began.

With his fist, as he had done in the single-engine plane that had first taken him into Chungking, Matthew rubbed a clear spot on his window. Outside, a land of which he knew almost nothing hurtled past. John Reed had been here and had dared to tell the truth as he saw it. "I have seen the future and it works," he said.

Matthew's report of the land of his birth, the land of his soul, the land of his beloved, would be a little different. I have seen the future and I will tell you only a little of what I know. . . .

Matthew's life as a politician began.

* * *

In an elegant penthouse suite overlooking San Francisco Bay, Harley Compton Fitch lounged at his spacious desk and sipped iced rum as he made a series of transglobal phone calls. With his wartime priority rating, his calls came first, before everyone except four-star generals and the President himself. Within five hours he had made over a hundred thousand dollars for Compton Fitch Enterprises. Who ever said that CFE needed Matthew Granger?

Exactly fifty-nine days ago Harley had strolled into his Washington office and was stopped at the elevator by his confidential secretary. "Oh, Mr. Fitch! We've all been so worried. . . ." And as he went past the receptionist, and the rows upon rows of typists, he'd been aware of a birdlike chattering—over a hundred women gossiping in muted tones.

"What is it, Mrs. Summer?" he'd snapped as soon as the door to his private office had closed behind them. "You might as well spit it out right now."

"It's Mr. Granger's secretary. You know how she makes sure to come in at least by six o'clock every Monday morning to take care of the weekend telexes. Well, she isn't here. Her door's locked."

"That's all it is, and you bother me about it?" His mind snapped back to a recent fling he'd had with another mindless secretary. She'd refused to use birth-control jelly because the other typists around could recognized the smell. When the dumb bitch got pregnant he'd had to spend good money to send her to the Bahamas. His father had been right—the only thing he was ever right about—when he'd told him never to dip his pen in company ink. With this still in his mind, he walked down the carpeted hall to Matthew's own suite of offices. "The door's locked," he said stupidly. "Where's everybody else?"

"That's what I've . . ."

"Get the security on the phone right now!"

The security man seemed to take forever. Harley tapped his foot impatiently, then walked in to find . . .

Nothing. Miss Hullinger's desk was there but photographs of her fat mother were gone. Even her blotter with the CFE logo of the bat eating a beetle was gone. Harley crossed the room to the bank of files that filled one wall. He yanked open a drawer, and the length of it clattered emptily out in his hand. Harley knew before he went in that Matthew's personal belongings would be gone as well.

Harley sat down in Matthew's chair and put through a call to Halcyon Hill. The maid said, after a moment's hesitation, "I'll put you through to Mrs. Granger."

He encountered Washington's aristocracy at its most unnerving. "Harley, how good of you to call."

"Val, put me through to Matt right away."

"Matthew?"

"I know he's there."

"I'm sorry, Harley, he's unavailable."

"Valerie, what's this all about?"

"I feel we must respect his wishes."

He slammed down the phone, and his mind went into gear. He remembered a self-centered, unattainable adolescent who felt infuriatingly sure she was the belle of Shanghai. Could Matthew have found Jordan? Immediately he dismissed the thought. A quarter of the earth's population lived in China and the odds of one person finding another one who was missing—dead?—were infinitesimal. No, Matthew must have finally learned the ways of the business. That was why the files were gone. He must have taken his information, everything he knew about the company, and offered it to another firm.

But the weeks went by and Matthew did not surface. Harley stopped calling Halcyon Hill. Rumors began to circulate around Washington that Granger had been sent out by the President on another highly secret mission—this time to North Africa.

Meanwhile, CFE went on. And Harley's money grew more effortlessly than ever. Who needed Matthew Granger! Harley poured another glass of rum and looked around his palatial, deserted penthouse. Harley needed Matthew because it was hell to be alone.

Angrily he brushed the thought away. All he needed was a good dinner and a few more drinks. On a whim, he ordered his driver to take him to the Green Gate of San Francisco's Chinatown.

Half-drunk, Harley roamed the narrow streets. The chilly air was redolent of ginger, garlic, barbecued duck, fried eel, the pungent odor of garbage. What was the point of going to the Far East when it had already been brought to the West by the Orientals themselves? Stick two Chinamen together and you've got a tong. Stick four Chinamen together and you've got a tong war. It irritated him when he realized that it was Matthew who'd told him that.

It irritated him even more when he stopped in at the Golden Buddha Restaurant and ordered a bowl of noodles. Harley had never acquired a taste for the true Chinese cuisine. His mother forbade it in the house in Shanghai. But when he and Matthew used to venture out into the Native City, his friend ordered peasant fare in a corner teahouse near the Willow Pattern lake. It was all part of the adventure then. The noodles brought back to him the sight of old gentlemen carrying their caged birds, family groups out to visit the City Temple, a Buddhist priest or two, shaven-headed, swinging their prayer beads, and what Matthew called "those painted girls" standing at open doorways, their amahs soliciting trade by praising their charms.

He washed the noodles down with a bottle of champagne; he smashed a fifty-dollar bill into the greasy liquid at the bottom of the bowl and hurried back out into the noisy street. His attention was caught by the bigger-than-life poster outside the Cathay Moving Picture Palace. The familiar eyes of his half sister, the glamorous Eurasian siren Tai-ling, looked into his. The black lace of her bodice barely concealed the nipples of her breasts. The film, *Bombs Over Hangchow*, would contain no scene like this. It would be all war orphans and propaganda. . . .

He bought a loge ticket and as the lights dimmed he returned to the womb of adolescent eroticism. Two hours later he came out, wild-eyed. Going to the taxi stand at the end of the block, he asked the first driver, "I'm looking for a house with jade girls who will do anything."

"You want Madame Lu's."

Dawn found the entire staff of Madame Lu's house pale and awe-stricken. Madame Lu herself made the call to the physician to bandage bruises and hurt feelings. In addition to his regular tab, which amounted to something like fifteen hundred dollars, Harley Compton Fitch paid an extra two thousand for medical and cabinetwork repairs.

Earlier that same night, a few hundred miles down the California coast, Tai-ling, naked under her white satin robe, sat on the balcony of her Malibu Colony beach house staring at the glistening path to the ends of the universe that the moon made on the sea. She, too, had been drinking.

This morning, on the set of *Peking Angels*, she had called for orange juice in her dressing room. As soon as the makeup man had finished, she had laced it liberally with vodka. All over Hollywood and, she guessed, all over the United States, people were drinking Moscow Mules and screwdrivers as a patriotic gesture. She simply made that gesture a little earlier in the morning than the people she knew.

She'd found a brand of lozenges in Chinatown that bathed her succulent mouth in a scent redolent of incense. Her breath was no problem, and of course her behavior on the set was disciplined and discreet. All day she fought off the Japs as a Peking Angel. This evening, at a cocktail party given by her producer, she'd waved a lacquered fingernail in dismissal as she was offered a drink. But in the powder room she had pulled a silver flask from her purse and had drunk deeply from it.

She wondered if the producer and his wife and their friends ever allowed a ghost of a thought about her well-being to cross their minds. She doubted it. To them, if they thought of her at all, she was no more than a money-making illusion, a mirror that reflected their own grossly inaccurate fantasies of the East. They expected her to drive off "mysteriously" in her limo with no company but her chauffeur, and she did.

During the long trip home, her feet arched high in delicate beaded sandals, her shapely legs appearing through the slit in their silver *baodai,* her neck and shoulders caressed by the softest silver sables, she sat on the jump seat and delicately ran the tips of her lacquered nails along Lee-on's neck. She saw the gooseflesh rise and subside on his youthful skin, but he said nothing.

Later that night, after she bathed and dressed herself in another of the soft satin gowns that set off her body to such advantage, Lee-on came to her, still fully dressed, with a bottle of champagne and two glasses. Together they thrashed and groaned in her huge bed. By the light of the full moon she saw his face tense with the search for his own physical satisfaction and contort with a loneliness even greater than hers.

Now, as Lee-on slept, she leaned her elbows on the railing of the balcony of her beach house, sipped what remained of the champagne, and studied the contours of her life. Her isolation was nothing new. She remembered the terrible tauntings in the courtyard of the True Heart School, the indelible knowledge that she was completely separated from the ordinary life of a Chinese girl. What the Grangers had taught her about a loving God was a pathetic delusion. And yet . . . she looked down into her champagne and watched the last few bubbles in the moonlight. This life, which she had learned all too well from her mother—a life of clothes and jewels and sex and alcohol, of sensuality that ended in surfeit—was that not a delusion as well?

She padded on bare feet back into her room and went to an enormous jewel box hidden in the wall. Diamonds, rubies, an emerald tiara; her fingers searched through them until they found what they felt for. A tiny bracelet made for a baby's wrist. She could not see in the dark, so she felt the pattern with her fingertips. She touched it with her tongue. The sign of a bat eating a beetle. Prosperity and good fortune triumphing over the ugliness of earthly things. Success. Love. Happiness. These things were as illusive, as absent from her life, as the father whom she had seen only as in a dream when she was a child.

For a brief instant she remembered Harley, then sighed. That, too, was part of the great joke.

Now, in America, she was even more alone than she had been as a little girl. "Mommy," she said out loud, first in Chinese, then in English. "Father?" And then: "Harley?"

The moon's path on the peaceful ocean looked so inviting. She thought that if there was anything in her life that she had ever truly loved, it had been the city where she was born. It had made no promises. It had delivered no chastisements. Perhaps she should swim home to it now.

Quietly, out on the balcony again, she opened the warped wooden gate to the stairs that in turn led to the sand. It was a very short walk to the line where sea foam rushed in. There she carelessly flung away her satin robe and dived into an element as indifferent and noncommittal as China itself.

Later, as she lay coated in sand and choking out salt water, she pondered the strange "luck" that had led Lee-on to wake up, to discover her missing, to find her robe on the beach, to demonstrate not only the strength of his regard for her, but also his considerable prowess as a swimmer. As she gagged and vomited, she saw that the young man was crying. "Don't," she gasped. "It's just part of the joke, Lee-on, don't you see?"

Gasping in one of Yenan's perennial dust storms, Andrew bent his face close to a perfect row of young millet sprouts that extended far, far beyond the vision of a six-year-old. Carefully he dipped a cup into one of the buckets of water which he carried and trickled the water about the delicate roots of the sprout, waiting as each drop soaked the parched earth. He would work all day, he knew, and never see the end of this row. His only comfort was that today he was not in Revolutionary School; today he worked only a few rows away from his mother and her husband. They worked faster than he, and as they came up behind him, even though he was not allowed to look at them, he strained with all his might to hear their words and understand their meaning.

"Is it true what you said last night? That I give you pleasure?" his stepfather asked.

"Yes," she answered. Her next words were carried away on the wind. Then Andrew heard, "You called me harlot. You said I had many lovers. I'll never forget that."

"The mind of a man clouds when faced with the loss of what he loves."

"You should have defended me against the insults of that Western running dog."

"You do love him then! You know as well as I do, that man is no dog, but a friend of China."

Andrew's mother returned resolutely to her hoeing and soon the two of them moved out of his hearing.

A true friend of China, the boy thought. That stranger was the only other Westerner he'd ever seen besides his mother and himself. Comrade Smedley and Comrade Snow he knew were from the outside world, but they were so old they hardly counted. But Mr. Granger had been received with respect and had been able to stand up to the mean old witches and even win.

Andrew *never* won. From the first day of his arrival, he'd been sent to the People's Child Care Center. He was only three, but already he knew he would never catch up. He was still in the split pants that babies wore so they could pee on the ground, but the teachers insisted that he change to regular trousers. The first time he wet them, the teachers locked him up alone for six hours. When they let him out they said it was because the Great Leader Mao forgave him. But forgiveness meant another year in split pants. When he had cried to his mother, she only laughed. "Step-in sit-outs are easy to take care of, and you can sit down anywhere to do your business. What is there to worry about?"

He'd learned the songs and dances that were part of the required performances before meals. He'd sung "We Are All Chairman Mao's Good Little Children," "The Communist Party Is Like the Sun," and "Communism is going up, going up, going up, capitalism is going down, going down, going down." But even when he got the words right, the teachers swatted him with switches for fidgeting, or not having clean hands, or for eating too fast or too slow. Day after day during the dances and skits, he'd been made to play out the hated parts of the evil landlord or the lazybones.

He finally graduated to the People's First School. With the other children he learned to write his first character—Mao. Of course even here—no matter how much time he spent at his studies—the teacher punished him. He'd spent long afternoons copying out a hundred times, "When I am big I will be a worker or a soldier or a peasant."

No matter how hard he worked in school he would never be allowed to play the part of the farmer who sows the crop, or the soldier who stamps out capitalism, or the worker who triples production in the factory. No matter how hard he worked in the fields he would never be praised.

He knew the reason why, but he couldn't understand it. They punished him because of how he looked. He saw the answer every morning when he peered into the polished tin to see if his hair was combed. They called him a slug and a worm and they were right. The skin on his face was white and dotted with pink spots. His hair was the color of cooking oil. And his teeth were like sticks in a badly made fence. But his mother, and Comrades Smedley and Snow, looked like slugs as well. People thought twice before insulting them.

He remembered what the stranger from the West had said about his mother's family. With an unaccustomed ache—for he thought he'd hardened himself against everything—he wondered if he had a real family someplace.

Did he have a grandmother who might someday take him on her knee and tell him stories of his father when he was a little boy? He had watched the Western stranger as he had argued with the old witches. Did Andrew have a father somewhere who might be something like that? Could it be possible? He spooned another cup of murky water from his bucket and watched intently as it disappeared around the roots of a fragile seedling.

He knew Chuen-yup didn't want him here. No one in the camp wanted him, even his own mother. Somewhere out there, there must be a father who wanted him. Andrew thought of sweets, and kite flying, and someone who would play with him all day.

The six-year-old boy sighed. He straightened his conical coolie hat, hoisted the bamboo pole from which two buckets swung onto his calloused shoulders, and started back down the terraced hill for another load of water. He still had three more trips to make before dusk.

"Grant mercy upon these poor souls, O Lord, and let perpetual light shine upon them." The Reverend Wilson Granger thought that he prayed aloud, but anyone listening would have heard only the incoherent mutterings of a man crazed by grief. He watched the emaciated bodies of two boys—the latest victims of a typhus epidemic which had raged through Japanese Detention Camp Number Two—as they were unceremoniously heaped upon a stack of putrid corpses piled up like cordwood on a flimsy wooden cart waiting to be dragged away and dumped in the common grave.

In the sweltering afternoon, Wilson Granger shivered and watched as his forearms turned pink with the rash of typhus. He knew that his suffering would be short, but an anxious conscience reminded him that he still had a great deal to do.

"Forgive me, O God," he prayed aloud, and others who saw him edged prudently away, "for all my sins. Shed Thy light over everyone here, for we are all in prison, even the ones who guard us. Watch over the little children and the old ones and especially forgive the monkey people, for they know not what they do."

Unsteadily, he staggered to a far corner of the camp, where he hoped he wouldn't be seen. He rebuked himself for the pride that had always been part of his character. It would have been more thoughtful for him to die by the cart. But part of that heavenly call, which had first singled him out as someone special enough to convert the heathen, gave him permission to reach for the luxury of dying alone. He went into a dim barracks, deserted now because of the epidemic, and knelt up against a urine-stained cot. He knew it was right that he should die on his knees.

"Father, forgive them," he began again, and then his exhausted face was suffused with radiant joy. "Elizabeth!" he cried out. "Is it you?" Before he crumpled, his arms stretched out to the unseen.

Book IV

REVENGE
1949

It looked like an ordinary river. But on this sometimes torpid waterway floated the most influential men of the most powerful nation in the world. Today Harley Compton Fitch, financier and munitions king—a billionaire, it was rumored, though he had yet to hit thirty-five—had put out in his yacht, the *Fortuna*, for an afternoon's cruise. Harley looked trim, in spite of having added a few pounds, in his double-breasted blue jacket, white flannels, and yachting cap.

The *Fortuna* was not his only vessel. He thought with satisfaction of her sister ships: the *Pepita* in Portofino, the *Golden Girl* in Sausalito, the *Yankee Lass* in the East Coast Newport, and the *Señorita* in the Newport out west. For the young magnate, these floating palaces were more than simply conspicuous consumption and settings for high-level meetings. Harley Fitch's strongest memories of freedom dated from over twenty-five years ago, when he would make the trip from his mountain boarding school in Kuling to the port of Shanghai and back. He had always wanted to be captain of a riverboat, to experience the adventure that it promised, and now he saw his small fleet as so many coins: tiny, valuable.

This afternoon, as soon as the *Fortuna* had swayed away into the center of the Potomac, Harley Fitch had gone up to the bow to savor a few minutes to himself before the obligations of his alfresco party began. He was the most eligible bachelor in Washington or perhaps America. Put another way, he, or his vast conglomerate, CFE, might eventually affect the fate of every living human being in the Northern Hemisphere. His fortune had increased geometrically from sizable to princely. Ah, it was good to be alive—and rich.

His guests today were a group of eight key senators, members of "The Club." These were—though Harley prided himself on being apolitical—exclusively Republican and conservative. The decade had changed; the war was really over. The three-and-a-half-term grip of Franklin Delano Roosevelt had been followed by his unprepossessing successor, Harry S Truman. The Republicans were regrouping for a fight. They knew that their choice for President, Dwight D. Eisenhower, with his overwhelming popularity and blinding smile, would assure that theirs would be smooth sailing for at least eight years.

These Republican senators were meticulously tailored. But there was one maverick in the crowd, an ugly duckling in an ill-fitting gabardine suit with wide lapels, wearing a bright tie liberally sprinkled with game birds. He drank blended whiskey straight. Though Harley knew this man must have shaved carefully just an hour or two earlier, his florid jowls and chin seemed grubby. He had been invited here today because of a series of speechs he intended to give in the Middle West. These right-wing Brahmins had intuited that this coarse parvenu might have something unique to offer.

Young women, the most expensive call girls in the city, lounged on the top deck under the awning, but their charms would not be needed just yet. The older men gazed with fascination at this swarthy Irish upstart who sang a siren song: "So, when I come into town what if I still don't know what it was they want! There'll be a big turnout down at the high school gym, and, hell, who knows what they'll be after? ya know?"

"You sound as though you've been at this for years, son. . . ."

"My boys'll give me two speeches. You know how it is, like sometimes a monkey needs more than one thing to choose from before he can eat, ya know?"

The senators listened.

"So one of 'em'll be on housing, and the other one'll be on—Jesus Christ!—Communism in our midst, the Red Peril! So, later the boys'll say I was drunk, but anyway, I'll go on out there, and I'll pick the speech from my left pocket. No! Ha-ha!

I'll pick the speech from my right pocket"—the laughter was polite—"and then I'll set 'em on their ass. I'll have those fuckers on the floor!"

Harley, listening from a few feet away, could feel almost physically the waves of unsatisfied vengeance that held the senators. This oaf, underneath his buffoonery, had tapped into the deepest well of their own hatred.

They had considered Roosevelt a fool at best; at worst a traitor to his class. By the end of the war their venom had focused on Yalta and its agreements, where, in their view, a cripple aproaching senility and a pompous bungler from a broken empire had given away much of the Western world to an Eastern despot. They did not doubt that after what seemed to them a lifetime of liberal rule, the bureaucracy of the Democratic Party sheltered "fellow travelers," as this Irishman insisted on calling them, and card-carrying Communists.

"So I'll ask them, 'Do you know who's teaching in your kids' schools and screwing around with your kids' minds? Do you know who's making those movies where all the Ruskies are bigger and stronger than we are? Do you know who's out there in foreign countries, and they're supposed to be on *our* side? They're supposed to be waving the red, white, and blue!'"

The senators stood mesmerized, swaying slightly from Scotch and the movement of the yacht, as Joseph McCarthy snorted in exultation. "They'll scream for more! They'll give me a standing ovation! The mayor'll say later he hasn't heard anything like it since their high school team won the tri-state basketball championship!"

Harley guessed that the Republicans had seen what they wanted. Joseph McCarthy, unless something better came along, might be the man for this decade. Harley waved to the girls, and they—clad in halter tops, tight-cut shorts, and spike heels—scrambled up to the senators.

"Oh, I'm sick of hearing all this Commie talk," one of them pouted. "Can't we just go off and have some fun?"

Stewards passed among the couples. McCarthy held two girls close to his ample middle. "I just couldn't do *that*!" one of them squealed. Harley grinned. It didn't matter to him what the senator did. It didn't matter who won the political battle. As long as there was strife, one side to play against the other, Harley would bank his ten percent.

* * *

With a sigh, Valerie Granger, still in the gown she'd worn this evening, removed first the emerald errings that had been in her family for four generations and then the double strand of pearls, set with smaller emeralds, that had been a present from her father when she'd had her second child, Paul. Her dress, a long-sleeved silken sheath of gray-green crepe, clung to her still slender figure. Her discreetly plunging V-neck showed just the hint of firm breasts. Her conversation, though adult in content, came from her lips in a girlish lilt.

"I knew that when you mentioned miners and all those safety things that you'd have Gig Wetherton in the palm of your hand. Before he went to Paris, you know, he attended a prep school nearby. I went to dancing school with Gig. You knew that, of course. And I really believe that the highlight of his life, until he discovered gin, was when his uncle took him down into one of the mines they owned. And forgive me, but I really must take credit for having the sheer inspiration of sitting next to Jessamyn Murdock after dessert. I hope you don't mind that I left the dais, darling. I simply told Jessamyn that we needed twenty thousand dollars, that this was a turning point in the political life of our nation, and that simply because the rest of the country was sliding over to that balding old general, there was simply no reason why *she* had to go along with it. Oh, I know you'll think I'm foolish, but I've seen Father at work all his life. I've seen him cut corners, but he's an honest man. I think that accounts in great part for his success."

She had removed a series of small jeweled clips that had kept her thick brown hair up. Now the curls sprang loose past her shoulder blades as she began her hundred strokes with a wire brush.

"It could be a simple matter of good looks and height. I'm so glad you're not short. I could never have married a short man. No, I think in a democracy one has to be tall." She paused for a minute and thought. "Do you know, I've no idea what might be a prerequisite for a woman senator? No, I think senators have to be intelligent, honest, handsome, and tall. At least, that's what I told Jessamyn. There's no point in spending money on a billiard ball that smiles. That's what I said." She paused, took a breath. "Matthew, darling, what do you think?"

Matthew, who had unknotted his tie and removed his onyx studs and cuff links, stared at her image in the mirror.

"What's that, Valerie?"

She sighed. "It's nothing, dearest. I just wanted you to know you were brilliant tonight."

He pulled his pajamas from a drawer and, standing against the highboy, gave her a tired smile. "I want to thank you for all you've done. I don't think I'd be able to get through it without you."

Now it was Valerie's turn to fall into silence. Still brushing her hair and watching her multiple reflections in the old-fashioned three-sided mirror, she pondered what he had just said. To get *through* it? To get through a night like tonight, when in one room the oldest, finest, most powerful American families gathered to give their support to a career that might change the course of history?

Matthew was running for Congress now. But in the last six years, since he'd come home from China and quit his job at CFE, the two of them had laid the groundwork for his career so carefully, so cautiously, so—intelligently—that this first election was calculated, not to give him two noisy years as a junior legislator, but to begin a stately progress that had as its ultimate—she prayed inevitable—goal, the presidency.

So what was wrong? Why wasn't he happy? She knew there was no point in asking. He would simply fend her off with polite answers as he had so many times before. No, there was nothing wrong. No, he didn't have another woman. No, he wasn't sorry that he'd quit CFE. Of course he loved her. And he adored the children. And so on and so forth.

Then that part of her brain that had known it was time to go up and sit by old Jessamyn Murdock took her to a tiny, black, rotten spot in their marriage. Something like a weevil in a nut meat. That woman. Matthew had not been the same since he'd come back from China. He had been perfectly honest with her, she was sure. He had told her about Chungking, Yenan, about meeting his old fiancée. When Valerie had asked him with all the courage she could drum up, "Do you want to go back to her, Matthew? Do you think that you belong with her?" he had said, "Of course not. I belong with you."

When Valerie had asked him if he loved her, he told her he would always love her. But—and here was the rotten spot—when she asked him if he still loved Jordan, he had not said yes or no but "How could I love a woman like that? She cares only about herself." Or, on another occasion—for she had asked him often during these last years when she had sensed him retreating in spirit from her—he had said, "What is love? It's a cultural convenience, that's all." When he saw her stricken eyes, he said, "But I do love you, Val."

She got up, went to the dressing room, took off her sheath, and slipped into a clinging nightgown of chartreuse chiffon. It was a point of honor with her that she be as enthusiastic a lover as she was a political partner and wife.

He was waiting for her when she came out. His tired face put on a smile. "You look lovely, Valerie. You are always lovely."

The lights went out and for a few minutes she was almost sure he was entirely hers.

Here in the capital, in a private reception room of Constitution Hall, national headquarters of the DAR, a group of conservatively dressed women had gathered for tea. They were, in essence, the elite of the China Lobby. Their guests of honor today were Claire Boothe Luce, playwright and wife of the most powerful journalist in America, and Tai-ling, the oriental movie star.

Mrs. Charlton V. Davidson, today's hostess, was saying, "It's important that we make our position known. Since the middle of the last century America has risen to her obligation to send her very best statesmen, diplomats, and missionaries to that faraway land so that China may learn to take its place in our modern world. We all know that years ago Attila the Hun, with his band of barbarians, was able to wipe out the Holy Roman Empire. Now, ladies, history threatens to repeat itself. Once again, from out of the northeast, the barbarian hordes reappear to stamp out Christianity and the civilized ways that have gone hand in hand with our beliefs."

From under her eyelashes Tai-ling surveyed Claire Boothe Luce. If rumor was true, she, too, had been little more than a whore. She, too, had lived in poverty with her mother who'd been abandoned, and she had suffered humiliation in school. But she had parlayed her beauty and wit to wrest a life for herself from the unthinking fools who comprised the American upper classes.

The rich and dowdy matrons attending this luncheon squinted myopically through dotted veils. The great unattractive sows. People like these rough-skinned *yang-gwei-tse* existed to give up their money like mother's milk. Impassively,

Tai-ling gazed at her manicure. Was Mrs. Luce, by chance, having some of these same thoughts?

"Everything you say, my dear," Mrs. William Kempton blathered, "is perfectly true. We must do everything we can to guard against the infiltration of our own people, even here in Washington itself, by godless atheists, and—what may be even more dangerous—innocent idealists seduced by deliberate propaganda. What else *can* we do?" These remarks brought on a chorus of agreement.

Tai-ling started. Claire Boothe Luce had actually given her a conspiratorial kick under the table. Acting on what was close to a whim, Tai-ling leapt to her feet.

"Ladies," she said, and used her old trick of seeming to pitch her voice low, while in reality it could be heard in the farthest corners of the room, "there *is* something each and every one of you can do. When you husbands come home tonight, you must make them understand that our leader, Chiang Kai-shek, educated by those very missionaries whom your generous country sent over, is now in great danger in his tiny island outpost. The Communists have him surrounded." She fell into the speech that she'd given at the end of almost countless propaganda films. "The spirit of democracy may seem to be beaten, but in reality God is on our side! You ladies open your hearts and ask your husbands with all the love that you can give them to open up their hearts to my poor country. . . ."

A few mornings later, in the Rotunda of the Capitol Building, delegations from foreign countries swarmed about the imposing circular space. As an impatient tourist guide shepherded her charges, politicians and their aides cut through the crowds with single-minded concentration.

Today was particularly busy because this morning promised a round of important Senate hearings on armaments and on the thorny problem of China. Jack Service of the "pink-tinged" State Department had lost it; how might it be returned to the hegemony of the United States? Liberals counseled patience, but Harley Compton Fitch was here to advocate the judicious use of force.

An eighth of a mile away, down a long, crowded corridor in the bowels of the Capitol, an up-and-coming young Democratic hopeful lectured to a bored Senate subcommittee on a new variety of enriched wheat. "It's hard to take action on this now, I know," he said to a half-empty room, as the senators present snoozed, conferred with their aides, or simply read the paper, "but climatological research tells us that the entire planet will enter into an extended period of drought within the next fifty years. The Ethiopians, for instance, exist entirely on an unappetizing grain called tef, which grows nowhere else in the world. When the drought comes . . ."

And pausing on the Ellipse of the Capitol Building, posing for photographers, generously signing autographs for gawking tourists, stood Tai-ling—brought in at the insistence of Mr. and Mrs. Henry Luce to charm the senators into more foreign aid for Chiang Kai-shek and his brave little band.

It was inevitable that the old adversaries should meet. Harley Compton Fitch strode out into the Rotunda. He had persuaded the government to send advisers to South Korea. Matthew Granger emerged, discouraged, with his papers under his arm. They had not listened, but at least he had told them. And Tai-ling, at the apex of an admiring entourage, came into the shelter of the Rotunda as onto a great stage.

Harley Fitch, after a minute's awful hesitation, crossed the floor to Matthew Granger. "Matt! After all these years! How they hangin', buddy?"

The other man looked at him for a long moment, then made a fist, and, lurching as he tried to bridge the distance between them, bruised the financier's nose. A trickle of blood stained Harley's hundred-dollar shirt.

"Wha . . . ?" Harley Fitch was stunned. His neck engorged. A vein protruded dangerously in his forehead. With all the strength he could command, he punched his old adversary in the solar plexus. Matthew Granger fell to the floor, his papers fluttering about him. For a moment, primitive as any caveman, Harley savored his second triumph of the day. To the victor belonged the spoils. And he turned, heavy with blood, to the only woman who could slake his desires.

She met his gaze and, taking advantage of the acoustics in the Rotunda, the awestruck crowds, and her own voice, she hissed, "You are more than stupid, Harley. You are a swine." She glanced around the great hall to make sure that the reporters had heard her correctly and that the press was taking notes. Then she left.

Harley Compton Fitch watched, helpless, as the others in the Rotunda shied away and left him alone.

* * *

Beijing—which had always been its name until the presumptuous foreigners started calling it Peking—boasts a great Summer Palace. For centuries the dynastic rulers of old China had sought solace from the heat and dust of the city by the shores of a cunningly constructed artificial lake, now the property of a new phalanx of rulers, the old guard of the People's Army of Mao Tse-tung. In January of 1949 the People's Liberation Army entered Beijing. Had they not earned this luxury? Did not the muscles that had toiled up and down the loess fields of Yenan deserve a respite in the splendors of the Manchu Dynasty? At first uncertainly, but then with increased assurance, Mao's comrades took possession of the seemingly endless courtyards within courtyards for their own relaxation outside the city.

Now the Long Corridor, which so magnificently bordered the lake, was inhabited not by strolling mandarins but bands of scampering children straight from the caves. With muted *ai-yahs*, revolutionary wives, traveling timidly in groups of two or three, entered draped seraglios and cried out in astonishment when they uncovered, hidden away in satin sacking, the silver pleasure balls—each weighted with a dollop of mercury—which the ladies of the court had introduced into their vaginas in order to sit rocking in special chairs while the rolling balls had teased them into repeated spasms of pleasure. What a way to spend the afternoon instead of watering millet!

Bah-wha could see that all too soon the army became obsessed with the rewards that were here for them. The wives dressed in yellow silks and squabbled over the best apartments. The men held incessant meetings and bickered over what place they held in the hierarchy. Her husband, now Minister of Agriculture, complained to her nightly about the slowness of bureaucracy and the obtuseness of his colleagues.

Bah-wha found the relics of empire impossible to paint. The others encouraged her to record these traditional scenes, but when she tried she produced old-fashioned scrolls. Mao and his men looked incongruous against these ornate backgrounds.

One afternoon she packed up her gear and went to the main entrance of the ground. Hiring a car, she told the driver to take her into the crowded quarters of the city. She found street vendors peddling their wares, children in odd corners amusing themselves with games of jacks, the whole animated stir of life renewing itself after the hardships of invasion and civil war. While in the Summer Palace revolutionaries celebrated with firecrackers, banners, and ethnic dances, the people of Beijing went about the real business of daily life. In sketch after rapid sketch she recorded scenes vivid with the everyday. The afternoon passed in a burst of creativity. It was time to return home.

Her satisfaction in having done her first good works since the caves was punctured almost immediately.

"Where have you been?" Cheun-yup demanded.

Before she had a chance to show him the afternoon's drawings, he launched into one of a series of tedious lectures on her inadequate behavior. "It's all very well to be a dreaming artistic visionary in an inland cave, but now you are the wife of a public official. You have a place to fill, a role to perform, that is your job." She knew he meant that her Caucasian blood, her foreign child were placing them all in danger. All foreigners but the Russian advisers had been forced to leave. . . .

Bah-wha sought the solitude of her small kitchen, where she began chopping the evening's vegetables. Her elder son entered with the slouch of an awkward adolescent and began to stare out of the window that overlooked the lake where his half brother and his friends swam. Bah-wha's nerves frayed. She turned on him as an easy target.

"Do you have to sit there like a big, dumb sloth?"

He didn't answer.

"Why don't you go out and play with your brother and his friends?"

This at least provoked him into sullen speech.

"He's not my *real* brother," Andrew said. "And anyway, they're just a bunch of babies. They don't want to play with me."

This exchange had been conducted in English. Although mother and son disliked each other, they had only once clashed openly. After the foreigner had come to the caves, Andrew had insisted—to the point of going on a silence strike for a week—that Bah-wha teach him his true native tongue. Now, after six years, he was close to being fluent and refused to acknowledge his mother if she spoke to him in Chinese.

"If you're determined not to go out," she said grumpily, "you can at least help me with the cooking."

He shrugged and picked up a cleaver. They spent the next half hour dicing green vegetables and pork. This life had become a cage for both of them—but for different reasons.

Living in this luxury, surrounded by priceless antiques and men and women set on personal gain, she felt divorced from the land, from China itself. Andrew had never fit in, and Bahwha realized that her time was up as well. As sure as she had turned inland when the bombs had dropped on Shanghai, it was time to turn outward now. The question was, how?

Senator Winthrop Eaton looked around the reception room of his suite in the Senate Building. Yes, they were all here—eight of the most powerful members of "The Club" and two representatives of the business world, with which those present enjoyed a symbiotic relationship. One of them was Roderick Brown, who dealt in East European and African interests, and the other was Harley Compton Fitch, who—if such a thing were possible—had the whole Pacific Arena in just one of his hip pockets.

An informal buzz already filled the room. Each man sipped a drink. The sterling-silver bowls held salted nuts—not for this group the arriviste farce of elaborately catered canapés and what he himself detested most, "dips and chips."

"I haven't asked you here," Eaton said, "to discuss how many representatives the District of Columbia should rate in the national conventions or what colors they should be." It was a standard joke, but it was an easy, a simple way to get their attention. He wasn't called "Easy-win" Eaton for nothing.

"No," he said, "we're going to have to drop that vital issue for the present and look at something a little farther away from home. It's community service, and this will be good for all of us when elections come up. We all know what's happening to China. The Communists have won, but the White House is caught in a bind. Even a couple of you here still have to keep pretending that the China Lobby line is the right one. You'd think after Mao held his jamboree in Tien An Men Square, and after the whole damn country is by now Communist, and Chang is sitting on a strip of land the size of Long Island, *everyone* would notice. What we've got to do now is get our own nationals out of there."

"Christ, I didn't know any American was fool enough to still be in China!"

"Quite a few," Eaton said. "Some missionaries, a few businessmen, some people married to Chinese—"

"Don't forget that Hinton woman," Harley Fitch burst out. "The dumb bitch who worked for Fermi and Oppenheimer on the bomb, and then decided it was a good idea to go out to China to try her hand at improving a breed of cows. You know, I was born in Shanghai, and the only cows in the whole country were owned by the Culty Dairy. That's the kind of crackpot you're going to be dealing with here."

"The problem," Eaton said patiently, "is that so far the International Red Cross hasn't been all that effective. They can't even get into China. We need—not a top-level, but a middle-level representative of our government, or at least someone with prestige, with clout, someone the Chinese would respect—someone who *could* create an incident if it came to that."

"You're talking political suicide," Wortham blurted out. "If he fails, he's a loser, but if he succeeds in dealing with Mao, then he's playing right into the hands of that junior toad from Wisconsin."

"Yes, but there's a ground swell of feeling among the electorate that we can't abandon Americans to a bunch of gooks," Eaton insisted.

Wortham spoke up. "Win, that still doesn't solve the human question. Where are you going to find a man to go in?"

"That's what I called you here for. If the shrewdest brains in the U.S. Senate and business world can't come up with an answer—"

Without waiting for him to finish, Harley Fitch broke in. "I think I've got your man. He knows the language—several dialects. He has political clout through his father-in-law. The Chinese would know they couldn't hold him without creating a real stink. It's exactly the kind of thing he could do."

"Who is this paragon?" Wortham asked. "He ought to be running for office."

"He is. Matthew Granger. Old FitzRandolph's son-in-law!"

"But, Harley, we've just said it would be political suicide. That man is up for election in three months!"

"Easy-win" Eaton kept a cautious silence. Fitch must have his own reasons for making this suggestion. Whatever they were, Eaton had no intention of probing for them.

"I've heard Granger is no dummy," Wortham said. "What makes you think he'll go for this?"

"You're right. He's no dummy," Harley said tensely. "But I've got a feeling about this. I'll lay odds on his saying yes—just leave my name out of it, though.

* * *

Less than twenty-four hours later, Matthew and Valerie sat over drinks in the family room. Outside, Paul and Joyce played tag in the reds and browns of fallen leaves, while in front of the fire a pitcher of martinis chilled. Valerie, though Matthew knew she'd been working as hard as he all through the day, looked relaxed and sleek as she sat with him on the couch. Tonight he confronted this staged harmony with a sense of unease. He listened to Valerie enumerate her little victories, which she set in front of him with the single-minded loyalty of a house cat lining up a string of mangled rodents in front of her queasy master.

"I talked to Sharon Locy all morning. You know how hard she it to get to and how much she can do for you if she wants. She's said all along that she likes you personally—well, of course, darling, they *all* do. Her husband's a lobbyist of course, and he's been very disturbed . . ." She stopped, blushed. "I'm sorry, darling, I know I do go on. It's just that finally she said that she'd give you eight coffee receptions of two hundred people each in the next two months. She said she doesn't even care about her new upholstery, even though it's taken her a year to get her house remodeled!"

"Valerie, I had a meeting today with some of the Foreign Relations Committee."

"Darling, that's wonderful! And here I've been going on about some silly women and their coffee!"

"There's something they want me to do."

"But that's marvelous! I'm so proud of you. Is it some kind of research? Is it official? I *told* Sharon this morning, the most amazing thing about you is not simply that you're honest, but that you *know* everything. You certainly don't find that in every public servant!"

"Val, I don't want you to make any plans for me. Tomorrow I'm telling my campaign committee to go on hold for a while."

"What on earth are you talking about?"

"The Chinese Government is shutting down, closing its borders, the way Russia did after the war. There are still quite a few Americans inside. Some of them don't want to leave, but some of them do. All the diplomatic channels are closed. So . . . I'm going in with a delegation of the Red Cross. I have to, Val. The Chinese know me."

"What about the campaign?"

"I'll certainly be back by November." He tried a lame bit of reasonableness. "This might work to my advantage. After all, it's a rescue mission. I'm going into enemy territory—though I won't have to parachute the way I did before. Other people have gone over, even General Marshall. I'll get my picture taken with world leaders—"

"Matthew," she said, "you don't know what you're saying. When Marshall went over, we still *had* China. Mao and his men are *Communists*, darling!" She looked at his stubborn face and sprang to her feet. "No matter how much you think you know, our country is against *Communists*! The fact that you're friendly with them . . . don't you see? You'll never get elected. You'll never get a chance to run for office again. Oh, Matt, how could you do this to me?"

She looked around. The great oaks outside, the carefully furnished family room with the children's pictures banked on polished tables in heavy antique silver frames, the merrily blazing fire, the martini glasses, almost empty by now. She had worked so hard.

"It's that girl, isn't it?"

Matthew's face twisted. "It's not that simple, Val. I know what my father would have done if someone had given him this project. He wouldn't have hesitated for an instant. He would have known hesitation was a sin! And he put his money where his mouth was. He and my mother had a chance to get out, but they stayed! They had to. It was their obligation, their duty!"

"That's *shit*, Matthew!" He had never heard her use such a word before. "It's that girl. You want to see her again, and you want to be the one to bring her out! Don't lie to me anymore!"

"She's married. She has a family. She probably doesn't want to come out. . . ."

Valerie's stubborn jaw locked. "Just tell the truth, god-damnit!"

"The matter is settled, Valerie," Matthew Granger said, and if he had been able to hear himself he would have been reminded of his father discussing tainted money. "I said I am going, and I will go, before the end of this wek. I'll be back in time for the election. Plenty of time."

"Do what you want!" she said. "But I would ask you to come out of your lovesick daze long enough to consider what you're about to damage, if not yourself and your career, then me, and the children. McCarthy is a power, Matt! Things will be very bad in this country. You keep your eyes closed to anything you don't want to see, but I'm out campaigning every day. I'm afraid, Matt! And so is Father. You'll be putting all of us in danger. And I don't care what your reasons are."

"Until dinner's ready, I'll be outside with the children." He rose, walked out through the french windows, and stood awkwardly, playing catch with his son, hugging his daughter as she swooped past him.

Valerie poured herself a double, and after she had watched her husband and children as long as she could bear it, she leaned forward on the sofa and stared at the fire. She said out loud, "All for a fuck."

The first leg of Matthew's trip took him from Washington to San Francisco. In the beginning it seemed like any other crossing of the continent, though he was still trying to sort out all his reactions to Valerie's outburst and his own real feelings about the children. He made no effort to deny that she had gone straight to the heart of the matter. Even in that first meeting with Eaton and the other members of "The Club," the thought of seeing Jordan again had come into his mind before he'd had any other real comprehension of what his mission was about. He could see now that Harley Fitch must have been behind this in some way. Who else would have known how to play on both his public and private sensibilities?

Matthew transferred in San Francisco to the China Clipper, which landed to refuel in Guam. He stepped out to stretch his legs. In the muggy darkness, he saw nothing but the lights of the airport building, but already Matthew fancied he felt the westerly winds coming off China, warm, damp, sensuous.

Then another landing, in Hong Kong, where more dignitaries boarded the plane, and where he was met by the International Red Cross officials, two Belgians and a Dane, who greeted him with obvious pleasure and relief, all too ready to transfer their responsibilities to his shoulders. They had with them a list of Westerners still in China, perhaps two hundred in all, divided by nationality. Looking at the roster, Matthew recognized a name here and there of persons he was sure could never be persuaded to leave. You might as well try to move the sphinx as to try and tell Brett Wingfield what she should do. And there was Terrence Laughlin, who had been working all his life on his revision of Chinese writing and romanization. Laughlin would never leave. Matthew suspected that some of the so-called businessmen in the Wuhan area had been so long entrenched with the local powers in all their shiftings that they would somehow manage to continue their way of life.

He searched the list again. There was no Jordan Logan-Fisher.

"Once we cross the frontier from Hong Kong to Canton we'll be able to arrange motor transportation direct to the Northern Capital," the Dane said. "To be perfectly frank, we aren't at all sure of our reception once we get there. We do not understand exactly why—"

One of his Belgian cohorts broke in. "Certainly one difficulty has been our problems with the language. We have not been confident in our interpreters. Though we come with the best will in the world, we can see that for the new regime we remain suspect."

They rode out of Canton in an enormous Oldsmobile previously owned by a foreign diplomat. The Belgians were pleased, but Matthew recognized this as an elaborate humiliation. "They are telling us we are capitalists and cannot stand the rigors of the road. They are reminding us that they are rich enough to give us this kind of convenience."

The roads between Canton and Beijing were fiendishly bad. The lanes that the Japanese had cut for the transport of their tanks had deteriorated. The peasants had reclaimed parts of their original fields and it took the chauffeur's utmost ingenuity to maneuver the heavy machine around treacherous, water-soaked areas beneath the thin asphalt surfaces, hastily slapped down by people's platoons.

More than once Matthew asked the chauffeur to stop in a village square. When the villagers came out to exclaim over this unusual spectacle, he queried them cautiously about what the last few years had meant in terms of their personal lives. He always opened these exchanges with the customary formal information, of his own birthplace in Shanghai, his father's title as a teacher.

In one village, though they were running late, the chauffeur stopped with a kind of stubborn pride. Matthew understood there was to be a public display. The entire village had turned out. The Belgians muttered fearfully that their might be an execution. What they saw was in some ways even more grotesque. Standing on a roughly constructed platform, the headman of the village and all his family clustered together. They had been made to wear their best clothes, and the women wore the family gold in their ears. One by one, each person in the village, from the oldest grandfather to the tiniest tot barely able to walk, went by the platform, scooped up stones and refuse, and flung it at the family. "You made your fortune from poor farmers! Now see where your wealth has come from." The chauffeur smiled. The car drove on.

A few miles later, Matthew saw human heads stacked in a ditch, but did not call his companions' attention to them.

Then, all too quickly, they made their way across China from south to north, crossing the Yangtze by ferry. Their first reception in the capital was full of formal speeches and toasts drunk to international goodwill. Matthew saw that his companions were completely deceived by this performance. He, however, knew that the presiding host came from the lower middle ranks. This host, though polite in the extreme, suggested that there might not be any foreigners who would want to leave China, since their minds and hearts were with Mao's revolution.

When it was Matthew's turn, he raised his cup of *mao tai* and said in impeccable Mandarin, "Let us drink to the truth. *Kam pei!*" He upended his cup and downed its contents in one swallow.

"My friends and I wish to thank you for the extraordinary courtesy you have paid us in allowing us to feel in our bones the very nature of your home soil. In village after village we have heard with our own ears, tasted in our mouths, the essence of the Revolution, of the new China. Time and again we have seen evil punished. We rejoice with you, and were it not for you thoughtfulness, much would have been hidden from us. We have seen old landlords replaced with new. We have seen that the peasants are no longer afraid to express themselves—even to strangers." As murmuring began, Matthew raised his voice. "We have even seen the decapitated heads of your recalcitrant counterrevolutionaries! We see nothing wrong with this! Every good requires an evil. But your lessons are best practiced on your own people, we believe, and not on foreigners"—here he paused, and continued ironically—"who will never understand your ways."

One of his hosts smiled.

"For the present, we wish to thank you for taking the time from your necessary assignments to receive us so generously. At our next meeting—whenever you wish to arrange it—your superiors will be ready, we trust, to discuss these matters further, on the level that the dignity of this subject merits and must receive."

One of the reception committee turned a raucous laugh into a diplomatic cough. "What's going on?" a Belgian asked. "Are things going well?"

"Things are going very well indeed."

Later, at the hotel, he relaxed alone with a glass of rice wine, glad to be relieved—if only for a moment—of the responsibility of his European companions. He peered from his balcony window to the busy street below, and his soul exulted. He was back in China, and nothing else mattered. When he heard a knock at his door, he cursed. A figure, dressed all in black, with a cap pulled down over his eyes, bowed and handed him a sealed envelope, then glided off down the hall. The message inside read, "Come to the compound directly south of the Forbidden City's Green Mosquito Entrance at ten tomorrow morning. You will find two people who require your services."

Matthew stayed awake until dawn watching the panorama below: the black limousines, the peasants hauling carts of food to the market, the bicycles.

Daylight finally came to the streets. To his left Matthew saw a group of elderly workers going through their morning exercises; the street filled with a mixture of vehicles; more and more bicycles appeared. Rickshaws had been outlawed, but a few pedicabs remained. In spite of the activity, a pleasing semisilence ruled the street: there were no motors, except for the occasional government limo, and street cries were muted; the hotel staff swept the steps and sidewalks. . . . Matthew's reverie was broken by a knock on the door. An attendant brought him a wooden bucket of hot water, towels, and a thermos jug of tea.

Within the hour, Matthew began his walk. Although he was a foreigner, his dark clothes, his very way of carrying himself kept him from being a focus of attention, and sooner than he reckoned he found himself at an ornate gateway that opened into a paved courtyard.

A gatekeeper barred his way, saying, "This is no longer a compound of easy access."

"I appreciate your concern," Matthew said, "but perhaps this will open the doors." He tendered the message with its crimson chop.

"The Minister of Agriculture himself has sent for you," the gatekeeper said. "You should have told me, and there would have been no delay."

Matthew crossed the courtyard with an escort who showed him into a large waiting room. Three bicycles leaned up against one wall, and an opened tin of Huntley and Palmer Social Tea Biscuits sat on a low table.

Matthew expected to be offered tea, but was left alone for a few minutes until a harassed assistant came in carrying a bottle of *mao tai* and two translucent porcelain cups. "The Minister sends his earnest greeting and apologizes for the delay. Please be at home."

It was not yet eight o'clock. Matthew eyed the *mao tai*, then poured himself a hefty slug. "*Nouveaux temps, nouveaux moeurs*," he toasted the empty air, then gasped as the liquor hit his empty stomach. The more he drank, the more bleak the room seemed. The dark furniture, the heavy drapes, the evident disorder combined to give a feeling of something sad, something finished. Here, *right* here, Matthew knew the Revolution was not particularly joyous. An inner door opened. Matthew blinked in the shadows and recognized the man he had been hoping to see, the man he'd been half expecting to find from the time the message had been delivered.

"The gods, even when one does not believe in them, are sometimes kind," Nyi Chuen-yup said. "I could scarcely believe my eyes when I read your name in the list of Red Cross idiots favoring us with a visit. Only you may be able to help me."

Chuen-yup glanced repeatedly around the room as he spoke, and shut the door behind him. He poured himself a cup of *mao tai* and gulped it. "There's no time for ceremony. I must appeal to you as a friend, as one who has shared your youth."

"How can I help?"

"I am now the Minister of Agriculture of all our republics. This is possible for me because of my years in Yenan, and all my years of work. But things are different here in the capital. . . ."

Matthew's skin began to tingle. He struggled to keep his face neutral.

"I have a wife who has worked as hard as I have for the Revolution. But—and perhaps you will find this ironic— although she's the daughter of a diplomat, she does not know when to keep silent, and I have been unable to teach her. Here in Beijing, it is far harder than in Yenan, since the evidence of colonial excesses are all around us. Bah-wha has only to open her lips, and the people remember the Opium Wars, the looting of the old Summer Palace, the burning of the great library. . . . She is like a kitten raised in a family with a child. She may *think* she is a human, but to everyone else she has fur, and mews."

Matthew opened his mouth to speak, but Chuen-yup cut him off. "It is just possible that I could persuade her to be a minister's wife, to be quiet and know her place, but, as you well know, she has a son, a hideous albino, scarcely human in the eyes of those around us. My wife is a strange woman. She dislikes her son, but she will never give him up. She keeps him—I don't know why she keeps him. I have many enemies here. Everything is still uncertain and"—he lowerd his voice to a whisper—"Mao has already been known to break promises to his old comrades-in-arms. I must rid myself of all risks, or I may end up as an enemy of the people, and my family along with me."

"Tell me what to do, and I will do it." Matthew could scarcely hear his voice for the pounding of blood in his ears.

"Now that the Red Cross is within our borders, it no longer needs you as its spokesman. I can guarantee your delegation a middle-level interpreter, and official permission to interview almost every Westerner on your list. But tomorrow morning you must be prepared to leave your companions, take the express train to Shanghai, and sail at dusk with what I believe is one of the last American ships to be leaving that port in some time. You will accompany two travelers. You must understand they can't be included with the rest of the Red Cross contingent. For the wife of a minister of the new government to *choose* to leave China would be an unthinkable loss of face. Already some have suggested she would be better off dead."

Matthew, wishing he hadn't drunk so much, perversely poured himself another glass. Chuen-yup joined him.

"You see what I am asking? Take her away *now*. She will be safe at your hotel. Then, tomorrow, take the train. Once she is on the ship, I will be able to sleep again, and to serve the Revolution in the right way."

Before Matthew could frame a reply, the inside door swung open, and there, dressed as a Chinese—but her face that of a furious Western woman—stood Bah-wha. Behind her, a boy tried to conceal himself, and another, smaller child rushed out to hug his father. The woman spoke in the rasping dialect of Yenan.

"Another bad joke, eh, Chuen-yup? I knew you would send me away, but how could you send me away with him? Could you not deal fairly, for once, and have my head removed, as you have disposed with so many others in the past months? I know you would not hurt your own child, but you would not give up an opportunity for revenge on me and my other son unless"—and here she gritted her teeth—"you found a revenge worse than beheading!"

She addressed herself to Matthew. "I have committed crimes, you see, against the Revolution! I have worked from sunrise until dark tending crops. I have aged until I look like a grandmother. I have worked harder than all of them! And in the night I told their story in pictures that will make them understood throughout the world. But I have committed a crime, foreign visitor! I have hair the color of flax instead of ink. Look at it! Perhaps you will remember!" The woman, in a practiced gesture, wrenched at the clips that held her hair in a tight bun. It was waist-length now, and golden, even in this light. "Yes, he could take pleasure in this body when we lived in a cave, but now that he is rich, he must give up a woman who has the wrong color hair!" She laughed out loud. "They call me an imperialist. But I have no use for all of this! I was happy in a cave. *I* am the revolutionary here! My husband is the self-serving bureaucrat!"

Chuen-yup looked at Matthew. "You see why she must go. I believe that fear has loosened her wits."

"Fear? It is *your* fear, not mine."

Matthew glanced at the blond boy just entering the gangling stage of adolescence. His eyes were cast down in an agony of embarrassment. He must have heard all of this before.

Without thinking, Matthew, half remembering his own children thousands of miles away, stepped over to him and put a hand on his shoulder. "I know how painful this is for you now," he said in Chinese, "but it will be better for you soon."

The boy surprised him by answering in English. "I don't see how it could get worse." He raised his eyes, and for an instant, Matthew was back in boarding school in Kuling.

"Your English is very good."

"That is because England, or maybe America, is my real country."

Now it was Chuen-yup's turn to cover his feelings with a blustering mask of rhetoric. "How much longer must I listen to insults and insolence in my own house? Have you packed your trunks, Bah-wha? I cannot allow myself to be distracted by personal matters for the rest of my life!"

But his wife had prepared for this as well. With an imperious double clap, she summoned her maid, who carried three items. She gave a hand-rolled cloth bundle, no bigger than a pumpkin, to Andrew. The other two she gave to Bah-wha: a cheap wicker suitcase and an enormous handmade portfolio bulging with drawings.

"I'm ready," she said. "I am not the first woman in China to be cast out by an ungrateful husband."

Chuen-yup stood between her and the door. "What are you *doing*, Bah-wha! You know you can't take those drawings. Mao himself ordered them and they are the property of the Revolution!"

It was the signal for which she had been waiting. She uttered a screech that made her previous tirade sound like a lullaby. She turned to her blond son and grabbed the bundle, spilling its contents on the floor. "Oh, generous husband, forgive me for trying to take a soiled homespun shirt for the child of the man who raped me. I knew I should not presume. I am far too worthless!" Then she ripped the flimsy bamboo bindings from her own suitcase, revealing, again, just one set of filthy peasant clothes. "I had thought to take some of the soil in which I labored, but I am too worthless even to take these as a dowry for another man, should he have me. Again, I presume on your generosity!" She turned to Matthew. "He gave me so much, and I am so worthless. Look! He gave me these earrings. He said they were proper for a good farmer's wife, but he should save them for his next one," and without flinching, she ripped them from her ears and shook her head wildly, splattering bright red drops. "And you want the drawings, Chuen-yup! Why should you not have them, along with my life's blood and the filthy garments in which I worked? But I will treat them the way you have treated *me*!"

In a frenzy of grief, her cheeks stained with gore and tears, still maintaining her shrill screech, she untied her portfolio and snatched up the top drawing. She held it in front of her husband, then tore it down the middle before he could stop her; tore it again, spat on it, and flung it at his feet. Then she reached for several more drawings, and stood on the rest, so that they could not be taken from her.

"Explain *this* to the Great Helmsman, cowardly running dog, revisionist bureaucrat, lover of riches, warlord's son!" She punctuated each epithet with another rip of her drawings, flinging them about, rubbing them against the draining wetness of her ears and eyes. Everyone in the room watched, from the servant woman—who, to Matthew's eyes, seemed curiously detached—to Andrew, to the smaller Eurasian boy, who, frightened and speechless, held on to his father's hand.

After what seemed an eternity, Chuen-yup stepped forward. "You were the mistress in this house. Take them, go."

As quickly as she had begun her tirade, Bah-wha stopped. She swiftly tied up her drawings and handed them to Matthew. Then, still weeping, she knelt before her younger son. "Do not believe what they will tell you about me. I was always your mother, your amah, your maid. Look at me closely. Try to remember me. You will never see me again, but I will always see you."

For one frantic moment, Matthew wondered what would happen next. He had visions of walking back to the hotel with a white-blond freckled adolescent and a woman in fury whose ears were bleeding, but Chuen-yup had a closed car at the gate. They made their way quickly across the courtyard. Chuen-yee had already begun to wail for his mother. At the car Chuen-yup took his wife's arm. "You know I do this only for you," he began, but Bah-wha cut him off fiercely. *"Tsa na ge gnang ke tso pee ah!"* Matthew brought up from the depths of his brain the translation: "Fuck your mother's asshole!" Then they were in the car and speeding away. Bah-wha ceased crying, though her breath still came in long shaking sighs.

"I have lost a son, but I have saved my work."

That evening, in a private dining room of their hotel, a strange group assembled. The guests at this improvised dinner party numbered twelve: the two Belgians and the Dane who were part of the Red Cross delegation, Matthew, nervously escorting Jordan and Andrew in borrowed Western clothes, four more bewildered Westerners who, by their expressions, appeared torn between relief at being allowed to leave and anxiety that the arrangements might collapse at the last moment. Matthew's successor in the delegation was there and another official to make the required speeches.

But the evacuation was going forward, and might be a

success. At the same time, there was an awkward silence. What was there to be said at a time like this? The elder Belgian stood.

"We are all good friends together. And we are embarked on one of life's great adventures. But what a pity that some of us scarcely know each other's names! I suggest that as we enjoy this delicious meal we go around the table and introduce ourselves, so that by dessert we shall be well on the way to being fast friends. My name is Baudouin la Fargue, lately of the Red Cross and always of Belgium!"

"My admiration for Monsieur la Fargue has brought me across the world," said the second Belgian. "I follow this modern Father Damien and try always to learn from him." (If the Westerners resented being compared to lepers, they did their best to conceal it.) *"Oh! J'ai oublié! Je m'appelle Jean-Pierre Mignon!"*

Jordan, dressed soberly in a cream colored blouse, was as pale as a fox-spirit, and as silent. But some inward part of Matthew smiled. That blond hair, long now, had been pulled back to show the mutilated ears. Trust Jordan to display her suffering! And her hair, so austerely arranged, was held in place by a series of intricately carved wooden combs. She had not spoken to him since her outburst, and her son had kept silent as well. One more guest, and then it would be her turn.

The next person was an elderly woman who worked for the YWCA. She gave her name as Olive Bentley. "I had hoped to be buried here. Perhaps this unfortunate situation will change soon enough for me to attain that wish."

Jordan stood. She addressed herself solely to the Chinese translator. Her arms formed the semaphore signals of the new Chinese peasant. "I come from the caves of Yenan," she began in Mandarin. "I am the truest revolutionary here. I have lived for years on gruel and red cabbage, with an occasional piece of dog meat as a treat. And this is my reward! To be banished! To be sent away with these fat crypto-reactionaries!"

Then her arms went limp. She stood quietly for a long moment, then said in English, "Thirty years ago my father came out to Shanghai to administer the funds of the Boxer Indemnity. I am an artist. This is my son, Andrew. I shall be returning to our family place in Oxfordshire. I was born— Jordan Louise Renalda Logan-Fisher."

The rest of the dinner guests stared at her as she whirled and rushed from the room. Matthew followed her upstairs. He tapped on her door, trying to coax her to answer him, then returned alone to the dining room.

Now Andrew was the center of attention. "Yes, it's true, we ate dog. We watered the plants one at a time. It was very terrible!" He glanced in triumph at the official. "They hate Westerners, you know. They made me wear a dunce cap! They threatened to kill me and eat me. It's true. They did. My name is Andrew. I don't have a last name. But soon I will find my father, and he will tell me what it is."

Baudouin la Fargue silently questioned the wisdom of his original proposal.

The Shanghai train left at daybreak. They rode first-class. Matthew, as he made last-minute arrangements at the station with Monsieur la Fargue, as he purchased an oily package of *bao tze* to help carry them through the trip, as he instructed Andrew to pick a compartment at the end of the car, as he accepted mementoes from the Red Cross, could not help comparing this coming train trip with his solitary trip across Siberia. Then, all had been unanswered questions.

He entered the compartment with dignity, called to the attendant to be sure they had tea, savored the initial lurch of the train as it left the station and crept through the outlying areas of the great capital city of China. People were just waking up, coming outside their houses, stretching, taking a look at the new day. A few waved at the train. Matthew waved back, and watched surreptitiously as Andrew did the same. Jordan sat wooden, facing forward, her hands clenched in her lap.

Although it was an effort, Matthew made himself be still. He knew that this journey would take more than two days. He had all the time in the world. However, he spoke at length to the attendants, saying that he was escorting two foreign guests of great distinction, friends of the Great Helmsman himself. After that there was no end to the stream of tangerines and sweets and little toys that found their way to the compartment.

Finally, Andrew could contain his curiosity no longer. With his newfound confidence and without even glancing at his mother, he asked Matthew, "How is it that you speak Chinese? And like a native?"

"I speak Chinese like a native," Matthew said, "because I am one. I was born in Shanghai, just like your mother, but in a different part of the city." He knew Jordan had heard, but she still gave no sign.

"What part was that?" Andrew asked.

"Just outside the Little South Gate of the Old Native City in the True Heart Mission Compound. Your mother, of course, was born in the International Settlement."

"The Settlement?"

"That was where most of the foreigners lived if they weren't living in Frenchtown. It was generally considered more civilized."

Jordan's breath came quicker.

"Did you know my mother then?"

"Everyone knew your mother. She was the uncrowned princess of Shanghai's English-speaking society."

Andrew looked at his mother in disbelief, but Matthew went on. "She was invited to every party, her dance card was always full—"

"I know what dancing is. You stand in a circle and—"

"Not that kind of dancing. Each man holds a girl in his arms and they move together to the music. Everyone wanted to hold your mother."

Two spots of red appeared on Jordan's cheeks.

"Why, I remember, at your mother's seventeenth birthday party, I was just back from college. Every important person in Shanghai had been invited, and your mother wore a silver dress, and shoes with very high heels. We were at the Country Club—"

"My mother?"

But Jordan burst out, "You can at least get it straight, Matthew! It wasn't the Country Club, it was the Cercle Sportif Français! It wasn't my seventeenth birthday, it was my eighteenth, and truly, my heels weren't all that high."

"Really? I remember a good four inches." Then he turned back to Andrew. "I remember everything about that night. The Japanese bombed the Native City. Your mother comforted her amah, who was crying. I fell in love with your mother that night. . . ." Before either of the others could speak, he continued, "Of course, everyone was in love with your mother, that's just what I've been saying. Why, simply to get a game of tennis with her, you had to book two weeks in advance."

"That's not true!" Jordan exclaimed, but there was enjoyment in her voice. They both tried to explain that particular game to the young man on the first leg of his journey into a world that some thought of as "civilized."

* * *

They pulled into Shanghai sixty hours later in the middle of the day. A courier met them at the station. Chuen-yup had arranged for accommodations at the Cathay Hotel, overlooking the Bund. For a few moments after their arrival, Matthew felt that nothing had changed. The Bund was alive with activity. Traffic went in and out of Nanking Road, still a center of commerce. The pedestrians still walked with the characteristic brisk speed of Shanghai natives. Some of them even came close to being fashionably well-dressed.

No evidence of bombing showed here on the Bund. No one had wanted to destroy the solidly built edifices that fronted on the river. Each side—*every* side—had hoped to claim them as the spoils of war, and use them for its own purposes. Soon these great hotels and business buildings—the Hong Kong and Shanghai Bank, with its imperial lions, the Customs House, the Shanghai Club, the Palace Hotel, the British Consulate, the Cathay Hotel itself—would be turned to the uses of the Revolution, but for the present they retained much of their original air.

The elevator boys in the Cathay Hotel still wore their plum-colored uniforms and snapped to attention as they greeted these new guests. Jordan and Andrew had been assigned a corner suite on the tenth floor. Matthew had been given similarly luxurious quarters two floors above. It seemed that the entire hotel had paused between the old order and the new. This place, which evidently was used to entertain foreign dignitaries, boasted amenities that might put New York, or even Paris, to shame.

"But, Matthew," Jordan whispered, while they were still in the elevator, "I have absolutely nothing to wear here. Neither does Andrew, for that matter."

Matthew's pockets were filled with government money. After they had taken possession of their rooms, and washed away the dust of the journey, he escorted the two of them to the basement floor of the hotel. At a men's shop he was able to find Andrew two very presentable suits. With these, and some shirts and a bathing costume, Andrew would be at least adequately clothed for the crossing on the *President Pierce*, which would sail within the next twenty-four hours. For Andrew it was an excruciatingly painful experience. He was all arms and legs—even the underclothing struck him as bizarre and needlessly binding. The sight of himself in a three-way mirror came close to unsettling him completely. He jerked his head from one side to the other, puzzled yet attracted to this strange figure that he had to believe was himself.

For Jordan the shock was in some ways even more difficult. Madame Poussant welcomed her into her *salon de couture* with little exclamations of delight. Jordan's years of hard labor and a meager diet had kept her more than fashionably slim, and, with the eyes of a revolutionary, she could not help but see the labor that had gone into these clothes. To her, silk meant eight- or nine-year-old girls laboring sixteen hours a day with their fingers in almost boiling water. But, as Matthew pointed out to her, she, too, had worked long and hard, and it was more appropriate for her to be wearing these things than the spoiled wife of a parasitic businessman. Jordan ended up buying two jaunty sports outfits for the ship, some silk underwear, which she and Madame Poussant giggled over behind a curtain, a tailored suit for travel, and a severely cut but stunning black dinner dress. All this would be packed in a commodious case ordered from the leather merchant down the hall.

Matthew sensed in Jordan's hectic laughter that this afternoon was taking its toll in subtle ways. She viewed the continuation of the world she had grown up in with a mixture of disdain and loss.

"My hands are the hands of a peasant woman."

"A simple manicure will take care of that," Madame Poussant suggested.

Jordan vanished into yet another shop, emerging later with her hair washed to a bright blond, her nails buffed and polished, her face discreetly painted for the evening.

Andrew looked feverish, and Matthew took him upstairs. "I know how you must feel, moving from one world to another."

"I never knew there was anything like this! How could my mother have made me live in a cave? How could she have let them . . ." He was unable to finish his sentence. "I don't feel so well," he said to Matthew. "I feel funny. I don't think I'm used to so much food."

Matthew left Jordan with Madame Poussant and took Andrew to the kindly woman who crocheted behind a counter of hastily assembled plywood. "I think I have a sick boy here. When I was sick long ago, right here in this city, they used to feed me rice gruel and arrowroot. That dish must be hard to find now in Shanghai."

The plump lady dropped her work and put her hand on Andrew's forehead. "You need to be in bed." She immediately turned into a solicitous amah. To Matthew she said, "You have nothing to fear. I can tell that the boy is as much upset in his mind as in his body." She cackled. "I can tell that you are a son of this city, just as I am a daughter of it. I can say to you, *Shanghai first!* Let the rest of the world take care of itself! I know where to find arrowroot, ginger, and the best rice. Tomorrow you will see that even this unsettled mind will share some of the wisdom of our city."

Turning her attention back to Andrew, she said firmly, "Heat chases out heat. Go sit in a hot bath in your room for fifteen minutes by the clock. Then wrap yourself in towels and get into bed. The sun is going down now and the lights are going on, so be sure to take the bed by the window. I will bring you supper, and sit on your bed and tell you stories until you go to sleep."

An hour later, when Jordan returned to her room, she took in a surprising tableau. Andrew lay propped up on pillows, his eyes half closed, listening to the hypnotic voice of the Chinese woman while, in the corner, Matthew, his long legs crossed, a Chinese newspaper opened on his knees, looked for all the world like a prerevolutionary businessman visiting the nursery before going downstairs to dinner.

And that—except for the fact that they went *upstairs* to the rooftop restaurant—was exactly what they did. Afterward, Jordan could never be sure exactly how it happened. How had she chosen, out of all the things she had bought, to wear the black dress? How had Matthew known to change into his dinner jacket? How had poor Andrew fallen into hands so inarguably competent that the best thing to do was to leave him in those hands?

The rooftop restaurant, recently renamed "Concrete Blocks to the Future," still retained all of the characteristics of the "Jade Dynasty" it once had been. Feathery bamboo had been grown in planters to at once shut out and reveal the lights from the city, the boats on the river. Cunning rock gardens, artificial streams with enormous carp from the *ancien régime*, and decorative camel-back bridges separated one set of tables from the next. A few nervous cadres sat uncomfortably trying to conceal their dismay over attempting to deal with a menu they could not understand. As members of the Party, they felt it beneath themselves to ask for help from this obvious lackey of the old corruption. The lackey, although in danger of losing his job and even his life, could scarcely keep his own contempt for their ignorance and crude ways from showing.

Thus it was that when Matthew and Jordan appeared, he thought he recognized people for whom the Jade Dynasty had meant something, and escorted them instinctively to the very best table in the house. Matthew, intuiting that under this glittering facade there must be some shortages of war, said, "Only you are familiar with the very best dishes of this region. All across the world people speak of this restaurant. We are privileged to put ourselves in your hands for this evening."

The Communist officials were reduced to asking the maître d', "What is it the foreigners are eating? We'll have that." As the evening drifted by, Matthew and Jordan dined on melon soup, followed by a tiny ramekin of river snails, sparrow wings in shallots and rice wine, flayed venison seared in Szechuan pepper and fresh lotus blossoms floating on a puree of crayfish, a penultimate dish cunningly calculated to revive the "Jaded palate" (an old restaurant joke, soon never to be heard again on this rooftop). After this came a fierce ginger sherbet, and with all, glass after glass of potent rice wine.

They said little this first night together, silently agreeing not even to recognize the old landmarks. At some point during the meal, a soft tropical rain began to fall, but almost before Jordan could put her hands up to her carefully coiffed hair, a series of translucent awnings were unfolded over the customers; the rain slid, in soft sheets, into the carp streams. By then a tired trio from the old days had taken their positions on the edge of a tiny, polished dance floor, and between courses Matthew and Jordan whirled—cautiously at first—to the strains of "Those Little White Lies" and "It Was Just One of Those Things."

With all this it was still early, no later than ten o'clock, when Matthew escorted Jordan back to her room, punctiliously shook hands with her, and went to his own bed to lie down to a sleepless night. The tenth-floor concierge was able to return to her desk in time to give some attention to a group of high officials from the north whose stomachs were upset by Shanghai's damp climate and rich food.

The next afternoon, as Matthew Granger asked the doorman of the Cathay Hotel to hail a cab for the dock from which the *President Pierce* would sail a few hours hence, they could have been any affluent Western family concluding a successful oriental tour. Jordan saw with a poignant sense of what might have been that Andrew, scrubbed, his new clothes impeccable, carefully followed the lead of the older man, even down to imitating him when he nervously ran his fingers through his hair. The luggage was piled in the back of the cab; the trip was made in a matter of minutes. The papers for Andrew and his mother were in order, and soon they found themselves on the boat deck of the *President Pierce.* Jordan oohed over the cabin that she would share with Andrew. The boy tested the mattress, looked out the portholes, and then stood, lounging easily, his hands in his pockets.

As they left the cabin, intending to explore the rest of the ship, two American teenagers raced down the passageway but came to a thundering halt in front of Andrew. "Hey! Wanna play shuffleboard? Dad says this tub won't cast off for an hour at least. I'm Tom Sturak, and this is my kid sister, Nancy. Our dad's in oil. What's your dad in?"

Andrew tried to force out some words, but the blond, hard-faced boy didn't wait for an answer. "Crumb! I'm glad to get out of this crummy country. This place gives me the creeps. Come on, you want to play shuffleboard or not?"

Tom's luckless sister began to wail, "Can I come? Can I come?" Jordan saw Matthew put a fatherly arm across Andrew's shoulders.

"Listen, Tom! We flew over here, and we've been up-country a pretty long time. Andy and I used to play shuffleboard a lot, but I know *I've* forgotten most of it, so maybe you can remind Andy how to . . . keep score, okay?"

"Ah, who *cares*," the Sturak boy snarled. "You just hit the disk as hard as you can, and keep everybody else from winning. That's how *I* play."

"I think I can do that. I think I remember!" he lied, playing along with Matthew's little deception.

The two boys loped off with the girl trotting eagerly behind. If they showed any resemblance to young Harley Fitch, Matt Granger, and little Jordan Logan-Fisher, the couple who stood watching chose to say nothing.

"I hear," Matthew said, after a moment, "that you can get a pretty good view from the first-class bar. May I buy you champagne? For old times' sake?"

She realized that for Matthew Granger, with his closed

face and correct behavior, all the old Western clichés about the Orient held. She would never know what he was thinking. He had always been masked, hiding behind various disguises of wit, knowledge, and, if all else failed, the conventions of the society in which he lived, the ferocious good manners that concealed his true emotions. It was partly this impenetrable set of defenses that had kept her from telling him about Harley's assault.

"Do you," she asked him, by way of accepting his invitation, "realize that I'm finally taking the last ship out of Shanghai?"

He put his hand under her elbow and guided her down the deck. "We'll have to hurry to get a seat by a window."

The ship was still tied up next to the Hongkew District. Looming upriver, the skyline of the Bund, which would always mean Shanghai to both of them, was silhouetted against a cloudy sky. Matthew's face, too, was cloudy. Then, coming to himself, he turned to her with an enigmatic smile.

"To whatever becomes of us!"

She and Matthew were together; strangers perhaps, but bound by obligations and memories of a past life that would be with them always.

He ordered a bottle of champagne.

"I haven't had champagne," she said, "since . . . our last party, our engagement party."

He didn't answer. The real Chinese were easy, accessible, practical people. She had a fleeting pang of homesickness for Chuen-yup. When he was angry, he was angry. When he was not, they made love or talked of the crops. But nothing ever had been simple with this man.

"When I thought you were dead," he said, "I thought my life had ended. But, of course, it went on."

"Have you been happy?"

"Look at China," was his answer. "Millions of lives, starvation, suffering, beauty. Do they bother asking if they're happy?"

"Long life and prosperity," she answered softly in Chinese. "And many children. That's all it takes. All the world knows this."

Hours later, after the ship had cast off, her body was suffused with champagne and the strange joy of being—in her own mind—exactly where she was supposed to be in this wide, unfriendly world. They stood outside his cabin. He whispered,

"Come in with me." She thought, *Long life and prosperity*—and an echo, barely acknowledged in her bones, and her womb—*many children*. Perhaps this act was not an impulse. She had lost a child to the country that had given her life. But perhaps China, and this man with a Chinese soul, would give her another to take his place.

For the next week Matthew surrendered himself to her. After that first night of lovemaking, Jordan left him asleep only to return, waking him with a whisper to say, "Andrew's already asleep. I must go back but . . ."

"But," he said, "not before we . . ."

"Before we talk, before we . . ."

It was as if they'd been given speech for the first time, speech and the private worlds of their own bodies. They could exhaust neither.

When Jordan finally left him in the morning hours, she said, "I know there's everything to decide, but not now."

"No, not for now," he answered. And with that understanding between them he plunged into sleep.

For Jordan, it was not quite as easy to ignore everything. She slipped into the cabin and once again shed her finery. Andrew slept in the other bed, one arm dangling to the floor, a leg thrust out from under his sheet. Jordan picked up her clothes, hung up her gown carefully. She reminded herself of what she had said to Matthew: there was everything to decide, but not now.

Not now, she told herself, relishing the soft silk of her nightgown, not now. She slid under the covers, and at last her eyes closed.

It was as if this new floating world arranged itself for them. Andrew went off every day with the Sturak kids. To Andrew's acute embarrassment, he found himself for the first time the object of a girl's affection. "Hey, Andy," Tom said, "take it easy with being nice to Nan. We'll have her around our necks the whole time."

Andrew blushed.

"Tell me more about that cave stuff. You know that's what Nancy thinks you should be—a real caveman." Tom almost crippled himself laughing at his own humor.

The Sturaks pratically made Andrew a member of their own family, delighted to have a companion for Tom and one that silenced Nancy.

For all of Tom's worldliness there was one big surprise coming. Once the Ping-Pong tables had been set up, he took it upon himself to teach Andrew.

"See, I bounce the ball, and bat the thing over to you, and you try to bat it back. Stand up closer, you dummy!"

Andrew had never been a star in China, but he drove Tom's patsy-like serve back to the very edge of the table.

"Hey!" Tom said. "That was a lucky shot. It's your serve now, but get closer."

"I think . . . I'll just try it my own way," Andrew said. The white ball came up off the service square with such speed and English on the bounce that it caught Tom on the forehead.

"Watch it!" Tom exclaimed. And then light began to dawn. "You've played this before, haven't you?"

Andrew shrugged. "Whenever I got a chance. It's almost the Chinese national game."

For the first time in his life, Andrew found himself in a position of superiority. He was now the teacher, but he was not a kind one. Just as he had been taunted and tormented his whole life by peasants who had always had the advantage over him, so, now that he had the advantage, he pressed it mercilessly.

"Hey!" Tom said, after Andrew had won the first game without allowing Tom to score a single point. "Don't be such a snot!"

"I won, didn't I?"

"Forget it!" Tom said, and, after flinging down his paddle, he sauntered away.

"'The dunce who loses at a game must look to how he lives his life!' *You* should be thinking about what you did wrong." Andrew hurried after Tom Sturak, his own face showing conflicting emotions—triumph at having won, terror at having somehow done something wrong, rage that his win had been spoiled.

"What are you talking about? I didn't do anything wrong. We played a game of Ping-Pong. It's just a game. . . ."

"It's *not* a game!" Andrew struggled with the language. "It showed that I . . ."

Tom looked at him with scorn. "Andy, what if I'd done that with shuffleboard? Or the caroms? Or the quoits? Or the gin rummy?"

Andrew's mind raced. Of course for a person like this life *was* a game. What did any of these people know about what life was really like? So stupid! They were more stupid even than he had been in the caves. All of his life *he* had been the foolish one. Now he was the one who knew, and he was living among fools. Now he had a weapon to use in this new world. In the caves they had always said, "The sharpest knife is painless," and, "The homeliest sheath hides the sharpest knife." He would have to learn to live behind a mask. "You're right, Tom," he said. "You're a real friend for teaching me that." He gave him a sugar smile, hesitated, then instinctively came up with the right way to assuage Tom's feelings.

"I bet *nobody* cares about table tennis out here in the real world. It's just something they play in caves."

Tom gave him a suspicious look, but Andrew's expression was so bland that there was nothing to argue abut. "Didn't you ever hear about sportsmanship?" the Sturak boy asked grumpily. By this time they were over by the quoits. Tom knew he would win this, but he could not shake the uneasy feeling that there had been another encounter between them that he had lost.

For Jordan and Matthew there came a time, locked as they had been for hours in his stateroom, when they had (temporarily at least) satisfied the appetites of their flesh.

"I thought when I said good-bye to you at the caves that I'd never see you again."

"But you . . . *you* said I wasn't beautiful! I could have killed you for that!"

"On the Trans-Siberian Railway, all I could think of was putting my fingers around your neck and squeezing. I really felt then that if I couldn't have you, I wanted you dead. And you went back to Chuen-yup."

There was an unasked question in his voice: *Did he give you pleasure? As much pleasure as I?* She answered, not altogether truthfully, "The Chinese don't care much for love, Matthew. I think the only women they really care about are their grandmothers. Chuen-yup protected me. But, oh! I love you, Matthew! I love no one but you!"

He sat up then, and opened another bottle of champagne. The late afternoon sun slanted in through the closed blinds and turned the whole world pink. It's now or never, he thought with clarity of drink and physical satisfaction.

"Jordan, why didn't you tell me about Harley?"

"I was ashamed. I was worried about getting pregnant. And I was afraid if you knew, you wouldn't marry me."

He had no answer for her. He tried to remember the fastidious, intellectual elitist he once had been. Would he have married a girl despoiled by Harley Fitch? He was afraid he knew the answer. But still there remained one more question to be asked.

"How—you don't have to tell me if you choose not to— how did it happen?"

Because they were so close, Jordan opened her eyes and began to talk. "I was so happy that night." Matthew needed no other words to know what night she meant. "It seemed that you and I were living in a perfect world. Those few weeks we were together . . ." Here she laughed and ran a careless hand across his back. "It seemed then that we knew all there was to know about love. Just a few kisses in the park, and you read poetry! At night after those afternoons, I'd go home to my family. I'd look at my mother and I'd think, I'll have a life like yours. I'll be safe, like you. And I knew you'd be successful. I'd be the wife of—oh, you know—someone prominent in world circles. Who *knows* what I thought! All I knew was that I was happy, and all I thought about was your mouth. Do you know, I never once, no, I promise you, this is really true, thought about you . . . there?"

She put a hand between his legs, and he shuddered. "I don't know what I thought our love would be, Matthew. I didn't know then that the body has its own rules, that there's that secret world none of us talks about, the world where *real* power is. How could you and I have known any of that, the way we were brought up? When I think of it now, how could my mother have let me dress the way I did? She must never have known that world, or forgotten it, forgotten what we have this afternoon. . . ."

She took a glass from him and drank. "I was *waiting* for you that night. And you were late, wasn't that it?" When he shook his head she went on. "All he wanted was one dance. And you know, he was always a wonderful dancer. I had expected him to be angry, because he always had a terrible temper. He expected me to choose him because . . ."

Again, her voice trailed away. Matthew could only listen and wait. "But he seemed all right. Oh, a little upset, but he always looked like a burning fuse. Then he asked me to take him up to my room. Of course, *now* I see . . . but then, we'd all played up there so many times."

"You don't have to tell me anymore."

"I just thought . . . well I don't know what I thought. Something like, I guess *I* showed *you*, Harley! But when we got upstairs he ripped my dress. He practically tore my body in half the way he tore my dress, and he did it to me like a dog, so he wouldn't have to see my face! Then he smashed down the dollhouse. That was how I learned about the other life. It was horrible. More horrible than I could have ever imagined. But I sometimes think it prepared me for—my life has not been easy, Matthew. But when you know the full horror, then whatever follows somehow seems bearable. Nothing they did in the caves could ever frighten me. I was stronger than all of them. I had been taught what the world is by an animal! That's why I never could love my son the way I should have. . . . Of course Chuen-yee was different. . . ."

Matthew heard her words, but no longer took them in. His mind had been caught by the sheer physical detail of the ripped dress, the smashing of the dollhouse—and, if he let his mind go just one step further—he could feel, beneath the revulsion, something that horrified him. Harley had brutalized this sweet flesh, torn it and used it. Nothing could change that. But now this woman, abandoned and undone by love, lay beside him. His vision blurred. Yes, this was Jordan Logan-Fisher, the girl whom he had always idolized, who had tortured him and tantalized him, Jordan, the belle of Shanghai, the incorrigible flirt. But here beside him was a woman who had come eagerly to his room the first night they had spent on the ship, who had deserted one son and cared little about the other, who stayed with him drink for drink, and who, during their long afternoons and nights together, had shown him ways to make love he had only imagined.

Jordan. Bah-wha. White flower. Was she a white flower, the woman who held the other half of his soul? Unbidden before his eyes, he saw another kind of flower, the crushed red rose of her ripped and swollen labia.

"I wish you hadn't told me," he mumbled, but she, her hand still upon him, looked at him in mindless delight.

"Again?" she slurred. "I don't know if I can stand it if you want to do it again. . . . " Her voice was low and seductive.

"Turn over," he said roughly.

It was early evening when she woke. She saw at once that Matthew had already showered and dressed, and was sitting in a chair just opposite the bed looking at her intently.

"Jordan, you know I have a wife and children."

She tossed her head restlessly.

"I'd like to be able to say that she doesn't understand me. In fact, she understands me too well."

Jordan took a breath, but Matthew stopped her with a gesture. "You haven't asked me about Val, and our life together. Jordan, when you said today you'd daydreamed about marrying a man in a prominent position—well, you weren't far off the mark. Jordan, I . . . I'm running for office."

"For *office*?"

"For the House of Representatives. It's my first crack at it."

She burst into laughter. When she could finally speak, she said, "I don't want to hurt your feelings, but I thought you might apologize for our last . . . session."

He colored. "I don't know what came over me," he said, as ready to take offense now from her insouciance as he had ever been in their youth together. "But what I'm saying is important. I'm in the midst of a campaign."

"And this is how you take the hustings? Going after the Yenan vote?"

"What I'm trying to tell you is, I'm in no position to— what's the old-fashioned term? Offer you anything. I have responsibilities at home."

"Would you have said all this," she asked gently, "if I hadn't told you about Harley? What is it, do you think I'm a 'bad girl' now? Or that I was never the good girl you wanted me to be?"

"I don't know."

"Reach me a drink, won't you? And would you mind handing me one of your shirts?"

He did as she asked, and that gave her time to consider her words carefully.

"Chuen-yup was good to me. He was a 'prominent man,' Matthew. There have been times in the last few days, when we haven't been making love, when I've tried to ask myself what's really going on with you and me. But I've learned a few things in the thirteen years since we've seen each other. Nothing can be thought of as permanent! Nothing, especially these days. Here is what I know. I know that once I loved you and now I love you. I know that we are on this ship. I don't care what you think of me, Matthew. You can live in the past and think of me as a silly girl. Or as a tramp. It doesn't matter to me. We've been speaking of prominence. Of prominent *men*. I'm not sure you realize that I have found my own strength. You've just finished dog-fucking the Official Pictorial Recorder of the greatest moment in modern history."

Now it was her turn to be quiet and watch him.

She smiled languorously and took a deep drink. "Matthew, I have no idea what these drawings will mean, to others or to me. But I know what the future is—it's unknown!"

A discreet knock sounded on the door, and an envelope skidded into the room under it. Matthew turned on a lamp to read its contents.

"The future is ten days further away from us," he said formally. "The captain informs me that the *President Pierce* needs to put into Pearl for repairs. Because of the secrecy of the rest of the China mission, we'll be staying in the vacant house of an officer on leave for a week."

"It's what I was saying, really. The world plans for us."

How could he tell her that even when they had kissed in the old days, he had been frightened quite as much as he had been excited by her; that the depths of his physical feeling had mocked the one thing he relied on more than anything else— his intelligence. But even as Jordan questioned his truthfulness, he saw the flaw in her story. He had seen her and Harley together! They shared a sexual coarseness that he would never understand. But she had said she loved him. And like it or not, he would forever be in bondage to her.

The following night, the *President Pierce* limped into the waters of Pearl Harbor. Matthew, Jordan, and Andrew kept to their cabins until late evening. A lone jeep pulled onto the deserted dock.

The lightning of a tropical storm lit up the sky. Andrew had always been terrified of lightning, and here there was no cave to run into. The wind whistled under the metal grating of the gangplank as the three of them ran, hunched against the rain, to the jeep and the waiting yeoman.

The ride up the precarious flooded roads was terrifying. Palm fronds flailed against the windshield, and finally the yeoman whirled the jeep into a shallow arc of a driveway. "This is it," he said.

Andrew, sitting beside the driver, glanced to the backseat for reassurance. He saw his mother and Matthew, their hands clasped, unaware of anything except themselves. He jerked his head forward.

The yeoman said, "It looks real spooky, doesn't it, kiddo? But just wait until I get the lights turned on." He jumped out and ran up the steps to the rain-slicked veranda.

A few moments later, this wide stretch was lit brightly. Then the interior lights came on, showing huge plate-glass windows. Running back through the storm, the yeoman called out, "Everything's set. I'll give you a hand with your bags, and in a couple of minutes you'll be high and dry, with plenty of room to spread out."

His mother and Matthew quickly disappeared into the back, looking for two rooms next to each other so they could Chinese-fuck in the night and pretend to Andrew that it wasn't happening. Andrew stayed alone in the living room by the front door, watching as great bolts of lightning appeared outside the french windows and the electric lights dimmed and flickered. He had never seen a room like this before; he wasn't sure it was a room at all. Indoor plants grew big as trees, guns hung on the wall, gray ship models loomed, and stuffed animals with glass eyes glowered—and he was all alone. For a moment he wished for Tom Sturak, and even Nan, but they'd flown away to the United States, like everyone else on the ship. Andrew hated his mother for putting him through this. For a moment he even longed to be back at the caves, where at least he *knew* the awful things that were going to happen to him.

The next instant the lights came up and his mother and Matthew, laughing, entered the room. Matthew saw the look of terror on Andrew's face. "What's wrong?" he asked. "Did the lights go out in here too? Your mother and I have been scouting out rooms. The admiral lives pretty well, it seems. We found you a room with your own bath and a view of the bay. Want to come and see it?"

But Andrew stood rooted by the door. If he went across the room, he would have to pass the bear. He saw his mother's face wrinkle. "Tedious beetle!" she began in sharp Chinese, but Matthew cut her off with a peremptory gesture.

"Jordan, I don't know about you, but I'm cold and wet. Do you think you'd be able to rustle up some coffee for us, and maybe some hot chocolate for Andrew?"

He shooed her out. "Go on, go on! And while you're at it, see if you can find some brandy." He waited until she was out of the room, then quickly crossed the vast expanse and knelt by the trembling boy.

"I bet I know what it is, sport. And your mother doesn't have the faintest idea. It's too *big* for you in here, isn't that it? Where you come from they don't have windows, and on a night like this, that seems like a pretty good idea. I felt the same way you did once. Only for me it was the other way around."

The big American foreigner crouched down so he could look deep into the boy's eyes. The room was uncomfortably hot, and the dampness brought a fine sheen of greasy sweat on the man's nose.

"Once I was locked up in a space, but it wasn't like this one. It wasn't too *big*." He paused for a moment so that the boy could take his point. "It was too *small*."

A bolt of lightning flashed so close that the air in the room sizzled with the acrid smell of ozone. The big man put his arm around Andrew.

"When I was just a little kid younger than you are . . ."

"Back in Shanghai," Andrew said in a disdainful voice.

"I was kidnapped by a vicious warlord."

"You were kidnapped?" Andrew echoed in spite of himself.

"It was a small room, with no windows. And even though I knew they probably wouldn't kill me, still I was very lonesome."

"Who kidnapped you?"

But Matthew changed to a different story. "I had trouble with space when I got to America too. 'The wide open spaces' they called it. And when we were on a train, just like the one you and your mother took to Shanghai, they laughed at me when I asked them about pagodas."

"They have pagodas in America?"

"No. They're just round towers used for storing grain. They're called silos. But there were so many of them I thought they must be some kind of temple."

"I wouldn't make a mistake like that."

"Probably not," Matthew said. "You've been through so much, I don't think anything could throw you. Now, why don't we go on out to the kitchen and see if your mother's gotten anything together to feed the men?"

Matthew heaved himself up to a standing position with a little grunt and kept a hand carelessly but firmly on the boy's shoulder as they walked across the enormous room. But halfway to the kitchen, Andrew stopped and looked up at Matthew. "Who kidnapped you?" he asked again.

And after a moment, Matthew said, "Of course you remember Nyi Chuen-yup. It was his father, Nyi Chuen-yao, a very wicked man."

"How did you get out? Why didn't they kill you?"

The lightning and thunder had abated with the suddenness of tropical storms and the room was quiet except for rain falling on the roof and the plants outside on the veranda. Andrew jerked on Matthew's arm, and repeated, "Well, how did you get out?"

Matthew took a deep breath. "Your grandfather paid the ransom."

Through the rest of the evening, while they drank hot chocolate and nibbled the admiral's cookies, and even later in the night as Andrew listened to the laughter and the sighs that came from his mother's room as she entertained the foreigner, the words simmered in Andrew's brain. Grandfather, which grandfather? And, if Matthew knew one of his grandfathers, he might know his father as well.

For the last week Valerie had been busy preparing for Matthew's return. First, her own charming notes had gone out, written on her own stationery, to the society and feature editors of every newspaper large and small in the state of Virginia and the District of Columbia. She followed up each note with a phone call, making her contacts woman-to-woman, saying in the gentlest possible way, "I wonder if your news bureau might not be interested in this as well. My father, Senator FitzRandolph, and some of his friends will be there at the airport for Matthew's homecoming. Matthew's been behind the Bamboo Curtain for almost a month. They say he's rescued some very important people. It might be an interesting story."

In the end it was television that made the return of Matthew Granger, the rising Democratic hopeful, and Jordan Logan-Fisher, the rescued beauty of Yenan, a national event. Millions of Americans saw the converted B-17 with military markings coming in for a landing. A sea of newspaper reporters, policemen, and the television crews with their sound booms and their enormous cameras flooded the airfield. Valerie felt a surge of pride when she saw her own father talking to newsmen, squinting against the flashbulbs, converting almost every sentence to something about Matthew, using that phrase, "the Bamboo Curtain."

The senator had brought his friends and Valerie had remembered to call a band. Everything was in its place. Everyone of any importance was here. Valerie monitored herself as carefully as when she used to take out old Molasses to take jumps and show his gaits to a discerning crowd. She dressed meticulously, no, perfectly, as a young congressman's wife. She wore a two-piece tailored suit of dull maroon lightweight wool with a maroon toque and pearl-gray gloves; a gray bag and pumps completed her outfit. She had fielded several wolf whistles as she came into the airport.

The plane coasted to a stop. The door opened and there was Matthew trying to smile, shielding his eyes from the lights, waving awkwardly. Just behind him was a terrified boy who froze halfway down the stairs. Matthew returned, talked to him for a minute, put his arm around him, and they descended the narrow steps together.

Good move, Valerie thought, but keep your chin up. Look right into the lights.

Only later would she remember that while her brain had been completely engaged in the orchestration of the moment, her heart had been somehow unmoved. Perhaps that was why she was so extraordinarily tuned to the spontaneous sigh of yearning and excitement that greeted the next person to appear at the door of the plane.

She was Western certainly, as beautiful as any movie star. Her hair was blond and shining, but her eyes, even in the unforgiving lights of television, were filled with mystery and pain. She hesitated and gave herself up to the public, letting them appraise her delicate, almost boyish body in her simple silken dress of Chinese cut. She stayed close to the top of the stairs in full view of the photographers and they greedily snapped her.

A reporter yelled, "I bet you're glad to get back to the U.S.A. What was it like behind the Bamboo Curtain?"

Now, Matthew, now, Valerie thought. Show them what you're made of.

But her husband only said, "China is a great and beautiful country. Vast changes are going on there, but I don't know much about them. You'll have to ask Miss Logan-Fisher. She lived for years in the caves of Yenan and I'm sure she can tell you everything you need to know."

As if in an unending dream of futility, Valerie watched her husband slip into the sidelines, his arm still around the boy. In a helpless rage, she saw the woman her husband had once been engaged to walk slowly and tantalizingly down the stairs and reach for a microphone that a reporter handed to her. "I've come from Yenan, where Mao lived before he took over China. I stayed there for ten years as . . . as the mistress of a warlord's son. Life was terribly hard. For months at a time we had little to eat, but I had my charcoal and paper and I made pictures of it all."

"And did you bring them out? Could you get them out, Miss, uh . . . ?"

"They called me Bah-wha then. That means White Flower. And yes, I was able to bring them all out."

By this time Matthew had made his way over to Valerie, been hugged by the kids, and stood in front of her with the hangdog look of a high school kid being sent to the principal. Valerie FitzRandolph Granger felt so angry, so betrayed, and so close to tears that she could only offer her cheek for her husband to kiss.

On board the *Fortuna*, Senator McCarthy and Harley switched on the television set. After he had adjusted the rabbit ears, the familiar face of John Cameron Swayze became clear.

"Now, before we look at today's news, and I know you're all going to be interested in who arrived today in the nation's capital, I'm fastening this Timex wristwatch to the propeller of this outboard motor. Then, in this tank, which I'm sure you can all see clearly, I'm starting the motor running, and it will run throughout this news broadcast."

Swayze, having started the motor, moved across the broadcast studio to his desk. "The top story tonight," he began, "is the arrival in Washington of a candidate for the House of Representatives from Virginia, Matthew Granger, who has gone to the heart of China on a mission to bring out the foreigners who refuse to live under a totalitarian government. Our Washington correspondent was on the scene at the airport this afternoon and we are now showing you the arrival and subsequent interviews with the latest figures to come out of that country."

As the picture shifted to the arriving plane, Harley said, "I wonder what sort of do-gooders Matthew has come home with."

The senator grunted.

Now the stairs were being wheeled out. The door of the plane finally opened. Matthew appeared with a towheaded youngster.

"Who the hell can that be?" the senator asked. "You think that's a mission kid?"

But he got no answer. Harley stared at the screen. What he saw was the frightened face of himself as a twelve-year-old.

As Matthew put his arm around the boy's shoulder to reassure him, Harley's memory clicked. He remembered the old days at the Kuling American School, the early mornings when he looked into the distorted shimmering mirror, splashed cold water on his face and hair, scrubbed his teeth with the corner of a coarse washcloth, saw his pink cheeks, his eyes that were steely even then, and told himself that whatever fight he might get into today, he would win, and grind the other kid in the dust and make him bawl for his mom. There, on the screen, was the reflection of Harley Fitch if he had lost one of those fights, *his* face, but scarred by life— afraid. Then, in shock, he saw a boy who had to be his son.

He knew that this must be the reason Matthew hated him so. All this time Matthew had known of this boy's existence. He blurted out, "If we're looking for Communists, how about that noble rescuer right there—what a hypocrite!"

He stopped. The camera had picked out the figure of a woman, now posing at the top of the steps. He recognized her immediately. With that recognition came the determination to see his boyhood friend destroyed once and for all for concealing what he knew.

As Jordan spoke, the senator said, "What about her?"

Harley said, "No, the real danger comes from Matthew Granger. Senator, you've got to see that he doesn't get elected. If you need any help count on me."

McCarthy nodded. He sensed a personal vendetta, but he was willing to go along with it. Harley Fitch would be a good friend in a campaign year.

John Cameron Swayze returned to the tank, stopped the motor, unstrapped the wristwatch from the propeller, put it first to his ear, and then, smiling smugly, held it directly in front of the camera for all to see the second hand still moving.

Jordan couldn't believe her own happiness. Life seemed easy and effortless. Everyone had been so kind. Although

Washington still suffered under a housing shortage, friends of Matthew's sublet her a town house in the heart of the city. The staff at the British Consulate did everything possible to facilitate the processing of mountains of paperwork that she and Andrew needed before they could return to England, or even remain legally in the States. The Red Cross arranged for a transfer of funds and clothes for her son.

In her first weeks here only one note of sadness had entered Jordan's mind. She'd spoken with her mother at The Beeches and learned that her father had died in a Japanese camp. But Madeline herself was fine and looking forward to Jordan's arrival at the family estate.

For Jordan there was no hurry. Just as she had hoped, the Americans took a tremendous interest in her work. Already she was considering offers from various galleries for exclusive showings. *Life* magazine had sent one of its senior editors to see if they could possibly arrange a feature article that would bring her work to the attention of millions.

She and Matthew managed to meet for a few hours each day. She had seen Valerie at the airport and knew that the time she and Matthew had together was certain to end. They had to break off their relationship, but neither one could make this decisive move. At the airport, Valerie had insisted that Jordan and Andrew join them for dinner at Halcyon Hill, but Jordan was unable to go through with the charade. Now, when she pressed Matthew on how things were between him and his wife, he refused to say more than "Somehow we'll have to work it out." But for now Matthew was using a string of weak excuses to come into the capital early and stay late.

This morning, Matthew arrived on her doorstep with coffee cake and a jar of Oxford marmalade. He had picked up the *Washington Post* as she opened the door to him. In the breakfast nook, while Jordan was making the coffee, the headline of the unfolded paper caught his eye. He tried to turn the paper over casually, but she was too quick for him.

"What is it?" she demanded.

"What do you mean?"

"You mustn't fool me."

"I had a feeling it was coming."

The headline of the article read, "McCarthy Accuses Candidate." The piece went on, "The senator said he had sources who would swear that Matthew Granger's recent visit to Red China was not so much in the interest of rescuing his countrymen as in maintaining subversive contact with the new Communist government." Matthew's was not the only name listed. Near the end of the article McCarthy praised Harley Compton Fitch III, referring to him as "a staunch and four-square patriot, unstinting in his service to the American people, who has not hesitated to come forward with any and all information that might lead to Communist traitors."

"So that's it," Matthew said. "I bet a subpoena to appear before the Committee is waiting for me at my office."

"Don't you see, Matthew, you can't do it that way?"

As soon as he was summoned, Matthew got in touch with Graham Williams, an attorney who represented not only Matthew but Valerie's father as well. "Certainly it's not illegal," Matthew said, "to take the Fifth Amendment. That way I can simply refuse to get tangled in the kind of mess that McCarthy is obviously interested in stirring up."

"It's not illegal," Graham answered. "But if you take the Fifth, you know perfectly well that everyone assumes that it's an admission of guilt. In this instance, it's not just yourself to be considered. There's your father-in-law. No one in his right mind could suspect him of Communist leanings. But if his son-in-law takes the Fifth, that's exactly the kind of rumor that will start making the rounds—the sort of gossip that the Washington columnists feed on."

"And this will mean the end of my campaign."

"Frankly, Matthew," Graham said, "the minute you decided to take that trip you pretty well wrote yourself off the ticket. I'm sure Valerie knows that, and it's high time that you admit it too."

"Giving up the candidacy would be letting McCarthy walk all over me. I'll have to think about what to do next."

Matthew stood in the bitterly cold, damp Washington wind outside his attorney's office building. He knew he should go back and confer with his staff; whatever he decided, they should be the first to know. No! Val—poor Val—should be the first to know. He considered calling Jordan, but he didn't want to see her now. How easy it would be! He would knock on her door, she would answer, as if her whole life was taken up in the act of waiting for him. He would kiss her, run his hands over her, touching silk and silky skin. She would take him to her bed, and nothing else would matter. They would be together in their world. . . .

"Are you going to *walk* or are you going to *stand* there?" A woman, her arms stretched precariously around bulky packages, wanted him to get out of the way. To fish or cut bait. Piss or get off the pot. Not stand there paralyzed! He needed a drink. I'm drinking too much, he thought. It solved no problems, but it kept them at bay. And maybe, in a week, when you looked again, they would have changed, or gone away.

But he knew the McCarthy purge was moving fast, too fast. Election Day came in November. Although Val's savvy was immeasurable, her patience was not. For a moment he almost hated Jordan, China, all the invisible ties that bound him as thoroughly, as inescapably, as Gulliver had ever been bound. He needed a drink.

Quickly he walked a few blocks to the Jockey Club. It was the kind of place he avoided, even though Valerie had repeatedly—if gently—lectured him on the importance of seeing and being seen. Ironic, that with his future, his career in shambles, he should come here now.

Once inside, he paused near the door, in the warm and noisy dark. To his right, the crowded bar, packed—standing room only, at not yet four in the afternoon. Washington was not an easy place to live, especially in what promised to become a reign of terror. Never, Matthew thought, had there been anything like this in the history of the United States. He had a sudden vision of the Reverend Wilson Granger staring down the fleshy, drunken, ill-bred junior senator from Wisconsin and grimaced. Father, he thought, what would you make of things now?

He found a stool and ordered a double martini. He knew that at some level he should be desperate. His life was breaking up about him, but all he could think of was his weariness, and Jordan. He would go to the door, she would be waiting for him, she would take him to her bed, and there would be no *thinking*, about anything, ever again.

But there was this. He could never leave Valerie, not as long as she wanted him. Because he was the son of his father and mother, and although he had never believed in God, he was forced to believe in "goodness," in honor. He looked at the furtive couples half hiding from the photographers. He had nothing but contempt for that kind of life. But, here he was living it.

He had to think about the Committee, the election, his career. His only real allegiance to the election was that he had promised Valerie. He *had* to think about how he would behave in front of the Committee. Here, again, the choices seemed odious. He was born and brought up in a country that had turned Communist, and yes, he had sympathy for the new government. Who would *not* who had seen Chiang Kai-shek's oppressive Chungking regime? But did that mean he loved the United States any less? To take the Fifth was a tacit admission of guilt. He was guilty all right, of marital infidelity, guilty of a growing exhaustion and boredom with his own life, but not, *not*, now or ever, of having been a Communist.

And yet, to be a friendly witness, to sit down in complicity with these low-bred thugs who were planning to take over America, to rule by fear . . . he couldn't do it. He thought of those few who had defied the Committee. They had been forced to leave the country or had been blackballed in their professions. He thought of Jack Service.

Forget it! He ordered another drink. He could phone Val. He could tell her he was staying late to plan a strategy with his staff, and must not, under any circumstance, be disturbed. He could call his staff and say he'd been summoned out of town on an important government mission, and they must, on no account, answer the phone. Then he could go to Jordan. She would answer her door, she would take him. . . . It was no good. It was *no* good. He was married to Val, and couldn't leave her, because . . . he was who he was. He would go home to Valerie, and have dinner with her and the children. He would discuss this whole thing with his father-in-law. It was what he must do.

He finished his martini, turned around to set the glass on the counter, and, in the corner he saw . . . he saw a glimpse of satin, the curve of a youthful shoulder, a tiny hat with a dotted veil bought at Madame Poussant's boutique on the basement floor of the Cathay Hotel. He saw Jordan. She was with Harley.

His instincts had always been right. When he saw—his *son!*—on those stairs from the plane, when he saw his old rival's arm around the boy, he acted without thinking. His blood told him how, and his blood was never wrong. In these past years he had built an empire; now he knew why. He had done it because he was Harley Compton Fitch III, son of a merchant prince of China, an outlaw, a buccaneer. Since that night when he had seen his own son on the flickering black-and-white screen, he had thought so many times of his own father: of sailing down the river, talking to the captain, exulting in being a man in the company of men, knowing that soon he would be in his own home. His father would pour Harley a drink. They would talk of school, and business. Blood called to blood.

So he'd sent Matthew to certain destruction. He'd called Jordan, confident that she'd see him. Deliberately, he'd asked her to meet him in a public place, partly so that she would be lulled into a sense of false security, partly so that she would be sure to come. He'd seen her, too, on television. He knew the artifice, the elegance, the ambition, the hauteur with which she greeted the world. He knew she wouldn't pass up a chance to confront her rapist, the father of her son, and one of the richest men in the world.

Still, he was not prepared for her glowing beauty, her smoldering hatred. She wore a smartly cut black suit and a satin blouse cut low to show her delicate, still youthful breasts. He felt himself swell, and elected not to stand up as she glided over to the table.

"You're as stunning as ever, Jordan. *More* stunning than ever."

He meant it, and leaned back to absorb the contempt she sent across the table. Sneer! he thought. Cry and scream! Do all you can against me! Because you remember how it turned out last time, and you know that it will happen again.

"Why did you want me to come here?"

"The Communists treated you well, it seems. I remember the Chinese cared for the delights of a beautiful woman as much as any Westerner. Even more, perhaps. Oh yes, your family was too good to know about the waterfront, the Shanghai basket—"

"You always were a pig, Harley. At least you make no secret of it."

He smiled amiably. "May I order you a drink?"

She asked for a Scotch, and he ordered another.

"It *is* like old times, you know. A pity there isn't an upstairs to this place. And a dollhouse . . ."

"What do you *want*?" She almost screamed the question, and several people turned curiously, then tactfully looked away.

"I want the boy, of course. He's mine. Anyone can see that."

"I gave my life to keep that boy. You have no claim on him whatsoever. There are some things in this world you can't own, Harley. Andrew is mine."

"Andrew. I didn't know his name until now. Thank you. Why didn't you name him after me"—he smiled teasingly—"darling?"

"May your prick be cut off and stuck in your mouth."

Harley leaned back and laughed. "Did the Chinks train you to be that wild between the sheets?"

"They trained me to kill capitalist pigs. I would love to kill you."

"Cut the crap, sweetheart. What's the price for my son?"

"You're so banal, Harley. Even your father had more finesse than you."

His face flushed dangerously, but still he smiled. "You can either give me the boy, or I'll take him from you."

"You were my rapist. There's not a court in this country, or any other country in the world, that would let you get away with that."

"Since you've been away, perhaps it may have escaped your attention that your 'rapist' is one powerful man."

She took his hand and dug her nails in deep until, with a grunt, he snatched it away. The back of his hand dripped blood from four cuts.

"Do you know who you're talking to?" she groaned out, half in Chinese, half in English. "Do you know, stinking bowl of porridge, that you are talking to a woman who fought for her life for *years*? Do you know that I have knifed men as they slept? Do you know that I have watched babies starve? Do you think that because you *ask* me, because you *order* me, I would *give* my oldest son to you?" Her voice had modulated into the unearthly speech of a wronged Chinese woman. She half whispered her insults, but the strange nasality, the chanting quality of a witch casting a spell, reminded Harley of his own early days in the Orient. He shivered as he dabbed his cuts with a thick linen napkin.

He knew he was losing in this exchange. Perhaps it was this that led him to play his trump card a little too soon. "I saw you getting off the plane. I saw you with Matthew, and if you think there's a future for the three of you, you're mistaken. He can't protect you. For one thing, he's married. For another thing, I'll ruin him in this town. I'll see to it that he'll never be able to get a job anywhere in this country. He's a Communist, remember, and so are you. In fact"—and he regained his good humor—"you're a regular Commie cutie. When you're penniless and alone with a boy to support, you won't be able to afford outfits like that." He reached across the table and wiped the back of his bloody hand directly on her breast. "When I get through with you and Matthew, you won't even be able to send that blouse to the cleaners."

Jordan broke into a laugh. "You're the fool! Go ahead and destroy Matthew. Nothing would please me more. It's the only way I'll ever have a chance with him. When we were kids, Harley, I was attracted to you, but I never loved you. I've always loved Matthew. It's my turn to thank *you*! Everything you've said, everything you've threatened, has made it clear to me. Now that I have Matthew again, I'll never let him go."

Harley cupped his beefy hand around the back of her fragile neck, and brutishly pulled her to within inches of his face. "You . . . !"

"It seems I can't turn my back on you for a minute."

Harley looked up to see Matthew Granger, swaying slightly, looking down at them.

Once again, Harley acted on instinct. "Matt, good to see you. Jordan and I were just talking about our future. And Andrew's, too, of course."

"Matthew! Believe me! It isn't what you think."

"Darling," Harley purred, "isn't it time to come out in the open?" But neither of them was listening to him.

Tears welled up in Matthew's eyes. "I had faith in you. I believed in you. I would have done . . ."

By this time the photographers had lurched out of their lethargy. The air came alive with the click and snap of flashbulbs. A reporter shamelessly ran across the room to hear the rest of the exchange.

It was eight-thirty in the evening before one of Matthew's aides drove him home through the gates of Halcyon Hill and up the driveway. Matthew saw, with a sense of foreboding, that almost every light in the house was turned on. The brightness inside only underscored his feeling of gloom, of defeat. He raised his voice against the ominous quiet.

"Val? Valerie? Where are you?"

"I'm here, Matthew."

She stood in the entrance to the living room. Beyond her he could see Joyce and Paul. They were at their homework, but now they lifted their heads from their books and eyed their parents apprehensively.

"It's time for you children to go upstairs. You can finish your lessons there. Your father and I need to talk over a few things."

Matthew tried to speak casually as the children passed him. "I'll be seeing you later," he said. But the children scooted by, sensing he was in trouble with their mom, and knowing from experience how strict she could be.

"Would you like some tea or perhaps coffee, Matthew? You look as if you could use something."

But Matthew crossed the room and poured himself a drink.

"Graham called and he told me what's happened. We have to talk about this."

"I'm not a Communist and you know it!"

"The whole town is *already* filled with gossip about you and that girl. I never expected it would happen to me this way, though it's the sort of thing every politician's wife knows can catch up with her. . . ."

"Valerie, I'm sorry. It's all over now."

"Obviously, Matthew, it isn't just the girl I'm concerned about. It's what you're doing to my family. I'm not going to play the injured wife." For a second her facade seemed in danger of cracking. "Have you any idea how you've hurt my father?"

Matthew put his head in his hands. "I'm sorry, Val. That's all I can say."

"It's a little late for that, don't you think? Now we have to look at things practically. You're going to have to map a clear strategy. I've thought about it. It probably is a good idea for you to cooperate with the Committee."

"Valerie . . ."

"You can't put this off any longer. Graham said on the phone that the preliminary hearing will be, *may* be, as early as the day after tomorrow. My father is waiting for you in the study. He's willing to help any way he can. And *you* should think about helping him for a change. FitzRandolph has always been a name at the center of political power in this country, from prerevolutionary days until now. The least you can do is try not to damage it any further than you already have."

"Val, *please* . . ."

"No! The time for 'please,' and 'thank you,' and 'I love you' is gone! You've got to save us, Matt. And yourself. And no one but you can do it. Now, my father is waiting for you."

Matthew went out into the entry hall and opened the door to the library. "Hello, Fitz," he said, heavily.

Their long night began.

Andrew walked along a street just north of the Capitol Building. He had come to learn that one way to deal with his fear of space was simply to enter it blindly, to walk through it, to learn what this new country looked like, what it contained. He particularly liked to get away from the tall apartment buildings, the luxury of the hotels, and the broad avenues that threatened him with their complex patterns of traffic. Nobody noticed an eleven-year-old boy. When he reached the drugstore, he lifted his eyes only to see his reflection, strangely distorted, in the plate-glass window.

He went inside, but the reflection remained. It wasn't his reflection. Instead, on a newspaper rack, a paper was folded to display the top half of its front page, and above his look-alike picture a headline asked, "Red Baiter Heartsick?"

Quickly Andrew fished in his pocket for change and took the paper to the counter with him. After ordering a hot-fudge sundae, he began to read.

"Last night the Jockey Club was the scene of a dramatic encounter between financial mogul Harley Compton Fitch III and Matthew Granger, Democratic hopeful for the House of Representatives and son-in-law of Senator Jerome FitzRandolph. Granger is slated to be deposed by young Joseph McCarthy. The two allegedly fought over Jordan Logan-Fisher, the beautiful artist from Red China, who just this month came to this country. Granger immediately left the scene. His aides reported that he was unavailable for comment. The Red spitfire physically attacked several cameramen in an endeavor to keep them from taking more pictures. Harley Fitch remained to give an interview to the press. 'It's a damn shame when they let Reds into the finest chop house in Washington,' he quipped. Then he offered everyone in the restaurant 'a drink on me,' and apologized for the 'unseemly interruption.'"

Andrew glanced at the mirror behind the soda-fountain counter. He flung the last of his change on the counter, popped the maraschino cherry into his mouth, went outside to the street again, and, for the first time in his life, hailed a cab.

"This Harley Compton Fitch," he said, showing his newspaper to the driver, "do you know where he works?"

"I know the building he owns, if that's what you mean, kid."

"Take me there."

The doorman, under the porte cochere of the thirty-five-story building that housed Compton Fitch Enterprises, was astonished to hear a voice both arrogant and anxious say to him, "Take care of the cab, will you? My father will pay you later."

Jordan had told Andrew this morning as she left around eleven that she would be gone only an hour. The owner of the Langsten-Struther Gallery scheduled their meeting offhandedly, saying over the phone that he would want only fifteen minutes of her time, but that she might want to bring a few of her drawings along so that she might have a quick look.

How well she knew from her years in the Orient the carefully feigned indifference as he offered her dark Indian tea in pale porcelain cups and left her portfolio standing in the corner of the gallery unopened. He chatted with her for an hour, then suggested that she might want to step out for a bite to eat. She should have called Andrew then, but in the ensuing commotion about where her portfolio should be kept for safekeeping, she found herself out on the cold winter street with Georgio Struther, striving to keep up with him on the slick sidewalks.

At the restaurant, she again thought to call her son. But as they passed the bar on the way to their table, Struther recognized, and then introduced her to, an emerging new artist, Jackson Pollock. Incredibly, he knew her name and asked if he might join them for lunch.

The next hour and a half had gone by in a haze of delight. For the first time in her adult life she was able to speak to someone who understood the activity that had meant so much to her over the years. It was as though everything else had fallen away, as she was able to speak to one of the leading colorists in the world about why she had been unable to use color; why the universe which she had been involved in trying to recreate did not require it. "I see now that's why I had so much trouble at the Summer Palace, and even in the streets of Beijing," she said. "It's because the caves, the people, their way of looking at things, were essentially monochromatic. . . ."

"I use color," he said. "I use abstractions, because the life around me isn't interesting enough to paint realistically. It's all been done before! I can't help but wonder how my techniques might have changed if I'd had a new world to paint, like you."

Once back at the gallery, she could have phoned, but Struther was saying unbelievably, "It would only be a short showing, a little less than a month, because we have Rothko scheduled for Christmas. But if you'd like to try it, I could schedule you for the beginning of November. I'd expect forty percent, of course. We'll stick them for thousands of dollars, Jordan, thousands. It's really quite amazing how even in the midst of this Communist scare, your own personal publicity has been nothing but favorable. A beautiful woman can get away with anything. We'll take advantage of that fact."

She understood that there was a 110 Shanghai Road in every city, and hers might be in this posh Washington gallery.

In one gust the night before, her happiness with Matthew had been blown away. She knew he would call, get in touch with her, but when? A simple reflex of self-preservation had made her get up at dawn this morning, glance at the morning newspaper, and hurriedly take it out to the trash so that Andrew might not see. She saw now that this Washington life—with all its comforts and its seeming conveniences—was filled with the opportunity to fall, to fail.

Now, coming up her stairs, Jordan tried out the vain excuse upon herself that she had neglected to call Andrew because she was not used to the telephone, having been away from one for close to seventeen years. The truth was, she had been thinking of something else, and this was just as true of her now in a modern Washington apartment as it had ever been in a primitive Yenan cave.

But for heaven's sake, what difference does it make? It was simply a matter of lunch. There was food in the refrigerator and in the cupboards. For Andrew, it was simply a matter of composing these unfamiliar things into something he could eat and put into his mouth. Surely he could manage that.

"Andrew," she said impatiently as soon as she came into the apartment, "I hope you've had lunch, and I'm sorry to be late. But really, I do have the most exciting news. . . ."

Her voice echoed strangely in the quiet rooms. She was alone.

Well. That was good. She knew that her son had been forcing himself to take short walks around the city. It was good that he had been going out to face his *bête noire* alone. At the same time, she thought, irrationally, he could have left her a note!

She picked up a copy of *Vogue* to fantasize about what to wear at the opening. She switched on a light, poured another sherry, and went carefully through the pages of *Town & Country*, memorizing the names of fashionable Washington matrons whom she knew might become her customers, her patrons, if all went well. She began to feel hungry—she had not eaten much at lunch—got up, went to the kitchen, sliced herself an apple and a few chunks of cheddar. What a treat to have cheese after all those years in inland China.

The anonymous, almost inaudible buzz of the electric kitchen clock caught her attention. It was seven twenty-five. Even allowing for the fact that she might have been later in coming home than she had admitted to herself, Andrew had been gone for at least three hours. If, as some sinking part of her knew, he had left the apartment just after she had, he would have been gone for eight.

Jordan hurried across the room and dialed Matthew's number. His wife answered. Jordan hung up. She could not inflict her troubles on that man any longer. If she were ever to effect a reconciliation with him, she would have to approach him as a reasonable human being. She hung up the phone, dialed the operator, and called the police.

"My name is Jordan Logan-Fisher," she said to the gruff voice that answered. "I'm afraid I may need some assistance." She heard her voice as an American might hear it—high-pitched, shrill, with a suspicious accent.

"What can I do for you?"

"My son, I believe, is missing."

"How long, lady?"

"Since this morning, perhaps this afternoon."

"How old is this kid?" the voice asked with concern. "Two or three? How did he get out?"

"He's eleven."

"Well, for God's sake, lady, he's probably out on his bike." And the phone slammed down.

There was only one other phone call she could make. She dialed the offices of Compton Fitch Enterprises, knowing that in the ordinary world of American business, both executives and workers would be home by now, deep in the consolations of domestic life. He answered the main business phone; he was waiting for her call.

"Yeah, what is it?"

"Harley, this is Jordan." She could not keep her voice from trembling. "Is Andrew there?"

"Yes, he's here."

"May I speak to him, please?" Again, the dreadful tremor in her voice.

A hand covered the receiver. She could see in her mind's eye its beefy outlines—the blond hair across red knuckles. Then Harley's voice came back at her, bland and cheerful.

"Nah, he says he doesn't want to talk right now."

And there was nothing in her ear but the dreadful silence of a phone that had gone dead.

Usually these preliminary hearings were held in closed rooms with a few deceptively cordial members of the Committee. At this level very little was ever written down. Attorneys on opposing sides bickered over details, as in an amicable divorce. If the witnesses were "friendly," the proceedings were kept a secret, so that the various committees might consolidate their information, yet keep it from the general public. In these past few months, families, friendships, even marriages had been split as each human soul called before these committees had to decide what was wrong and what was right.

Was America plagued with Communists within its own government? Was democracy being eaten away as by a monstrously growing cancer? Or were these tiny cells seen under the congressional microscope simply projections of a lunatic fear far more dangerous than any "Communist conspiracy"? Matthew didn't know the answers and he was fairly sure that no else did either.

Today would not be the usual confidential first step. He saw Harley's hand in this when he realized his appearance had been scheduled for a public hearing room of the Senate that included a visitors' gallery—filled to capacity this morning with curious onlookers and members of the press. McCarthy himself was here this morning, busy, bustling, full of jocose asides to his aides, reeking, even from twenty feet away, of Scotch.

Matthew stated his name, his age, his occupation, his birthdate, his place of birth. At the mention of "Shanghai," the senator huffed and looked around at those assembled as if to say "You see, there's almost no point in going on." Then came the all-important question, "Are you now or have you ever been a Communist?"

Matthew heard his own voice—or was it his father's?—full of hauteur, condescension, white Protestant to the core. "Absolutely not. Never."

The senator cleared his throat. He wiped his eyes with the back of his hand. He'd obviously had a bad night. "Good. Now, since we know you were raised in a Communist country and did your college work in a university that is rife with fellow travelers, you won't mind giving us the names of those who have been and are still conspiring to rip our great nation from its foundations of democracy?"

Again Matthew spoke exactly the same words in exactly the same tone. "Absolutely not," he said coldly. "Never."

Murmurs of disbelief rippled through the room.

"Mr. Granger," Senator McCarthy said, "you know very well the rules that pertain here. If you choose to hide behind the Fifth Amendment, you may. If you choose to cooperate, you may do that as well." The senator's voice took on a familiar bullying tone. "But you cannot have it both ways. Otherwise, you will be held in contempt."

"Perhaps that is appropriate, because I have nothing but contempt for this Committee and all it stands for."

The senator's face grew blotchy. He took a rasping breath and began to speak, but Matthew went on.

"Senator McCarthy brought me here today because he professes to have doubts about my loyalties. In some ways I agree with him. There is a grain of truth in what he says."

A low rumble went through the chamber.

Matthew, moving quickly, snatched up a few sheets of paper. "I'm reading from my prepared statement," he said. "It's a short one, and it has relevance to the Committee." He glanced about the room. "Earlier this year, ladies and gentlemen, I went on a mission to China. I went to rescue Americans about to fall under the tyranny of a Communist power. To my considerable surprise, I found some Westerners who wanted to stay in that country. They felt, ladies and gentlemen, that a good crop had been sown there. They knew what Chiang Kai-shek had reaped from his own sowing of terror. I don't have to argue that," Matthew said sharply over the noise. "If Chiang had been a popular leader, he would still be a leader, instead of a puppet of our own government. No, I say to you, that what he reaped was the hatred of most of his people. Now the Chinese wait, as they have waited for centuries.

"In private life, I've dabbled at farming myself. No farmer

is foolish enough to judge his crop when it is still little beyond the stage of seedlings. You know the old story of the impatient farmer who kept pulling up his plants to see how they were prospering. Day by day he was so delighted with the increase of growth that he had pulled up over half his planting before he had anything to reap."

The senator could take no more. "Does all this rigmarole mean that you approve of the totalitarian government of a power-mad thug, a pawn of Moscow?"

"Anyone who would call the ruler of China, which contains a quarter of the world's population, a *pawn* has a pitiful sense of history. I'm saying a new crop has been planted! What it will grow into, we cannot tell. But whatever it is, we cannot judge it until it has begun to ripen."

"I'll have you jailed for this," McCarthy shouted. "You've just admitted treason."

"One of my father's favorite sermons was about the tares among the grain. When I was a child that sermon irritated me, because to a child every growing thing is beautiful. And for a long time I never knew what a tare was. A tare is simply a weed. Only when I became a farmer and was trying to make the earth yield up a living did I realize what damage tares could do. They were harsh, they were ugly, they were lawless. They bullied the grain. They disrupted the order in the field."

The junior senator from Wisconsin broke in, "We don't have time for this bombast, this rhetoric."

"You cannot argue with a tare, Senator. You cannot reason with it. You cannot be silent about it in the hope that it will go away. You must put on your working clothes, ladies and gentlemen, go out into the uncomfortable sun and pull tares up by the roots. The senator would suggest that he is weeding out the tares of Communism. I would suggest that the fine golden fields of democracy, which were sown with such hope almost two hundred years ago, are now, in fact, infested with the tares of reactionary corruption. It is because of this infestation I have begun to doubt my own country. As of this moment, I am withdrawing from my campaign for public office. I am publicly repudiating this Committee and all that it stands for. And I . . ."

Matthew looked around the room, seeking to establish eye contact with as many people as he could. "I am not a man of public action. It is up to the people of America to . . ." He looked up to the balcony at the scribbling journalists, the intent politicians, his wife, who listened with her head held high and her face a mask of composure. There, in the first row, returning his own stare, were two faces in some ways almost identical, faces that recalled his own deepest feelings of inadequacy, betrayal, and helpless rage. Harley Compton Fitch III grinned down at him, and in the protective curve of his father's muscular arm, a young boy nestled—Andrew, Jordan's son.

"I . . ." Matthew started, "I believe I've finished now."

After his aide dropped him off at Halcyon Hill, Matthew went straight to the library, where according to their plan of the night before, his father-in-law was waiting for him.

"I've been to your safe-deposit box this morning," Fitz-Randolph said. "I have your passport and fifteen thousand in cash. I'll open a bank account for you where I can send more money as you need it."

"You don't have to do this—"

The senator interrupted him. "Listen, Matthew," he said. "If I were a different kind of man I would have stood up there right beside you. But I'm a practical politician. It's my whole life."

Matthew rubbed the heel of his hand on his forehead. "I feel that I've let you down. I know that I've let Valerie down terribly."

"It's true. Valerie's upset. She's a very intelligent woman, Matthew. But all young girls are alike. Valerie led a very sheltered life and when she met you she thought she'd met the man of her dreams. *Her* dreams, Matthew, not yours."

"I can't shake the terrible feeling that for one moment of so-called idealism I've thrown away everything that should matter."

"*Should*," the senator said heavily. "That's the word that stands out to me. Those things *should* matter to you, Matthew, but I'm not sure they do." The senator sighed. "I'm going to miss you, Matt. This is the kind of thing we could have spent long evenings talking about. But there will be no more of them for us until all this blows over. Valerie and the children are waiting for you upstairs. She has your things packed. I took a gamble and made a reservation for you on the afternoon flight to San Francisco. You have to move quickly. Get out of the country while you can. Others have already had their passports revoked."

"Senator, I'm asking Valerie to go with me."

"Good luck! I hope she has the guts to do it. Go on. She's waiting for you."

Matthew thought he'd been prepared for the pain, but nothing could have prepared him for the agony of this separation. Valerie had kept the children home from school. Little Joyce was crying, which was bad enough, but Paul seemed not to understand at all. When Matthew knelt down to tell him he'd be going away for a while, the boy said, "Will you bring me back a present?"

Matthew looked into that sweet face so devoid of guile or suspicion, knowing that it would be months and more, probably years, before he would see his son again. Joyce reacted far differently. She stiffened against his embrace and cried out, in the manner of a Washington princess already burdened with an overdeveloped sense of right and wrong, "Don't touch me! Everybody at school has been talking about what you were going to do. Yesterday afternoon Miss Gussenhoven talked about what it means to be un-American. I couldn't go over to Betty Taft's yesterday to play and"—her lips began to tremble uncontrollably—"I know how you've hurt Mama. So just don't touch me."

Now he and Valerie were alone.

"You may hate me for this morning, but in one way I did what you said, Val. I don't think you father has anything more to worry about."

She didn't speak to him, and he remembered how many times—as in any marriage, he supposed—she had retreated during an argument, especially when she had something to conceal, into a shell of wifely righteousness.

"Your father thinks it's best if I go away, and so do I. We thrashed it out last night. You and I—all I can say, Valerie, is that we should have more time to talk about this. It's terrible that we have to be quarreling now—"

"You coward! You're leaving the country, Daddy told me! I heard you with my own ears admit that you don't love America. And you pulled out of the election without even asking me! Can't you stand up and fight like . . ."

"Like a man?"

"That's it, Matt. I thought I'd married a man. But you—"

"That's *enough*! What you think of me, what I think of you, for that matter, is not at issue here. I told you last night

I'd given up Jordan, and I mean it. You're my wife, Valerie, and we have two children to think of. I'm not leaving the country on a whim, and I'm not the only one leaving. America may be on the brink of a dictatorship." His lips twisted. "You think you're ashamed of me now, but would you relish having a convicted felon for a husband? I'm leaving before they revoke my passport. I want you and the children to go with me. We'll go anywhere you say. Lausanne, Mexico City, Paris—anywhere you want. We can start over, Valerie. On your terms."

"On *my* terms! On *my* terms? My terms were these! That I could be as proud of my husband as I was of my father! That you'd go beyond him someday, that . . ."

"That someday you'd be the First Lady. That was it, wasn't it, Val? I could have had a thousand mistresses if only I'd given you the White House! Well, I can't. And I won't." He looked squarely at her, and at their ten years of marriage, which seemed to fade, even as he spoke, from the present and into the past.

"I'll write when I have a chance," he said. And then he left.

"I've tried the police already," Jordan said. "Don't you understand? Of course they called Harley Fitch and he told them that the boy was his son, so there was no reason to give him up. They told me there was no problem—a boy can be with his father."

"And this man, then, actually *is* his father?"

"I thought I'd made that clear. . . ."

This was the third time this morning that Jordan had gone through the same telephone conversation. As soon as an attorney heard Harley's name he lost interest in helping her.

Her eyes rested on the piece of paper beside the phone. It was a contract with the Langsten-Struther Gallery for a one-woman showing of the pictures that she had brought out of China. All it lacked .was her signature. Mr. Struther had written, in an accompanying note, that time was of the essence. They should mount the show as quickly as possible to catch the pre-Christmas buyers. What had brought her such happiness on first reading now seemed totally unimportant. She was ripped by conflict: Should she sign it now? What could she do to recover Andrew? Should she get in touch with Matthew?

The harsh ring of her doorbell cut through her confusion. "Western Union for Jordan Logan-Fisher."

Jordan tore open the yellow envelope. She read, "I must leave the country while I can STOP we must each make our own future STOP I hope you find happiness in yours MATTHEW"

Jordan's indecision was gone in an instant. The gallery could wait. As for Andrew, by the time she'd come back, he would have learned what kind of a man his father really was, and would want to return to her. She had lost Matthew twice before. She could not let it happen again. She loved him, she had always loved him, and she knew where he must be going now.

That same afternoon, Senator Joseph McCarthy conducted a press conference on the steps of the Capitol Building.

"I know what you boys want to ask me, and I'm ready to answer. You want to know about the destructive forces working in our society. Some of you, or at least your newspapers, have said that I'm just making all this up. But I'm here to tell you today that I've already rooted out one traitor just this morning! He's betrayed his class and his country. If the State Department wasn't so riddled with the 'pink network,' we might have brought him to justice. But Matthew Wilson Granger will be able to use his passport to leave America!"

"Senator," one of the reporters asked, "are you sure that Matthew Granger really is a Communist?"

"What paper are you from?"

"The *Washington Post*."

"That doesn't surprise me! Your paper prints more lies about me and what I'm trying to do for this poor sick nation than almost any other."

The reporter persisted. "But, Senator! What if Granger is telling the truth? What if he's an innocent man?"

"The truth!" the senator exclaimed, his face blotching. "How can that subversive crap be the truth? It's the good citizens of America, like my friend Harley Compton Fitch III, who are the guardians of the truth."

"Give us something we can *print*, Senator. What about the woman? That white-flower babe? She really *is* a Commie. What are you going to do about her?"

"Ah, boys, she's a limey to begin with, and you know how they are. Besides, she isn't important. She's been off in a cave, as I understand it, for the last seven years. Off the record, boys, she's just gash. A piece of tail."

"Forty-love," Harley called cheerily. "Your last chance to take a game off your old man." Harley tossed the ball into the air and served a clean ace. "Good game, son. You're getting the hang of it. You'll be winning in another year or so."

Reluctantly, Andrew approached the net to shake hands.

"Come on, now. Be a good sport. And put some feeling into that grip."

Harley assessed the figure that his handsome twelve-year-old son cut here on the tennis courts. After a fight with Jordan, and Matthew's debacle in Washington, Harley decided that the best thing to do with Andrew was to take him away to a completely new place, so that they might have the opportunity to get to know each other as father and son. What could be better than California, where traditionally all sorts of people had come to start new lives?

They checked into a suite of rooms at the Ambassador Hotel on Wilshire Boulevard. Harley knew that with the dubious legal help that Jordan could hire, her chances of finding them were minuscule. Every day that Andrew remained with Harley, he became more of a son to him. In this, as in everything else, possession was nine-points of the law.

After a few weeks, their days settled into a pleasant routine. Harley got up at six to keep an eye on the New York Stock Exchange and to make his international phone calls. He taught Andrew to scan *The Wall Street Journal* so that he might get at least a glimmer of understanding of the vast empire which he would someday inherit. Only after these financial exercises, a source of unaccountable pleasure to Harley, did he allow breakfast to be served.

He took particular delight in the way Andrew had developed a taste for Western food. "Eggs Benedict again, Andrew? It's okay, but you've got to be sure to work it off. Do a few extra laps in the pool."

As soon as breakfast was finished, Harley sent Andrew off to another set of lessons as important to a businessman as a head full of figures. A straight back, a hard body, a good game of tennis, the sheer physical energy to keep going after everyone else was exhausted—these were the attributes that Harley's own father had preached to him, and that he recommended now to his newly acquired son.

After lunch came Harley's favorite part of the day, when together they addressed the ball on the tennis court, to see what Andrew had learned from the pro. Though Harley took pride every day in his son's advance, he felt that he, himself, must never play below his own top level. The boy must learn to win, and win on his own.

"That's four hundred and thirty-five dollars you owe me. But you'll win it back, son. You know there's no point in doing anything without a profit motive."

The boy looked at him neutrally. Harley noticed again how trim he looked in his tennis whites, how well his skin took the tan, now that his diet had improved.

"Dad," Andrew said, "I feel a little thirsty. Can we walk over to the outdoor bar and get a drink?"

"Sure. We have plenty of time before we change for dinner."

Only a few swimmers remained in the pool at this hour. Languid Hollywood wives frittered away the time, sunning themselves, listlessly turning the pages of *Photoplay*.

"What's this game?" Andrew asked, stopping by a green table. "It looks a little like what we've been playing, only much smaller."

"Oh, that's just for kids, Andrew. Ping-Pong. There's no point in learning that."

"But, Dad"—the boy looked up at him with long-lashed big blue eyes—"if I'm a kid and this is a kid's game, I might have a better chance of winning."

Harley laughed politely and went on toward the bar. It had been hot on the court and he was looking forward to a gin-and-tonic. His son lagged back at the table, picking up a paddle in one and and a ball in the other.

"Come on, Dad. I bet I can win this. I really think I can."

"*Andrew.*" But Harley couldn't think of a reason to deny his son.

"I heard something on the court today. 'Double or nothing.' I'll play you double or nothing, okay?"

"Son, that's a wrong move. That would just leave us even. You should always play for profit. Let's make it double both ways. There's no point in playing if you don't play to win."

Harley came over to the table and picked up a paddle. "Now this game is very much like tennis, and . . ."

The boy called, "My serve."

Harley lost his first point. In less than five minutes the game was over. The score was twenty-one-love. Even the languid wives put down their magazines to watch the blistering defeat of the handsome tycoon.

Andrew shook his father's hand firmly, smiled ingenuously up into his eyes, and said, "The drinks will be my treat, Dad."

"Great game, son!" And even more proudly: "You really put one over on me."

Andrew felt a surge of blind rage. What was this game? Andrew had dealt his father a beating he knew both of them would never forget. Yet at the end, his father had smiled. He had lost no face at all.

The Hollywood Bowl was filled to capacity. Madame Chiang Kai-shek kept her audience waiting for a full ten minutes while the tension and excitement grew. Tai-ling shifted in her seat on the dais and wished that the December sun might curb its unseasonable warmth. She looked out at the crowd and smiled professionally as she counted the motley groups represented there. She'd forgotten how many Protestant missionaries had retired to this mild climate. She could spot them by the sobriety of their dress. And, once again, all of Chinatown had turned out to get a glimpse of their female idols: Tai-ling and Mei-ling Soong.

Before Tai-ling had a chance to reflect further on the reasons for this sellout audience, the slim, elegantly dressed figure of the Generalissimo's wife swept onto the stage. The roar that greeted her was a physical shock. But as Chiang began to speak in her cultivated Wellesley accent, Tai-ling found her attention wandering. It was the same old rhetoric: "I am not here to panegyrize the great American people, or to thank them for their generosity during this period of my great country's agonized suffering. No, I am here to tell you of China's perilous plight, of the danger of the *true* China being obliterated. I am not here to remind the government of this great land of its promises made to my people. . . ."

But that was exactly what this designing woman was doing. After all the millions that had been poured into her country, only to be dissipated by Mei-ling's family and their corrupt cohorts, Madame Chiang could go on making her eloquent appeals. She would be applauded by the missionaries, and by those businesses that still hoped to recover their Chinese investments. But Washington, she suspected, had already decided that enough was enough.

Tai-ling fixed a look of rapt attention on her face and let

her mind drift to the events that had been promised the honored guests later on in the afternoon and evening. They were to be whisked away to the Ambassador for a reception and dancing.

Soon enough, it was finished. She turned over her limo to Madame Chiang and rode with the Chairman of the China Friendship Society to the hotel. She was happy for once to be at the center of a circle of still admiring fans.

At the Ambassador, she cooperated with the photographers at the main door of the hotel, but then, as the others made their way in gabbling groups to the Coconut Grove, she took a quick turn to her left into a small bar used mainly by the habitués of this hotel. More and more these days, she felt that life, such as it was, could be made bearable only by the solace of a drink.

The bartender, who knew her, acknowledged her presence with a solemn nod and turned to prepare her usual champagne cocktail. Then, although she thought she was alone in this room, where there were stools for no more than five patrons, she caught the scent of another presence. Scotch, Bay Rum, pipe tobacco, tweed, fresh sweat, and—she could explain it in no other way—the smell of Shanghai.

"Would the mission girl prefer a Ramos Fizz?"

She felt for a moment that she might faint, and put the palms of her hands on the bar for support. She could tell the bartender was waiting for a signal from her to throw the masher out. She heard her own voice, not the voice of the world-famous actress, but the singsong voice of the half-breed schoolgirl who had turned to her rescuer for protection from the brutal Sikh.

"A Ramos Fizz, please."

"If your public could see you now," Harley said.

She saw that he, too, was trembling.

They had said no more than a few sentences to each other when they were discovered by a boy who burst in and said, "Dad, I've been looking all over for you. Henry Stone's parents have an extra ticket to *South Pacific* down at the Philharmonic. They said they'd take me to dinner at the Pantry. May I go, sir?"

Tai-ling saw Harley's face crossed by an expression that was foreign to her—a look of almost boyish pride.

"Of course, son," he said. "Remember to thank the Stones

for their invitation and I'd like to see you home by one
o'clock."

The boy was off in a flash. Almost at the same moment,
from the inside door that led into the main lobby, a group of
about a dozen journalists came in.

"Say, Mr. Fitch, we didn't know you knew Tai-ling!"

"Tai-ling, honey, how about just putting your elbows back
on the bar and crossing your legs so that we can get a shot of
those sexy gams?"

"What's that you're drinking, sweetheart? We thought you
were a champagne kind of girl."

Tai-ling cast her eyes down as Harley reached in his
pocket and pulled out a thick wad of bills.

"Trouble with you boys is you work too hard," he said. "I
know for a fact you've been at it all day." As he spoke, he
pressed a crisp hundred into each man's hand. "Why don't I
just have the bartender close up for an hour or two and let you
boys take a much-needed break? I used to know Tai-ling in the
old days, and I'll level with you, we haven't seen each other in
years. Give us a chance to get acquainted again and we'll be
grateful."

Before any of them could answer, he put another handful
of hundred-dollar bills on the counter and said to the
bartender, "That will be all right, won't it, if I give my friends
here a little party? Drink up," he said steadily to Tai-ling. "I
hear music over in the Grove. Wouldn't you like to go and
dance?"

He took her by the arm and they left the bar, closing its
doors behind them. As they crossed the spacious lobby, she
said in a half-whisper, "Your son is made in your image. I
should like to meet him sometime."

"Not tonight."

"You're bold."

"It's the boldness of twelve years."

Then they danced, and in the dark she could have been
any Chinese girl; he could have been any man. Their bodies
glided effortlessly across the dance floor. Every turn, every
dip, even the slightest shift of weight, she seemed to
anticipate. Before they had been in each other's arms for five
minutes, their bodies had fallen in love—again.

"People are beginning to leave." She put her hand on the
back of his neck, and brought his head down so that she might
whisper to him. "What shall we do now?"

He pretended to hesitate. "You shunned me in the Rotunda the last time we met. . . ."

She laughed. "It was good for you."

They ended up driving out to the beach to Thelma Todd's Restaurant, looking out from the upper windows across the Pacific Coast Highway. They had driven here in Harley's limo; they drank champagne on the way, and ordered more. Tai-ling discovered that she was ravenously hungry. They ordered oysters and Mexican lobsters drenched in sweet butter. She watched as he ripped the meat from its shell and, fully aware of the sensuality of his gesture, laid the strips of white succulent flesh on her plate. The energy between them was thick and electric. In the candlelight, she gazed at the fine blond hair on his solid wrists. She was aware of every movement of her own body underneath its silken sheath.

He raised his hand to call for more champagne, but she placed a glittering fingernail at the base of his throat. "My home is very close," she said, "and the moon is out tonight. Why don't we finish our meal on my balcony, over the waves?"

He paid the bill, and in a matter of minutes they were in a room on the second floor of her Malibu home. Now it was his turn to be overwhelmed by images and scents from the past. Beaded curtains tinkled in the sea breeze; the aroma of sandalwood rose, old silk rustled. She was a queen; she was a panther.

She opened the champagne and poured two glasses, very carefully. Her hands were steady, but he folded his arms so that she wouldn't see his uncontrollable shaking. She turned to him, handed him his glass, and sipped from her own. He watched in the moonlight as her fingernails reached for the silken buttons that fastened that flimsy silk, first at her throat, then her shoulder, then . . .

As he kept his eyes focused on those nails, so red and hard, to keep from staring at her delicate breasts, he realized, with a feeling both of defeat and of triumph, that those half-forgotten nights of rage and lust when he had rampaged through brothels of "Chinatowns" all around the world, those hours trying to satiate an insatiable appetite, to obliterate the memory seared on his brain of that one unforgettable, forbidden coupling, had been futile. All that had only fed the fire of his desire, his longing, his lust. This was why he had never married. It was because he was in love with his sister.

"Tai-ling," he said huskily. "Don't. Please don't."

She smiled, and seemed to coil, a beautiful serpent of the night. "*You* know that, Harley"—and her skin, entirely free of its *chi-báu*, gleamed in the moonlight as if it, too, were made of silk—"and *I* know that. Yes, we are brother and sister. But you and I are the only two persons left in the world who know."

This first time was over as quickly as when he had been twenty-one and she an innocent mission girl. When he came back to himself, she lay under him, her half-closed eyes both lazy and amused. "There's no need to hurry now" she said, and her voice was like syrup. "There's no one to disturb us. We have all the time in the world."

Her hair, so carefully coiffed earlier in the day, had come undone and swirled about her on the pillow. "Bring me some champagne. . . ."

He handed her the bottle. She took it from him and trickled some of it between her girlishly small breasts.

"Aren't you still thirsty?" she muttered in a voice so low he could barely hear her.

She continued the bottle's thin stream. Wantonly, she let the stream fall between her fragrant thighs. And he drank deeply of her. Hadn't she said they had all the time in the world? He brought her again and again to the brink until she was almost wild. Then she became the aggressor. She mounted him and became mysteriously still. With her inner muscles it was her turn to tug and caress until he cried out in a harsh voice, "Stop!" But she wouldn't. He cried out again as he came, in a voice filled with anguish; she would give him no chance to rest. By her relentless movements she kept him stony hard; the sensation now was more pain than pleasure. He wanted to beg her to stop, to wait, to give him a chance. But he realized that she was more than a woman now. She was an agent of fate, a reminder of all the times he had imposed his own conscienceless lust on those whose desire had faltered. Then she commenced an eerie wail, dug those red nails into his chest, tore at his flesh. More pain, close to agony for him, but it combined exquisitely with his joy in watching her face contort as she reached her own ineffable height of physical pleasure.

After a moment's pause, he searched her face for any sign of remorse or regret. Still sitting astride him, she reached across for the glasses and adroitly, still holding him in, poured the champagne.

"When you have sucked these clean," she purred as she

extended her fingernails incrusted with his own blood and flesh, "you may have your reward of Dom Perignon."

She took the Clipper to Hong Kong, landed at the airport, boarded the *Star Ferry* to the Kowloon side, and checked into the Peninsula Hotel. She dined At Nathan's, slept easily and long between crisp white sheets, and set out early the next morning, glad to be in the oriental streets, at the gates of China. She relished the teeming crowds, the sharp contrasts between the jewelry shops specializing in rope upon rope of pearls and the frank squalor of the street vendors who sold great vats of gray fish paste and dog meat as a special delicacy. She loved hearing insults addressed to her in almost every dialect and enjoyed even more her own retorts, leaving merchants and peasants alike agape.

At the Chinese Consulate, she sifted through all the recent American visa applications, having paid a hefty sum to do so. The People's Republic frowned on such practices, but practiced them nontheless. Almost immediately she came upon Matthew's name, and a little farther down the list, the red official chop that showed his visa had been issued. Then in crude, penciled characters, the information that he had taken the Canton train only ten days before. All that remained was to apply for a visa herself.

After two weeks, the visa had still not come through. She thought it prudent to move from the Peninsula to the Wanderers Hotel. She ate Chinese breakfasts—jook and dried fish—to keep her filled until nighttime. She caught a nasty cold, which was made steadily worse by her daily walks to the consulate. Her back ached constantly. She went to an herbalist. He gave her a newspaper-wrapped handful of dried grasses, with the warning that the infusion from this would turn her urine red. It did, but it didn't make her feel any better.

She woke at night drenched in sweat and riven with doubts. What was she doing here? Why was it taking so long? Every day someone at the consulate demanded more money. When she got back to China, she'd make sure that Mao himself heard about this! Then her heart constricted. Hong Kong was small; China held a quarter of the world's population. How would she find him? What if he had decided not to go to Shanghai?

When she woke one morning, a tropical rain was falling.

She forced herself to get up, and vomited in the sink. Again, she walked to the consulate. When the clerk held out his hand as usual, she said, weakly, "I have almost no more money. Just enough to pay my hotel."

He spat eloquently. She realized that a decision had been made at some point in the hierarchy to shut her out, possibly by the Chairman himself, but most likely by former comrades—the brave soldiers with whom she had spent ten years. On the way home she had to kneel in the gutter twice and be sick again.

When she got back to the hotel, she found that she didn't have enough cash to cover the week's bill. The management was amicable, but insisted on keeping her luggage.

She staggered out onto the street again, but her weakness invited harsh remarks and the derisive attention of ruffians. She had tottered no more than a few blocks toward the waterfront when her purse was snatched. She remembered the YMCA, just across the street from the Peninsula Hotel. Barely able to reach the building and step inside, she fainted.

She regained consciousness in a small, clean room. A soberly dressed lady sat beside her. "Don't try to talk," she said. "You've been ill for several days. We had the doctor for you and you have two pieces of good news. The first"—and here her lips curled in a smile, as if to say she would never understand the Chinese—"is that you will probably not die. The second"—and here her eyes softened with compassion—"is, my dear, that if it is carefully attended to, hepatitis does not affect pregnancy."

Jordan pulled herself up on one elbow and began to retch. The woman was immediately beside her with a small tin bowl.

"Evidently," she said softly, "even the doctor was puzzled for a while, since the symptoms of one condition mimic the other. You're not to worry. Just tell me your name if you can."

"Jordan Logan-Fisher. I'm traveling on a British passport."

"We'll send someone down immediately to report its loss. It will take a few weeks to replace, but you may think of that as good news as well, because the doctor has said it will be at least a month before you can travel."

During the next few days, Jordan settled into a drab and seemingly endless routine. A continuous bland diet of sweets and boiled rice soon calmed the worst of her nausea, but she was so weak that she could barely stagger across the room to the bucket that served as a commode. Her mind, if possible, was even more tortured than her body. She had failed to get into China, failed to find Matthew, failed as a mother to both of her children, failed as a woman. She had even failed as an artist, giving up a chance for fame to go off on a harebrained escapade that she must have known, had she chosen to think about it, was doomed from the start.

So far she had resisted the well-intentioned entreaties of the people at the Y to send a message to family or friends or anyone who might be able to help her. Every day they offered help; every day, with a stubbornness that even she recognized as pitiable, she refused it. She would conquer this illness on her own; she would have this baby on her own; she would . . .

Somewhere in the middle of the eleventh or twelfth day she began to see the pattern, the colossal ego involved in all this—the narcissism, the arrogant drive that had blinded, allowing her to see the vast and wondrous world only in terms of herself. When she was a child in the Logan-Fisher compound, servants dropped everything and came running when "Little Mistress" cried for her doll. When she walked on the street, the Sikh policeman, recognizing the daughter of a British emissary, singled her out either for a bow or a smart salute. At her eighteenth birthday party, when the Japanese dropped their bombs, she had seen the destruction of Shanghai as a lively fireworks display.

Yes, but your life has been hard, a voice within her cried. You were the victim of rape and you lost the man you love. But another voice answered with relentless rationality that it had been she who flirted with Harley, she who used him to tease Matthew, she who rubbed herself against the virile youth, simply for the fun of feeling his body change and thinking he could do nothing about it. She had thought that she could stay in China, have the baby and abandon it, then return to Matthew with him never being the wiser. No wonder Andrew hated her. She could say all she wanted that Andrew was the child of a rape and the son of a brute, but the real truth was that she used him as well; she kept him because China had closed and she had no one else.

She writhed in self-loathing. Not only had she planned to abandon Andrew, she had succeeded in deserting Chuen-yee, a son she loved with all her heart. How could she have done it? Was she a monster instead of a woman?

She had a sexual connection with three men in her life. Harley was an animal and never tried to conceal it. Matthew was an idealist, and thought too much for his own good. Between the two of them—dark-skinned, straightforward, her scout, her champion—had been Chuen-yup. In China there was no such thing as romantic love. She and Chuen-yup were friends, comrades, partners in the truest sense. She had trusted him with her life and he never betrayed her. Even at the end she had been wrong in putting her motives onto him. He was not a person who worked as she did, from a position of narcissism. He had asked Matthew to take her away for her own good, her own safety. Why had she not taken away her other son, little Chuen-yee?

And the dark, self-serving little voice within her said, It was too inconvenient. After a decade of defending a blond outcast in the caves of Yenan, it would be too much, simply too fatiguing, to defend an oriental half-breed on the croquet lawn of The Beeches.

Adding to all of this self-absorbtion was the amoral egotism of the artist—that mindless, thrusting ambition that made her do anything, even maim her own flesh, to take those drawings away from China with her.

It was not until at least another week passed, after she cried futile tears for all of them, all the lost ones in her life—Matthew, Chuen-yup, Chuen-yee, Andrew, even Harley—that she began to see her own arrogance, her tantrums, as masks. As a daughter of the British Empire, she had been reared in the belief that feelings, or the show of them, were common and in poor taste. She thought again of her birthday party and the Japanese bombing, of comforting her amah, all too aware that she did it to catch the attention of the aloof and haughty boy at the far end of the balcony who tried as ineffectually as she to keep his emotions in check. She remembered that with Chuen-yup, too, there were strong emotions that neither of them cared to face. Now, from the enforced objectivity of this bed, she looked back upon a scene somewhere in an official house in Beijing: a Chinese husband, an American courier, and an English woman screaming at the top of her voice.

That poor woman, Jordan thought with detached compassion, she screamed because she was losing a beloved child. She screamed so as not to shame her husband with tears. She screamed because a combination of circumstances and her own flawed character would keep her forever from her own true destiny. Because her spirit would forever belong to only one man. Matthew Wilson Granger.

Once she recognized this and admitted to herself that she'd never find Matthew, she saw that the time to grieve had ended. She must set about planning the future in the best interests of their child. If, in her past life, she had been self-centered, she would try this time to place herself and her coming child in the context of the larger world. She would use her art, not in the quest of fame, but to share what little wisdom she had with others. If her first two sons had been out of place, marked with mismatched parenting that would forever make their lives difficult, she knew that the child within her had exactly the right father. And she knew, now that the illness receded ever so slightly from her, that the child might grow up in a perfectly appropriate home, and come into a bountiful heritage.

The next morning when the kindly matron from the Y came in to ask—as she did each day—if there wasn't a person to whom Jordan might want to send a message, this time Jordan said, "Thank you very much, and yes, there is. Would it be possible to send a cable to Madeline Logan-Fisher at The Beeches, Abingdon, Oxfordshire, England?" She would ask her mother for airfare to take her finally home to England. The conventions that kept her away during her first pregnancy—the stigma of being an unwed mother—still pertained, but if she used her head, she could make her reputation as an artist and an eccentric pay off. She was no longer a simple English girl. She was Jordan Logan-Fisher, and she didn't give a bloody damn what any of them thought.

In the full sunlight of a June day, a tall figure clad in peasant dress walked along the path that led to the Lungwha Pagoda, an old landmark ten *li* to the west of Shanghai. His straw-sandaled feet kicked up puffs of dust with each step. As he drew nearer to the elaborate old structure, he saw that it had been sadly neglected. The paint on the unswept eaves of each tier had faded, weeds had sprung up in the courtyard and around the crumbling walls. He was therefore surprised to see a stooped figure come out from the gatehouse.

"Old Father, I am happy to see you. For a time I thought there were nothing but ghosts around here."

"Sometimes my woman and I think we *are* ghosts. So

many landowners disappeared in the war and the fields are unplowed. Still, the new government has appointed me guardian of the pagoda."

"So I see," the stranger said. "They can't think very highly of it if they let it fall to pieces."

"That's true. They do not like it because they think it is part of the old false religion, but it is so powerful in the minds of the few people still left here that cadres are afraid to do anything against it."

By this time the stranger, whose face was concealed by a coolie hat, stood in front of the old man. As he put his head back he pulled his hands out from the protection of his Chinese sleeves.

"*Ai-yah!*" The gatekeeper exclaimed. "*Yang-gwei-tse,* foreign devil!"

"I'm not really a foreigner, although you may think I'm a devil come to join the other ghosts. I am, no matter what I look like, a son of the city."

"A turtle proclaims himself a peacock, but that does not put feathers on his shell."

"May a weary pilgrim beg for a cup of tea while we discuss the matter further?" the stranger said.

And as they sat in the broken-down arbor, a moving cloud of dust appeared on the horizon.

"Now what?" the gatekeeper grumbled. But the visitor watched the approaching cloud with equanimity.

A prewar, gunmetal-gray Essex chugged through the gates of the grounds of the Lungwha Pagoda. When the door opened and the official alighted, the gateman bounded to his feet and commenced a series of frantic bows.

The stranger got up and lazily ambled over to the uniformed official, who said to him, "I see they've already made you welcome." And then ferociously to the gateman, he barked out, "Have you made this honored guest of the People's Republic welcome? Have you opened all doors, swept all the rooms, straightened the pillows on every bed?"

The gatekeeper gasped. The official drew himself to his full height. "Everywhere I go," he roared, "I am hindered by the muddy backwaters of bourgeois revisionism, and the laziness of people with slothful ways. There is only one way to deal with this! To water the ground with their blood!"

"Honored emissary of the sun—"

"Enough!" the official roared. "Must the Minister of

Agriculture of the People's Republic of the New China encounter insubordinance and disobedience at every turn?"

"Sir, I—"

"It is not for you to think, corrupt custodian of the fossils of the dead way of life. It is for you to work as hard as you can to change your retrograde mind into a gear that will go forward and onward."

"What shall I do?" the gateman whimpered. "Just tell me."

"At the far edge of this property there is a compound that used to belong to the Fong and the See families. As I am told by my informants, they lived here many years until they went to the United States to make their fortune. This property is attached to a hundred hectares which come up to the gates of the pagoda itself."

"Yes, sir, you are right! There has always been a circle of untilled fields around the pagoda."

"Go now," the official said ominously, "and do not presume to be carried in a litter like a gentleman of old. Walk honestly on your own two feet to the closest village. Inform the population that the grounds surrounding the pagoda and the grounds that extend from here to the banks of the Whangpoo, including the Fong-See enclave, have been turned, as of this moment and hour, into the Number Seventeen Millet and Soy Growing Outpost under the aegis of Comrade," and here he faltered, "Liang-fei 'Fertile Grain.'"

The gatekeeper looked at this mysterious visitor whose face was still partially hidden under his broad farmer's hat. "What shall you require for your evening meal, sir?" he quavered. "We are poor, but I shall scour the countryside for ducks and *foo-yi*."

"Absolutely not," the visitor said. "I shall require rice, and rice only. There shall be no feasting until all your village and you and I feast equally from our own crops. And do not prepare a large room for me. I shall require only a small outbuilding and a fire of my own."

Perhaps even more bewildered than before, the gatekeeper stared back and forth from one man to the other. The official clapped his hands.

"Is it my fate to wait all day?" he shouted. "Am I surrounded by donkeys that cannot even understand what it is to carry a load? Your new superior and I shall pace the fields that have fallen into such disgraceful disuse. If all is not ready when we return, we shall fertilize these fields with bonemeal. You need not ask whose bones they will be."

The gatekeeper ran off at a dead gallop on his hard, horny feet to relay this astounding news to his home village. Only then did the stranger raise his face and grin at the Minister of Agriculture. "Ah," he said, "this reminds me of old times. The honorable and noble son of the warlord Nyi Chuen-yao comes at last to restore order and decorum to the countryside, just like his father."

"As *your* father might say, I established righteousness in a good cause."

Chuen-yup snapped his fingers at his driver, who got down from the car and pulled out a few modest provisions— some steamed buns and rice wine. And then he unloaded a few cases of supplies—hurricane lamps and kerosene, a carton with cooking utensils, an idiosyncratic choice of Western groceries (stone-cut oatmeal, six cans of Boston clam chowder, oregano, peanut butter). From then on the unloading was more prosaic: hundred-pound sacks of seed—millet, wheat, Ethiopian tef, and drought-proof barley. Finally, two tin trunks, which held scientific data.

The two men ate in a companionable silence, which Matthew finally broke.

"There were times in Beijing when I thought you'd never be able to accomplish this."

Chuen-yup gazed at Matthew almost with fondness. No one had been more surprised than he when Matthew had turned up in the courtyard of his official home in Beijing explaining that he was a political exile and making the enigmatic announcement that he wanted to live out his life farming on Chinese soil. Common courtesy, as well as curiosity, had forced Chuen-yup to make Matthew a guest in his own home. What had started out as cautious exchanges, tinged with suspicion, had ended in many long nights spent over bottles of *mao tai*. Matthew had explained his ongoing agricultural experiments. He pointed out how China, so exploited over the centuries by the Western outsider, might benefit now by the small contributions that these agricultural breakthroughs might make. After only a few evenings of this, however, they had fallen to talking of the subject dearest to both their hearts—the headstrong, imperious Jordan Logan-Fisher, Bah-wha.

Delicately, Chuen-yup had queried Matthew on Jordan's

whereabouts and listened, unbelieving, to Matthew's story. "You're telling me now that she's coupling with that red-faced, masturbating capitalist?"

Drunk, Matthew would only say sadly, "I loved her, and I had her for only three months. You lived with her in the caves for ten years, and you don't even believe in love. What a waste!"

"We're two old bachelors now," Chuen-yup had said, "and we might as well get used to it."

"A woman is as slippery as a fish and just about as trustworthy. Now, when do I get my land?"

And Chuen-yup, out of the bonds of old acquaintance and a shared lost love, out of the certainty that Matthew loved China as much, or perhaps even more, than he, took the long-term gamble that these agricultural experiments might actually someday affect national production. Against the counsel of his advisers, he was able to find Matthew a patch of arable land.

Later that night, at Lungwha, after Chuen-yup had noisily motored away, Matthew stared into the tiny fire he had made from bits of thatch and twigs, alternating slugs of fiery *mao tai* with teaspoons of his precious store of peanut butter. His life had changed for good.

"Keep it up, Andy. Keep it up and keep running! That's it. The wind's taking it. Good, good, now let her out. Now turn around and watch. Good, son, great! Watch the wind take her. It's aerodynamics, don't you see? Once it catches the wind, a kite has nowhere to go but up. It's the same principle that makes a plane fly."

"I know how to fly a kite, two-headed snake!" Andrew whispered under his breath in the mountain dialect he was sure no one within three thousand miles could understand. Then, raising his tanned face, tossing back his white-blond hair, and giving his father a wide smile, he said, "Gee, Dad, this is fun! Where'd you ever manage to find a dragon kite anyway? The only ones you can find around here are those dumb triangle things and anyone can fly those."

"Tai-ling bought it for you when she went down to Chinatown this morning."

Andrew gazed at the slight, elegant woman dressed in white linen who watched them from the balcony of her beach house. "That's certainly very nice of Tai-ling."

His father also looked at the woman in white, and said, his voice suddenly thick, "You just run up and down here and fly the kite."

Andrew did as he was told for all of two minutes. Then he reeled in the kite, and after setting it quietly on the stairs leading up to the balcony, sneaked around the side of the house and hoisted himself up by one of the pylons. On tiptoe, he made his way around the narrow ledging that separated one story from another until he reached a high narrow window, well above the eye level of the people inside the house. He swung close, mashing his face against the glass, and peered down into the gloom.

There, in the half-light of the boudoir, the glamorous movie star Tai-ling had glued her painted lips on the red-veined and wrinkled skin between his father's thighs. Carefully holding on to the ledge with one hand, Andrew unzipped his pants and coarsely, quickly, whipped himself to his own conclusion.

Proud that he had beaten his dad in this contest, Andrew quietly and quickly retraced his steps. When Harley and Tai-ling brought brandies-and-soda out on to the balcony to enjoy the sunset, they were able to survey with pleasure the spectacle of Harley's son adroitly keeping the elaborate, long-tailed Chinese paper dragon high in the air.

"It's good to see," Harley said to his companion, "just how well the boy's adapted to our way of life."

"Monckton, dearest, I *know* you like the one with the dusty cliffs. But don't you see, since Mr. Beaver is redoing the drawing room in sheep's wool and chrome, we *have* to have some color. I prefer this picture of the peasant teaching his boy to fly a kite. Oh, darling, *do* say you like it. And there's no need to quarrel, is there? Because you can buy the dusty one for the snuggery."

In a far corner of the gallery, two dealers dickered. "Look here, Bosley, I'll take the whole crop of them off your hands for fifty thousand pounds straight up. I'll put them away in a vault for twenty years, and then bring them out for a real killing."

Arthur Thompson Bosley smiled enigmatically. "I have a good idea they'll be worth a good deal more than that. You're looking at these pictures from a historical perspective alone, but these are much more than pictures from a revolution. This is only one period, an early one, in the career of an artist whom I intend to back until the end of either her life or mine."

And indeed the paintings of Jordan Logan-Fisher seemed beyond any taint of vulgar, ephemeral publicity. These scrolls—caught sometimes in thrusting black and white and sometimes in the pastels of native dyes—spoke not only of a serious artist, but of a visionary, a prophet able to see into the deepest substrata of the world's experience.

Bosley, owner of this posh West End London gallery, priced all these pictures very high, but wisely marked the series on children as "Not For Sale." There was an aching sadness inherent in these pictures of the children of Yenan, a sadness that seemed to be the very heritage of displaced children everywhere. It had been argued through Paris, London, and Rome in the past three decades that there could be—except perhaps for Mary Cassatt—no major women artists because of their personal preoccupations with motherhood. But like Cassatt, Logan-Fisher had turned that liability into a stunning asset. There were those here tonight, sophisticated, jaded Londoners, persons of taste who felt they had seen it all. But it fell to the most worldly to be struck dumb at this spectacle of real experience wedded to perfect art.

For Jordan this moment—triumphant as it was—seemed oddly anticlimactic, or, more accurately, simply one point on a long continuum that began six months ago and stretched out to the end of what she had reason to believe would be a very long life. She knew that Bosley signed her to a lifetime contract because he sensed this resolution in her. She had deliberately taken a turn in her life, a turn that led through the valley of the shadow of death, and from it to a home that was waiting for her.

Several months before, Jordan's long car had crunched over the gravel of the driveway to The Beeches. Her mother, sensibly dressed in tweeds and wearing her best pearls, stood at the top of the flight of steps leading to the entry together with all the members of The Beeches' considerable staff. Her mother held her close for a moment and Jordan felt tears on her cheek, but all her mother said was, "Next time, my dear, I shall know better than to send you belowdecks unaccompanied."

Jordan's mother knew gallery owners, art lovers, and the best obstetrician in London. Jordan fell easily into a rigorous regimen. She worked all day and attented her mother's dinner parties at night. When her first showing came, it was essential that the right people be there to look and to buy.

In the midst of a day of painting, Jordan felt the first pangs of labor. She was at work on her kite-flying series, drawn from memories of Chuen-yup teaching their son. Chuen-yee had been too small to run fast enough to launch the delicate structure of bamboo and colored paper. Chuen-yup had lifted the kite, letting the boy think that he was doing it, and Jordan had striven through the hours of her labor to commit that gesture of parental concern to paper while tears streamed down her face and her mother and the servants clucked about her with cups of strong tea and admonitions to lie down and rest.

Even after the doctor arrived, Jordan kept him waiting while she worked, until she finally gave it up and staggered— like any Chinese peasant woman—into her room to give birth to her child. The boy burst from her within a matter of minutes.

"I couldn't get their faces," she sobbed to her mother. "They wouldn't come back to me."

But this would be the painting that critics would single out as an acknowledged masterpiece, and by the end of that day of suffering Jordan had found a new face to dote on, a tiny, wizened combination of her own and Matthew's features, a lusty little boy who began howling as soon as he hit the air.

Jordan stood now in a circle of awed admirers speaking of her work, but her attention, and her love, were focused primarily on the pram in a corner of the gallery. She had made mistakes, she knew, but Desmond—that was the name she had chosen—would profit from them. It is in our children, she thought, that our best dreams lie. We can only do so much. Surely they must surpass us.

It was this thought that she tried to explain to those experienced critics who found themselves touched by the apparent simplicity of a father building up his son's confidence so that in later years he might find the courage to move the world.

Book V

REVOLUTION
1967

The fog was a suffocating, damp blanket. It stopped up the nostrils and irritated the eyes. The northern moisture was tainted this early morning by the acrid effluvia of a major spill of crude oil, spread with the coming tide from a leaking tanker anchored offshore. The pungent oil washed up in black sticky ropes onto the sand outside the bay's entrance. Now, with each shift in the chilly waters, it crept farther into the calm clean bay itself.

On the end of Pier Fourteen in the heart of the industrial loading zones, two vigorous men in their early fifties tried to gauge the intensity of the slick. Between them a five-year-old girl, dressed for this morning's excursion in leggings, boots, and an emerald-green coat, looked up adoringly from one grandfather to the other.

"Horace, why don't we send a few of our smaller ships and let them unload the cargo at sea?"

"Harley, old buddy, you know a lot about business, but you don't know diddly squat about shipping. If we send freighters out there, they're going to be running into each other in this soup."

The two men discussed the arrival of the *Argonaut*, a freighter out of Djakarta by way of the Aleutians on its way to a final call at São Paulo. This was only one of a series of lucrative business interests that combined the ships of Horace Walton Westphall and the raw materials of his partner-by-marriage, Harley Compton Fitch.

Six years before, Pamela Westphall had married Andrew Fitch, and it had been the talk of San Francisco. Three years later, the alliance had faltered. Malicious whispers circulated about this *mariage de convenance*, but to the two patriarchs, the divorce was of almost no consequence. They could remain partners, and they enjoyed the almost unlimited company of their beloved granddaughter, Angela. Men of such power had few other men whom they could meet as equals, so they continued to enjoy their relationship.

"So why can't we just bring the ship in? Every hour it stands offshore we lose five thousand dollars!"

"Because, Harley," Westphall answered patiently, "it breaks up the oil in the slick. It spreads it to other ships. It would kill more birds—"

"We'll *pay* for the boats, and *fuck* the birds!"

"Grandpa!"

"Sorry, Angela."

"Besides, Harley, the harbor master has halted all shipping."

"You mean to tell me that guy's never heard of a bribe?"

"Not old Perkins. I've tried off and on for twenty years. He'd rather see California fall off the continent and sink into the sea than to bend one of his rules."

"Well, we'll just go ahead anyway! We don't need his permission!"

Horace clapped his partner on the back. "You don't, but I do. Shipping's my game. I can't afford to lose my docking priviledges in this bay. You're just a privateer at heart."

Harley took this as a compliment. "So what do you suggest, Captain?"

"Ever hear of L.A.? They've got a harbor down there too. We'll lose a few bucks, but we don't want to risk a head-on confrontation."

Their exchange was interrupted by impatient tugging.

"Grandpa! Grandpa!"

Harley swept his granddaughter up into his arms. What was a paltry hundred thousand compared to this precious angel? "What is it, sweetie?"

"Grandpa, look at that lady on the other dock. She's carrying a birdy all wrapped up in a blanket. Why's she doing that, Grandpa? Why? Why? I want to go see!"

The two men exhanged looks. "Not today, honey."

"But, *Grandpa*! I need to! I need to see what that lady is doing with that bird!"

"Don't you worry, little honey," Westphall said, "Grandpa Pushover will take you over there to see what's going on. I've got to get back to work." Horace gave his granddaughter a kiss, said good-bye to his partner, and disappeared into the fog.

"Grandpa Pushover" walked, with his granddaughter riding his shoulders, from the end of Pier Fourteen to the head of the adjacent one, where a rickety shed had been pressed into service as a makeshift first-aid station. Dozens of young people worked at what Harley perceived as a quixotic project. Out at the end of the pier, people leaned off into the water netting dead and dying birds from the slick.

The birds, immersed in oil, couldn't move, except to peck resentfully at their rescuers. In the shed, big tubs of detergent had been set up. Volunteers took the birds, dipped them in suds, and tried to wash them free of the goo, as if they had been recalcitrant children playing in the mud. An ever-growing pile of carcasses filled a corner of the shed.

"Let me down, let me down, let me *down*!"

Angela's feet beat a tattoo on Harley's chest until he had no choice. She slipped from his grasp and dodged between clumps of unkempt people. Distraught, Harley moved forward to retrieve the little girl.

An unwashed hippie put the heel of his hand squarely on Harley's chest and said, "Butt out, old man. People like you aren't wanted around here."

Harley reacted instinctively and pushed back, snarling, "You're the trespasser, asshole. I own this dock, that dock, and that dock."

A young woman in a shawl stepped forward. "If you're the one who owns all this, then you must be the one who's responsible! You're the one profiting from this disaster."

Harley tried to muster the arguments of common sense—that certainly there was no profit for him in an oil spill, that he hadn't planned it.

Little Angela came running out of the shed, her cheeks streaked with tears. In her arms she carried a dying tern, the holes in its beak clogged with oil, its eyes crusted shut with more Indonesian crude. Its head lolled back like a newborn infant's. Agonizingly, the bird still breathed.

"Grandpa, Grandpa, it's sick. They're all sick in there. You've got to make them well."

"He's done enough already," the hippie said.

Angela burst into a storm of tears. "Grandpa can fix anything he wants to. Isn't that right, Grandpa?"

Harley held his bearded adversary in a baleful stare. "You're absolutely right, honey! I can do anything I want. By lunchtime we'll be sure those birds of yours have a hospital."

Angela looked up. "See? I told you so!"

As Harley and his granddaughter turned to go up the dock, he became aware of a truly hellish sound, a chorus of high-pitched moans that sounded almost human—the birds calling in their makeshift first-aid station. Why doesn't somebody put them out of their misery? he thought irritably. Isn't that what you're supposed to do to a sick animal? Even I know that!

Once back in the comfort of his limousine, Harley reached over and patted his granddaughter on the cheek.

"All right, honey, we've seen one end of the business this morning, although I'm sorry our ship didn't come in. But you have to remember, the other side is just as important. And that's why we're going to a—"

"A board meeting," the little girl crowed. "Oh, I'm so excited! Will I get to see Uncle Max and Uncle Joshua and Uncle Tim?"

"Of course, honey, and your daddy will be there too. After the meeting he'll take you home."

The little girl absorbed that in silence. Finally she said, "Well, anyway, I bet we make a million dollars today."

With his granddaughter cuddled in his lap, Harley Fitch put the unpleasant moments of this trip from his mind, leaned back, and savored their trip through the streets of downtown San Francisco to the stately edifice that housed Compton Fitch Enterprises. Defying the earthquake doomsayers, Harley had been one of the first to coat a building in sheets of reflecting glass to a height so great that sometimes San Francisco clouds hid the Compton Fitch logo—a bat eating a beetle, modernized over the years into a filigree of abstracted circles.

A uniformed doorman opened the door of the limo. Three bodyguards lurked unobtrusively in the far shadows of the porte cochere. Harley looked cautiously around as he half hid Angela under his greatcoat and hustled her inside. The fear of kidnapping always haunted a family as wealthy and, in certain circles, as thoroughly hated as the Fitches.

They went in a side entrance reserved for VIPs. Out in front, at the main entrance, demonstrators had clogged the streets for days. The hippies were acting up again.

Harley and Angela rode up the private elevator and arrived in the board room just as the clock struck eleven. They joined the dozen directors of CFE, who had flown in from all over the world for this monthly gathering. Even though Harley and Angela were on time, the other had arrived at least a half hour early. God forbid that any one of them should be late.

Harley's affairs advanced swimmingly. CFE stock had gone up another three dollars a share in the last month. Financial analysts attributed this to the escalation of the war in Vietnam, and in part this was true. But Harley always kept his interests diversified. Almost nothing could happen in the world without his company making a profit. Whether a house was built, or a child born, or a gun fired it was all grist to the CFE mill.

As the meeting droned on in a steady hum of masculine voices, a small piping voice trilled in accompaniment. "Uncle Tommy, have you missed me? Can I sit in your lap, Uncle Josh, if I'm quiet?"

Most of these dour tycoons had seen fit to include in their thousand-dollar briefcases a tiny toy rabbit or a miniature coloring book. Joshua Van Ransaeller III topped them all today by having had the foresight to bring not one but two trinkets for his darling—a diminutive kaleidoscope no bigger than a cigar, which kept her completely entranced for at least twenty minutes, and one of the new-fangled Chelsea Morning Crystals that caught the rays of the sun and turned them into bright bands of red, yellow, and blue. Since little Angela was no saint, she saved this toy until her father began to speak, casting the bars of light against his handsomely chiseled face, his fashionable new-age mustache, and even into his glinting blue eyes—not often enough to provoke a reaction, she knew him too well for that—but often enough to bring a grin of amusement to her adored grandfather's face.

"I've been asked to report on the state of the demonstration and what they have been pleased to call a 'vigil' outside the main doors of the company for the last seven and a half weeks." Andrew shook his head impatiently as the light caught his eyes. "My figures show that the crowd has never exceeded two thousand demonstrators, except on weekends. There have never been less than three hundred even in the hours between midnight and four in the morning. There's been absolutely no littering. They request that we divest ourselves of our chemical division. They confine themselves to a single comment to our workers as they come into the building, and that is"—here Andrew grimaced—"'You look way too nice to melt children for money.'"

"They may have a point," Joshua Van Ransaeller interrupted, resting his jowly chin on top of Angela Fitch's auburn curls. "I'm talking about public perception of CFE. How can we expect to sell consumer goods to these people ten years from now when—"

"Poppycock and balderdash," Tim Holt said stuffily. "CFE has made its name by doing business in the present and this country is at war in the present. We can't go off on some harebrained Utopian scheme—"

"Andrew," Harley said, "just what percentage of our interests are tied up in the chemical division?"

"Seventeen point nine," Andrew answered like a shot. "But twelve percent of that is in bacteriological research that has absolutely no bearing on Vietnam. It's obvious to all of us, I'm sure, that these figures should not go outside this room."

"What do you think about it, Andrew?" his father asked with deceptive amiability. "What do you think we ought to do?"

His son's face froze. "I'm afraid I don't have either the expertise or the power to make that kind of decision. I have to leave that up to you."

"Andrew!" Harley leaned forward, putting his elbows on the table. For the moment he stopped baiting and testing his son. "Andrew, what I want you to do in the next couple of weeks is to see if you can get to know some of those demonstrators on a more personal basis. Learn what their policies are, and how we line up on their list of enemies. Are we just a token corporation that will look good on the six o'clock news, or do they really have it in for us? At next month's meeting we'll be better equipped to discuss what's best for us to do in terms of the company as a whole."

"Yes, sir." Andrew snapped his briefcase shut. Of all the assembled men he was the only one who had not brought a toy for Angela. And he was the only one whose lap she avoided.

Almost as an afterthought, as the other members of the board filed out, Harley stood over his son, dictating in an undertone. "A couple of other things need to be taken care of. In case of future bombing, we'll be wanting to liquidate our assets in Cambodia and put them over into Brunei. And see if you can find about two hundred thousand in petty cash and a building somewhere around here. Angela's been worried about the birds that have been dying in the oil spill. . . ."

Harley picked up Angela and tousled her curls. "See, honey, Grandpa told you he'd do something about it and he did." In a lower, more indifferent voice, he addressed his son again. "Find a couple of ornithologists and get a TV crew in there. We ought to get some good out of that. Our little princess has a great head for business."

Then Harley and Angela toddled off to spend the afternoon in Grandpa's office, putting through phone calls to see if indeed they could, in Angela's words, "make a million dollars today."

Goddamn little brat, Andrew thought as he walked back to his office. He knew that as a father he should love his little girl and he supposed that at some level he did—about as much as his mother had loved him. It was not simply that Angela was a miniature of her now-famous grandmother, Jordan Logan-Fisher. . . .

The old man managed, with his usual acquisitiveness, to undermine Andrew's authority with the child. Even Pamela, the girl's own mother, was not allowed a say about Angela when Harley was around. In his darker moments, Andrew felt that Harley not only alienated Angela's affection, but had destroyed his marriage as well. He constantly promised his son a full partnership and reneged on his promise time and again. Pamela watched her husband repeatedly bested in family confrontations and corporation politics. No wonder she stopped responding to him as a woman. To take on Harley Fitch was, *de facto*, to lose.

Now, as always, Andrew was alone—orphaned by his parents and ignored by his child.

He went into his office closet, took off his three-piece suit, pulled out Levi's washed to the desired shade of pale blue and a surplus work shirt that had undergone the same treatment. He reached into a small refrigerator, took out a Coors, then sauntered to the mirror in his dressing room and appraised the face—full of frustration and discontent—that looked coldly back at him.

His father's idea of dressing him up as someone who might

pass in the hippie community was distasteful, but it would probably work. Since he was almost thirty, he marveled that his face, once thought to be so ugly that people turned away and hissed at it, was considered handsome. He looked like an aging surfer. Thirty! Kids today said that you couldn't trust anyone over thirty. When his dad turned thirty he owned half the world. That was the rub.

Andrew opened a small drawer and pulled out a handful of trinkets his secretary had bought for him in the Haight-Ashbury district—a "peace symbol" on a leather thong, a string of beads that had probably been made in a progressive nursery school, and a feather choker. His secretary said with a simper that she bought it because the feathers matched the color of his eyes. He knew he could have fucked her right there on the desk, but just the thought of it tired his back. He let his forefinger caress those fine blue feathers. He picked up the choker, tied it around his neck, looked in the mirror, and, even in his foul mood, had to grin. He looked outrageous. He looked fine.

He finished a beer, opened another, and, enjoying the slight cloud of mellowness that the beer gave to his bad temper, walked purposefully to the VIP elevator. He stepped out the side door, barely nodded to the security guards, and strolled around the corner, making his way up the long block that marked the boundaries of the vast CFE building to where the demonstration had been going on peacefully for days.

Four out-of-tune folk singers finished up to a smattering of applause. A boy in his early teens, with a harmonica hitched around his neck in the manner of the artfully tousled Bob Dylan, got up, blew a few tentative notes, and was gently hustled back down the stairs. His turn would come later. Now, in time to catch some of the workers going in and out of the building, they chose to put on a speaker who, Andrew thought, looked strangely familiar. . . . The spokesman appeared to be just a few years younger than Andrew, but the similarites ended there. Where Andrew was muscled, this man-boy was delicately formed, tall and slim. He tossed his head carelessly as he talked and his thick mane of black hair brushed the bottom of his shoulder blades. He spoke softly, stringing his words on a fine wire of emotional intensity. He was a spellbinder. Dumpy secretaries paused as they made their way down the steps of CFE in cheap high-heeled shoes and turned their youthful faces to listen to this stranger's message.

"They call us flower children," he said. "They call us the generation of love. Those phrases are nothing but clichés, and only fools would march to their destinies by those catchwords. We've been singing for weeks now. We've been talking. We have had love-ins, be-ins, teach-ins. And, yes, we dress a certain way and we talk a certain way, but we all have the same body underneath our clothes. We all have hearts and lungs. We all want to be loved by our parents. *No!*" he said, to the few who snickered. "We may think we hate them, but we want their love. We'd be lying to say otherwise. . . ."

"What shit," Andrew grated.

"Sometimes it's hard to remember why we're standing here. We're here because this company sells chemicals. It sells them to the military. It sells them to people who drop them in bombs on people exactly like you and me."

"Whaddya sayin', butt-fucker? You sayin' we're like a bunch of gooks?" Andrew recognized a delivery man from the mail room. "My brother's in 'Nam! He says gooks ain't worth shit!"

Right on! Andrew thought, but the speaker silenced the heckler with a gesture that might have come from a pulpit. "All of us are afraid of people who seem different from what we are, but at least you have the courage to say it."

The speaker waved to a tired typist on the edge of the crowd. "Do you think I'm not scared to death of you? Do you think I don't *envy* you, with your job and your skill? Why do you think I wear my hair like this? To be scary, that's why!"

He had the crowd nodding in agreement by now. "Yes, it's silly. Just because somebody wears a straw hat, and carries water on a pole, that's not a good reason to fry him like an egg."

Andrew felt his gorge rise. That was *exactly* the reason to fry them. He could listen to no more. His handmade boots clicked sullenly on the pavement as he hurried back around the block and ducked into his waiting limo. He opened the bar in the backseat and poured himself a huge slug of Scotch. Why was he so angry?

He had been lectured at length, over hours, weeks, days, *years*—by his school friends, girlfriends, even his wife, Pamela—on the subject of "everything." You have everything, they kept telling him, everything you could possibly want or need. You have your penthouse, your yacht, your limo, your Santa Barbara ranch, your lovely wife, your beautiful child. And you're bound to inherit everything, anyway! When your father dies, you could be one of the richest men in the world.

It was true. He had everything—except power. He existed as a figurehead. No one actually listened to him when he proposed one of his ideas. Everyone acted polite, but he knew it came from fear of crossing someone who carried the Fitch name. His father was not afflicted with that fear. He would sit through any proposal of Andrew's, sometimes not even acknowledge it, but simply go on with what he had been talking about. Yes, Andrew thought, it always came back to his father.

It had been a mistake to let anyone get close to him in the first place. Pamela seemed a decent-enough person, but when he began to confide in her late at night, to expose the wounds of his childhood, expecting some kind of healing comfort, she had drawn back. "It's time to forget all that, Andy," she would say. "Look at what you—we—have. And anyway, that was ages ago."

As far as he was concerned it was as fresh in is mind as if it had happened yesterday. And none of them understood.

Andrew tapped on the glass. "I won't be going home yet. Take me to the Buena Vista." He sat back. In the old days, if you wanted sex without paying for it, you had to "sell" yourself—your good looks, your manners, your promise of special performance, shared pleasure, perhaps, even later, affection. At the very least, you had to buy them dinner. Now, with this sexual revolution, women were as easy to come by as the free dinners the Diggers, those new radicals who saw money as energy, gave away every night down on the Panhandle, and just about as appetizing. He went to parties in the Haight, where dumpy women in caftans said in a normal conversation, "Anyone want to ball?" It was a mark of the times that there were no takers.

He preferred, now, to hunt among the straitlaced, if he could find any. That way a challenge remained, something to overcome. That was the reason he chose the Buena Vista.

Tossing back a couple of Irish coffees on top of his Scotch, he approached a shy woman at the end of the long bar. They exchanged remarks about the fog, the superiority of San Francisco over Los Angeles, her job as a legal secretary. Her name was Wilma. He asked her if she was hungry, but she said she was on a diet and would prefer just another Irish coffee. Andrew felt his dark spirits lightening. They had two more drinks. As the after-work crowd began to empty out in search of dinner, he said, "I've got a nice place near here with a great view of the harbor. What would you say to . . ."

She smiled up at him, then whispered in his ear, "I don't go anywhere without my girlfriend." He looked around, and three places down the bar saw a slim and friendly-seeming blonde in a pretty print dress.

"Bring her along," he said thickly, in a guilty rush of anticipation. "The more the merrier."

Eight ounces of caviar and a bottle of champagne later, the great view had been pretty well forgotten. Andrew found himself spread-eagled, flat on his back on his own bed. He had scarcely had a chance to undress himself as the four hands of the two girls fumbled over buttons and dealt with the zipper of this trousers. They seemed to gain skill as they went on, pulling off his shoes, stripping his socks, until he was mother-naked. Now their hands stimulated him without mercy, jabbing their fingers into his anus, whipping his cock back and forth like a pump handle, jamming their tongues into his mouth, both at the same time—a feat he would not have thought possible without experiencing it.

They pinned him to his own sheets. His cock was relentlessly ridden by the brunette, who whooped like a cowgirl, and the demure blonde sat on his face. Her crotch gave off an animal odor not cut by any perfume. "That's *good*," she said, "that's the idea!" Then, turning back to her companion, she said, "Lucille, you've got to try this—but not yet!"

An hour later, Andrew lay propped up on his pillows with some medicinal champagne. He felt as if he'd been to the dentist. His face, his whole body, had been stretched, pummeled, and had grown swollen.

Sitting shyly at the end of the bed, the girls, each having pulled a Brooks Brothers shirt out of his closet, held their knees up under their chins, munched caviar on toast points, got crumbs on his bed, and told him their story.

They were each barely seventeen, and that's why they dressed "grown up." They had been school friends in Yuma, Arizona, and had gone together in 120-degree heat last summer to buy the Rolling Stones album *High Tides and Green Grass*. Together, in a stifling back bedroom on the edge of town, Lucile and Wilma had listened to Mick Jagger sing, "Let's spend the night together," and decided to take him up on his invitation.

They took after-school jobs for the rest of the summer, saved every penny, and in February, after having collected every possible Christmas gift ("Stones albums or money, please"), they boarded the bus for L.A. They carried plaster of Paris in a separate suitcase to make casts of the cocks of the musicians they slept with. L.A. was a dead town, they told him, but they had good times with Canned Heat, who had asked them to be permanent "boogiers," the Rivingtons—it really was true that some black men were bigger—and met up with Spirit in Topanga Canyon.

"So we heard Mick was up here, and we just got off the bus, and everyone said we should go to the Buena Vista for Irish coffee!"

Andrew realized with a sick feeling that they planned to stay the night. "You don't belong here," he said, "I think you belong down in the Haight."

"Don't you want us to do a cast? It'll be a keepsake!"

"I'll remember you," he assured them. He went into the kitchen, filled a sack with oranges, vitamin pills, and packages of instant cocoa. Then he pressed a hundred-dollar bill into each of their too-familiar hands, and phoned down to this chauffeur to take them away, *please*.

After shutting the door, he looked for a few moments at his famous view, illuminated now by streetlights, the beams of moving cars, and the eerie glow of dock-bound ships. He slumped into a chair and turned on the TV. It was only eight-fifteen. He sat through *Daktari* and *Mod Squad*.

At ten o'clock the phone rang. He was almost too drunk to talk, but Pamela didn't reproach him for it.

"Angela's birthday is coming up," she said, "and you know how all of our parents feel about that. So, I'm giving a birthday party. You don't have to do anything. I just want you to write the date down. It's on May the eleventh, and it will be on my father's lawn. It's a zoo theme. There'll be animals in cages. Andy? Are you listening? Are you writing this down?"

"Pamela," he said, "I've got a great view over here. Wanna come and look at the boats?"

"Andrew, please . . ."

"The television is nice. The ten o'clock news comes up any minute. You don't want to miss out on that."

"Andrew, have you heard me?"

"Okay," he said. "If you don't want to come over, be sure to save a trapeze for me in the monkey house."

He heard the receiver go down at the other end of the line. Dutifully, he wrote down, *May 11. Westphall Lawn. Afternoon. Zoo*.

* * *

Tai-ling put down the phone and turned to Harley. "Your ex-daughter-in-law certainly observes the proprieties. Pamela's as considerate of me as if she and Andrew were still married, as if you and *I* were married!"

"What did she want at this hour?" Harley lounged in silk pajamas in Tai-ling's penthouse living room watching the fog come in through the Golden Gate. The remains of a late-night snack littered a silver tray. With the remote control, Harley flicked off the sound of the ten o'clock news.

"Is this my wild lover, who worries about people calling after ten o'clock at night?" She laughed at him fondly. "You know, she's probably called your place several times, and only phoned here as a last resort. It's about Angela's birthday party. . . ."

"Does she think we'd *forget*?"

"Harley, she's just a little nervous. This is a big party, after all. Angela is going to be five. And I think in any family, after a divorce, there's even more concern."

"More concern than that son of mine ever showed in his life about anything."

Tai-ling, who had been at such pains to make excuses for Pamela Westphall, let this slight to Andrew go unanswered. What had started out so promisingly sixteen years before—the unconventional triad of Harley, Tai-ling, and Andrew—had been sabotaged far less by the taboo of incest than by Andrew's seething discontent. Tai-ling had long ago given up trying to make peace between him and his father. On the other hand, she was fully aware that Harley, having amassed his vast empire, and still in the very prime of life, mulishly refused to give any of his holdings to his son.

Harley had insisted that Andrew start from the bottom, as box boy, mail boy, gofer. He subjected Andrew to endless, maundering lectures on the history of the company, from its dim New England beginnings to its growing importance in Shanghai, the accomplishments of Harley Compton Fitch II, the ruthless merchant prince of the Orient who had loved the East even as he plundered it. Harley expounded, countless times, on the history of the company logo. A bat symbolizes good luck and prosperity to the Chinese mind, and with sturdy commerce, a bat will always eat the beetles of everyday troubles and pain. . . . Harley promoted his son to assistant manager. To junior vice president. And now to Information

Officer in Charge of Public Relations. It was a meaningless title for a meaningless job, and both father and son knew it.

Like a boxer feinting in an empty ring, Harley expected Andrew to challenge him, to fight him for his share of the spoils. But Andrew sulked like a girl: *Give it to me!* was his silent, unmistakable message. Tai-ling usually blamed this churlishness on the fact that the boy had been raised by the arrogant Jordan Logan-Fisher. On other occasions she dismissed the whole problem: Andrew was simply an awful person with serious personality defects, but it wasn't her business.

Tai-ling's life for the past sixteen years had been embroidered in a careful pattern of her own creation. She had found a man whom she loved passionately, and he returned her love. She lived now in a material monument to that attachment. The Sea Gate Towers, the most exclusive luxury apartment building in the city, had been built with twin penthouse towers separated by a hanging garden that cascaded from an elaborate sky-walk. Harley lived in the west tower, Tai-ling in the east. Tai-ling told herself—had been telling herself for years—that no one really guessed at their liaison. Each evening Harley went "home," to the west elevator of the Sea Gate, then came out on the roof and walked to the east penthouse, where, like a good Chinese wife, Tai-ling waited with dinner. They were meticulous about thier social life. If on a Tuesday they went together to the opera, on a Thursday they would attend a banquet separately. It was imperative that the world never guess they were lovers. But neither of them resorted to "beards"; Tai-ling told him she would kill him if she found him with another woman, and Harley could not bear for her even to speak to another man.

Most of their evenings were spent in the delicious monotony of sex. Neither of them could get enough of the other. Each of them lived in theoretical dread that the world might thrust them apart again. And yet that was foolish. After sixteen years, they were both in middle age. Here she was, having just put down the phone from a conversation with Andrew's ex-wife, and Harley, who an hour before had been a demanding lover in bed, was watching the news and grumping like any grandfather.

"I know you've ordered the cages," Tai-ling said, "but have you arranged for the animals? Have you checked with Pamela's father that everything will be ready?"

When the Westphalls had decided on a zoo theme, Harley knew that the appropriate gift to his beloved grandchild would be a miniature zoo, the beginnings of one at least. For the past few weeks his transoceanic business calls had included arrangements for small, exotic animals, one for each of Angela's years: a koala from the Australian outback, a spider monkey from Malaysia, a miniature sloth from Burma, a Tasmanian devil, and a San Francisco ground squirrel.

"It's all taken care of," Harley told her, but Tai-ling fretted.

"There's something missing in all this," she said. "A little girl wants to open presents!"

"You're not suggesting that I call a paper mill for enough tissue to *wrap* those beasts!"

"Don't be silly, darling. I just think . . ." Tai-ling, who had been sitting on the chaise across from him, got up to go into her bedroom.

"You stay right there," she said, and returned in a moment with an enormous jewel box.

"What Angela needs," Tai-ling said, "are little things, baubles, presents that she'll like now, and that in later years will come to mean something special to her. Five little boxes, one for each year."

She sorted through a tray, while Harley, reclining across from her, gave himself up to a familiar pleasure—a combination of drink, soft lights, sensual satiation, and the pure aesthetic appreciation of watching his beloved in the act of being beautiful.

One after another she held up tiny treasures for his inspection. "My mother gave me this ring when I won honors in English at the True Heart School." She smiled wickedly. "A man who rescued me from a Sikh gave me this gold chain one afternoon. I do wonder what became of him. And I think my father gave me this baby bracelet. . . ."

"This is the end/My only friend, the end. . . ." The Doors wailed about incest and the end of the world, but the sound was curiously satisfying, the atmosphere domestic. The old house on Telegraph Hill was chockablock with residents and guests. Dinner had been cooking for the past five or so hours. The air was thick with incense and marijuana. On one wall Day-Gloes of the Dead, the Airplane, and Jimi Hendrix glimmered. On the opposite wall more images called for a sterner, different set of values: *What have you done to improve the world today?* Gandhi seemed to ask, one finger held up in Christ-like benediction. Malcolm X glowered; Martin Luther King looked pensive.

Beneath all these household gods, a half-dozen bra-less girls scurried, dressed in madras bedspreads made into saris, dresses dripping ribbons, even some army surplus pants and jackets, robbed of their militarism by haphazard clusters of buttons that stated *Make love, not war* and *What if they gave a war and nobody came?*

But just as in any household, the men sat in the living room and waited to be served. Stokely Carmichael said that "the only position in the movement that women could fill was the prone position," and his audience roared in agreement.

The intoxicating thing about being alive in 1967 in San Francisco, the very epicenter of this new revolution of youth, was that no one really knew what anyone's correct position was. One knew that an unconscionable war dragged on in the jungles of Vietnam; one knew that tasting a tab of a certain invisible chemical could plunge you into a deeper eternity than anyone ever dreamed possible; one knew that truth and love stalked the streets, but that death was not far behind; one knew that a shining new world was being created, and that the people who lived in this apartment were among those building this world.

Finally, at ten-thirty, dinner was served out of wooden bowls on the living-room floor. Earlier, food had been taken in huge tin pots to those keeping vigil all night on the steps of CFE. The girls who had put together the repast were understandably proud. It was vegetable curry—quite tasty—over brown rice. The rice had been given away today at one of the Haight's free stores. For the rest, the girls foraged in the garbage bins of supermarkets.

"Sunshine stood outside the bin while Johanna just jumped inside and shut the lid and used her flashlight. Did you know that more green things get thrown away than anything else, and those are the things that are *good* for you?"

"A guy caught us and wanted us to throw them back in," Johanna said, "but Sunshine just waved some spinach in his face. "'You want it so bad, *you* eat it,' she said."

Paul Granger, sitting quietly at the center of the group of men in the living room, responded, "I'm not so sure if it's right to make them feel shame. People aren't happy if they have to act out of a sense of shame."

But Sunshine curled her lip. "We got the spinach, and the broccoli and the carrots, and everyone here tonight is eating well because of it." She stood in front of Paul Granger and held his bowl just out of his reach. "Listen to *this*, my friend! Johanna and I went to another supermarket and while she was begging for some curry powder, I *stole* two jars of chutney, stuck them right in my blouse where people would think they were my knockers. So . . . are you hungry or not?"

"I'm sure you dealt a telling blow to the capitalist system," Paul said lightly, "and I'm sure you contributed to our happiness by the skill with which you prepared this, okay?"

He took the bowl from her, but she didn't budge until he took up his spoon and dug in. Sunshine Liebowitz had been *Rachel* Liebowitz until ninety days ago when she'd moved in. Paul Granger, who had put in his time at Sunday school, and who had a grandfather who had been a Presbyterian missionary to the heathen Chinese, knew all too well the New Testament story of Martha and Mary.

"One side can't exist without the other," he said.

Sunshine stared at him. "Huh?"

"We can't think, we can't act, we can't change the system unless we have the energy to do it. And human beings get their energy from food. To put food in another person's mouth is to contribute just as surely as to act, or pray."

Dazed, she still stood before him.

"To contribute *good* food," he said gravely, "is to act with love. And this curry is excellent. Thank you."

"Uh, thank *you*, too." When Rachel-Sunshine Liebowitz returned to the kitchen, she hugged Johanna and Jill and Rain and Marina. "He likes it! I knew he would. It's my mother's recipe."

Out in the main room, they talked about energy.

"They were right to take those vegetables," said a boy who liked to be called Fast Eddie. "Those vegetables were an insufficently used product. If the system tightened its belt, humanity's work load could be cut in half."

"What then?" said a young man named Simon Dale, who had studied economics in his first and only year at the universtiy. "Then you have the problem of unused leisure time. . . ."

"Let the leisure take care of itself. Put lysergic acid in the urban water systems. *That's* not the problem!"

A fatuous environmentalist spoke up next: "Forget the

people! The trees were here first. Pressed cardboard along with synthetic gasoline will put the ecosystem into balance. We can live off existing sawdust for the next fifty years. Experiments show that furniture made of pressed cardboard from sawdust thrown into the Colorado River—"

"Lasted eighteen hours. Or *more!*" several of them chorused sourly.

"Well? Just because I've said it before doesn't mean it isn't true."

"You're absolutely right," Paul Granger said. "We have to keep in mind all the possibilities. Energy takes all kinds of forms. It's not just things like electricity and oil and steam power. The most important kind of energy comes from the mind." He gestured to the picture of Krishna Murti on the wall. "That's why we've got him up there. He's a transcendental spirit. He shows us a new kind of energy. I had a grandfather I never met who was a missionary in China. He spent his last years in a Japanese concentration camp. His favorite story from the New Testament was the miracle of the loaves and the fishes."

"I'm Jewish," Fast Eddie quipped. "Fill me in."

"Five loaves, Eddie, two fishes, and as many people out there on the mountain to listen to this prophet who had as many new ways of doing things as there are at any be-in. They were too far outside of town to go for food, and they were hungry. So . . . Jesus *thought* about it, and after a while everybody had enough to eat, from two covered baskets of loaves and fishes."

"I hate fish," Fast Eddie said morosely. "Does the New Age have to have fish in it?"

"What we need now," Paul said, "is to get a sense of what our purpose—not just our policy—should be. Our real job is to change the direction the human spirit is taking. That's the only thing that will make political solutions work. My mother is a senator and I'm very proud of her, but I'm convinced that as long as she keeps working on the material plane alone, she'll be incapable of effecting any real changes. We have to disengage from material life! We really do have to remember that we are children, not necessarily of some god with a beard, but of the universe. We are orphans on this earth! My stepfather is successful on the wordly plane. He is an anchorman on television. But he can only *report* the universe."

By this time two joints had been lit and were making their

way about the circle in opposite directions. The girls finished their work in the kitchen and clustered around the entrance of the main room with a joint of their own. Someone put on a Ravi Shankar record. With his first deep inhalation, Paul recognized that he was as much a victim of his own enthusiasm as the man who wanted a world full of cardboard furniture.

He was a man who was searching for goodness as assiduously as any desert saint who ever wandered in the wilderness in search of a cranky God. He was also—and half the time he got the two completely mixed up—a son in search of his father. Paul had grown up contented with his mother and her second husband, Bill Tarkington. Paul knew he was lucky to be of America's privileged class, and he was intensely proud when his mother ran for the Senate—and won. She was a natural politician, like her father before her. There were never any family secrets. He and his sister, Joyce, knew they had another, a "real," father, but Bill had been there for both of them, and so affectionately that Paul never felt the need to find out more.

Last summer at the tag end of a somnolent family picnic, Paul had astounded them by announcing that he wasn't going back to college.

"Not *going*? Not going back to school?"

"Oh, Mother, he just thinks he's being a nonconformist. It's just a stage. Don't pay any attention to him." Joyce had gotten up with great dignity and left the room. She was home for the weekend from Bennington, and Paul found her almost unbearable, a stupid caricature of all the worst traits of their mother.

But when he was alone with Valerie and Bill, he'd almost wished for Joyce's protection. His mother badgered him about his lack of ambition, his "idealism," and until that night he never realized that she held idealism in such low esteem. She'd grown more distraught until finally, as a trump card, she said, "But what about the war? If you're not enrolled in a university, you'll be drafted."

He had pronounced the unforgivable words "I just won't go, that's all. I'll go to Canada. They can't make me do something I don't want to do."

For the first time in his life he saw his mother lose her composure. She picked up a heavy pigeon made of Steuben glass and hurled it at him with all her strength. He ducked, and it whizzed past to shatter against the wall.

"You're just like your father!" she'd cried. "A *coward*, a . . ." And she had run from the room.

Bewildered, he'd looked to his stepfather for some kind of explanation. As always, he came through. "Your father was a complex man, Paul. When he went before the Un-American Activities Committee, he showed great courage."

The next day he took his stepson down to his television newsroom. The two of them spent the morning running old film clips. Afterward, there was little to say. Paul was stunned to discover his real father—if only in bits and pieces of celluloid images—and the specter of evil that McCarthy represented.

"What really happened?" he asked. "Where did my father go?"

"Valerie's father kept in touch with him for a long time before your grandfather died. I have a hunch that Matthew probably went to the Orient, but in this family no one ever talks about it. If your mother has ever heard from him, she's never told me."

"I've got to find him!"

"I knew this day would come, Paul. I can only wish you luck. I do know that the man who framed Matthew does business out of San Francisco. Harley Fitch was always insanely jealous of your father. If anyone in the world knows where he is, Fitch does. Whether he'll tell you is another question."

"I'm going to San Francisco. I'm going tonight!"

"No! You can't do that to your mother. I won't allow it. You'll graduate from college and go to graduate school. She won't like that, but she'll understand it. And you will not discuss this with her, ever again."

His stepfather put a hand on his shoulder and said, "I have to speak to you as a man. This was never a simple political fight. There was another woman involved. Your mother always felt that your father was in love with someone else. That's why the glass pigeon almost put you out of your misery last night. Not to be loved enough—that's something a woman never gets over. I don't care if she's a senator, I don't care if she's President of the United States!"

So Paul took civics classes in his last year at Wesleyan. He graduated and headed west, to find Harley Compton Fitch, and then his father. He found a country in revolution, torn apart by its youth—a generation that chose to avoid an unjust war, or at least protest against it. He came to San Francisco and found a new society burrowing up out of the confines and strictures of the old. He watched theater in trucks, ate free food on street corners, and listened to the Grateful Dead at Fillmores East and West. He dropped acid; in the last few years he had learned that far more people than just himself thought of Harley Compton Fitch as the embodiment of evil— or at least of error—in the world.

Paul looked around. He, more than anyone else in this room, saw that his personal search and his larger quest were inextricably combined: to show Compton Fitch Enterprises the error of its ways, to find his father, who had taken a stand against evil once, and ask him what to do next. That would take a miracle, but he had come this far. He knew he could do the rest.

The smoke had overcome him. . . .

"Nevertheless," he said, continuing his conversation, "nevertheless, we must continue to work on this earthly plane until the Man comes with the two covered baskets of loaves and fishes. We have these things to talk over." And in the next few hours they dreamily discussed how their own energies should be spent: Cesar Chavez was having trouble with his strike in the Central Valley, several of them would make trips down there and picket; the girls should boycott lettuce even in the rubbish bins, and make lettuce cairns outside supermarket doors. An organization called United Orphans Relief asked them for money and help; they would withhold both, since without the war there would be no orphans, and to support the orphans would be to give credence and legitimacy to the war itself. But everyone living in this house would take turns working at the aid stations set up to care for the birds caught in the oil slick. And they would continue the demonstration at CFE, but they would do everything they could to keep it peaceful.

The pictures of Jimi and Krishna Murti and Martin and even Malcolm seemed to gaze down on them with approval. Someone put hash oil in this joint. Paul looked at the face next to his. Someone turned the lights down. He could hear the music on his skin. The record changed. George Harrison: "Turn off the lights, relax and float downstream/This is not dying, this is not dying." Tiny sparkles bounced off the teeth in the face next to his. He caught one, and stuck it in his own mouth. He would get closer to those sparkles, catch them, swallow them, and he did. His soul shivered and giggled, his arms, a hundred of them, reached out for the soul next to his. For a moment he hoped that the girls had come in to be a part of this circle. Then he forgot, and surrendered to the cosmic jokes that the universe was forever telling. All you had to do was listen, and catch the burning sparks.

"Yams! I shall not be able to face the people in the village when they hear of this latest abomination, this crime against nature and the human digestive tract!"

Matthew Granger listened tolerantly to this outburst from Lu Wei-fu, formerly caretaker of the Lungwha Pagoda near Shanghai. He recognized the joke that had grown between them for—could it really be that long?—the last sixteen years. Since they were spending the morning in calculation (how many hectares to be given to sorghum, to millet, to winter wheat, and now, to yams), and since Matthew had the abacus in his hand, he nimbly counted the years he had spent in China. He was fifty-one now. *How could such a thing have happened*? He had, *click*, spent his first seventeen years in China, then, *click, click*, four years at Stanford, three at Oxford. And, *click*, eleven years in Washington, and then, the last sixteen years of his life as administrator of the Fong-See compound by Lungwha, one *li* from the brown tidal waters of the Whangpoo. That meant he was Chinese at last. Only eighteen years of his life in the West and thirty-three years here. If his father were alive, he might have something to say about *that* number!

"I see that you must be ashamed, too, since you offer no excuses for this beggar's food you plan to grow," Old Lu insisted.

"Now, Old Father, you know that's exactly what you said when I began to grow millet. You said it was fit only for half-tamed northern barbarians. But what is it I see you eating with obvious pleasure each day for your early morning breakfast?"

"I knew you would throw that back in my face," Old Lu said. "Before you came, I used to be a man of taste and refinement. I ate white rice and meat once a week. My name drew respect when I went into the village. But now, I have grown used to ridicule."

Matthew recognized a reference to the first difficult months of his stay at this then-deserted, uncultivated Fong-See holding. In those days, and nights, there had been no jokes. Lu avoided him, except when he was sent for. He persisted (in spite of any talk of a "revolution") in addressing Matthew as *Si-sang*—"Professor"—to his face, and "the Crazy White Earthworm" behind his back. When Matthew went into the village of Lungwha—no more than fifteen one-story buildings with one teahouse and one butcher shop—every building appeared empty, as abandoned as the farm he had taken possession of. The handful of villagers remained behind locked doors.

He had sent Lu to buy provisions, knowing that the villagers' fear of foreigners stemmed from the brutality of the recent Japanese occupation and their equally fierce resentment of the international community in the nearby city of Shanghai. Westerners had started with the Opium Wars, forcing "foreigners' mud" upon the people, extracting China's wealth, and leaving miserable poverty behind. No wonder they regarded each of Matthew's new ideas, even now, with despair and outrage only slightly blended with trust and humor.

Yes, he had sent Lu, sixteen years ago, ordering unpolished rice for food and asking if there were men of the village for hire to work his fields. No one, however poor, however desperate, came forward. Lu had delivered these messages, standing at attention, his teeth clenched, to *Si-sang*. When Matthew invited the old man to sit down while making his report, Lu refused, or ignored the request. Matthew stood, talking on and on about crops and plowing until Lu fled.

In those early weeks, Matthew occupied his time until the first sowing by whitewashing the inside of his tiny house and repairing the windows. Lu persuaded a man from the village who had worked for foreigners in the old days to come out to the farm as a cook. On his sixth night in the house, Matthew had sat down to a table groaning with fives dishes: a whole steamed fish from the Whangpoo, bean curd with black mushrooms, green peas, pork with pickled vegetables, and a large tureen of soup.

With what was to be his first and only show of temper, Matthew summoned Lu and his new hireling. "I have asked you both to come in here because I am not at all pleased with the way things are going. I want both of you to understand that we are going to change many things that were done in the past."

"Whatever *Si-sang* requires," Lu said smoothly.

Matthew took him up instantly. "*That* is one of the first things we change. My name is Liang Fei. I am here on the same level with you. We are all together in trying to find the best use of this difficult, wornout soil. The old ways are no help in this. Neither are these foolish titles. Beyond that, to serve five dishes to one person is not polite. Do you think I am too stupid to understand this kind of insult?"

Lu stammered, "It was not I, *Si-sang*, who suggested such a thing. It was our dog-headed cook."

"Never mind," Matthew said. "*You* hired the cook, and you are both interested in 'squeeze.' But there is to be no squeeze in this house. You are both such dunces. In these new days, when you squeeze, you rob only yourselves."

He looked at the steaming dishes with distaste. "Do you think I am still such a round-eye that I can't see what you planned to do with this meal? There is a great cauldron of rice cooking in the kitchen, am I not correct?"

Lu and the cook kept a prudent silence.

"You would wait as I picked at these dishes, then take all that remained, together with the extra rice, back into the village. You would all think yourselves very clever for feasting at my expense. But it is really at *your* expense!" He snapped his fingers. "Bring me a cup of that rice and a pot of tea and take all the rest of this away to the village *now*. Later on, when the harvest comes in, we may be able to feast together." To Lu, he said, "Take this man away. He is fit to cook for a corrupt emperor of the old regime, not for a hardworking farmer of the new!"

Matthew jumped up, went to the kitchen, filled one small bowl with rice from the huge pot that indeed was there, took it with a pair of chopsticks to his cot, hunched over his dinner, and began to read by the light of the one kerosene lamp. After a few embarrassed moments, Lu and the cook cleared away the dishes. Later that evening Matthew checked to make sure that the cauldron was gone.

The next day when he went into the village, he saw a few people come out into the dirt street and stare at him with their characteristic, slack-jawed, expressionless gaze. His reputation as an eccentric madman who claimed against all evidence to be "a true son of Han" was well on its way.

Matthew plowed alone. He sowed alone. He realized early on that these plots were not good for rice because no matter what the weather conditions, the water table was not high enough to ensure a good crop. Of the twenty-five hectares that he planted that first year, only one field was used for rice and the rest seeded with his own drought-resistant millet. From time to time he saw the farmers of the village gathering to jeer at his strange-looking crop.

That year there was a drought. Rice paddies dried out. Other people's *bah cha* withered, and bitter melons shriveled on the vine. Matthew labored in his fields from dawn to dusk over his millet, hand-cultivating, hand-watering. Finally, in the crisp days of October, he harvested—all alone—an enormous crop.

The day came when Matthew asked Lu to call back the cook. "I seem to recall that you are renowned for taking fish as big as babies and steaming them so carefully that not one scale is out of place. And I have heard you have a way with eel." He pulled out a small sack of gold coins. "I wish to repay the people of the village for their hospitality in these past months. I have been able to save my vegetable garden with the water I would have ordinarily used for rice. So, Cook, take these coins. Purchase fish, some ginger, some wine. Borrow some bowls and platters. Have Lu set up tables outside. But don't buy rice. We are going to eat my millet."

"A banquet with millet?"

"Please have the kindness to invite the whole village for tomorrow evening as the sun sets. Buy a lantern for each table! And cook your spiciest dishes, your dishes fit for a wedding or a New Year's feast."

The villagers came, seduced by the smells. Matthew greeted each of them with perfect courtsey. The village survived that first winter and many more on what had first been the crack-brained idea of a successful Washington bureaucrat. Soon families began lending him their younger sons so that they might learn his techniques. Within a few years the entire village started to prosper. Word spread, as daughters married out of the village, across the delta of the Whangpoo, and even into the city of Shanghai itself, of the village of Lungwha that seemed impervious to nature's usual bad jokes. Year in and year out, Lungwha was able, in spite of drought or flood, to grow a surplus of hearty grains.

Matthew Granger, "Fertile Grain," thought often of how he fled America. He could rationalize all he wanted that the United States was not his real home, or that he had done the best he could under difficult circumstances; there was no point in reliving the past, but whatever happened, Matthew put down his roots—both literally and figuratively—in the pungent earth of the Fong-See Compound. He made friends; he saw his theoretical agricultural experiments come to fruition. He was respected in the village; these people became his new family.

He could say now, to grumbling Lu, "Yams are a source of natural sweetness! They are as round and orange as the sun! They will put eternal springtime into your brittle joints!" and go on this way until the old man threw up his arms in resignation and scurried back to the kitchen to bring tea. In Lungwha everyone respected "Fertile Grain" but sometimes his ideas were as outlandish as persuading a cabbage to sing.

In the May of 1966, after a little more than fifteen years of the revolutionary rule of Mao's Communist regime, the aging leader looked about him and became convinced that China was sinking back into its old ways of bureaucracy and corruption. The traditional oriental respect for age once again asserted itself; the fierce soldiers of Yenan became the entrenched politicians of Beijing. Mao Tse-tung decreed a change, a "Cultural Revolution," calling on the youth of China to save the country with the strength of its new thought. His wife, Jiang Qing, saw an opportunity to wrest power from the men who had been scornful of her in the old days. She leapt at the chance to be her husband's zealous handmaiden in the Cultural Revolution, whose agenda seemed to be to wipe out every gain that the Communists had made. The cold draft of malicious change, of disrespect—in a land that for millennia had been built upon respect—lashed and whipped through even the most remote villages of China. In the great cities a generation of callous youths had grown up disdaining all the actions and thoughts of their parents and grandparents, denouncing the revolutionary past that made the new China what it was.

Each week brought new visitors to Lungwha from the cities—sometimes to play and sing new songs, sometimes to recruit for Young Pioneer groups, sometimes to hold mandatory evenings of self-criticism for the peasants. The new cadres never criticized themselves for bad manners or preying on the countryside like locusts. Always it was the bent, exhausted farmers who were criticized—those who had been working the fields since before dawn and would not see their beds again until they accused themselves of wrong thinking, revisionism, romantic thoughts, or an excessive love of sweets.

One evening in this spring of 1967 the Cultural Revolution finally came to Lungwha. Six loud and overbearing city youths brought thick white sheets of poster board, nailed them up to the outside of the public hall, then mounted a dais to harangue the crowds.

"In the past," one of them shouted, "a hundred flowers bloomed! The intellectuals stated their complaints. The Helmsman decreed that weeds among the flowers might spring up and be pulled out. How can we recognize wrong thinking until we see that which we think?" His voice was hoarse from previous meetings. "These posters have been brought here for you to state your feelings boldly. Loy-wei has brought paints, buckets of them, and large brushes. We will teach you how to make known your oppression to the whole world." The boy coughed and spat. "We have, traveling with us this week, the special Committee on Agrarian Reform from Beijing. You know their faces and they know yours." His voice took on a menacing whine. "Do not think that because production in the village of Lungwha is up that there are no evil thistles here. Where production is up, pride and smugness are often a problem. In the following weeks you must feel your neighbor's arms and those of your children and parents. If they are plump from overeating, you must report it here." Dramatically he dipped a brush into a bucket of black paint and inscribed quickly "Serve the people" across the poster board. "Calligraphy is nothing!" he said. "Do not be afraid if you cannot make you characters perfectly. The truth, courageously written, is fertilizer to the crops."

Ever since the mention of the Beijing Agrarian Committee, Matthew—while he kept his hat tilted down and his face as impassive as those of all his neighbors—searched the hastily built dais for the slight, compact figure of Deputy Chief Wong Sumoy.

Ten years before, Sumoy had come to Lungwha on a visit. She had heard of his farm both from her superior, Nyi Chuen-yup, in the capital, and out here from the peasants' word of mouth. All though the first day they met he had kept her tramping through the fields. That night he had forgone his millet and let the cook make them both a simple but delicious meal. Matthew and Sumoy exchanged stories by lantern far into the night. Every member of her family had been destroyed during the war by either the Japanese or the Nationalist armies. Sumoy was an orphan whose only family now was the Revolution. Her life was gross national production and a fiery passion for her own country. Matthew, for the first time in six years, had been able to speak about how the sweep of national events in his own country had deprived him—in a different way—of his family and everything he loved. They shared a bottle of wine and spoke of their childhood; they talked through the night, until dawn quickened the air and a thousand birds began to sing.

"I have to sleep now," he'd said awkwardly. "We must be up in the morning to finish our tour."

Sumoy went to the corner, unwrapped her bedroll, peeled off her clothes, and lay down on her back.

"Can it be that you're a bourgeois revisionist?" She caressed her naked breasts with her calloused farmer's hands. "The Revolution says that we shouldn't be taken up with selfish concerns. But the Revolution never said we could not show affection for our comrades."

During this past decade they had seen each other no more than two or three times a year. For all that, they were still strong lovers and fast friends.

As Matthew listened now to the cadre's unpleasant rhetoric, he knew that soon he would go home, roll out the bedding, bring out the *mao tai*, and scrub himself with harsh farmer's soap made out of ashes, lye, and kitchen fat. He would make himself ready for Sumoy.

Later that night, after the mandatory self-condemnations, she came to him. He blew out the lamp once again. After their first coupling, they began to talk.

"You looked demure yet stern on the dais, my forever youthful comrade," he murmured to her. "But all I could think of tonight was when we would be together."

"That kind of thinking could lose you your head," she said apprehensively. "Weren't you listening at all to what those hooligans said?"

"Every week they come. But every week they go away. I have no time for shouting children and their meaningless slogans."

"Is that not both unwise and obtuse after what happened to you in your own country?"

"Yes, but the man in America who started all that was a powerful politician. As I understand it, these boys are being sent out by Mao's wife. It's simply a means to make Jiang Qing feel useful. In my country, we had a President's wife, Eleanor Roosevelt, who used to go off and talk to the poor. . . ."

"Jiang Qing is no ordinary Chinese wife. She is ruthless as a she-dragon. She carries the spirit, if not the blood, of the old Dowager Empress." Sumoy sat up in bed. "Mao is an old man now. His Great Leap Forward resulted in famine. His Hundred Flowers were a reign of terror. Each Five-Year Plan has put us five years back in the past instead of firmly in the future. Now Mao hopes that his wife may accomplish what he couldn't. . . ."

"But it doesn't make sense," Matthew said. "To exterminate intellectuals, to close the universities, to stop production, to send roving bands through the countryside, to destroy the artistic heritage of the country and replace it with Peking operas about the Revolution. . . . What good can that possibly do for China?" He thought nostalgically of Harley's lurid, imaginary brothel at 110 Shanghai Road. During the first Revolution it might have housed needy orphans. But under Madame Mao's current austere vision, it might turn into something unattractive—for instance, a ship-building institute, all thoughts of pleasure forever banished from the Middle Kingdom.

Sumoy spoke quietly. "There are those who say that Jiang Qing was a movie actress here in Shanghai before the war. They say she has made a list of all those who humiliated her. Now she is taking her revenge, and she has a long memory." Her chapped palms touched his face. "Next week, if the cadres come back to the village, be careful."

During the past few weeks, since the safari set up in the flat lands close to the delta of the Tana River in the heart of Kenya, she had discovered that the lion was not the king of the beasts, nor the lioness the queen. The lion did not pace the jungle unafraid. Nor did the lion or lioness make the day-to-day kills that kept food in the mouths of their young. Packs of jackals, yapping, shrill, and enterprising, hunted together and brought down the appealing ibex or the wildebeest. The lions loitered on the outskirts of each kill, as aimless and bored as lower-class English families waiting for their neighborhood pub to open. They held back until the jackals filled their small stomachs and then moved in to feast at leisure. What they lacked in fierceness, they made up in domesticity. If lions could read, they would read the *Daily Telegraph*; if they could follow a plot, they would watch the telly. The parents grew stodgy and spent long days bickering with their children, fighting a losing battle against the insolence of youth.

Jordan Logan-Fisher's guide reminded her that lions hunt at night. He sent her out on several nocturnal expeditions, carefully lit and expensively set up. However, after she saw lions waiting at the kill—their hats in their hands so to speak—she had insisted to her white hunter that she wanted to paint lions in the day.

"Jordan, you silly dear," Farrell had said. "Lions nap in the daytime. They rest with their children and they mate. There's no danger in painting them then, no risk, no truth."

"Leave the truth to me, Farrell," she retorted. "If I paint in the day, we shall have the nights to ourselves."

And that was why she was here on this vast plain, at two in the afternoon under the African sun, filling papa lion in with yellow pastels. How shabby he looked in the daytime, how pitiful, how unemployed. Jordan sketched in a mother lion as she cuffed her cubs and growled at them.

It had been Jordan's custom every year, since she returned to England and civilized life, to spend three months doing a series of paintings on a subject that "saluted the larger world." She donated the proceeds from these paintings to a cause. Five years ago she spent a summer traveling in the southern United States sketching in bold black and white the first civil rights marches. She divided the proceeds, giving half to the followers of Martin Luther King and the other to benefit poor white children—as oppressed in their own way as any black children.

Invariably, she began each expedition with one set of beliefs and came back with another. In India she found that although Mother Teresa was undoubtedly a saint, she was also bossy, dictatorial, and controlling, much like Jordan herself. On the ice floes of Labrador, where she had gone to record the slaughter of baby seals, she returned with the Newfoundland hunters to their outpost villages and recorded the deaths of their children from scurvy and tuberculosis.

This summer she was in darkest Africa for a series of drawings that would raise money for the Foundation for Endangered Species at the London Zoo. Her gallery agent disapproved of these jaunts, her mother worried, and her son, Desmond, was—as always—embarrassed for her.

When he had been a boy, he had wanted her to dress in skirts like the mothers of his friends, but she had lived too long in China to give up the natural elegance of pants. She had fashioned a wardrobe of loose trousers and tops, and put two-carat diamonds in her ears. Her admirers told her she looked like a young Kate Hepburn, that she would never go out of fashion, and she was inclined to believe it. But when Desmond grew older, he took to criticizing her vulgar earrings and urged her to buy new blouses.

Dear Desmond. She sent him to school—to Eton, naturally, like every other Logan-Fisher since the beginning of time—in the winters. The summers were for Desmond. She'd carried him on her back to the Mount Everest base camp and he'd developed an ear infection. Three years later, in Newfoundland, he'd kicked out a boy's tooth and there'd been hell to pay. He'd wandered off in the mines of Northern Italy for a day. In the ruins of the Good Friday Alaska Quake, he had climbed down into a crevasse and refused to come out. She thought that the onset of puberty would channel some of this irrepressible energy into a simplistic chase of the female sex. But in Papua she and Desmond found that although the native girls were compliant, their fathers nursed a grudge against British imperialism. Mother and son retreated from that island idyll in a flurry of mutual recriminations and domestic disgrace.

Dearest Desmond. He was a perfect traveling companion and a wonderful boy. When she suggested this May that perhaps he might like to stay at home, that the African jungles carried the threat of billharzia, elephantiasis, and yaws, he simply said, "I'll stay out of trouble this time. And I'll carry only my knapsack, my new electric guitar, and a generator to go with it." The bearers puffed cross-country taking turns with the generator, but they crowded around Desmond at night. Jordan and Farrell sipped their vodka like old folks while Desmond sat as part of the circle of joyous natives and composed songs for the bearers who had lugged the generator that day.

So far, Jordan thought, it had been a perfectly splendid trip. Only one case of dengue fever and two of Lhasa; everyone else as sound as a dollar and plenty of good work done.

Suddenly the lion stood and, motionless and alert, sniffed at the eastern breeze. Jordan felt the hair on the back of her neck rise and glanced at her watch to check the time. These were nocturnal animals and she knew that the lion family had eaten heartily the night before. What was happening? Was some incautious beast about to cross the foreground of her painting and ruin a perfectly constructed design? But the

aroma the lion had caught before Jordan was human sweat cut
by generous doses of lavender water.

"Have I the honor of addressing Madame Jordan Logan-
Fisher?" A portly Britisher in ill-fitting Bermuda shorts had
trotted up behind her.

"Don't be a bloody ass!" she snapped. "And keep your
voice down. I don't want the cats spooked more than they
already are."

The courier stiffened and bowed. "I have the honor of
presenting you with this communication from Her Majesty the
Queen."

He handed her a long blue envelope, only slightly soiled
from its arduous journey and bearing the royal crest. Jordan
ripped it open and laughed triumphantly. The lions, annoyed
at last, loped away into the underbrush.

Jordan took off at a confident pace, leaving the sweating
stranger to carry her easel and paints. When she reached the
camp, she called out, not in the shrill complaint of the Chinese
revolutionary or the narcissistic tone of the Shanghai belle, but
in the joyous full throat of someone who knows herself to be
forever vindicated:

"Desmond, Farrell, Jolly Bob, we'll all be drinking
champagne tonight. Break out the best rum. A messenger,
whose name I'm afraid I didn't catch, has brought some rather
exhilarating news. Desmond, you're good at writing songs. Do
you suppose you could whip one up—something along the
lines of 'My Mother the Dame'? Her Majesty is creating me a
Dame of the Order of the British Empire. I should so like,"
she said, and happiness blurred her words, "for there to be
dancing and singing in the camp tonight."

When the messenger came panting after her into the
camp, she turned to him with mock reserve and said, "It's not
too soon to be calling me by my new title, sir."

Doffing his pith helmet, the messenger bowed deep and
said, "It's an honor to be the first, Dame Jordan."

From the windows of their second-floor apartment,
Chuen-yup and his wife looked at the busy Beijing street.

"Now that spring is here everyone is happier about
getting out and doing his duty," he said irritably. "Look at that
group of older workers performing their morning exercises."

"It's been some time since I've seen you practicing any of
the correct positions of the Tai Chi Chuan."

"You must remember," he said, "that I have an important administrative position."

"All the more reason for you to keep up your strength."

Chuen-yup turned away from the window. "I'm too busy to spend mornings waving my arms and legs. I'm already late, and you still haven't served me my meal."

Outside the second-story window, the plane trees were in full leaf. The sultry monotones of a million cicadas singing during the night were replaced by the cheerful sound of bicycle bells. The view from this apartment was as calming as a day in the park. In the distance the turnip-shaped white Tibetan dagoda showed above the low roofs of the surrounding buildings. The spring morning sun was absolutely perfect, giving only a hint of its pitilessness during the summer. Chuen-yup could smell the freshly dampened earth, the aroma of a street vendor's cart.

All was as it should be. Why, then, did Nyi Chuen-yup, Chief of Motorized Vehicular Production and fifteenth in line in the Politburo, feel such a sense of anxiety? He looked at his wife chewing last night's rice stewed into a lumpy porridge. By such daily economies she showed her right thinking and saved the family's precious rice coupons. Poor Zizhen. She had never been very attractive, but her enthusiasm and gratitude when Cheun-yup came forward to marry her lit her features with an inward glow. It was a wise and fortunate marriage. She took the name Zizhen, the name of Mao's second wife, who so selflessly had given up four of her children to friendly peasants along the path of the Long March.

Chuen-yup and Zizhen had been married for over ten years now. Zizhen had been a politically astute wife, but she seldom laughed, and the Beijing winters were not kind to her. They had chosen not to have children. As for Chuen-yup, he knew only too well the domestic strife that children in the post-revolutionary family structure could cause. Now Zizhen had become an "Old Mother." Her pomegranate, as the soldiers in his father's camp used to say, held no more red seeds.

Their childlessness had been wise—Chuen-yup was sure of it. They saved their *yuan*. Zizhen spent her days as Assistant Head of the Committee for the Preservation of Art Objects Over a Thousand Years Old, and Chuen-yup had been promoted from the agricultural side of production to Motorized Vehicles.

Everyone called it a promotion. The truth was, Chuen-yup had never been happy about it. He mastered two areas in his first forty years. Four areas really. To his embarrassment, he knew a great deal about Christianity. To his advantage, he understood Dialectical Materialism. In Yenan he learned, through drought and flood, to be a good farmer. And from his warlord father he learned the rudiments of how to amass a fortune: find someone weaker than you and steal everything he has. Unfortunately, none of this transferred to the burgeoning industry of motorized vehicles.

The Helmsman had read that America and Australia used assembly lines. He would not be content until China had its own assembly lines. But a line like that demanded workers who knew what they were doing, and parts from other regions of the country—made by workers who knew what *they* were doing. Motorized vehicles of socialism needed designs that appeared to copy neither the revisionist autos of the Soviet Union nor the imperialist beauties of the United States. It was impossible! Chuen-yup dreaded every inspection of every factory. The truth was, he didn't understand the workings of the internal-combustion engine.

He woke often at night, next to the gently snoring Zizhen, in a drenching sweat about the delivery of carburetors from Harbin, or the tires that Sukarno had promised them from Indonesian rubber, but then had been sold instead to an American conglomerate in San Francisco. None of this kept Chuen-yup from wanting, more than anything else in the world, a motorized vehicle of his own. In the night, when he fought his way out of troubled dreams of spark plugs, he would remember the automobiles of his childhood—his father's fleet of highly polished American cars. He remembered one of the most exciting nights of his young life—forever tinted pink in his mind by the flames and smoke of the bonfires of his father's military compound and the red flares that lit the way of the Packard belonging to the American merchant pirate Harley Fitch, wasn't that his name?—when he had been taken for that wild ride through the midnight streets of old Shanghai. There had been flags shimmying in the wind on that car, and burly bodyguards on the running board. . . .

In the first good days of the Revolution, when the victorious armies had come down from Yenan to Beijing, they had given him a government car to ride about in—a Chevrolet confiscated from the Canadian Consulate. That had been a good car. He drove it for years, until 1966, when, for no good reason, they had seen fit to take it away from him.

"They say here that the production of our small-model car, the Red Star, has dwindled to nothing," he said indignantly. "But I know for a fact that the factory in Wuxi turned out five last month and three of them are in perfect running order. For an agricultural nation we have made great strides. There is no reason why every single member of the Politburo shouldn't have a car of his own."

Zizhen looked at her husband over her rimless bifocals. "We have four thermos jugs, two bicycles, a polished pressed-wood armoire made in Shanghai, an eight-inch television set, four indoor heaters, and still that is not enough for you. Instead of worrying about another bourgeois plaything, you might set your mind with more advantage to the vexing question of why you, out of all the members of the Politburo, have not been invited to the banquet in honor of the Romanian delegation."

"Maybe there is not enough room," Chuen-yup said, but his stomach clenched with apprehension.

His wife grimaced. Sometimes he allowed himself the thought that she was as tired of him as he was of her.

"Not enough room in the Great Hall?" she asked him. "It seats only three thousand people!"

"Party invitations and automobiles! It is the same conversation every morning."

They looked up to see Chuen-yee lounging against the doorframe in embroidered pajamas and robe. Though he was twenty-six, he still lived with his father and stepmother and contributed very little to the family funds from his job as a ticket taker in a local movie theater.

"Is that all you can think about?" he continued. "You with your finery and your bourgeois appurtenances!"

"But that's what the Revolution is all about," his father retorted. "We work hard and we get rewards—equal rewards."

Zizhen sighed and got up to clear the breakfast bowls. This was an argument she'd heard for longer than she wished to remember.

"Do you think an automobile is fair recompense for your contributions to the state?" Chuen-yee quipped.

"And what have *you* done for the Revolution lately?"

"Right now I am writing a verse play on the change of the old thoughts to the new."

Both of his elders looked at him sadly. Zizhen asked, "Since when does that put rice on the table?"

Chuen-yee ruffled his hair and brought the scent of Kitty Kat hair oil across the room. "It is the fate of the fool to be forever divorced from the masses. Rice, cars, silk, it's all the same to you. You measure your victories in terms of riches and government banquets."

When he failed to provoke any further response, he took a Turkish cigarette out of a Russian birchwood case and lit it with a flourish. Without saying anything further, he stepped out on the balcony, ostentatiously communing with nature.

"That half-breed son of yours," Zizhen muttered, "never brings us anything but trouble."

It was with these troubling thoughts that Chuen-yup pedaled to the ministry. It was true that Chuen-yee was a cause for concern in these days when anything Western was suspect. And it mattered not a whit that Chuen-yee's mother, Bah-Wha, had been Official Pictorial Historian of the Yenan period of the Revolution. Those days were far behind. Although Bah-Wha had been a particular favorite of the Helmsman, she and Jiang Qing never got along—both of them strong-willed, with much more rooster than hen in their makeup. And Jiang Qing was crowing now.

His austerly furnished office, painted in shiny, cream-colored enamel, housed a cheap desk and production figure charts that were so bad that sometimes Chuen-yup was tempted to turn them upside down. He paced back and forth and riffled through the latest disheartening reports. They were national in scope and covered all industries. The gap between the projections and the realities was ludicrous. Turning the pages, he saw that no significant unit, either industrial or agricultural, had even begun to reach the assigned level of achievement. In the far north and east, the country was dangerously close to famine. Only one district had met projected agricultural levels and even exceeded them—a section of the Yangtze Delta watered by the Whangpoo River, in the area of the village and pagoda of Lungwha.

Chuen-yup rubbed the back of his neck. *He* was the one responsible for Fertile Grain being there, and he knew there was no chance he would get any credit for it. In fact, the foreigner was an embarrassment, a continual reminder that Western ways, even in the hands of one man, always seemed to work.

He stepped out of his office. He had learned, a few years before, that a diet of fish and rice caused stomach cancer. Chuen-yup went to great lengths to procure red meat for his family, and especially himself. Now, they wrote that red meat caused heart attacks. Since he read that, he had trouble breathing. A breeze ran through the hall, open, these spring days, at each end. And also, in the hall, he might find someone to talk to.

He was lucky. Wang Dong-xing, a deputy assistant to the Minister of Textile Production, was also taking the air.

Dong didn't even bother to say hello. He held up a hand in mock warning. "Don't talk to me about vehicles. At least you are bound by the laws of physics—four wheels and a chassis. But I, *I* have been instructed to come up with a uniform for every woman in China, with a full skirt and what they call a 'cinched-in' waist. Can you imagine planting rice in such a get-up? Our women will cry to have their bound feet back."

Cheun-yup nodded in silent commiseration. Neither of them was imprudent enough to name names, for it was Jiang Qing who had thought up this so-called national costume.

"There is no help for it," Dong said. "We must take each day's simple pleasures as they come. At least later this week we get a state dinner in the Great Hall."

"Are you referring to the Romanians?" Chuen-yup asked stiffly. "I am afraid that Zizhen and I have not been invited to that function."

For a fraction of a second, terror contorted Wang Dong-xing's face. In this new climate talking to the wrong person could mean political ruin or worse. Then he recovered. "Who, in your opinion, is more dull? An Estonian, a Romanian, or a Latvian? In the olden days, the Buddha never had to worry about these questions."

Their destination was the airstrip outside Kapini. During the long trek out, Desmond watched the harsh Kenyan plain soften into sloping green hills. Near the strip the bearers stopped their chatter and ceased singing the verses of Desmond's songs. During these long days they had woven the lyrics into the carrying chants of their tribes. Desmond learned far more from the members of the Ebo tribe than they learned from him. Hour after hour he heard his melodies and lyrics improvised upon, shifted into minor keys, and braided into the tribe's elaborate oral history.

The time he dreaded most during these expeditions, the moment of departure, was near. Desmond knew that he and his mother were simply two bright beads on a long necklace of time. The Ebo would remember them, but only in verse, only in song. Already they were being cast out of the real life of the tribe.

The trees opened up in front of them, and they were out on the edge of an airstrip that ran to the eastern horizon, ending abruptly in scrubby sand dunes bordering on the ocean. He saw a twin-engine plane circle the field and land.

Farrell shouted orders and supervised the loading of their mountain of gear. His mother saw to her crated paintings, and Desmond leaned against the side of the hut and watched her. She cared for him, loved him, fretted over him, protected him until he felt he'd go out of his mind. Then she would crate him like her paintings, ship him off to a life that was "good for him," while she turned her attention and energies to her art.

At Eton he'd heard friends complain about their parents; that they were "uptight," that they didn't understand, but he was cursed by a mother who was too cool. She'd gone to California and dropped acid with Aldous and Laura Huxley up underneath the H in the Hollywood sign, even before it was against the law. His mother's picture was right there in the third row on the jacket of *Sergeant Pepper's Lonely Hearts Club Band*. Last summer in Papua, when he'd knocked up that chick, his mother had paid a bride's price of thirty-eight pigs. Whenever he came home from Eton full of theories, she would hear him out respectfully. She was so cool, she didn't need a husband and so he didn't have a father.

Oh, he had one. "The love of my life," she was fond of saying. But during his lifetime he had seen one of those during every expedition.

He knew that his mother had—along with generous gifts—given directions to the headmaster on how her son was to be fed, housed, and educated. No matter how hard he tried not to take advantage of his special privileges, no matter how rigorously he entered into playing rugby for the Oppidans, his fellows always set him a little apart.

Oh, what was he complaining about? He was only sixteen, and he had already seen the world. He went to the best school in England, and his mother loved him. But he knew very well what it was. "What do you want to do," his mother once asked, "more than anything else?" And he answered, "I want to sit in the kitchen with you. I want to watch you make cookies." He had been almost everywhere on this earth. He'd seen the very rich and the very poor. But he'd never played badminton out on the lawn. Or watched a tennis match on the telly with anyone. His mother had taken him to Africa, but never spent an afternoon with him at the London Zoo. Sometimes he felt he had seen every kind of life except the real one.

Matthew walked along the dirt borders of the rice paddies on calloused feet the ten *li* from Lungwha to Tse-pou, home village of his old amah and her husband, the Granger household cook from thirty years ago, Da Sze Foo. On and off, for the last sixteen years, he made this trip, as dutifully as a son.

On his first visit, he got no farther than the outskirts of town, where he was greeted by snarling half-tame dogs.

He wasn't frightened by the dogs, but as he looked at the group gathered at the village entrance, he saw a tall figure making motions from the rear—Da Sze Foo. He clenched his fists, raised his voice, and shouted at Matthew, "We have no place for imperialist pigs here! You have pillaged and stolen too much already! You have made the land barren by walking upon it! I piss in your teapot! And so does my wife."

One of the villagers bent down to pick up a stone. Matthew looked at Da Sze Foo's anxious face, and turned to go back. At least he knew they were alive. That night Matthew heard a timid knock at the door. When he went to open it, at first he saw no one. Then he looked down and saw a tiny figure kneeling in tears in front of him.

"Don't kill me! My grandfather, Da Sze Foo, sends you his greetings and apologies. He says that if he were to welcome you, they would take away his hectare of land and put him in the stocks for a day. He begs you to forgive him and to accept this gift of three eggs, except"—she burst into fresh tears—"I broke one on the way."

"Come inside, and have some tea and rice."

"No, I am afraid."

Matthew took the eggs from her. "Wait here while I wrap up some sticky rice and sugar cane to return to your grandparents."

When he came back, he insisted she eat a ball or two, and it was obvious that she was famished. Those eggs had been a real sacrifice.

"My grandfather says that the next time he sends me to visit you, it will be safe for you to come to our village."

Four months later, after the harvest, Matthew had his caretaker, now almost a friend, go the the village with a wheelbarrow full of grain.

"Do not waste a barrow of grain on those who deny you," old Lu said. "Properly used, this would be enough seed for an entire crop."

"Exactly," Matthew said. "And remember, do not give this to anyone but the headman of the village. Do not say it's from me. This is simply a gift from our village to theirs."

"There is no one more dull than a foreigner. We were right to expel them."

"Lu, you must remember that these are my Chinese parents."

"The state is our parent now."

That night the girl came back with a gift from the headman and an invitation to visit Tse-pou. Matthew was formally received and taken to visit three households—one of them belonging to Da Sze Foo.

The old couple made tea, and a bowl of special Shanghai-style pan-fried noodles, Matthew's favorite Chinese dish. From then on Matthew sent, after each harvest, a wheelbarrow of seed grain and made a point of visiting the village at least twice a year.

In the last five years, his amah, now well into her eighties, and suffering from arthritis, had taken to her bed. Her work-worn hands had drawn up into tiny claws. Matthew brought her Tiger Balm and ginseng, but he knew she appreciated his attentions as much as the remedies. Da Sze Foo had worked hard during his long life and was looking forward to an old age filled with respect, which was the traditional reward in both the old days and these new ones.

Now as Matthew neared the village, the local boys, perched on the backs of water buffaloes, turned their heads away. With an increasing sense of disquiet, Matthew hurried on and saw pasted on the earthen walls big character posters denouncing "parasites who live off foreign gifts."

The wife of the headman appeared at the door of her house dressed in torn strips of white mourning cloth. "It is you," she sobbed. "It is you who have cursed our village. My children won't speak to me. I am an outcast."

Matthew hurried on to Da Sze Foo's house. A dreadful

stench emanated from the usually clean main room, the unmistakable odor of death. On a pallet lay the lifeless figure of his old amah. As for Da Sze Foo, he was just barely alive—bloated and pale as a white sausage. The stories of dreadful punishment circulating through the countryside were true. The unfortunate couple had been thrown into the common cesspool.

Matthew put his hand on Da Sze Foo's shoulder. "What has happened, Old Father?"

"Last week, Jiang Qing, the queen of evil, came here," he gasped. "With her words she aroused old hatreds. She said all those who once suckled at the foreigner's teat drank corruption. Because of this corruption, my wife and I were put into a cesspool until we saw our wrong thinking. I was able for some hours to hold her in my arms, but these arms are old and have little strength in them. She slipped from my grasp. The exrement closed over her head, and before I could rescue her she was gone."

Matthew's eyes filled with tears.

"Perhaps it was best," Da Sze Foo went on. "The screams I heard echoing through the night should not have been heard by anyone. They lopped the headman into thirteen pieces and sent his parts flying to each end of the village so that he will never meet his ancestors. They pulled all the teeth of the schoolteacher because she said—"

"Don't say any more."

"Oh, Young Master . . ." And then he was gone.

That night in Lungwha, Matthew suffered agonizing remorse. His father had come over from America, full of naïveté and good intentions. He had devoted all the energies of his life to helping the Chinese. Matthew saw now that he had tried to do the same, and it had come to this. Instead of a new life, he had brought death.

"Don't take it so hard," Lu said. "The butterfly flaps his wings and expects a good meal. The ground squirrel hoards his grain. The people in that village should have taken care of themselves. If you hadn't been feeding them, Liang Fei, they would have all been dead long ago."

But Matthew was inconsolable. All night he stayed up crying while Lu offered what meager comfort an old friend could give.

Until the television cameras arrived, the demonstration had languished. At ten that morning, Mario Savio had come by and given a speech, but after he realized the press was not there yet, he went home. Angela Davis spoke for a fiery ten minutes, suggesting that until every black had "more than equal" rights there was no point in protesting the war or chemicals or anything else.

Andrew kept track from an office only five floors up, monitoring the gathering. In reality, he was looking for just one face.

It was a slow news day in San Francisco, because at about twelve-thirty the trucks of two or three local television news crews began to arrive. From his vantage point Andrew saw an immediate effect. The raggedy cadence of "We Shall Overcome" swelled and became more confident. Odetta came to the center of the crowd. Even through double thicknesses of industrial glass, Andrew could hear her majestic voice grind out "If I Had a Hammer." How standard it all was, Andrew thought petulantly. That's why he was inside and they were outside.

Then an incautious sound man pushed his microphone to within six inches of a demonstrator's face. He had picked the wrong demonstrator. The stocky redhead took the sound boom and snapped it in two as if it were a twig. Forgetting about the elevator, Andrew ran down the emergency staircase, taking the steps two at a time. As he looked out from the third floor he saw several police cars, their red lights flashing, converging on the scene. By the time he hit the mezzanine, the block had been cordoned off, the police were beginning to use their nightsticks, and already a girl lay sobbing and bleeding on the steps. Andrew galloped, his feet thudding across the marble floor of CFE. With every bit of theatricality of which he was capable, he threw open the doors.

"Not that!" The television cameras, in their tropism for news, obediently turned in his direction. "Compton Fitch Enterprises has never countenanced violence and it never will!"

He heard boos and hisses. Someone asked, "Isn't that one of the Fitches?" and an answer: "Nah, it can't be."

Andrew tried to face each camera in turn. "My father, Harley Compton Fitch, believes in free speech and in the American right to dissent."

The redhead who had broken the sound boom yelled, "Go back inside, faggot!"

Before the cameras could turn again, Andrew shouted

out, "There's no point in confrontation. We must learn from each other. My father has asked me on his behalf to invite twelve of you to come inside for a conference."

"Divide and conquer," somebody called out. "That's what you're trying to do."

Andrew answered, "You, the person who said that, will you be the first to come in?" He tossed his hair as he spoke, glad that he had let it grow long.

"Compton Fitch Chemicals kill women and children," a girl shouted. Andrew took the chance, walked into the crowd, and squeezed her upper arms with both his strong hands.

"We need someone to speak for the women and children," he said. "Won't you come inside?" Then, his heart pounding, he looked up at the oaf who had ruined the sound boom. "Might I interest you," he said, clearly enough for the television crews to catch, "in a cup of tea?"

The mob began to break up into groups and each group pushed forward its own spokesman. Andrew soon picked eleven. They stood nervously with him on the stairs. Then, though he was sure there was no God and he had certainly never prayed, Andrew's whole being focused into one pulsating wish. Please, he thought, please! He scanned the crowd.

"You," he said to the boy who had spoken a few days before. "You've been here before. Will you come in too?"

The boy stepped forward. Andrew addressed the rest. "My father's boardroom seats only thirteen or I'd ask you all in. As it is, my father asks you please to go on with your demonstration. And he asks the police please to avoid all violence. . . ."

Dispirited, the demonstrators took up where they'd left off; the television crews picked up their equipment and drove away. Andrew's gamble had paid off. Then thirteen of them were in the cavernous lobby of Compton Fitch Enterprises. His twelve guests gawked in awe at the enormous three-dimensional logo of a bat eating a beetle.

"It's the Chinese symbol for prosperity or something like that," he said. "My grandfather was a robber baron out in China. That's where all the money comes from." He spoke to them as equals, and in truth they were all approximately the same age. He stopped in front of the security guard, who sat gaping behind his desk, and scribbled a few words on a pad of paper. "I'm sending a note to my father to ask him to come in and meet us." In additon to that Andrew had scrawled, "Herb tea to the boardroom ASAP."

The VIP elevator whisked them all to the twenty-third floor. Some of them hadn't taken a bath for some time. Some, like the street urchins they were, held hands and closed their eyes against the ride. When the car stopped and the door opened to the top floor and they spilled out into the sumptuously carpeted foyer of the boardroom, the big fellow who had broken the boom asked in a subdued voice, "Hey, man, is there a place to take a leak?"

Andrew handed him a key to the executive rest room. He was amused that while some of them were overawed by the conservatively elegant surroundings, others settled themselves confidently in the mahogany armchairs almost as if they had found their proper place in life at last. So much for the Revolution. He could see them in a few years, conservatively suited, each with a pigskin briefcase. . . .

It had been his father's particular conceit when he planned this room that the man at the head of the long table would be able to make himself heard perfectly all through the room. Everyone else sitting the length of the polished mahogany surface would find his own voice slightly distorted.

"Nice place you got here," said one of the demonstrators, and his voice echoed as if he had spoken from a well.

The girl who had shouted about the women and children took hold of the table with one hand and said, "All this wealth rightfully belongs to somebody else." As she heard her own echo, her forehead wrinkled.

A uniformed cafeteria worker came in with herb tea and whole-grain cakes as Andrew spoke soothingly to the distraught girl. "You're absolutely right, of course. All this *does* belong to somebody else. That's why we're here, isn't it—to discuss a more equitable distribution?" Before anyone could answer, he added, "It takes courage to sit down and talk to the other guy." He was rewarded by looks of sympathy from eleven of the twelve. The only one he cared about remained watchful and aloof.

"Our whole organization is going through a series of important changes. We're doing our best to get out of any industry that might be thought of as even marginally destructive. We want to invest in industries of the future." It was all bald-faced lies. Again, eleven persons nodded. One kept his own counsel.

Of all the things that Harley Compton Fitch III had learned during his fifty-one years, he had learned best how to make an entrance. When the legendary magnate entered the room, the very air seemed to shimmer, and the demonstrators—shabbily dressed to begin with, certain only of their beliefs—seemed to turn again into what Andrew had always thought them to be—no more than bums off the street. They shrank, they diminished as Harley Compton Fitch pulled up a chair right next to his son's, put his hands, palms down, on the table.

"I won't beat about the bush with you people," he said, and his voice sounded like a priceless musical instrument. "We've had our fingers in pies we shouldn't have. We've rowed our boat faster than the other crews. We've kept our asses in gear while everybody else's has broken down. But we've got to change the way we do business. Frankly," he went on, "I'm surprised that you're *here*. Do you know where you should be? You should be down at the docks protesting against our oil slick. Yes, I'll admit to you right now, we're responsible for that one. And it was my own granddaughter, my lovely Angela, who burst into tears when she saw those birds and said, 'Grandpa, we have to help them.' I think she was right. What we've done is set up a whole hospital to take care of all the Bay Area species that were caught in that oil disaster. We have 'beds' in the hospital for two thousand birds and we've had a success rate of . . ."

He stopped in mid-sentence and flashed an angry glance at a young man with a strikingly handsome face and an air of confidence who had just stood up.

"Why, this is perfect!" the young man said, his voice as garbled and strange as a record being played at the wrong speed. "This is really very good. It's a terrific feat of acoustical engineering." As he spoke he kept on moving, and with each step his voice changed slightly in pitch and density. "You see, the farther I am away from the chairman of the board, the stupider I must be and the stranger I must sound. So I don't talk very much. The closer I get to the head of this table, the further up I am in the company. I'm closer to power. I must be smarter and my voice takes on resonance."

By this time he was standing directly on Andrew's left. "When I'm up here," he said, and his voice was as spellbinding as the man's in the seven-hundred-dollar suit, "my word is law. It's a little like singing in the shower. We all sound good there. But when you get out into the real world you're off key again just like anybody else."

Harley jumped to his feet. "Who are you?" he asked. "And how did you ever . . . ?"

"It's an old trick," the young man said. "I was born into a political family. My grandfather was a senator and now my mother is one too. I was practically raised in the corridors of the Capitol Building. I know the tricks sound can play there."

"Granger!" The name burst from Harley's mouth. "You're Val Granger's son. I was there the night you were born. . . ." He broke out in blotches and sweat began to pour down his neck. "What the hell are you doing here?"

"Thank you very much, Father," Andrew interrupted coolly. "We know how busy you are."

The vein that had bulged dangerously on Harley's temple diminished.

"I know you've got that delegation from the Arab Emirates waiting for you, Father. You know how a man in a burnoose hates to be kept waiting."

Harley stared down at his son for perhaps a full second. "Of course, of course you're right." Then he left the room.

Andrew glanced around quickly to gauge the mood of the demonstrators. "How'd you like to have that for a father?"

Paul Granger cut in. "It's all very well to placate us with *mu* tea, to play silly games with acoustics, and try to be hip about your dad. But you're not against him. You're *with* him and *against* us. What we still want to know is, what is CFE going to do about napalm, about nerve gas, about the warheads for atomic bombs—"

Andrew stopped him. "We can talk about all that later. And we will, I promise you. But let's start with something we have a chance to agree on. Come with me to the bird hospital. You'll see we aren't as bad, as evil, as you think. Will you come with me tomorrow?"

The girl spoke up, brave now. "I know a couple of volunteers down there. I didn't know CFE had anything to do with that." Her voice wavered on the periphery of Andrew's consciousness.

"Will you come with me or not?" Andrew asked in a baiting tone.

Paul's deep brown eyes bored into him. "Yes, I'll come. But what will you give me in exchange?"

When Andrew finally got back to his desk, he found an urgent message for him: "Come to my office. HCF."

Andrew welcomed the coming encounter. He knew that he and he alone had saved a ticklish situation back there in the boardroom. His father's temper, which almost always worked to his own advantage, had, in this instance, come close to defeating their plans for sabotaging the demonstration. Andrew jauntily went into the executive suite, prepared to face his father's wrath.

"Out of a thousand people to choose from, you had to pick Paul Granger! How do you do it, Andy? How do you manage to be so thick? Don't you have eyes! Couldn't you see who he looks like?"

"You think he's Matthew Granger's son?"

"Yes, you idiot! Even you ought to have been able to figure that out."

Andrew hesitated, somehow taken up in the sheer wonder of it all. Then he said, "So Paul is actually the son of Matthew Granger, the man who brought me and my mother out of China. Somebody else has to be pulling the strings—"

"You imbecile! Of *course* somebody else is pulling the strings! Paul Granger is pulling the stings! I've worked my entire life to consolidate my father's shaky empire. I've met every threat head-on. I've had a rule in business that's worked for me for over twenty years. Any rival, any enemy, who challenges my power gets taken care of in one of three ways— hire him on, buy him out, or—if neither of those works—put him out of business, destroy him!"

Andrew stared at his father in morbid fascination. Someday, he thought, a heart attack will put an end to him.

"I have people who dislike me," Harley rushed on, "and people who think they can do better"—he gazed meaningfully at his son—"but in all the world, I can truthfully say I have only one enemy. I had to fight him to get you, Andrew! Matthew Granger wanted to bring you up as his own son. He found out what happens when you cross Harley Comton Fitch! So you know where he is now? He's rotting on a mud flat outside Shanghai, not thirty miles away from the crack-brained mission where his father thought he could bring salvation to a bunch of self-serving Chinese. I put him there, Andrew! I drove him out of the country because he wanted you, and you were my son! So this is the way it stands now, Andrew! I have one enemy in the world. He is five thousand miles away on a mud flat, and today *his son was right here in my boardroom!*"

Andrew regarded his father with outward calm. Someday,

he thought, you'll be dead. All this will be mine. Including this office, these *objets d'art*, this toothsome secretary . . .

"Well, say something! What have you got to say for yourself?"

"Isn't it better to know, Father, where your enemy is?"

"Yes. You may be right, for once. He must be here for a reason. Well, I hope at least you strung him along with that bird operation—"

"He's agreed to look at it. Tomorrow."

"Good. I'll take care of this. I'll take him in a limo, we'll stop at the Yacht Club, I'll get him drunk, find him a girl, and after a few hours of that, I'll have him in my pocket."

"No!" Andrew spoke with a firmness that startled both of them. "That's *my* job. You know how close you came to blowing the whole thing today?" Then he allowed himself an unprecedented impertinence. "You may find this hard to believe, but there are people who don't enjoy your lectures and your girls and your drinks, and I believe Paul Granger is one of them."

"Hold on now. I know how to handle this kind of thing."

"Don't be so sure of that. Remember, it took Paul Granger something under three minutes to get so far under your skin that you looked as if you'd burst open right there in front of them."

Harley gave a lopsided grin and said grudgingly, "You know, in all the years we've had meetings in there, I think that boy's the only one who figured out the acoustics, or at least the only one who had the guts to call me on it."

"Look, I know you never want to give me any real responsibility. But even you ought to be able to see that I'm the one to deal with Granger. I'm close to his age. I speak his language."

Harley's face changed into a familiar look of low cunning. "I don't see what he can do to us, but he's obviously out here for something. In the old days, all of us used to be friends. His father used to work for me, and I spent plenty of weekends with Matthew and Val—that's Paul's mother—out at her old family home. She's a senator now, and she may be behind this." He rubbed the back of his neck. "Our books are in perfect order. We can stand any investigation. So what could she want? *Are you listening to me, Andrew?*"

"Yes, Father, I'm listening. Frankly, I think I'm ahead of you on this. I think Paul is here for something more than his mother. I think Paul is his own man."

"Well . . ."

"If, as you say, his mother comes from an old political clan, would she do anything so obvious as to send a member of the family to feel things out?"

Nothing was so irritating as his father's habit of taking someone else's idea and commandeering it as his own. "Fine. Here's what I want you to do. I've decided to put you completely in charge of taking Paul Granger on this so-called hospital expedition tomorrow. You speak his language. You won't have to bully him. You can find out all about him, why he's here. Why would a politically savvy person send out a member of her own family? I don't think Paul is the kind of person who responds to yachts and limousines. Take him to a cafeteria. Find out what he wants."

Andrew jammed his hands in his pockets so his father wouldn't see his fists clench.

"Yes, I'll do that." To himself he thought, The old bastard's always been a quick study.

"And, Andrew . . . handle this right, and there'll be something in it for you. I'm talking stock. I'm talking a better seat on the board."

"Certainly, Father. I'll go with Paul tomorrow, and report back immediately. And I look forward to my promotion. It's very good of you."

In San Francisco in 1967 the prevailing belief was that there was a governmental conspiracy behind everything. The war in Vietnam was out of control; everyone knew that. But how many people knew that the man who had invented strobe lights had a government contract; that the salesman who persuaded the management at Fillmore West to use them in their nightly "happenings" had a fat federal grant? Yes, somewhere in the city Ken Kesey came in from time to time and hobnobbed at parties with some Hell's Angels; his great experiment: Would enough acid induce those famous socio-paths to put down their chains and wrenches and *smile*?

But there were other parties, in other parts of the city, where officers of the Air Force, dressed carefully in chamois fringe, laced lemonade with megadoses of lysergic acid, waited patiently until their subjects were stoned to the eyes, took them to bedrooms and subjected them to wall-to-wall pro-jected films of the earth burning and the moon spinning, the wings of their planes falling off, until they shrieked with grief.

Later, they were locked in closets for a week to see how they came down off the drug. Because of this, and a few attempted suicides, acid got a bad name, and the government was satisfied.

Everything was owned by somebody else. Everyone was part, wittingly or unwittingly, of a larger plan. The would-be revolutionaries knew it, but who among them knew *how* to fight it? Who could be sure that the grapefruit in supermarket bins had not been planted there as part of another experiment? Who could be sure that the Angels would not be hired by the CIA to bludgeon victims to death at Altamont, to give rock a bad name, to induce people to shave their heads and go to Vietnam?

How many people at the improvised bird hospital, housed in a crumbling three-story warehouse on the ocean side of San Francisco, knew they were part of the larger plan? How many dedicated young men and women, working twenty-hour days cleaning the eyes of shore birds with Q-tips dipped in Prell, knew that the warehouse became available to the earnest veterinarians courtesy of CFE? How many knew that while the first two stories of this rat-infested building were given over to the scrubbing and feeding of thousands of sick birds by hundreds of hippies, the third floor housed chemists direct from CFE? How many knew that while some scientists tried their best to bring the oil-burdened birds back to life, others, with equal interest, took thorough notes, stood by impassively, and watched the birds die?

This morning, before Andrew sent for his car, he made two phone calls, one to a veterinarian, Bernie Hansen, who answered, his voice strained with fatigue, that he would see visitors, but that they shouldn't expect anything resembling order. "It's a charnel house down here," Hansen said. "We've been working twenty-four hours a day." Andrew's second phone call was picked up by a person who did not say hello. He spoke into the electronic silence, "I may be coming down with a member of the counter-culture. For God's sake, try to look humanitarian, if you can."

"Have you checked this with your fath—" but Andrew had hung up.

Andrew drove himself to a little house on Telegraph Avenue. Paul was waiting for him on the sidewalk, his Levi's clean and freshly pressed, his work shirt's open collar turned up to reach his hairline. His long carefully combed hair ended in a ponytail and he wore a tweed jacket.

Paul got into the car without saying anything. Andrew watched him checking out the leather seats, the wood steering wheel of the beautiful old Mercedes. "Nice wheels," he said grudgingly.

"It's a collector's item." Andrew slid easily into the Berkeley traffic and headed for the bridge.

"You don't need it," came the stern response. They took the rest of the drive in silence over the Bay Bridge, the spring fog skimming just beneath its ironwork, and across the whole of San Francisco until they reached the ocean and the Cliffside Restaurant. Andrew made a sharp left, heading down along the bottom of the cliffs to a part of San Francisco few tourists saw. Here the shore was lined not with resort hotels or boutiques, but a string of old warehouses. Andrew switched on his fog lights and continued for a few blocks to a building where a sign read "This Property Is Condemned." A few yellow lights inside shone through broken windows and cracks in the wall.

Andrew locked hs Mercedes, then took off his tie, rolled it up, and put it in his pocket. They looked at each other through the thin wash of fog and surf spray. The moisture had beaded on Paul's eyelashes. Andrew sighed, then unbottoned the top button of his shirt and flipped up his collar. He and Paul became almost exact lookalikes.

"Have you been here before?"

"No," Paul said. "I'm waiting for you to show me."

"Come on then."

The warehouse was enormous. The ceiling that originally separated the first and second stories had long ago disappeared. A wide balcony—a veranda on all four sides—remained. Thousands of cardboard boxes were stacked up along the walls to the mezzanine, then began again on that level to the farthermost recesses at the top of the building. Each box sat on its side. Each one housed a number of seabirds. Each bird squawked out its own tale of woe, and the noise was both heartbreaking and unbearable.

Here, a young man labored carefully over a bird, scraping oil from its feathers with a scalpel. There, three teenagers, their clothes drenched, held a soapy pelican underwater. Some of the birds, definitely at death's door, had been wrapped in baby receiving blankets while girls—a few of them weeping—tried to force-feed them with medicine droppers. Too often the food—a mixture of flaked fish and Pablum—dribbled uselessly out onto their oil-caked necks. Over in the corner of this first floor perhaps a dozen pelicans and cormorants on the road to recovery waddled about in what looked like an enormous playpen made of sagging chicken wire. Clowning boys flung handfuls of live smelt from tin tubs to the voracious survivors.

Bernie Hansen came to walk with them.

"These birds here look well enough to be let loose," Andrew shouted, but could barely hear the sound of his own voice. "Why are you keeping them around?"

"The girls did their job too well during those first few days," the veterinarian yelled back. "They put birds into hot water and plenty of detergent. It took away the crude, but it took away the birds' oil too. These fellows would sink like stones now if we put them in the water. We don't know what to do with them."

"Who paid for the building? How did you get in here?"

The veterinarian looked at the new questioner intently and his face lit with recognition. "You're Paul Granger!" he said. "I've heard you speak. Some of the girls from your house have been helping out. To tell you the truth, I don't know who paid for it. On the second day of the spill someone called me up and said we had to do something about the birds. They said I could come down here, and stuff has been coming in ever since. I haven't been out of this building in over ten days. People have been bringing birds in by the carload."

"So whoever has done this has done it anonymously, not even asking for credit," Andrew said pointedly.

"I don't know a thing about it. All I know is that we've taken care of twenty thousand birds and the survival rate, as near as we can calculate it, is somewhere around eighty percent. Over at the university, they aren't doing any better than thirty-seven."

"May we see the second story?" Paul said.

"You have to understand," Bernie Hansen said, "I'm only responsible for the birds here."

They walked up a rickety staircase to the mezzanine. Here, too, they ran into something like the smell of fish, but Andrew realized with a start that the moist and murky odor was actually the smell of sex. Hundreds of people must have had sex up here. That smell—at once attractive and repellent—mingled with the smells of real fish, of dead birds, of incense and marijuana. Here the birds were stacked up facing the center of the warehouse. Behind them, bisected by tiny walkways, wooden packing crates had been made into temporary homes. The sounds were disconcerting—low laughter and the moans of love.

Paul disapperared into the smoke-laden air.

"Don't go in there," the veterinarian said. "I can't be responsible."

But Paul gently pulled back a madras bedspread that curtained off a crate. Andrew, against his will but drawn by a force he couldn't control, was there at the hut's entrance with Paul, glancing in at two men lost in ecstasy. One body lay on its back, its legs splayed, a head full of dank ringlets locked into its crotch. A voice groaned. Hands clenched convulsively in the dark cascade of curls. The hands showed brown, strong, masculine, thick.

"Don't," Andrew said, and thrust Paul's hand away from the curtain. For a fraction of a second, Paul's arm met his with equal strength. Suddenly Andrew realized that *he* was the one being taken on a trip, shown sights he was not equipped to deal with.

The veterinarian babbled as they made their way back to him. "I can't be responsible. We're doing good work here. Nothing dangerous has happened."

Andrew pushed past him and, taking Paul's arm above the elbow, walked to a freight elevator marked "Out of Order" and punched a button. In half a minute they were on the third floor, where the air stank of Lysol, every surface seemed made of stainless steel, and banks of fluorescent lights turned every human face a sickly gray-blue.

"CFE is in charge of this operation," Andrew said shakily. "CFE owns all of this."

Paul gave him a lazy smile. The second half of their tour was considerably less stimulating than the first.

The Westphall family mansion stood on the north slope of Nob Hill. Its large grounds and solid stone construction saved it from the San Francisco earthquake and fire, and it now stood as a bastion of Bay Area society. Today, for Angela's birthday party, the first and second terraces were turned into an improvised zoo. Llamas, peacocks, and pygmy horses mingled with the guests. Children jockeyed to ride the elephants and camels. The third and lowest terrace held the caged animals— big cats, bears, monkeys, and a huge aquarium filled with

California species—seals, sea lions, and a dozen lively otters. Inside, on the gallery walls, generations of Westphall family portraits had been removed and replaced with Jordan Logan-Fisher's wild animal drawings from her recent expedition to Kenya. And all of this was for Angela.

"I want to open my presents now," the little girl insisted. She was dressed in five full yards of tiered organdy, which caused one sharp-tongued guest to remark, "All the Westphall and Fitch sugar and spice still can't begin to make Angela nice!" It took all of the tact of the family servants to keep Angela's demands from ending the party before the program began. At no small expense Horace Westphall had brought in some of the animal acts and jugglers and clowns from Ringling Brothers, Barnum & Bailey Circus to entertain the assembled guests.

When at last the time came to open the gifts, Pamela pleaded with her daughter, trying to prevent a tantrum. "Now, sweetiekins, please open them one at a time, and make sure you give Mommy the cards."

Pamela's entreaties were lost on the little girl, who ripped open gold- and silver-paper-wrapped gifts of jewelry, stocks, bonds, porcelain dolls, stuffed animals far bigger than she. And there were the big presents from both grandpas—the miniature zoo from Grandpa Fitch and a two-week cruise for four down the Amazon "to see animal life in its natural setting" from Grandpa Westphall.

Pamela sorted through the mess. In the midst of this she turned to Andrew and said, "Wouldn't it be a good idea for you to take care of these small things, the valuables, so that they won't get lost?"

"Sure," Andrew said. "Just let me out of here."

Even the "smaller things" filled a good-sized box, bulging with envelopes and peppered on top with a dozen velvet cases of various sizes and shapes.

Andrew drove with such determination out of the circular driveway that his wheels skidded on the gravel. No more than half a mile from the gate, he pulled the car over to the curb and put his head on the steering wheel. For three hours he'd been put through almost unendurable torture. He'd suffered his own father's contempt coupled with the stiff reserve of Mr. and Mrs. Westphall, who felt strongly that he had betrayed their daughter. For three hours he'd seen his *own* daughter cosseted and flattered and spoiled. They were turning a sweet little girl into an intolerable little bitch.

Andrew thought back to his early years. He hadn't known what a birthday was. He had never received a gift. His own mother had never loved him. Was he doomed to repeat that isolated pattern all through his adult life?

Andrew had a vision of himself alone from the very moment of his birth until the instant of his death. A person who would never find happiness, never even be able to make a friend. Poverty and riches seemed reflecting images of the same tarnished coin. He knew he should do something. It was pointless to let this kind of thinking go on. He knew he shouldn't have left the party, but he just couldn't face it.

He started up the car and drove at random. He stopped at the first liquor store he came to and bought a six-pack of Bud to wash the taste of Dom Perignon out of his mouth.

He sat in the car, clicked open a can, drank half of it, and idly plucked among the little boxes to see what his daughter had so thoughtlessly received. Here was an ankle bracelet from the Hearst family. And a miniature cameo from the Crockers. And a truly execrable poodle pin, a mother and three puppies on gold chains studded with emerald eyes and a diamond pouf. The card to it had vanished.

He cracked open another can and picked up a nest of red lacquer boxes still carrying wisps of its traditional red paper wrappings. These could only be from Tai-ling. Such tiny pieces! His hand looked enormous against the ring, the pin, the hair clips. Could this actually be a bracelet? He jammed two fingers through it, and was oddly touched to see that the gold was soft enough to carry baby-tooth marks. His fingers felt a slight irregularity, and he held the bracelet to the light to read the inscription: "To Tai-ling from her Daddy." There was also a Chinese character—probably the engraver's chop. Something made Andrew examine it more closely. It was tantalizingly familiar, it was . . . a primitive form of a bat eating a beetle. The Compton Fitch logo!

It took him the rest of the six-pack to come to terms with what this might mean: the dates, the places, the bits of gossip overheard, all these leading to only one possible conclusion. . . .

Across the asphalt parking lot he saw a pay phone, headed for it, and dialed Paul Granger's number.

Half an hour later the two men met at a North Beach bar. Andrew arrived first and drank two whiskey sours before Paul joined him.

"Sit down," Andrew said. "Have a pew."

Paul glanced at him warily and ordered a beer.

"What I want to know is this," Andrew said. "Why have you camped out on our doorstep for the last six weeks? And don't give me any shit about chemicals and children."

"A waiting game."

"Games, games, games. I'm sick of playing games. I already know who you are, Paul Granger! I want you to tell me why you're here."

"When I was a boy, my father walked out and he never came back. I know part of what happened. I have to find out more. Your father destroyed my father. What I can't understand is *why* it happened. That's the reason. To find out why."

Andrew studied his drink. "Do you," he asked, "believe in good and evil? Would you entertain the notion that your father was good—I knew him for a while, Paul, were you aware of that?—and that my father is evil?"

"I've never known an evil person. My mother and Bill—he's my stepfather—have been good to me. I don't believe that stuff about not trusting people over thirty. I don't think there are evil men, only ignorant ones."

Andrew snorted. "My dad brought your dad down because he hated his guts from the time they were boys." Andrew ordered another drink. "Do you know what my father says? 'Hire them, buy them, or destroy them.' He tried all three on your dad."

"Why would a person do a fellow human being such harm?"

Andrew pulled out a golden circlet from his pocket and put it on the bar. "Tell me, Paul, if you had the opportunity to destroy your father, what would you do?"

"Why would I want to destroy him? I just want to *find* him."

Andrew held back his information that Matthew was living in China, outside of Shanghai. "Put it this way, then. If you had the opportunity to destroy my father, what would you do about that?"

"Maybe you've had too much to drink. I'm not getting across to you. I just want to find out what happened. I want that more than anything else. I'm not interested in revenge."

"I am," Andrew said. "I'm very interested in revenge."

Paul's hand reached out to touch Andrew's, then drew back. "But why?" he almost whispered. "Don't you know, don't you really know, that revenge, or hatred, or even war, never solved anything?"

"There's another business saying of my father's," Andrew said intently. "Listen to this one. 'Revenge is the best revenge.'"

"How can you say that? How can you even think it?"

Andrew tried to keep the beautiful young face in focus. "Because you're your father's son. And I'm my father's son."

Although the architectural outlines of their penthouses were mirror images of each other, Tai-ling, like a mother who has given birth to identical twins and wishes to define their separate identities, took great pleasure over the years in decorating their respective dwellings in terms of polarity—the Yin and the Yang.

Tai-ling's sunny breakfast room glowed with flamingo-pink walls and baseboards of shiny black tile, white venetian blinds, and exotic ginger jars in salute to her own cinematic career and Shanghai past. Harley's morning room reflected Tiffany-box blue with with a pearl-white ceiling. Huge vases of white gladioli and blue agapanthus were replenished every morning—blooms that the florist had assured her were particularly masculine in tone. The nights they spent in passion, bordering on the unnatural, were consummated in Tai-ling's enormous bed draped in swaths of apricot satin. After they had eaten hungrily of each other, they could make their way—knees shaking—to Tai-ling's cozy breakfast nook and feast on delicacies that slid and spurted in their famished mouths.

Occasionally, they would stay up all night and talk, regaling each other with stories, getting gloriously drunk, plotting sales and sell-outs. They spent these nights in Harley's apartment, where his ticker-tape machine clicked merrily along in the den, like a trusted member of the family. Often they would curl up on one of his commodious sofas at nine in the evening, armed with a scratch pad and a couple of telephones, and by five the following morning be several hundred thousand dollars richer. In those exhilarating dawns they craved wholesome breakfasts and Tiffany-box blue.

This Sunday morning they breakfasted on cantaloupe with lime and Corsican squid in virgin olive oil. They had bankrupted yet another Southeast Asian nation and were gleefully speculating on how long it would take before the bloody overthrow of the martinet in charge.

When a loud buzz interrupted their meal, Harley said, "It's Sunday morning, for God's sake!"

Tai-ling, for all the world like a mollifying oriental wife, answered, "Dearest, please. Don't upset yourself. No one would dare bother a man of your importance unless it was an emergency."

Harley excused himself and went to the intercom. When he returned, he said, "It's Andrew. I told him I was busy, but he said that this time he knew I'd want to see him. I told him to come up."

The door chimes sounded and Harley disappeared, to return in a few moments with his son, who also had obviously been up all night, but not in pursuit of financial gain. He reeked of whiskey, his hands shook, he had neither bathed nor shaved, and there were traces of vomit on his shoes.

Harley stared at him. "Is this how you dress for a social call?"

"You know, Father," Andrew said, "Pamela trusts me. I've always been able to get along with women, just like you. Do you know what she did yesterday at the party? She put me in charge of Angela's gifts." His face twisted in hatred. "I don't mean the crap," he said. "She put me in charge of the gifts that meant something—the stocks and the bonds and the jewelry." He looked over at Tai-ling and smiled grimly. "Do you suppose I might have a drink?"

Tai-ling obediently left the room.

"What is it, Andrew?" Harley asked. "What do you want? What do you think you have?" He spoke in steel tones.

"Tai-ling has exquisite taste in jewelry, Father." He leaned across the table until his face was only three inches from Harley's own. "And your father had good taste."

Tai-ling reappeared with a shot glass of whiskey on a small silver tray. Andrew took it with a flourish and repeated his sentence almost exactly. "You have exquisite taste in jewelry, Tai-ling, and so did your father." He bowed formally in the Chinese manner. "Your father," he said to Tai-ling, "and your father," he said to Harley. "That would be Harley Compton Fitch II, wouldn't it? Tell me, Dad, is it fun fucking your sister? In the old days when I used to watch, you seemed to enjoy it."

Tai-ling moved swiftly from her chair. She picked up what was left of the Corsican squid and hurled it at Andrew's face. "Pig's abortion!" she snarled in Chinese. "Red-faced masturbator!"

Instinctively, Andrew answered her in the language of the caves. "Incestuous rodent! Corrupt civet cat! Your hole gives off fumes."

Harley came up from behind and dealt his son a savage kidney punch that sent him sprawling. "You don't know what you're talking about. You're drunk. Now get out!"

Andrew dragged himself up and leaned heavily against the wall. The bright blue lent his oatmeal complexion a nasty pallor. "I have a child's bracelet, Father, and I can recognize any version of the old Fitch logo. After all these years, I know a bat eating a beetle when I see one."

As Harley moved toward him with his fists up, Andrew laughed again. "I'm not fool enough to have brought it with me. It's in a safe place, and it will remain there until you see fit to—let's say—give me controlling stock in the entire conglomerate, and you can start with Compton Fitch Chemicals. Then I may give the bracelet back, or who knows? I may save it until Angela has a little girl of her own. She'll love the story that goes along with it."

He turned to Tai-ling. "And, Auntie, you'll appreciate from all those gangster films you used to make that it will be your job to make sure your lover doesn't send out someone to kill me. Because, believe me, the version I've written down is even more lurid than the reality, if that's possible."

Tai-ling opened her mouth, but Andrew put up his palm to hush her. "No more street language from you, young lady!" he said waggishly. "It doesn't reflect well on the family. And, Dad, don't worry. You'll always have a job with the company. You know what fun it is to have a punching bag at those board meetings."

He gave them both his most winning public relations smile. "Catch you both later!" Then he wheeled unsteadily out the door and was gone.

For a long moment brother and sister, partners and lovers, looked at each other over the breakfast ruins. They had been inseparable for the past eighteen years. They didn't need to articulate the alternatives. Tai-ling could go away; both of them remembered her luxurious, lonely life on the coast at Malibu. Or, she could disappear utterly. Andrew would have no scandal. Or, they could hire a thug. Or, buy the bank with the safe-deposit box. Or, they hadn't invited the Hearsts to Angela's party for nothing. A few phone calls from Harley and the story would never see print. Or, they could give the pig's abortion the stock he wanted. Or . . .

"You get the paper, and I'll get the pens. You make more coffee, and I'll get some vodka out of the freezer. I'm good for twelve more hours. Aren't you? Let's give the kid a run for his money."

Tai-ling threw back her head and laughed. "Shall we dateline our calls from 110 Shanghai Road?"

Breakfast had been early and large. Pecan waffles made from whole grain, with fresh fruit and herb tea. The occupants of the house gathered together to thank the universe for its abundance. After they ate they prayed, but briefly. Then most of the men and women went out for the day to the bird hospital and the ongoing demonstration at CFE. Only a half dozen remained to pick up the breakfast dishes, to work in the vegetable garden in the alley below, to doze, to dream.

Paul helped Sunshine with the dishes. He put on a record of Paramahansa Yogananda singing "Oh, God Beautiful" to the accompaniment of his harmonium. The day seemed perfect.

Then all that shattered as someone pounded on the front door with such force that the whole house shook.

"Narcs?" Sunshine asked. "At this hour? Just tell me what to flush, Paul, and you hold them at the door as long as you can—"

But it was already too late, and it was not the narcs. Lurching against furniture, Andrew staggered into the house, calling out for Paul.

"I'm here. I'm here." Paul found Andrew on his knees in the dining area, his head in his hands.

"What is it?" Sunshine appeared in the kitchen doorway. She appraised the situation. "Maybe I'd better go and leave you two alone."

"I did it," Andrew sobbed. "I did what I said I was going to do. I destroyed him. I humiliated him. I brought him down."

"Your father?"

"Yes." Andrew looked around wildly. "I think I'm going to be sick."

Paul took him into the large old-fashioned bathroom on the ground floor, held his head while Andrew puked, then busied himself putting ice cubes into a towel. "Put that on the back of your neck. You'll feel better."

"All I wanted," Andrew said, "was . . . I don't want the company!"

"What did you want?" Paul asked quietly. He lowered the bamboo blinds to cut off the bright sunlight, lit a stick of incense, and began to run a warm bath with a generous dollop of patchouli oil.

"When I was a kid," Andrew said, "I always thought that when I found my father he would want me and everything would be perfect. But from the very beginning, all he cared about was competition. When we went swimming, he would splash me in the face until I couldn't breathe anymore. '*Do you give, do you give, do you give?*' When he taught me how to play backgammon, he made me play for money. I lost thousands of dollars and he made me pay it all back. But still, all I wanted was to be with him. But when I found him, he found Tai-ling. She's all he's ever cared about—Tai-ling and my daughter. So, I had to do it, so he'd be proud of me! Because I've won now. I've definitely won." Again, he was forced to stop because of tears.

"Of course you've won," Paul said. "And you're not alone now. You're with me, and you're going to be all right. But you know what, Andy? You need a bath, real bad, brother. Let's just get some of these clothes off you. . . ." He unbuttoned Andrew's shirt and plucked something from the hollow of his collarbone. "What's this? It looks like a baby squid!"

"It is," Andrew said. "Tai-ling threw them at me." Then, like a little boy, he allowed a small smile to replace his tears.

"I want you in that tub when I get back," Paul said. "And put those clothes outside the door. I'll get you some clean ones."

Paul went to his private stash and pulled out two joints of the very best uncut Mill Valley sensimilla. He found some matches and returned to find Andrew already in the bath. He splashed water on his face and hair, and the cleansing oils began to melt the care from his features. Paul lit a joint, inhaled deeply, then, kneeling by the tub, passed it to Andrew.

"I've never . . ."

"Come on, it'll do you good! It'll relax you and it won't give you a hangover."

In silence, broken only by the sighing of a few enormous eucalyptus trees outside, by the occasional rustle of a bamboo blind, by the slightest ripple of water as Andrew moved first one leg and then the other in the bath's healing warmth, the two men smoked. The joint went from a pair of full, almost brutal lips to a mouth as soft and yielding as a young poet's. As the benevolent drug produced its effect, the colors in the room grew lush. The textures of the toweling, the slick enamel, the iridescent shimmer of oil took on lives of their own. This seedy Berkeley bathroom turned into a tropical island.

Paul watched as the lines of tension, malice, and grief etched on Andrew's face faded into a weary calm. "You're cleaner now," he said, referring to Andrew's soul as well.

Still, from time to time, a tear would make its way down the once tormented face. Finally Paul said softly, almost like a mother, "Time to get out now," and held a towel to wrap around his new friend.

Andrew stood quiet as a child while Paul patted him dry, his mind a million miles away perhaps, as sleepy, as mild, as a tot before his nap.

"Time to get some sleep, maybe?" Paul guided the naked man to his own room, and they lay down on a low bed flanked by pillows. Andrew's face turned impassively to the ceiling. Then the tears began again.

"Don't cry, don't."

And then Paul was kissing him.

She came into town on the first Thursday of June. It was already an open secret that her patternless, seemingly random errands and visits followed a decipherable code. The enemies of the people whom Jiang Qing denounced were simply those who, in the early Shanghai days when Jiang had been a movie actress, assigned her the second lead or shortchanged her last paycheck or said her eyes were too close together or gave her a bad review. It was said that Madame Mao's ambivalence toward the West stemmed from those months during which she had played Nora in a production of Ibsen's *A Doll's House*. If she could not be hailed as an immortal in the world of Western culture, she would expunge every trace of Western culture from Chinese life.

She circled through the flatlands of this delta city. The farmers who worked in Matthew's neighboring fields spent more and more time at the Fong-See Compound conferring about seedlings, plowing, and the division of crops. Often they spent the night wrapped in sacking inside Matthew's home. Whether they stayed for curiosity or because they cared, Matthew was unable to tell. He knew inevitably that she would be coming. He also knew that unless they got this new beet crop in by the middle of June, he would be unable to measure its moistureproof properties.

That Thursday he and his comrades rose before dawn, plowed thirty hectares before breakfast, and then went home, where together with a dozen of his most trusted associates, Matthew laid out his strategy for a maximun harvest. Although they were not a real commune yet, he and the villagers devised a plan in which fields overlapped private properties in order to make the best use of the soil. He made blueprints for his own use, but used the dirt floor of his main room to scratch out with a stick his new suggestions for the location of the droughtproof wheat. Their meeting was interrupted by the pad of bare feet on earth and the wail of an old man as he keened, "Hide all your possessions! Tell your children to run away! Offer them your mother-in-law to rape and pillage. We're done for."

"Is this the mudhill of the fat Western termite? The swollen leech that sucks up the blood of our people? Tell him to come out into the sun, into the harsh light of justice. We will render up his fat in the skillet of correct thinking."

Matthew looked at the men around him. Their faces betrayed nothing. "Lu," he said to the trembling caretaker, "it sounds as if she has brought people with her. Be sure there is enough tea, and slice up some cold sweet potatoes for those who need refreshment. I shall receive Madame Mao on my porch, but for those who have other duties, there is a back entrance to this building."

Matthew stood for a moment with bowed head, took a deep breath to compose himself, and stepped outside onto the tiny veranda.

"My home is honored by your visit," he said quietly in perfect Wu. "My friends and I have prepared simple refreshments for you."

The woman before him was gaunt and wild, her hair unkempt. Her steel-rimmed glasses had made sores on either side of her nose. On her left wrist she wore an expensive gold watch, and gold teeth glittered in her mouth.

She began to scream, turning from time to time to the thirty or so journalists who had shuffled along in her wake to this rural outpost. As her tirade swirled about him, Matthew caught phrases that accused him of lying in bed all day, taking his pleasure with children of the neighborhood, and requiring himself to be carried, even as the gentlemen of old, from one side of the room to the other.

Matthew thought that when she had finished, he might be

able to say something. But in fact, here in the morning sun, he could not marshal any response, could not, in a sense, remember what his argument might be. Then Wang-fu, one of his neighbors, stepped forward.

"This 'termite,' as you call him, has plowed fifty hectares by himself this morning."

Lu came out, carrying a plain wooden tray with tea and sliced cold potatoes. With what Matthew would always remember as incredible courage, Lu passed in front of Madame Mao and offered tea to two of her male aides.

"Spare me humiliation," he said loudly. "Take some of this unattractive refreshment. For weeks I have begged this man"—and here he pointed his chin at the foreigner—"to lay in some supplies for possible honored political guests. But since he eats such miserable fare himself, he thinks the whole world lives on cold tea and roots."

"It's true," a teenaged boy spoke up. "When I was very small I had my first taste of meat because this man sent his feast to the village. He refuses such fare. All he uses, even for seasoning, is a little horseradish. He grinds it himself."

Suddenly there in the sun, the peasants who had declined to write on the big character posters pushed forward to tell a separate story of the foreigner's disregard for self-indulgent ways.

"He has no furniture," one of them said. "You would see that if you went inside. He has given it away piece by piece as the young people of the village married."

Another declared that in the sixteen years he had known the foreigner, he had seen him eat rice only once; that he was rumored to live on berries, nuts, and air. And another said that when he had asked Matthew for a loan, he was unable to give him money because he had none, but that he had come in the night to work in this man's house as a common laborer, whitewashing walls and cleaning out septic tanks. "Money is nothing," the foreigner had said. "A man's time is his only real possession, and I will give you as much as you need."

All these stories bypassed Jiang Qing. They were delivered to the journalists, who, with the reflexes of their trade, began to jot down notes. Jiang Qing, crazed as she was from her own enforced stays in Moscow's mental hospitals, her husband's flagrant infidelities, and a difficult menopause which deprived her of sleep and all rational thought for some months, was still nothing if not a consummate politician.

"Behold!" she proclaimed, pointing to the fields about her. "The sweet green breast of Mother China, which suckles even the dwarfed atrocities of Western birth and turns their twisted limbs and sickly thought into something comparable to our own men of merit!"

"You speak truly of one thing," the foreigner said at last. "China is my mother. I was born here and intend to be buried in this earth. I have accomplished little, but whatever I have been able to do, the credit is China's, and China's alone."

The tiny, bespectacled woman gazed shrewdly at her adversary. She could detect absolutely no sign of fear in this man. How she despised foreigners!

"You see," she shrilled to her entourage, "how austerity and good conduct go hand in hand! This man has no paintings, no music, no furniture, and no food. Yet see how the people love him! I shall make this place a model farm for our own bloated and decaying intellectuals. They shall be doubly chastised to have to learn from a Western dog about correct thinking. Now see that you try these yams! And refresh yourself with some cool tea. Just squat down there in the dirt. Do you see how easily journalists can turn to the life of the soil? I shall go back to the hotel now and rest. Meet me at dawn tomorrow, and together we shall ferret out more crimes."

After Jiang Qing's truck had left, the journalists were invited to sit in the shade of Matthew's sycamore trees for some cold sticky-rice and several cups of homemade wine. Madame Mao dined in the quiet of her suite on baby shrimp and shark fins in candied ginger baskets, and went to bed early with a splitting headache. But she was as good as her word. In the coming months she would send at least twenty intellectuals from the Beijing bureaucracy to sort out their thoughts on the banks of the Whangpoo.

Before the Revolution, the Bud of the Lotus was notorious for its panoply of low and disgustingly delicious pastimes. It offered these to both visiting foreigners and the few Chinese prosperous enough to sample its varied and decadent services. The three-storied building housed three separate restaurants, a mah-jongg table, an opium den, and on the top floor a brothel full of girls, boys, and a few perfumed domestic animals. The owners claimed to cater to everyone's most rarefied whim.

Naturally, after the Revolution, the Bud of the Lotus was one of the first places to be closed. Just as naturally, as the years of the new regime slipped by, the Lotus was one of the first places to start reopening—petal by petal. Now it boasted a teahouse on one floor, gambling rooms, and private restaurants where some furtive sexual favors were exchanged. On the main floor, at what was once called "the world's longest bar," a new generation came to drown their frustrations in imported Russian vodka, which this year was cheaper even than *mao tai* because of the precarious balance of trade between the two Communist giants. Here in the Bud of the Lotus a young group of dissidents, who referred to themselves sarcastically as the Gilded Youth of Beijing, gathered nightly to exchange their grievances. They had even coined a saying about themselves: "How the gilded have become tarnished!"

They loved to recount tales of how their relatives who left for America, that corrupt "mountain of gold," created instant antiques by burying new brass objects in shit. They perceived themselves as part of a social system that fed upon itself until it, too, turned into shit. They were just intelligent enough to perceive their utter unimportance in the scheme of things.

"My father keeps two cases of tinned pâté in the basement," one young man said. He wore a Rolex watch and twisted his wrist compulsively in the bar's dim light so that the gold might better shine.

"My mother spent the better part of last evening thrusting her ugly legs into a pair of Western 'panty hose'—she wore them all night, and woke up smelling like a wild boar."

"All day at school we hear about the Revolution and tales of the Long March. 'When I was a boy I walked eighteen thousand *li!*' But now he sits and dozes and complains that we are not the first in our neighborhood with a new bicycle. Tell me how this has changed from the old days! Tell me, and I will buy you another Stolichnaya."

"Even this," Nyi Chuen-yee said, peering down into his drink, "even these distilled spirits are simply another example of round-eye decadence. Tell me, just tell me," he said pugnaciously, "that a Russian factory is different from an American one, that a Russian official is smarter than a—"

"Quiet down, Chuen-yee," said a friend uneasily.

He knew better than any of them that he had nothing to lose. He was here only on sufferance; he was a source of disquiet to his friends and a burden to his family. His green eyes stood out in his face like beacons. In the old China he would have been put out as a baby into the killing-walls for the wild animals to eat. As it was, he could never look at anyone directly in the face. The most enlightened of his intellectual friends would involuntarily put out their fingers to ward off the evil eye. "His mother was a witch," they would say behind his back, and even *to* him when they quarreled. He could not deny it. He was the whelp of a foreign devil.

Chuen-yee raised his voice. "Do you know what the Revolution means to my father? A car! Nothing more or less. Do you know how my stepmother registers success? By party invitations. Oh, my friends," he said, "we are cut off from the old ways and divorced from the new. At least the ancients, corrupt as they were, could write down their sorrow, and others would read it or hear it."

"You forget the big posters, Chuen-yee."

"But Madame Mao is behind those," another said. "How can anyone take a woman seriously?"

A wave of sobriety washed over them.

"The Helmsman is very old," one said. "His wife grows in power every day."

The conversation once again took on its whining tone. Chuen-yee nursed his vodka. He knew that in the hot months his family took up residence in the Summer Palace and that Madame Mao herself frequently visited that pleasant resort.

Two months later as the sun came up, Chuen-yee, with the ostentatious scorn for his elders that is so common to young men everywhere, left his family to eat their breakfast and fret about mundane concerns. He strode the arcades of the Summer Palace that bordered the artificial lake so loved by China's last empress dowager. He breathed in the fresh air as he paced the Painted Gallery, and tried with all his might to invoke his muse. He had read that the rebellious poets in the Western world a hundred years before gained their inspiration by communing with nature. But try as he might, all he could see were the blossoms of the wisteria vine coming into bloom and the reflection of the ancient empress's marble "navy" mirrored in the lake's turquoise waters. He marched, he waited, he agonized.

Then a morning came when, in an instant, he knew exactly why his life would change and how. As he strode from west to east, squinting into the rising sun, he saw a group of five marching toward him under the arcade. The light shone behind them as if they were emperors of old. At their center, a tiny figure glittered. He recognized, in the marrow of his bones, the distinct sound of her assertive voice—sharp as a cleaver cutting through lard. He stepped behind the twisted wisteria vines to let Jiang Qing and her entourage pass, but at the last moment he threw himself in front of her and bowed his head to the ground in the ancient gesture of servitude.

"Daughter of the sun," he said, "only you can help me. I molder. I die. My life is meaningless without you."

Jiang Qing stared down at this attractive supplicant, and somewhere in her the empress that she might have been in another life stirred. "No need to be so sad, my brave young puppy. Get up. Get up. Come with me. I shall have them make tea for us, and I will show you my monkeys."

The blinds had been drawn and the windows shut tight against the insistent summer sun. Chuen-yee's eyes watered. He brushed tears away from his cheekbones and sneezed uncontrollably several times in the acrid air of Madame Mao's apartment. When one or another of his parents' friends brought in an ill-tended child, the smell of ammonia came with its blankets. And afterward his stepmother would sniff, "A child's rotten bottom betrays his parents' low origins."

Madame Mao deduced part of his thoughts. "You are wondering about my children. They are a lonely woman's only consolation." She clapped her hands sharply.

"Bring them in," she called. "Bring in my children to show my new friend."

Two servants, wearing medical masks, appeared in the gloom wheeling something that was four feet across and just brushed the ceiling.

"Unveil them," she cried. "Unveil my little poppets."

The servants drew away the drop cloth and disappeared into the murky air. Chuen-yee found himself at eye level with three scabrous spider monkeys who eyed him with boundless cynicism. They reminded Chuen-yee of the three monkeys from the shrine at Nikko in Japan—those cheap souvenirs sold everywhere, even here in China—those monkeys who admonished a sinful populace to "see no evil, hear no evil, speak no evil." But these monkeys looked as if evil was all they heard, saw, and spoke.

"My babies, my little ones, my darlings," Madame Mao crooned, and then said to Chuen-yee, again with a combination of the demonic and the real, "These are my friends, my only children. You see I am lonely. I was *forced* to go out into the countryside of China to make my mark."

A masked servant now wheeled in an elaborate tray of syrupy liquors and sticky sweets. Chuen-yee's stomach heaved.

"Sit down, young man, and tell me of yourself."

"I want more than life itself to be a poet and serve the people in words made new for our times."

A monkey picked up a wad of its own dung and hurled it with unerring accuracy at the back of Chuen-yee's head. He flinched, but went determinedly on.

"But my parents think only of material acquisitions."

Madame Mao's eyes narrowed as he desperately continued with the speech that he had only recited inwardly so far. He spoke now as if a Nikko monkey had snatched its paws away from sealed lips.

"This may be madness, but in my dreams I think of you, not simply as the wife of your husband, but as the modern embodiment of Quan Yin, our ancient Goddess of Mercy. Through you, and *only* through you, I hope to set out upon the correct path of art."

He was able now to see a little better in the thick air. He could watch Jiang Qing consider, gaze at him calculatingly, and then issue an invitation. "There's an opera tonight—a corrupt one, I'm afraid—that I'm forced to attend and inspect. You will accompany me."

He sent more than two hundred telegrams. He hired the best catering company in the city and had the walls of the reception hall of Compton Fitch Enterprises banked with thousands of dollars' worth of day lilies. He hired a strolling mariachi to wait by the main doors of the lobby and serenade his guests as they came in. He hated the din of spic music, but somehow it seemed right. He had bought a new suit expensive enough to finance a Central American country for a year and instructed Tai-ling to dress to kill.

Everyone would be here, including his shipping partner, Horace Westphall, his wife, and all of his children, including Harley's own ex-daughter-in-law, Pamela, who would bring his granddaughter, Angela. He asked every financier in northern California, every banker, every industrialist. But the real guests of honor were the members of the media—the press, radio, and television. Harley staked everything on his primitive, but effective, knack of establishing an immediate rapport with the press.

Harley spent not even a moment in needless worry since his son had dared to confront him with his measly little threat. No, Harley simply did what he did best. Now he waited, happy with the thought that one of the first telegraphed acceptances had come from Andrew.

Harley knew the names of every guest and every reporter. For a full hour he roamed the marbled lobby and the carpeted reception hall, shouting over the strains of "Escaleras de la Carcel" and "La Balla Perdida" to "Have another Scotch," or, "Try some of this champagne," and "Don't let that caviar go to waste! I had fifty pounds of it flown from Beirut just this morning." An old-fashioned ice-cream soda fountain served Angela and any of the young people who might want to make themselves a hot-fudge sundae or a double-dip sugar cone.

Harley fended off questions about the purpose of this lavish display. "It's a celebration," was all he said. "Just a celebration that's long overdue."

When he judged it time to speak, he thanked his instincts for remembering the mariachi, who provided him with a strenuous, if slightly off-key fanfare. Harley unbuttoned his jacket and thrust his hands deep into his pockets. He grinned with unfeigned good cheer as he surveyed his audience.

"We're all friends here," he began, "and it means everything to me today to be surrounded by friends. Of course, we've all been living through trying times. . . . " He treated them to exactly eight minutes of platitudes, about the sanctity of the family, the undesirability of war, the inviolate borders of this great democracy. Then, when he judged them all to be close to a harmless coma, he said, "Sometimes I feel that the fight has gone out of me." He was greeted by groans and half-derisive laughter. "No, I mean it," he said, and waved his arms in a joking, helpless gesture, although his mind was coiled as tight as jeweler's wire. "There are those who've been saying I'm out of touch. . . . " And the bankers eyed him narrowly, tabulating changes in their own investments should the chemical division of CFE be phased out. "What this company needs is a new point of view, a fresh emphasis, an exciting change that will let us move smoothly into the future. Now, I don't want you all to think I'm going into complete retirement, but . . . " He stopped and looked around the room.

Every pair of eyes in the place was fixed on him. But Harley watched his son. Andrew's jaw hung slack as he breathed through his mouth. Harley fancied he could hear each raspy exhalation.

"I'm deeding over a controlling interest in Compton Fitch Enterprises to someone all of you already know—the astute, the incomparable, the adorable Tai-ling!"

The hubbub rose around him. "Don't you think it's time we began to let some women have a say in how we run this great country of ours?" He called up Tai-ling and put his arm around her waist.

"There's a little story attached to all this," he said after the noise had died down. "I don't think many of you know it, but Tai-ling and I have been friends for a long time. When I built the Twin Towers it was with Tai-ling in mind." He had their attention now. "Don't think I haven't heard some of those stories over the years that Tai-ling and I were more than just friends. Well," he said directly to the reporters now, one good buddy to another, "you were right about that one. Tai-ling and I *are* more than just friends. We're family! Tai-ling and I share the same father." Through the chorus of ohs and ahs, he raised his voice. "I guess you could say that's why I believe in Pacific commerce. In Compton Fitch Enterprises, Asia and America have been joined at the hip for a long time!"

Tai-ling waved modestly. She was dressed in precisely the style of Madame Chiang Kai-shek—tailored suit, high-heeled sandals, a lavaliere of exquisite jade. "You're looking at more than just a pretty face," Harley boomed jovially. "The blood of Harley Compton Fitch II circulates in this lovely woman, and I'm proud to be able to pass my holdings on to her, because"— and here he struck the pious note he had sounded earlier in his speech—"family means everything to me."

The party went on for hours. It was axiomatic to the press—once they had called in their stories over special phone lines installed for them by Harley—and the financial community alike that it was foolish to leave until less than a pound of caviar remained; and every time this seemed to have happened, a pair of husky retainers staggered out carrying yet another crystal vat of the freshly imported black gold.

After his speech, Harley made his way through the crowd and found his son standing beside the Westphall family contingent. Andrew's former in-laws and ex-wife edged discreetly away, but little Angela, not knowing any better, stayed, reaching up to hold her daddy's hand.

Harley put a social smile on his face and spoke through gritted teeth. "So you call yourself my son, you slimy little shit! You disappointed me. Tai-ling and I spent a fair amount of time anticipating your moves. That you would go to the press with a series of leaks. That you'd try to beat us to the shareholders. We even had plans in case you'd unload your own stock this morning to devalue the shares. That, at the very least, you'd start a round of rumors on Wall Street, or Hong Kong, or London. But you didn't do shit!"

"Dad, I—"

"You're no son of mine. I said a while ago that family meant everything to me. But it doesn't mean shit! My father was an incompetent crook, and my mother was a crazy lush. I had to fight to build my empire and there isn't a faggot in the world who can take it away from me—not even you."

He threw back his head and laughed, and to outsiders it looked as if father and son were sharing a joke. "While Tai-ling and I were working—naturally we had you followed—you were sticking your dick up some kid's ass!"

Angela whimpered as her father's hand tightened over her own. "You hurt me, Daddy!" She pulled away and put her arms around her grandfather's knees.

"Don't worry, Andy, I'm not going to disown you. I'm not even going to fire you." Harley's smile changed to a feral snarl. The telltale veins began to bulge in his neck. "This wasn't just another round, you ass-licking butt-sucker! This wasn't a game of Ping-Pong, or some penny-ante rubber deal in Malaysia. This is the real game. And you lost. Do you know what you tried to take away from me? My empire! My woman! Do you think I'd give those up to you because of some empty threat? Do you think I created this company by cutting out paper dolls? Do you think Tai-ling would love an ordinary man?"

Andrew struggled not to cry while his father watched in disgust. "You really are a pansy. I wish there was some way I could get rid of you, but I can't." Then, changing his tone, Harley said, "Come along, Angela. We should see to our guests. Doesn't your mother always tell you to circulate?"

The airport at this hour seemed almost completely deserted. Paul and Andrew trudged along determinedly, Paul outfitted in the manner of a pilgrim of the sixties, with layers of jackets made of sacking, carrying a bundle across his shoulders. Andrew puffed beside him, hugging an enormous knapsack labeled conspicuously in black crayon, "PAUL GRANGER, GENERAL DELIVERY, San Francisco, Singapore, Kuala Lumpur, Delhi, and"—the last scrawled in a burst of hope—"Tibet."

Then, all about him teemed a shifting mass of Orientals pushing, calling after lost children, and jostling for position in a barely perceptible line. Paul turned his head and grinned.

"A good part of these people are Indonesians," Paul said. "I've been reading up on my itinerary. The Indonesian word for line is *malam*. Do you know what it really means?"

Andrew shook his head.

"It means to mill about and shout and have a good time. That's how Indonesians stand in line."

Andrew said sourly, "They could use an efficiency expert here."

"That's the materialistic American businessman in you talking."

For Andrew at least, these banalities covered an aching sense of loss. As he put one hand on to the back of Paul's belt and with the other pulled the enormous knapsack along the floor, he thought of the many talks he and Paul had had over the last three weeks. Paul assured him many times over—sometimes even as they lay in bed—that virtue was its own reward. In this instance, Andrew thought bitterly, it would have to be.

The night after the gaudy reception at CFE, Andrew sought out Paul. He wept in his lover's arms. For Andrew, no matter what his father thought, this last battle hadn't been about the company or Tai-ling. He wanted his father to pay attention to him and to realize that he was a man worthy of trust, a man of power and imagination. Andrew saw now that he had played it out all wrong, and there would be no more battles. He lost everything: his wife, his daughter, his position, any hope to ever run the company, and finally he lost his resilience.

Paul said, like one uncertain little boy to another, "At least you have a father and there's always a chance to work it out later. You have someone to go up against. My father just came into the solarium one day while I was playing with my sister, said good-bye, and that's the last I ever saw or heard of him. Do you know what I'm saying, Andrew? Your father cares enough about you to give you a fight."

Oh, sure, his father would be ready to go at it again tomorrow, but Andrew just didn't care anymore. He didn't have it in him. . . .

"I know where your father is," Andrew blurted out, and that was the bitch of it. With that one sentence he'd lost the one person he'd ever loved.

Andrew had gone on to tell all he knew. As he did he could feel Paul pulling away from him, murmuring over and over, "You really know where my father is?"

Matthew Granger was in China, on a bank of the Whangpoo River near the pagoda and village of Lungwha outside Shanghai. He was a farmer and, as far as anyone knew, he was still alive.

In those first few moments, Andrew thought he was safe. China's borders were closed. Inevitably, Paul—even as they kissed and drank and smoked and went out for a walk and came back to make love and lie together exhausted—began to make his plans to continue his search for his father.

Andrew was amazed by Paul's tenacity. *China was closed.* No one from any Western country could get in. At the same time, Andrew remembered the determined little kid that he, himself, had been, recognizing his father from a scratchy newspaper print and hailing a cab to take him to the man who had given him life. A lot of good it did him.

"What if you do get through and you really manage to find your father, and—how can I put this, Paul?—he turns out to be, not necessarily just like mine, but completely indifferent? Suppose he doesn't care about you at all?"

"That's what I've been living with ever since he walked out. I feel that he loved me. But is that just a dream? If he doesn't care about me—if he left because he didn't love us anymore—well, I just want to hear it from his own mouth."

They had three weeks, the happiest time in Andrew's life. He took time off from the office, and he put all of his own energies to work—using his contacts at CFE—to prepare Paul for his quixotic trip across half the world to find his father. Andrew remembered back to his own days in China when he listened to dissatisfied revolutionaries whispering about "other places." The knew that their long northeastern border led only to Russia; Hong Kong was far away and involved an often fatal trip by water. Instead, they dreamed of the south and the southeast: the lush fields below Canton, or the icy peaks of Tibet, and ultimately, anonymous Burmese jungles where any man who could weave a hut and find a native woman could be his own man, his own king. Why shouldn't Paul attempt this trip in reverse?

Together they mapped out a plan. He would fly first to Singapore, to acclimatize himself, then Delhi, then make his way north to Katmandu, trek across the Himalayas, and into the isolated regions of Tibet, which had been occupied by the Communists since 1951. The Tibetan Autonomous Region shared a long border with China. It was Paul's hope, since many men in that oppressed land had been monks, and had now been pressed into indentured labor, that he might find a guide who, out of a spiritual affinity, would take him into southern China. From there, Andrew arranged a series of possible "safe houses" from the old oil connections of his father.

Together the two of them went into strenuous physical training. The actual details—the tickets, the visas, letters of introduction to Indian agents—had been easy to accomplish. But the trip would be as arduous as climbing Mount Everest. They took twenty-five-mile hikes daily around Mount Tamalpais. Andrew nursed Paul through the side effects of inoculations for typhus, cholera, smallpox, malaria, and hepatitis. Paul gave up being a strict vegetarian; he ate thick steaks every night and liver in the morning to build a high iron level. He increased the loads in his knapsack until he reached a hundred and twenty-five pounds.

After their short weeks together, though Andrew thought Paul was far from ready, he also knew that his lover would wait no longer. So, tonight, two young men, one blond, one dark, stood in the pulsing mayhem of the airport under harsh overhead lights. One smiled, already deep into his adventure; the other feigned indifference. Then, after forty-five minutes, the moment was upon them.

The two gazed into each other's eyes. "You'll come back to me?" Andrew asked. But it was Paul's curse always to be truthful.

"I'll try to. I don't know. I can't read the future."

They cast aside all caution and clung to each other. The Orientals who stood about them clucked to each other in their various dialects, and an Australian voice called out clearly, "Christ, Harry! It's a couple of poufters."

Then Paul was gone.

Andrew ordered a brandy, and stayed to watch the plane

take off over the Bay. He took a cab to a well-known gay bar and got drunk as quickly as he could. There were plenty of young, inviting faces, and compact, tiny butts. All of these boys were willing, God knew. But it was too intimate here. "I like your eyes," one said coquettishly, and Andrew remembered when Paul said the same thing, running his fingertips across his lashes.

Andrew asked a question of the bartender, who directed him down the street to a place called the Adonis Bath House. After paying, he went to a large locker room, undressed, was given a towel, and sent down a long, dimly lit hall. It was lined with small rooms meant for couples. In a larger room, perhaps fifteen oiled male bodies writhed in a heap. He could not join in, shuddering at the thought of that suffocating contact. But along one of the walls he found the glory holes he had heard about in prep school. He felt an enormous erection, a delicious surge of shame, and then he stuck his cock through the hole and into a waiting, faceless orifice.

Chuen-yup drained his glass of *mao tai* and looked around him in the Great Hall of the People with a combination of physical contentment and emotional dread. After weeks of brooding over why he was not included in the Romanian reception, after months brooding over possible failure, even as he *seemed* to succeed, it appeared that his worries were for nothing. Just this afternoon a messenger had come with a handwritten note from Madame Mao deploring the mix-up in invitations and hinting broadly that if he and a few friends would stay after the Westerners had gone home, they would enjoy a midnight supper for the elite and a surprise for the whole family.

His wife, Zizhen, fretted endlessly over what she would wear this evening. She had vacillated between her plain cotton blouse and pants that were the standard uniform for everyday and state occasions alike, and her one silk gown that she kept for appearances with foreigners. "When Wang Guang-mei went to Indonesia with her husband, Jiang Qing suggested that she wear black velvet. Jiang Qing wanted her to sweat to death! But perhaps Guang-mei should have worn the velvet so she wouldn't be rotting in prison today!" Finally Zizhen settled on her silk dress, saying, "I have so few occasions to wear this and surely it will be appropriate for the Romanians."

And it had been appropriate. The Romanian women were stuffed into yards of heavy brocade and skirts decorated with native embroidery. The banquet had been a full twelve courses, stretching out over four hours of interminable Romanian conversation and speeches requiring the use of translators. Chuen-yup grudgingly admitted that he'd worried over nothing. Though the food was good, the entertainment, if it could be called that, was dull and routine. Only the thought of his "surprise" kept him from falling into total apathy. Could it be his car at long last?

After the toasts and the formal withdrawal of the Romanian delegation and at least two-thirds of the guests, servants escorted those invited to stay to tables immediately in front of the platform. More *mao tai* was brought out and platters of cold snacks—candied walnuts, pickled kidney, and iced almond curd.

Madame Mao rose to propose the first toast. "This is just for the few of us. Even my own husband has gone home. Affairs of state press upon him. You also know that I have been asked, against my will, to purge the cultural life of our country. We have burned bad art, but what shall we replace it with?"

Chuen-yup looked around the table at his companions and saw the fixed smiles on their faces as they anticipated a good quarter hour's harangue from the Helmsman's rudder.

"Some new writers have been composing a new kind of theater to cauterize the running sores of capitalism which have drained our strength like boils. They *know* their words must be a strong disinfectant!" She glanced into the wings and started a round of applause.

Chuen-yup clapped dutifully, but his hands stopped in midair when he saw that the young man who came out onstage, peering nearsightedly at his loose sheaf of papers, was, in fact, his own son, Chuen-yee.

> *"They thought our country was a mother.*
> *They made her into mother termite.*
> *Soft, white, fat, and breeding maggots.*
> *Writhing, pulsating, disquieting to watch."*

The assembled guests stared off into space.

> *"Was this what they meant*
> *Those pioneers in the hills*
> *Who gave away their children to friendly peasants?*
> *Was the cure, after all, worse than the sickness?*

Was the disease of hunger cured
Only to be turned into the syphilis of materialism?"

Chuen-yup's wife buried her face in her hands.

"Is this the Revolution? Toasters?
Is this the Revolution?"

One by one, shamefaced, the assembled guests fell into the chant *"Is this the Revolution?"* Onstage Chuen-yee gestured dramatically at each pause and shouted, "Bourbon whiskey!" "Armoires!" "Golden chopsticks!" "Electric rice steamers!" "Bicycles from the West!" "Upholstered easy chairs!" "Automatic can openers for foreign delicacies!"

Finally, when Chuen-yee had worked himself up into a frenzy and sweat misted his spectacles so that he could no longer read, he flung down his papers, drew himself up, and shouted, *"Motorcars!"*

Chuen-yup could smell it even before he saw it. He heard the creaking of wood upon wood as several bureaucrats who had supposedly already left, and still dressed in their best clothes, wheeled out an ox cart, crudely gilded, heaped to the top with fresh dung.

Madame Mao ran up onstage and draped a friendly arm across the narrow bony shoulders of her protégé.

"Here is a reward for someone who has worked hard for it. The vehicle that he's plotted for years to receive!" She, in turn, pulled out another sheaf of papers. "I have letters he has written requesting this reward, even as millions of our own people starve from the famine that is ravaging our communes in Szechuan!"

Flamboyantly, she took one of the letters and began to read. "For many years I have labored . . ." Chuen-yup heard his own carefully constructed sentences shouted out ". . . to build our country, but my workday has been cut from fourteen to twelve hours bicycling in heavy traffic from my apartment and waiting for public transportation to take me the many *li* outside the city."

Were the catcalls he heard obligatory, or was there an undercurrent of real rancor? No one in this room had a car yet, except Jiang herself.

More letters followed. Then Jiang Qing pointed a finger directly at Chuen-yup. "But do not worry, Nyi Chuen-yup, our country rewards the deserving and your reward is coming."

Chuen-yup felt himself lifted up from his seat by the elbows and hoisted above the heads of his bearers. The next instant he was flung down into the still warm and steaming dung.

"Now, Chuen-yup," Jiang Qing shouted, "you may do as you have always wished—ride to success and riches on the backs of your own people!"

Some of his tormentors—old friends from the caves—started to pull the cart around the perimeter of the Great Hall.

If he could just control himself, this would be over soon. But there were to be three clattering rounds; the last one he would never forget. Jiang Qing went directly to his wife, ripped the silk gown that Zizhen had so carefully chosen, exposing her frail back. Jiang Qing walked over to the cart, commanded Chuen-yup to stand up, then handed him a whip. "Go ahead! Enjoy your triumph! Trample them all beneath you! Flog the workers, soldiers, peasants, your patriotic son, and especially your wife, who for so long endured your petty tyrannies and materialistic longings."

Two men roughly placed Zizhen between the shafts of the cart and shouted at her to pull. She could barely move it. "You must whip her, Chuen-yup! You must apply the goad! Only by force and intimidation will you extract the last ounce of strength from those you wish to exploit!"

Chuen-yup used the whip. He had to. The wife of the Foreign Minister hadn't worn black velvet to Indonesia's tropical hell, and she now languished in a solitary cell.

"Harder!" his son called out. "Whip her the way you did at home!" And the thick pink welts rose on Zizhen's back.

Once they were back within the temporary safety of their own home, Chuen-yup scrubbed himself raw in tub after tub of steaming water that he hauled in himself. The servants had vanished during the course of this evening and taken their belongings with them. So everyone had known what had been coming!

Zizhen sobbed, her face down on the bed. "I have a sister in the interior who must take me in. I shall start out as soon as the sun comes up." Chuen-yup heard her use of "I." He knew he could no longer count on any member of his family, or any of those he thought were his friends in high places. Was there no one to whom he could turn?

As he scrubbed away at his body, his mind brought up, and finally settled on, a single fantastic possibility.

* * *

He spent the night in a freezing guest house where the fleas and lice were ravenous, where quarreling mountaineers drank too much and vomited where they fell. When Paul went outside for air, a horde of beggars maimed deliberately by their parents surrounded him. When he kept his coins to himself, they hit him viciously behind his knees with their dented tin cups. A nasty intestinal bug sent him squatting behind low rocks many times. He was weak and dizzy. An excruciating headache plagued him—whether from the altitude or dysentery he wasn't sure. He cursed himself for forgetting his folding umbrella. Standard baggage, since beyond the timberline there were no trees to hide behind while defecating. He was mocked by churlish Sherpas as his bowels groaned audibly for mercy. Only the idealized vision of his father, ever receding, gave him the courage to continue the sharp climb up loose shale to stagger on to the next meager shelter.

"If only 'Fertile Grain' would get his mind out of the dirt and up into the realms of greater learning, our stay here would be less taxing," one of Beijing's formerly most prestigious economists griped.

A renowned cellist on his knees next to the economist ranted softly as he extracted one by one the weeds that clogged "Fertile Grain"'s crop.

"If I have to hear another word," the cellist whispered, "about the bright orange of the yam and the dark green of the mustard leaf combining to form the copious soft brown stool that assures a healthy peasant . . ."

"Personally," remarked a professor of foreign languages weeding in the next row, "I have found these last weeks a stimulating interlude. A hundred years ago in the American Northeast this same experiment was tried and found wanting. Reading Nathaniel Hawthorne's *Blythedale Romance* in translation has given me an important key to what is happening now in our own country."

"Stuff a yam in that man's mouth," said the first weeder, "and do not pull it out until the evening."

It was the custom at Matthew Granger's commune, the former Fong-See Compound, to spend the daylight hours in manual labor. Only in the evening, after an austere but nourishing meal, did these disaffected intellectuals, exiled from the Northern Capital by the Cultural Revolution, feel free to assume what they felt were their proper roles, trading *bons mots* as they speculated on the state of the country and their own fates. They cherished the learned atmosphere and drank in the abstruse learning of the foreign scholar who was their host. But if they stayed up late, they knew they would be roused all too early by the caretaker's gong. And after a hasty morning bowl of gruel they were back again on their hands and knees, complaining eloquently about their assigned tasks in what became a ritual almost as satisfying as their evening flights of fancy.

Here, on "Fertile Grain" Granger's farm near the Lung-wha Pagoda on the banks of the Whangpoo, close to twenty ostracized intellectuals had been sent for reeducation. These few, who later would write memoirs of these golden years, thanked their ancestors that what had been meant as a prison was instead hospitable soil in which their loftiest thoughts could flourish.

This morning their cultivation of the yam field was interrupted by Tsiang Oo-zong, former chairman of the Department of Economics at the University of Beijing, who, coming to the end of the row of yams, by the irrigation ditch, straightened up so fast that he pulled a ligament in his back.

"May the gods of the ancients protect us!" he grunted, thus showing one reason for his expulsion from Beijing's academic halls. There, cowering before him in the ditch, crouched a mud-encrusted stranger, in hiding from the roaming cadres.

Two learned workers extended their arms and pulled the stranger from the ditch. One of them peered at the newcomer closely.

"You were in the caves? After that, Motorized Vehicles—isn't that right?"

The professor of foreign languages said, "Didn't you take in a Western bastard child? What an interesting connection with the West!"

"Whatever I was once," the stranger said, "I'm worse off than a leper now. My one hope has been to find . . ."

They helped the exhausted man to stumble across the fields of plowed earth. As they neared the whitewashed walls of the home compound, Matthew Granger, who spent his morning sharpening plowshares, looked up in irritation.

"If those yams aren't . . ." he began. Then his eyes widened. "Is it really you, Nyi Chuen-yup? It's true some word of disaster has reached us, but I thought it was only gossip."

"Whatever you have heard could not come near to reaching the truth," Chuen-yup replied, his voice close to breaking. "I don't even know if I have the right to ask for refuge here."

Matthew sighed. "No matter how strong the individual, the government is often stronger. This is something we can discuss at length during our evenings together." He looked up at the two who had brought in this refugee. "Please take him in to Lu and let him have a bath, a meal, and a good rest. Tonight," he said to Chuen-yup, "you can tell us of your adventures." To the others he spoke with grim humor. "Don't think you can get out of your morning's work simply because you've recruited a new member!"

One morning the following week, as the summer sun beat down on the compound, Matthew Granger contemplated what new methods he could bring to the farm. Crop rotation could be introduced, rivers dammed, irrigation not so much improved as extended. All of a sudden, he felt the ground begin to vibrate. At first he thought it might be a minor earthquake, but as he straightened up he saw it was a rattletrap jeep, left over from World War II. It ran as much from sheer determination as mechanical know-how. Clouds of choking oily smoke escaped from under the hood; from time to time the exhaust backfired and the vehicle listed alarmingly to the left as it drove. Eight soldiers weighted down the tired springs as the khaki-colored machine creaked into the compound and shuddered to a halt.

"Ho there, farmer!" the apparent leader shouted impudently, and then gestured involuntarily to ward off the evil eye as Matthew's coolie hat tilted back to reveal the face of a *yang-gwei-tse*.

"We know you are sheltering a traitor here!" The stream of Chinese that poured from the leader's lips was a crude dialect from the canal people of the southwest, the same tribe of hooligans that floated up from the river into the canal near Shanghai's old South Gate. They had often reviled Matthew's father and Matthew himself. He found the leader and his speech equally offensive.

"What are you doing on dry land?" Matthew asked sharply. "I can tell from your filthy speech that you're nothing but a canal rat, not even fit for a running river. No wonder the machine rebels against you! You would have trouble with any boat bigger than a sampan."

The leader's companions began to giggle and lean out of the jeep to look at Matthew more closely. The leader was not amused. He stepped down from behind the wheel, drew his handgun, cocked it, and held it pointed at Matthew's head. "We know you're giving shelter to that running dog of the old ways. You must turn him over to us, and we will give him more of the public punishment that he deserves."

Matthew stood at exaggerated military attention. "Are you referring by chance to the former Minister of Motorized Vehicles, Nyi Chuen-yup, the son of Nyi Chuen-yao, reowned warlord of these parts, who, in the old days, kept the canal pirates from extorting money from passengers who attempted to work or travel upon the waters? I've heard that his son is even more ferocious and uncontainable than his father. It is true! The government has sent that wild dragon to this harsh land where he can snort out his blasting fire and hurt no one but those of us who till the soil."

The crew of raw-wristed youngsters looked around nervously, but the leader flushed the crimson of an overripe plum.

"Of course," Matthew went on, "I can awaken this sleeping dragon. You may take him if you can. But I assure you, you will need more than this pitiably inadequate machine. And he will be difficult to tame. That is why Madame Mao, who only three weeks ago designated this a model detention camp . . . I can say only that if you offend *her*, you will find yourself attacked by both a male and a female dragon."

"It's because of you that our people have fallen on hard times," the cadre whispered venomously as he lowered his gun.

"Go back into the menstrual crotch of your canal, which gave birth to you and the stinking clots that make up your family!" Then, pulling out all the stops, Matthew switched to English. "I've had it with you and everybody else like you! People like you have tried to bully me since I was a kid at school. I've been persecuted in two countries. And enough is enough!" He watched their eyes go round with horror at the demonic syllables, and he began to sing. "Mairzy d'oats and does-ee d'oats, and little lambsee d'ivy," he intoned and jumped up and down on the hard-packed earth in imitation of an angry demon.

The boys in the jeep set up a howl. "It must be a curse so ancient that it came before the Middle Kingdom was created!"

The leader jumped back into the jeep, dropped his handgun on the seat, and desperately turned the key in the ignition, but without result.

Matthew danced beside them. "Peter Piper picked a peck of putrefying pipsqueaks," he taunted, "who can't even start their own car."

He roughly pushed the leader across the front seat, reached under the dash, and hot-wired the car, all the while continuing his wild patter. "There was a young man from St. John's, Who was constantly screwing the swans. One day said the porter, 'Here, take my dorter, Them swans is reserved for the dons!'" The motor started, but the driver was too afraid to move. Matthew stuck his thumbs in his ears and waggled his tongue at him with a guttural babble. Then he said once again, in Chinese, "This commune is under the personal protection of Madame Mao!" The driver let out a high whine of terror, shifted over, and put the jeep into gear, flooring the accelerator. The jeep lurched, made a wide circle around the compound, and disappeared in a volley of backfires.

After a moment or two, Nyi Chuen-yup shakily stepped out from one of the storage sheds. "I knew you were brave when you came by yourself to the caves, but how brave I had no idea of until now. I have no words to express my gratitude. And what a mastery of two tongues!"

Matthew grinned. "An Oxford education comes in handy now and then."

Nyi Chuen-yup's unpleasant experiences that day were far from over. When Lu drove up later in the commune's supply cart—each Thursday he took fresh produce into the city and bartered for cooking oil, soy sauce, and cigarettes, as well as the week's supply of *mao tai*—the old man's face looked wan and more drawn than usual. "There is bad news, I am afraid, from Beijing for our new guest." He opened the morning's paper and handed it to Nyi Chuen-yup, who read it and cried.

"She said she was going into the interior and that her sister would take her in. But I cannot blame her for playing the game of power. Jiang Qing was right about my defective character. I have played that game for many years. My friend, I believe you were right this morning. The blood of my father runs deep in my veins."

Chuen-yup's wife quickly found a proper new mate. In a public ceremony in Beijing she renounced her husband—no need to divorce him, she said. The disgrace that he had heaped on her made him less than a human being, unworthy of legal action. Instead, Zizhen chose for her new marriage a general, a widower who possessed substantial land holdings. She also changed her personal name to Siao Jiang Qing, or "Little Madame Mao," so that as long as Jiang Qing remained in power she would be safe.

"Love in this country is very trying," Matthew said consolingly. "In my other country we have a saying that politics make strange bedfellows, but there it is just a saying."

Chuen-yup only shook his head.

Later that night, Matthew and his intellectuals staged a surprise party to do what they could to rally Chuen-yup. The group made short work of the week's supply of *mao tai*. Tsiang Oo-zong, famous for his calligraphy, used his art to create a handsome bill of divorcement, with congratulatory flourishes on the husband's escape from the cruelties inflicted upon him by his faithless wife.

Eventually the others staggered away, leaving Matthew and Chuen-yup with the last bottle of *mao tai*. It wasn't long before the two turned to the subject that has puzzled men from the beginning of time: women. As Matthew refilled their cups, he said, "I suffered the tortures of a castrated choirboy when I went to the caves and Bah-wha wanted you instead of me."

"Why shouldn't she?" Chuen-yup asked. "I was a dragon in the old days. I lit up the caves."

"You should have seen my first wife. She was as cold and unfeeling as last winter's pumpkin in a neglected root cellar."

Chuen-yup poured another drink for each of them. "My wife, Zizhen, was infected with maggots. . . ."

"That's why you feel so good tonight."

"When I was young I thought life was just heroic deeds. But every day I live I see more and more that it's just a bad joke."

"I feel like you, Chuen-yup. More and more I feel that my life has become a long joke without a punch line."

His knees buckled beneath him. He had taken nothing but boiled rice and buttered tea for the past week, and the rice left his exhausted body in the same state as it entered it. Paul knew that he was nothing more than a gutted shell by now, but still his goal eluded him. He found little of the spiritual peace for which he always yearned. Most of the time it seemed he was farther away than ever from the father he sought.

Paul backtracked and backtracked until he knew that he was completely lost. He sank to his knees. Muttering an inchoate prayer to whatever deity might be in charge of this forlorn moonscape, he lay down for what he thought would be a short nap. Thirty hours later, he was found by two Sherpas, who argued the merits of robbing or rescuing him, and decided in favor of the latter. They hoisted the unconscious body into a sling. Hours later, Paul was left at the gate of the Lamasery of the Thousand Buddhas, which until now—by its inaccessibility—had been overlooked by the occupying armies of the Chinese.

The monks took him in. Paul's delirium brought him images as exquisite and seductive as anything he had seen in his drug days. Incense assailed his nostrils. The whir of incessant prayer wheels sounded to him like the very heart of the universe itself. The Buddha who had sprung into life by turning twelve times around was with him now in every manifestation. What a dream!

Soon it turned into a nightmare. Soldiers snatched him away. Warmth was replaced by cold, swatches of red and gold by sweating gray stone, and the nourishing aromas of incense gave way to the stench of urine and feces.

"Spy, spy, spy, spy, spy," a voice repeated to him "Tell us your name and why you are here."

Somewhere in a corner of his brain Paul considered that he might very likely die here in this room of typhus. He had memorized some words in Chinese, but English was all that came to him now.

"My father, Matthew Granger, lives in Shanghai. My father, Matthew Granger, lives in Shanghai. . . ."

"Spy, spy, spy, spy!"

"My father. Matthew Granger. He'll know why I'm here."

A scant two months later, after Nyi Chuen-yup had found a home at the former Fong-See Compound, word came from the head of the extended province of Shanghai that the city intended to honor Matthew "Fertile Grain" Granger and the fine work his commune achieved. Even before the "cleansing" of the Cultural Revolution, over the past sixteen years the Lungwha Commune had doubled its production three separate times, and was able to ship drought-resistant seed into the depths of the interior. In addition to his own accomplishments, he cheerfully reeducated the rotten apples under his care and set an example to other peasants in the countryside who balked at sheltering those who worked with their brains.

As a special honor to the peculiar but extraordinary foreigner, the municipal authorities arranged to hold a banquet in Matthew's father's mission compound. But the old True Heart School no longer existed. The buildings had been turned into the campus of a new "vocational" school, where high school students were dragooned into serving their country by learning agriculture's homely skills.

At first Matthew refused to attend. He was not political, he insisted to his Chinese friends. He was devoting this latter half of his life to tending his gardens in a purely Voltairean sense. But the professor of Western languages laughed at him. "Are you *mad*, simple farmer? Are you really so naive as to think you can escape politics by crossing something as paltry as an ocean?" Matthew finally accepted on condition that his "rotten apples" could come with him.

And so, on a blistering August morning, just days before their greatest harvest at the commune was to begin, Matthew and a hundred Lungwha villagers, as well as his gaggle of intellectuals, dressed in their cleanest clothes, were driven in trucks to the old mission. It has been a full thirty years since Matthew left his boyhood home. He deliberately avoided those buildings, not wishing to awaken old memories. When he had returned to China he had made the decision to give up his past, and that meant all of it. He would narrow his life to a few *li* and a few friends, and hope that he wouldn't fail in this smaller world.

But here he was. In spite of his anxieties, he discovered that his first memories were cheerful ones. In this he was helped by Chuen-yup. Matthew was punched playfully in the ribs as Chuen-yup said to him, "Do you remember how funny all of the Chinese—all of us—felt when we learned that the mission contained a house set aside for single ladies? How those old women used to whip me when I didn't know my Bible verses!"

"Served you damn well right!"

"*Judge not that ye be not judged,*" Chuen-yup answered primly.

Matthew had no time to answer, for both he and Chuen-yup stopped where they were at the sight of the arch facing them, decorated with paper flowers and characters cut out of red paper for long life and happiness. On each side of the arch, blackboards carried praise for Matthew in carefully made characters of colored chalk. Beyond the decorated gate, a chorus of high school girls burst into a song of welcome: "Greetings to the revolutionary farmer!"

Everyone clapped at its conclusion and Matthew bowed in thanks. Another three steps forward and the dean of the school appeared. He delivered a brief address. At its close, the students drew up in two columns along the path leading to the dining hall. As the party passed between them, they called out, "Welcome! Welcome to the Revolutionary Agricultural Achievers!" Matthew and his retinue were escorted to the head table on the dais, seated beside the dean. Before long the noise of conversation and eating filled the room where, so many years ago, students sat and sang that Jesus loved them.

"White rice for a change," Tsiang Oo-zong remarked, and all the dissidents, using their most cultivated manners, snatched the tiny bits of duck, beef, pork, and shrimp that hid under the mountain of fresh vegetables.

A brigade of Young Pioneers, aged eight to fourteen, whirled multicolored ribbons as they sang a song written especially for the occasion:

> "Right sayings make men grow strong—
> Right dung makes wheat grow strong—
> 'Fertile Grain' plows his fields with both!"

The bird imitations began. A man close to a hundred years old, who had survived every regime since the Dowager Empress because of his knowledge of wild canaries, whistling swans, and the mating call of the stork, was interrupted as he prepared for a duet of two bulbuls by a messenger sent from the central government offices of Shanghai. He handed Matthew a note.

During the rest of the ceremony, Matthew, though he responded with automatic courtesy, sat abstracted. He waited until the final toast, briefly gave his thanks, and apologized for what might seem abrupt behavior. He asked the other members to stay on, and excused himself from the celebration.

A guardsman waved the black Daimler limousine through the iron gates of Buckingham Palace. It pulled up at the entrance.

The Honourable Madeline Logan-Fisher was enjoying this ceremony the most, thought Jordan. Madeline, highly powdered and rouged, looked like a survivor from the Edwardian court in her picture hat decorated with pheasant wings and a full veil drawn tight under a diamond choker. Jordan, too, was pleased, though a trifle nervous. Looking at her son, Desmond, facing them on a jump seat, she could see that he was uncertain of what role he should play. At first he rebelled against renting court dress. But once he put on his black satin knee breeches, silk hose, and patent-leather pumps, he was immediately transformed into a proper son of the aristocracy.

"You know," he'd said, "it's just like dressing up for a costume party, isn't it?"

Jordan had chosen a black silk Chinese imperial gown embroidered with the exquisite blind stitching that caused the loss of sight of countless generations of young Chinese girls sold into that craft by their impoverished parents.

A footman escorted the Logan-Fisher party down a long hallway and kept them waiting for a few moments before another functionary asked Jordan to follow him. The footman showed Madeline and Desmond to seats in a semicircle near the rear of the room.

As the ceremony began, they stood for a few minutes with the others—fifty to be honored and their family members. A page opened a door to the left of the brocaded throne. Two trumpeters played a fanfare, and, as the Queen entered, they heard the strains of "God Save the Queen" played by a concealed chamber group. After the Queen seated herself, one of the heralds called the roll of those to be knighted. Man after man, who in one way or another had served the Empire, was announced, walked up the steps, and dropped to one knee. With a ceremonial sword, the Queen tapped him on the shoulder and bade him rise as a Knight of the Order of the British Empire.

Only two women were to be honored today. The other was Helen Louise Gardner, the first woman ever to hold a professional chair in English at Oxford University. Her elegant exegeses of T. S. Eliot's poems and John Donne's devotional works had won her international recognition in the world of scholarship.

When the herald announced Jordan, she stepped forward. How much her father would have enjoyed this honor. If anyone had truly served the Empire, it had been Andrew Logan-Fisher. Now she, like the others, sank to one knee. She felt the light touch of the sword and heard the Queen say, "I bid you rise, Jordan Louise Renalda Logan-Fisher, Dame Commander of the British Empire." As Jordan rose, the Queen reached out and touched her on the wrist. "My dear Dame Jordan, you cannot know what pleasure it gives me to honor one of my own sex. Prince Philip would like you to know that we greatly admire your work. One of your line drawings hangs in our family drawing room at Balmoral."

"Thank you, Your Royal Highness, I am honored indeed."

At the end of the ceremony, the long hallway filled with groups of family and their newly titled members. Jordan approached the Merton professor and said, "I know that you have been honored here today as a scholar, Dame Helen, but I have heard through friends of my son that your prowess as a teacher is also formidable. May I offer my compliments on your ability to make one of England's most unintelligible poets attractive to the young?"

Dame Helen scorned to acknowledge the compliment. "Unfortunately, I'm not acquainted with your work except by reputation. I understand that your family home is near Abingdon. I have recently purchased Myrtle House in Eynsham, a small place that dates from the sixteenth century. I hope that one day you will join me there for lunch. I live near a trout farm of fine reputation. And I believe I make the finest martinis in all of England. I have heard rumors that the Royal Family cares little for the works of Eliot but a great deal for my mixture of gin and vermouth."

He had soiled his bed repeatedly. He was far too weak to travel the endless distance to the other side of the cell. Even as he slept, he felt a prickling around his cheeks and lips. When, with enormous effort, he lifted his hand to his face, he brushed away hard-backed beetles that were feasting on his saliva.

A band of pain sliced into his forehead. His eyes stayed shut; the light, even in this shadowy cell, inflicted searing sensations from his pupils to the back of his eye sockets. Even when the pain began to lift, Paul knew he must be hallucinating, because a voice came to life in his brain, a voice not his own.

Gradually he became aware that days turned into night, that he was being gently rolled from side to side so that his bedding could be changed. It seemed to Paul that he was a child again and safe—that he lay on smooth sheets smelling of the sun, covered with one of his mother's soft quilts. He believed he was with his teddy bears and toys, and that his father had come in late to hold his hand and say good night. He was half asleep the way he always was when his father came home. "Sing me to sleep, Daddy. I can't go to sleep until you sing to me."

His father would sing, in a cracked, humorous voice, "With plenty of money and you-hoo-hoo, there's nothing that I couldn't do-hoo-hoo! In spite of the worry that money brings— just a little filthy lucre buys a lot of things!"

It was so safe here, with Daddy. He could go to sleep now, and not be afraid of bad dreams. He could hold on to that strong hand, and feel his hair being pushed away from his face.

When he did come to, it was that gray time between day and night. He woke with a feeling of dampness, and health, of the same sort of relief he'd had when he was a kid just getting over pneumonia, and his father was there. . . .

"It's Dad, Paul. I'm here." The gray light came from one small window in this cell. The smell of sun-fresh linen had not been a hallucination. The man who sat there beside him looked drawn, his black hair thinly streaked with silver. Paul saw a faded-parchment face. It was his father's, but so much older than the face he remembered—so much sadder.

"I'm better, Daddy," Paul said, fading in and out of consciousness. "But I can't go to sleep. Sing me the money song."

An inexpressible sense of longing, of all the things in life that are lost, or spent, or misplaced, or forgotten, a yearning for the past, and a tentative joy in the present crossed the face that looked over at him now. Had Paul really traveled so far to ask this man for an *explanation* of his conduct, of how he had lived his life? They were together now, and explanations were unnecessary. "With plenty of . . . money and you," his father sang. Paul lay there, a child full of trust under a blanket of safety.

The three weeks that followed brought explanations aplenty. Explanations, logistics, plans, counterplans, intimidations, bribery. For the first time Paul heard his father speaking as a true Chinese. He saw his father wave money inches away from a truculent official's nose. He heard his father speak with scathing contempt to the people who ran this lamasery turned house of detention.

"What did you say?" Paul asked at one point, after Matthew arranged to have him taken on a litter up a winding staircase of ancient stonework to a tiny room in a high tower with windows on three sides opening out to the grandeur of the snow-capped Himalayas.

"I said only that if the Buddha has a thousand eyes, nine hundred are focused on those who seek him, and that my son, having come through hell to find me, deserves a taste of heaven."

Now came their time to talk. They exchanged stories with the intensity of those who meet on an ocean voyage or share a trench in a war. Both of them knew that a parting must come soon. Both tried desperately, each in his own way, to put off that moment.

Matthew asked questions about Joyce and Valerie. Paul confided in his father as if they were best friends. "Dad, I think Joyce was born bossy. I look at her and I know just what she'll be like when she's a mother. But Mom, I think she'll be young forever. She's a senator now and she's against the war. She gets up every day full of plans." Paul looked at Matthew. They sat together in the tower room. In one direction snow whirled about the peak of Annapurna and in another direction the sun shone on blankets of fresh powdered snow, a carpet of diamonds. The world was ineffable and full of change. "Dad, how could you have . . . why did you?"

"People act first, and think up reasons later. I could tell you it was Senator McCarthy. I could say I was helplessly in love with another woman, but that would make me out to be a worse person than I really am. It was only after my first few years in Shanghai that I realized it was where I belonged. I'm a farmer, Paul."

In the end, inevitably the world pushed them apart. Matthew received word that he was needed in Shanghai to supervise the fall planting. When Matthew asked Paul to come and visit for some months, Paul surprised himself by announcing he couldn't stay in a totalitarian land. China contradicted the spiritual values *he* most cherished.

"Do you see what I mean, son? I love you. You love me. But . . ."

"I know, I *know*," Paul said. And he did know. He had found what he had come for. "I *get* it, Dad."

Nevertheless, at dawn the next morning, after he had slung his father's luggage onto a filthy northbound train, Paul clung to Matthew. Then he straightened up, shook the exile's hand, waited until the train clattered down the northern slope, and headed south, on foot, to begin a self-imposed exile of his own that was to last for years.

The school term began on the following Monday, but Desmond knew when he'd taken the seven o'clock train that he would have eighteen hours before the master of his form would notice his absence. He was ravenous. His mother had given him just enough allowance to last him two weeks. He had spent almost all of that on the train fare from Oxford to Liverpool. The railroad station looked dreary beyond belief. If it had ever been summer in this grimy city, it was impossible to find evidence of it now. The few people who scurried past had pallid, exhausted stares. Desmond walked through the station, both timid and appalled. Finally taking his courage in his hands, he approached a woman, a char lady, coming home from work.

"I beg your pardon, madam," he said deferentially, "but would you be so kind as to direct me to the nearest inexpensive restaurant?"

A soot-filled rain drizzled down into the gray, uninviting streets. The wind picked up, and Desmond shivered. He knew that he had exactly two pounds six pence between him and either destitution or a humiliating phone call to his mother. He trotted along the wet streets, and veered into a battered storefront that advertised fish and chips.

He went in to a blessed if stuffy warmth, ignoring the curious glances of the few customers in the place. At the counter, trying to appear at ease, he leaned on an elbow and said, "I'll have . . ." and stopped.

He had dined on witchity grubs in the Australian outback, flank of ibex in Africa, flayed seal in the Arctic Circle, but never in his life had he tasted the dish that the "other England" lived on.

"Fish and chips," he said.

"Wha?"

"Fish and chips."

Two girls in the corner giggled. The man behind the counter snickered in their direction, then wrapped a huge order of the batter-fried plaice and potatoes in a triangle of newsprint. Conscious of his knapsack and guitar bumping on his back, Desmond put his change on the counter before he picked up his serving. He held it, he realized, exactly like the bridesmaid who has caught the bouquet. He and the man stared at each other. There was still something he hadn't done, but Desmond didn't know what. Then, snorting in contempt, the proprietor grabbed the newspaper back and drenched its contents in vinegar before taking Desmond by the arm and pushing him toward the corner.

"I got a live one for you birds." The girls in the corner clutched each other and smirked.

Desmond took a deep breath, walked over to the table, put down his food, unleashed himself from his guitar, and sat. This was no time for pretense.

"Good evening, ladies," he said. "My name is Desmond Logan-Fisher and I am a musician from out of town. I rather doubt that you can understand my accent, but I'd thank you for any kindness. I'm looking for a club in which to play."

The girls wore imitation leather. The eyes of one were ringed in lavender and the other in bright turquoise. Their scrawny bodies, and the way they clung to each other in delight at the sound of his voice, reminded Desmond of lemurs he had seen in the jungle. Inspired, not waiting for a reply, he picked up his guitar. He could sing in their dialect even if he couldn't actually speak it.

"You're my little lemur, you're my little chimp," he sang to the lavender one. "And you're a little devil, yes you're a little imp. Be my monkey, baby!" He hummed the next few bars, then continued, "Wrap you funny tail around me," and watched as they dissolved in helpless laughter.

"Coo-ee, some toff!"

And the other kept saying, "Gore!"

Several hours later, they took him down murky streets to the unmarked door of a basement club, the High-Hat. He sniffed the air and realized that it was time to share his grass with Patti and Tricia.

During the first break, the bass player of the wretched group that had been performing came up to talk to the girls. Desmond still had trouble following the dialect, but he understood the fellow to say that their lead guitar player had been knocked unconscious by a brick.

"'E c'n ply."

The bassist looked doubtfully at Desmond. "But 'e's a toff."

"Aye, but 'e c'n ply an' 'e's foony. *Try* 'im Keithyboy!"

Once Desmond was onstage, he knew exactly what to do and he did it. He seduced the natives. He composed songs about "the toff what run awigh, too doom to eat 'is fish 'n' chips." He sang a love song to "Patti 'n' Tricia," and toward the end of the night he sang a couple of his African songs.

"I gave up everything in the world," he said, and he realized he was pretty well stoned, "to be here with you."

The group played until five in the morning. They took him home. He made love to Patti, or was it Tricia. When he woke he found a message by the bed with a pound note pinned to it—his share of the earnings from last night.

"You were wunderful," Patti had written in a childish scrawl. And, on a neatly folded page of the Liverpool *Gazette*, she had put out breakfast for him—slices of white toast spread with anchovy paste that spelled out "I LUV U."

Nothing was more despressing than coming home. Nothing was more depressing than taking responsibility. Nothing was more depressing than facing once again the irrefutable fact that he was essentially alone and would very likely spend the rest of his life without a family. His father would have had something to say about all this, perhaps a short sermon on the text "As ye sow, so shall ye reap." At least he had seen his son, but that had torn the scab of his defenses away from his gaping wound of loneliness.

What rot! He was going home, and he would get to work, and he would serve. His father might know, in his Presbyterian heaven, that Matthew was living a good and useful life.

He took a bus from Shanghai's South Railway Station to Lungwha, and set out for the commune on foot. The sun had already gone down, but a pinkish haze lingered over the land. Even in this light he could see that the field to his right— already planted—needed irrigating. The one to his left had been plowed in a pattern that guaranteed flooding. How could they have been so careless after all his careful instructions?

From a quarter of a mile away he saw the glimmer of at least a dozen kerosene lamps on his veranda. I go away for a month, he thought angrily, they don't do their chores, and they stay up all night partying like children. Then, as he got closer, he saw that his veranda was occupied by strangers, by foreigners. If anything, his irritation increased.

"Lu!" Matthew shouted. "Are we running an orphanage? Have we not enough misfits already from the Revolution?"

A blond stranger stood up, extended his hand, and said in heavily accented English, "I am Per Christensen. I am very happy to meet you. We are journalists. We have heard of your good work here. You are one of the few foreigners ever to be honored by the municipality of Shanghai. We have been waiting for you."

"Eating our rice?"

"Millet," an Englishman said. "But not to worry. We've brought our own Johnny Walker—Black Label, of course. Still a couple of cases left."

"*Buenas noches, señor,*" said a man who introduced himself as Raul Martinez. "*Es un honor grande.*"

"*Il n'y a pas des nouvelles en la cité,*" and elderly, dapper French reporter said, "*et avec Madame Mao, c'est toujours la même chose. Alors, nous sommes ici.*"

Matthew took a hard look at this seedy group of reporters. He saw that they were as lonely, as homeless, as he.

"Lu!" he shouted again. "Where are our manners? Bring some glasses! With your Black Label and my glasses, and whatever dishes Lu can throw together for us, we must have a party. I suppose you're the ones who have led my intellectuals astray in their watering of the fields. We must get to the bottom of this."

The following week reporters caught transportation into Shanghai and filed their stories. In Portuguese, in Danish, in Spanish, French, English, and in Swedish, glowing reports went out over the press wires celebrating the achievements of "the Albert Schweitzer of the East."

Perhaps it was because the globe was in the grip of a cultural revolution that youth in both East and West had begun to question their elders, or perhaps it was because the populations of many countries shared a hatred of oppression, as well as a need to identify with one courageous individual. Whatever the reason, newspaper readers all over the world took heart from the story of a quiet man who had wanted nothing more than to be a farmer—but who, at the same time, kept his integrity and defended his right to do and say exactly what was right. Whatever it was, the recluse had become a celebrity.

Book VI

REUNION
1983

Coming to Oxford as a Rhodes Scholar had been a dream for Angela Fitch during her four years as an undergraduate at Harvard, but she had never believed, except in her most secret heart, that she would be one of the first women elected to a scholarship. It meant more to her than it did to some of her classmates. It wasn't a question of finances; she knew that her Grandfather Harley Fitch was eager to support her and would have happily paid all her expenses. But doing it alone gave her a sense of independence, a feeling of exhilaration that was the climax of her four years as an undergraduate at Harvard. And now here she was, punting on the Char, as she had in her dreams so many times before. She was no longer simply the spoiled and pampered granddaughter of two strong-willed men. Now she could see that her mind counted for more than good looks, or all the millions in the world.

Her thoughts were interrupted by the drawl of her companion, Cedric Carstairs of Balliol College. "And just what are you thinking of?" he asked. "Don't you know that you should be appreciating this rare sunlight?"

Angela smiled. "I am appreciating it. And it *is* good to see the sun at last." She settled herself in the cushions as Cedric pushed on the pole, sending the punt up the river at a slow glide.

"What really astonishes me," he said, "is that instead of reading English, as most women do here, you've chosen all those truly dull volumes of philosophy and political science, and worst of all, economics. Can you explain that to me?"

"I suppose you think it isn't ladylike?"

"I wouldn't say that," Cedric said, with such instant politeness that she knew she had hit the nail on the head.

"Whether it's ladylike or not," she said, "in my country, though most of the men don't seem aware of it, women control much of the economy. They're the ones who look after the households. Almost everything that's bought in terms of consumer goods is bought by women. According to your outdated nineteenth-century English laws, Cedric, a family inheritance went right through women, like water through a sieve, from father to son, leaving females at their mercy. In America, from the very beginning, women have been able to inherit fortunes, and women own the majority of the country's wealth. I intend, when I get back, to use that fact to my advantage."

"Oh, American men, look out for Angela Fitch!" Cedric answered dolefully. "She's going to do you out of your rightful heritage!"

"Anyway," she said, "it seems much more practical to me, to be doing what *I'm* doing, than to be trudging through the 'classics' the way you are."

Cedric looked defensive. "That may very well be true," he said. "But a 'First' in what you Americans insist on calling the 'classics' opens up almost any career."

"But that's so silly," she said. "In China before their Revolution, when the elite studied *their* classics, it cut them off from everything that was alive about their own country!"

"Be that as it may," Cedric said. "The Chinese have nothing to do with us. After all, Plato in *The Republic* . . ."

Angela finished his sentence for him: ". . . provided Hitler with a perfect model for the Third Reich."

"That's really a bit thick," Cedric said. "We English don't take anything that literally. We muddle along. Our real excuse for this sort of education that it gives the country a ruling group who have a common language."

"Muddling along is even more dangerous than it's ever been. We don't have time to muddle in the atomic age!"

"There are great crimes and small ones," Cedric said cryptically. "I'm afraid that you and I have been guilty of a very great one right here in this punt."

"Whatever in the world are you talking about?"

Cedric guided the punt into the shade of an overhanging tree and half beached it before he answered. "We must never let this secret get out. Don't you realize that ever since we set out we've been talking shop?"

Angela grinned. "The parties I've been to here might have been more interesting if people *had* talked shop instead of nattering along in your famous English way."

"You may be right."

After a long silence Cedric said, "Now what are you thinking, Angela?"

She gave him a sunny smile. "We're not very much in love."

"Just jolly good friends."

Angela allowed herself the enjoyment of the moment: the waters of the gently flowing Char, the barely perceptible pat of the leaves as they fell upon the river's surface, the lovely green and gold light that seemed to tint the very air. Hundreds and hundreds of years of tradition made up this world.

"I'll tell you what I'm really thinking about. It may be shoptalk, but it's a shop all its own."

"What would that be?"

"It may not mean much to an Englishman," she said, "but this summer the eightieth anniversary of the Rhodes Scholarships is being celebrated. There's going to be a huge reunion from every part of the globe. They've never had a bash quite like this. It'll be a three-day celebration. Black-tie dinners, and the Queen is coming! I've been dragooned into hostess duties because I'm a girl. And frankly, Cedric, I've even, in my darkest thoughts, entertained the notion that they've so recently begun giving these scholarships to females because they knew this reunion was coming up."

"Take heart, Angela," Cedric teased. "I've heard they're tearing down the wall between Rhodes House and Wadham Garden stone by stone. Perhaps you can strike a blow for sexual equality by volunteering for *that* job instead of passing round tea."

"All this fuss, just so the Queen can pass through without using thirty yards of public sidewalk. You'd think we were back in the sixteenth century."

"It's damn decent of the Queen and Prince Philip to attend a do that includes all you ex-colonials!"

But she wasn't listening. "Nine in the morning, the Queen arrives. Ten-thirty to twelve, reception for the Warden.

Twelve to three, lunch for the VIPs. *We're* not invited. By this time," Angela recited, "all of the scholars and their wives will have congregated in Wadham Garden. Hats and gloves for the women strongly recommended. At quarter to three the Queen and her entourage walk down the gravel path from Rhodes House to that *hole in the wall*. The band plays 'God Save the Queen.'"

"And then you brash Americans and all the darker colonials will have a chance to see what's made the British Empire great. The Queen shall pass among her subjects . . ."

"You needn't be so damned *English* about it, Cedric. I'm not a barbarian. My own grandmother is a dame."

"Don't flaunt your titles at me, you hussy," he said. "Your grandmother's a damn fine woman in her own right and she mixes an abolutely top-drawer martini. I say, did she learn that from Al Capone?"

The punt tilted dangerously as she kicked at him.

"Well, what am I going to do there?" Matthew grumbled in Chinese. "I hate the cold weather. I can't stand small talk. I don't have the proper clothes. And I've got to get back to the farm. We're in the middle of the growing season."

"Don't you know you're a victim of the cult of personality, Matthew Granger, *your own* personality? You think you're too indispensable to leave China on a four-week trip?"

"I've been here at Tsingtao for ten days as it is. Every time I go away I come back to find my farm in shambles," Matthew said peevishly. At that moment he looked like an old man and sounded like one, although the years had been kind to him. His constant work in the sun had left him as lean, brown, and strong as a man in his forties. At night by lamplight, as he laughed and joked with his friends, his brown eyes shone, but the moment he was confronted by something he didn't want to do, he managed to turn into a crotchety hermit.

"The last time I went to Europe, I got a very serious case of pneumonia. You know that, Chuen-yup."

His friend's eyes twinkled. Chuen-yup himself had carefully dressed for this trip from Beijing to Tsingtao and then to England in a three-piece gabardine suit with a wide tie that had "friendship" printed on it in three languages. "Well, you did get the noble prize the last time you went."

"That's *Nobel*, and you know that too. And what does that trip have to do with this one? My celebrity lasted for two weeks. My bronchitis went on for six months. That's no laughing matter."

Chuen-yup looked at Matthew sympathetically. "The life of a Nobel Prize winner is hard. Yes, a free round trip for you and a guest to Oxford University for the Rhodes Scholar Reunion, paid for by our Politburo and featuring a dinner invitation from that bourgeois English Royal Family is—how would they say it back at the mission?—a terrible cross to bear. But alas, we have to do it to serve the people!"

"I remember how you served the people in Stockholm, comrade. Drunk in a snowdrift for fourteen hours and the only reason you got out alive was because you were insulated by bar girls and schnapps. Serve the people! All you're interested in is serving your cock!"

"It's true, my fiery dragon enjoys world travel. So should yours, Matthew. Or is it curled up forever in its dark cave?"

Matthew could only shake his head. They headed up the gangplank of the renovated freighter *Cormorant*. He mused on the discomforts of his situation. "You interrupted my first vacation in three years. . . ."

"What about your two weeks in Beijing last winter?" Chuen-yup answered back amiably. "Or the three weeks at that farming conference in Bali? I do not even count that villa in Trieste where you stayed in 1980."

"That was *work*," Matthew said. "All I can say is I don't like being ordered around by anyone's committee."

"You'll have fun once you get there. You'll see your old university chums. Be brave about it. You have had ten full days in Tsingtao. The Politburo gave you the use of your old family summer home. You cooled your brittle bones in the northern surf. You rested. I understand that a tanned skin is a mark of the pampered rich in the Western world. You will look as though you have done well."

Indeed, Matthew had done well. Several years before, he'd won the Nobel Prize for his work with droughtproof grain. True, he'd had to split it three ways—with a man who had isolated some virus and another who perfected an anesthetic. Since then he had entertained dozens of deferential altruists and agronomists from every land. Though he fled civilization, Matthew Granger garnered more fame than most men gained in a lifetime.

The circumstances of his daily life improved immeasurably. The Fong-See Compound prospered. They now had such modern amenities as refrigerators, a tractor, and a black-and-white TV. With the downfall of the Gang of Four—Madame Mao and her three cohorts—and with the death of Mao himself, China entered a new era of modified capitalism. By 1977 the eleven years of the Cultural Revolution had come to an end. As always, Matthew held himself haughtily above any government changes, and thus emerged unscathed, but he missed the daily banter of the intellectuals, who had gone back to their regular jobs and came to the farm only for vacations of their own.

His only real friend now was Chuen-yup. With the practical ruthlessness of a warlord's son, he, unlike Matthew, thrived on politics. Chuen-yup had looked for a vacuum in the power structure and adroitly maneuvered himself back into the Politburo. He never remarried, but had many concubines. His travels turned him into a man of the world. The incident in Stockholm was not the first but only the most celebrated.

Matthew finally responded to Chuen-yup. "I know why you want to come along to Oxford with me. Besides being a cryptocapitalist and eager to taste the forbidden delights of an English university town, you want to send your boy a postcard from yet another capital, assuring him that *you* at least are having a good time."

A flicker of hurt crossed Chuen-yup's sleek, well-fed face. But then he said blandly, "We all know a revolution is not a dinner party. The boy crossed me. I hope he will have the long life and prosperity to see his own son attempt to overthrow him."

Chuen-yup had waited for the proper moment in 1979 and then suggested to the government that his son, the notoriously bad poet, Nyi Chuen-yee, was not a criminal—taken in as he had been by the satanic machinations of the "White Boned Demon," Madame Mao—but that he was undeniably unstable and could profit by a few years in the mental-health clinic in the bleak northern town of Harbin.

By now the boat had slid out of Tsingtao Harbor, taking swells that signaled the high seas. A brisk westerly wind ruffled Matthew's still thick hair and he felt his mood begin to change.

"Aren't you done up like the dandy," he said, looking at Chuen-yup. "Where are your twenty-one pieces of matching luggage?"

"I sent them on ahead." Chuen-yup smiled. "And don't worry about your wardrobe for Oxford. The Politburo put through a call to Oxford. Hall's Tailoring establishment will have clothes ready for you when we arrive. We sent the message that you're as trim as you always were, but for them to be sure to cut your trousers as skimpily as a girl's, because surely your dragon must have shrunk to the size of an earth-worm from lack of use."

The bottle of Dom Perignon exploded across the bow of the *Angela*, Harley Compton Fitch's spanking-new, state-of-the-art, one-hundred-and-twenty-five-foot yacht. The vessel slid easily from dry dock into the waters of the upper Hudson. Harley was sixty-seven, but as he watched the sleek yacht glide into the water, and Tai-ling, who had done the christen-ing, decked unashamedly in more than a million dollars' worth of jewels, her hair glistening from the fine spray of champagne, he knew that this moment marked a milestone in his life.

He was a magnate, family man, far more powerful than either his father or his son, and now the owner of the most expensive private ship in the world. He'd named it after his granddaughter, and it was appropriate that the *Angela*'s maiden voyage would be an easy run across the Atlantic to meet its namesake. They would turn into the Thames and go as far upriver as they could. Harley wanted to dock at Henley, where they would stay for the annual regatta. Back in Shanghai, when old Logan-Fisher had given his very British picnics and held boat races, Harley had thought that was the "real" Henley. In a sense, Harley had bested Logan-Fisher too—bested them all, and on their own terms. Before the regatta, Harley, Tai-ling, and a small party of friends and family would attend the Eightieth Rhodes Reunion. His beloved Angela was one of the very first women chosen for that honor. She would be both a participant at the reunion and hostess to men renowned for their good deeds around the world. Angela had finally given to Harley what money could never buy. Honor. Respect. And at long last, a sense of pride in the family name.

With the *Angela* launched, a crowd of what Tai-ling cynically called "seven hundred of our closest friends" began to file up the gangplanks for the bon voyage party. A steward met each guest with a hand-blown crystal glass of Dom Perignon. Each woman received a pair of half-carat diamond earrings; men were presented with solid-gold cigarette light-ers. Up in the bow of the ship, a big band began to play the optimistic tunes of the forties.

From the scaffolding on the dock, where Horace West-phall stood next to his business partner, Harley said, with his old boastfulness, "Horace, I'll bet you've never seen a ship like this. There isn't another one like it anywhere in the world—gold and silver fixtures in every bathroom, our own brand of CFE saltwater soap, marble floors on every deck, every bathtub made from Carrara marble. We've got armor-plated windows, a missile detection system, a freshwater swimming pool, and our own helicopter pad."

"Harley, why are you going to this reunion? I love Angela as much as you, God knows, but we can both visit her anytime. Why do you go to this gathering of elitists when, if you'll pardon me, you weren't a Rhodes Scholar? Why should you court any possible slight?"

"I want them to see me. I wasn't a Rhodes Scholar, but I can buy their university. I can buy their shitty country if it comes to that. I want them to know it." *And Matthew will be there, and I want him to know it too.*

The two men switched the topic to safer ground. A shipment in a Westphall Shipping convoy would parallel the *Angela* in her course across the north Atlantic. It contained three cases of firing devices—very fragile, floating in jelly, resting in a special compartment, controlled by a gyroscope. The devices would arm the nuclear missiles that the President of the United States planned to deploy that fall in England and Western Europe.

"You *bitch!*" said Andrew to the tanned boy who had just remarked that Andrew's anus was so loose that fucking him was disconcertingly like doing it to a girl.

"No, really, Andrew, it's true. You're going to have to do some exercises to tighten up. In the dark, with a bra full of sponge rubber, no one would know the difference."

This barb was, in fact, a kindness in disguise. Andrew Fitch was plainly ill, and his friends worried about him.

Today, though, was a day to put worries aside. Thirty or forty of Andrew's friends had been invited by him to join in what had become, even more than the pursuit of vice, his reason for being: to rub his father's heterosexual nose in the irrefutable fact of his own homosexuality. Accordingly, Andrew's friends, most of whom had daytime jobs in the straight world, were dressed for this launching, as they loyally put it, like "queens for a day."

Andrew asked for a makeup table in his suite, and when his father furiously refused, Andrew said, in the most mincing and spiteful tones, "All right, then, I don't want a room at all on your silly boat and I'm going to tell everbody why."

But as it turned out, Harley hired a designer whom Andrew had met in a notorious San Francisco bathhouse to decorate the interior of the yacht. Jacques Lauren had gleefully thrown himself into the project of hoodwinking his macho employer. Not only had he tarted up Andrew's suite of rooms, he had also dotted corners and niches of the good ship *Angela* with insulting messages that only the cognoscenti might grasp: Jacques had ordered five hundred custom-designed hand-painted Portuguese tiles, which he had assured the elder Fitch were nautical good luck signs but actually bore the phrase "Harley loves to suck" in Syrian lettering. These tiles appeared at random throughout the ship along with less offensive logos of squid, manta rays, and lobster.

And Lauren had taken special pains with Harley's own bedroom suite. For the mirror, which Harley always insisted upon above his king-sized bed, Lauren had ordered a delicate embroidered scrollwork at the borders, again commissioned from his favorite artisan in Lisbon. What looked to be a simple gold filigree spelled out in several different modern languages "Harley's dick is noodle-weak." Lauren told Andrew's assembled guests about these pranks, and they were convulsed with laughter.

Andrew leaned back, smiling tiredly. He raised his glass for a toast. "To my friends," he said. "To all of you, to Raphael, Georgio, Jacques, Don, Phil, Chris, you've been more than just friends to me. . . ." This remark was greeted by sly yips, but he overrode them, saying, "Be serious for once. We've been friends, we've been lovers. You've been the only family I've had. Here's to you all." Silently he added what he couldn't say aloud: Thank you for giving me my means of revenge. As long as I'm alive, there'll never be a day when my father will wake up happy.

The fund-raiser was a great success. Desmond Logan had chartered a freight barge and charged the very wealthiest members of the international peace movement two thousand pounds a head for this afternoon's performance. In return for their investment, the guests were treated to pints of "half and half" and a generous pub lunch of Scotch eggs, kidney pies, bangers and mash. Desmond had already done his stint—forty-five minutes of new songs composed for this occasion, songs in which he had tried to use his own image to the best advantage. His favorite was "Put Down Your Nukes and Fight Like a Man." He had delivered it with clenched fists to a standing ovation.

In the fifteen years of his career, Desmond had cloaked himself in the manners of the working class. He evolved from his early roots in Liverpool to something approaching the tender masculinity of Bruce Springsteen. Over the years he had become an arbiter of mass culture. If Desmond Logan chose to stand for peace, then it must be the right thing to do. Journalists were now saying that the activists of the sixties had been ineffectual. But the way Desmond saw it, some of those same activists held positions of power and had the money to make their opinions felt. A generation so desperate for a sense of meaning in their lives that in America they accepted a movie actor as a father figure was only too glad to take Logan's musical sermons to heart, to breathe them, live them.

In America, they called Springsteen "The Boss." In England, Desmond was titled "Rev," for "Reverend." At first he was embarrassed, because he knew his own inadequacies. But he cherished the civilizations he'd seen in his youth; he was committed to stopping the destruction of the world. It was only in the past months that he'd begun to realize just how much combined energy it would take to beat the war machine, and he loved his new name now because of its double meaning; "Rev" for "Reverend," and "Rev" for "rev it up." "We've got to put the peace movement in gear," he said today. "We've got to win this race. We *cannot* lose it!"

The sun was setting on the Thames. The city of London rose on either side. Barges passed. People waved. An occasional television helicopter swooped overhead to shoot footage of the festivities. Desmond leaned back against a bulkhead and put down half of his pint of Guinness Stout. It had been a good afternoon, but it was only the beginning.

In a matter of weeks America would begin to deploy missiles all across Europe. He knew that there would be millions of demonstrators in Europe and England. He also knew that because they would be mostly women, children, and the poor, the odds were they would fail. It was up to him to make *men* work for peace. It was up to him to enlighten the rich as well as the impoverished. In a few weeks he would participate in a peace concert outside Abingdon Air Base. A few days later he would be a part of the Queen's Command Performance for the Rhodes Scholars Reunion. Today had been successful far beyond his hopes, and he could only assume that students at Oxford would be equally responsive. There must be a way. He would unite the two Englands, rich and poor, and he would set that united England to the task of taking down nuclear weapons.

A freighter sailing under the Liberian flag, outward bound from Buenos Aires via the Azores to Southampton, carried only eight passengers—all jealous of their privacy. Two tables for four were set up in the austere dining room. One of them bore a hand-lettered card that announced tersely "In Retreat." No conversation was permitted at that table. Paul Granger, man of letters, sometime professor at the Center for Asian Studies at Yale, sat at the "In Retreat" table for every meal. This voyage would last thirty-three days. He needed the time and quiet to finish an academic paper on the Alpha state as it is perceived in the Far East.

Paul divided his time between writing, meditation, and prayer. In the years since his rescue from the Tibetan prison by his father, he had been on what he could only call an incessant spiritual quest. But soon, once the ship landed, he would allow himself a single pleasure. He would once again see his father.

This morning, Paul, wrapped in an army blanket and stretched out on a deck chair, watched the heaving gray swells of the North Atlantic. He knew that his grandfather had been thought of alternately as a fanatic and as a saint, that he died a martyr's death in a Japanese prison camp. Many are called, he thought, but few are chosen. What did that even mean? Didn't all men—and women—yearn for union with the infinite? Paul ruefully remembered the days when an orgasm and a few jolts of whatever drug was on hand would kick him right up into the celestial realm. But was it the drug, the spasm, or the sense of literally and spiritually touching another human being? Paul had never known his Presbyterian grandfather, but the longer he lived, the more he began to understand Christ's stern warning "Strait is the gate and narrow is the way. . . ." Paul had long since given up alcohol, drugs, and sex, not because he believed they involved sin, but because those three anodynes turned into cheats. They promised the divine, but they delivered little. For the last decade Paul Granger had searched for the greatest high of them all—union with God.

"*Salamat pagi!*" Paul looked up to see a shivering Indonesian boy offering him beef tea. Paul stood up, took off his jacket, draped it over the boy's shoulders, and made him take a long nourishing draft of the drink he was serving. The boy, astonished and shy, thanked him.

Dame Jordan Logan-Fisher puttered about her library putting together the last-minute details for the tea she was giving for her granddaughter Angela and her friend Cedric. Today she arranged to order the smoked trout with which Dame Helen Gardner had enticed her fifteen years ago. The scones were baked by a woman in the village just this morning, and there was clotted cream from the village dairy, together with blueberries picked by her own hand, a generous tin of caviar from the grocer, who kept a special stock for Jordan, and a sweating pitcher of excellently chilled, very dry martinis.

Jordan appraised the room with an artist's eye. The library had the darkness of a secular chapel. Careful lighting pointed up only those things she wished to be noticed. On the mantel an enormous medal awarded her by the Queen of the Netherlands. A few of her own paintings, modestly framed, perfectly lit. The chairs—which sat around the antique table where tea was set out—were covered in traditional country chintz. But in a corner, under another light, stood a two-foot statue of Quan Yin that would have cost her thousands of pounds had she not bartered some of her own paintings for it. After all these years she had finally brought to an apotheosis her own style, a combination of her beloved Orient and the domesticity of her English forebears.

She sighed and gave herself a little shake. She was bored beyond words with the internal voice that kept repeating, *For what, for what, for what?* She looked around the cozy library, a stage set designed for actors to play out a series of meaningless charades. "For my work," she said woodenly, her voice echoing in the perfect room. "I always have my work."

Restless, Jordan walked into another, wider, lighter room—the part of The Beeches that, when her mother was alive, had been used as a solarium. For the past five years Jordan had made it her studio. More than once she thanked her stars that she had had the wit to take her pictures of the Chinese Revolution out of the country that they celebrated. Her paintings by now might have been destroyed a dozen times over with some shift in Chinese domestic politics.

Strangely enough, Jordan's approach to art had been transformed by a remark of Madame Mao: "Do you ever see black flowers?" she had ranted at a painting exhibition. "Do you ever see black earth or black trees? No! I say that the artists who paint these things must be black-hearted and counter-revolutionary!"

Jordan never liked Jiang Qing, even in the best of times, and this demented remark had sent her back to an examination of the Chinese traditionalists. How much they'd been able to do with a block of ink, a swatch of paper, and just the barest hint of color. She had followed that lead to a private revolution against the pseudo-realism of what critics called her "Communist period."

But Jordan's subject matter was always the same: China, her China of the mind, her 110 Shanghai Road. But now her treatment was impressionistic, achingly nostaligic. Raging rivers and cliffs wet with spray. Eastern and Western styles merged. Jordan eyed her latest, half-completed work—a picture of her childhood home, a bastion of British respectability in international Shanghai. In the street, locked away from prosperity, a few Chinese lounged, the domestic staff exchanged gossip with a rickshaw boy and a produce bearer. Jordan knew that her style and her vision were close to an almost perfect marriage, but still, to her eye, something was lacking. Perhaps it was China itself. She knew what it was like, but God help her, there were times when she couldn't exactly remember.

Her manservant's announcement of her granddaughter distracted Jordan from this melancholy turn of thought. She returned to the library in time to overhear Cedric whisper loudly to Angela, "And are we to meet the Rev today?"

"I'm afraid not," Jordan said. "Desmond usually comes by once or twice a week for tea. But he's been fund-raising for the peace movement and he's rather done in."

The afternoon turned pleasant. As they talked about Oxford and Abingdon, Jordan wondered just exactly how much Angela knew about her grandparents and whether she cared. Angela paid a formal call, her first one, only months before, carrying with her a letter of introduction from Harley. The girl never mentioned, and Jordan never brought up, the circumstances by which Angela was related to Jordan Logan-Fisher and Harley Compton Fitch as grandmother, grandfather. Jordan and Angela had never discussed the other man they had in common: Andrew Fitch—Angela's father, Jordan's son.

Jordan watched Angela teasing Cedric, keeping his martini glass filled, stuffing him with smoked trout, then badgering him mercilessly for making a pig of himself. She's like my own mother must have been as a girl, Jordan thought, journeying without a care in the world to a new country, sure of her welcome.

At least two hours passed before the lively conversation hit a lull. Only then did Jordan remark that she'd received an invitation from the Queen to join the Royal Entourage for Oxford's Rhodes Scholar Reunion. "Of course, I'm flattered, but you and I, Angela, are the kind of women who need entourages of our own. And *you* know, Cedric, that these days being part of a Royal Entourage means nothing more than walking backward at a very slow pace in front of the Queen, tripping on rug fringes, and backing into people to whom you must apologize. It's a thankless task." Already part of her mind was bored with the sound of her own voice, bored with her life as it was occurring at this very instant. "What being in an entourage *really* means is that at every social occasion, one's duty to the Queen entails searching out the absolutely dullest person there and then engaging him in conversation until you swoon from ennui. I shan't go."

Angela leaned forward. Jordan realized that her granddaughter was just the slightest bit tipsy. "But, Grandmother, you must! Don't you realize that Rhodes Scholars are made up almost completely of stuffy and complacent white males? Don't you remember, Grandmother, what Virginia Woolf said about women not being allowed to walk on the lawns of Oxford or Cambridge? She *couldn't*, Grandmother! The finest woman novelist in England, and she couldn't walk on their grass. You must come, if only to make those men sorry."

The older woman sipped her martini, stared at the medal on the mantelpiece from the Queen of the Netherlands, and thought of the woman she used to be. She was adventurous and ready for any journey, and yet the world outside The Beeches now held only people she did not wish to enounter. She read about Harley and his gaudy yacht. She knew that Andrew was coming to England with his father. She knew what pop psychologists would say—that her son was a homosexual because she had rejected him. She knew it was true, but what was one to do about it now? Worse than all that, somewhere out there, beyond the hedges that kept The Beeches away from the rest of the world, there was a Nobel Prize winner who had rejected her far more cavalierly than she had rejected her own son.

Jordan remembered the spring five years before as her mother lay dying in a hospital bed in the solarium, delirious and incoherent. Desmond was on tour, unable to come home. Rain pounded against the glass walls as Jordan, alone, held her mother's hand and watched Matthew Granger peer out at her on television, mouthing platitudes about saving the world as he pocketed thousands of dollars in Nobel Prize money. He had been so close. Only two hours away by plane, only a day and a half by boat and train, and seconds away had he bothered to pick up the phone. She had sent him a telegram and flowers, and waited. Even as her mother was dying, Jordan's anguish centered in the bitter fact that Matthew never tried to seek her out, never cared enough to send her a note. . . .

She surprised Angela, Cedric, and most of all herself by blurting, "I rather think I *will* go. I'll walk upon the grass. I'll create a sensation, Angela. With any luck, I'll be an embarrassment to you. I hate to think of exciting things going on without me."

A few miles down the road and across the toll bridge, a very different kind of social occasion was in progress. Long ago, during World War II, brash Americans had come here, swooping their planes over the British countryside like hardshelled insects. They expanded Abingdon Air Base. The doughboys married English girls and took them home, but the base remained. Now Abingdon was a chess piece in a far grimmer war, the war that might end in worldwide conflagration.

The hopelessness of the equation communicated itself to the demonstrators who shivered outside Abingdon's forbidding gates. Soaking from the drizzle, a tired spokesman, exhausted from organizational problems, tried to rally them.

"Remember," he shouted hoarsely, "we are only one group at one air base. All over England, all over France, all over West Germany, Italy, Norway, and Spain, our brothers and sisters are demonstrating with us."

Joseph Simpson and Raymond Barnes, together with their classmates who came up from the London School of Economics, had heard the speech a hundred times. They huddled together, sharing a mackintosh square, covering their heads with a tarpaulin, and listened to a pop station on their transistor radio. Across the airwaves, Desmond Logan sang of peace. But Joseph and Raymond, committed as they were to the movement, knew that as thousands, even millions, sang and held hands all across Europe, each new sunrise here at Abingdon would see another American transport plane—fat with the hated missiles—landing behind the base's secured fences.

In all the time that Raymond and Joseph could remember of their short lives—neither had yet reached his twenty-first birthday—they had never seen the peace movement stronger. Everyone they knew was doing everything they could do. And still, it was not enough. The American missiles would be deployed, the Russians would counter the threat, and the world would take one more step toward extinction.

The Rev sang on. Water dribbled down Joseph's neck. He yearned for a beer or a sandwich or an easy lay. He picked up a rain-soaked tabloid from the ground, carefully opened it, and began to read. "World Leaders to Visit Oxford!" Much good that would do, Joseph thought. With the combined scorn and jealousy that the working class feels for the aristocracy, he read through the sodden pages. There would be physicists, bankers, professors, the Queen. . . . Then, in a sidebar, a feature story caught his eye. "One Family to Shine. Young Angela Fitch will be a lucky lady at this reunion. As she hurries about Oxford busy with her hostess duties, her handsome uncle, Desmond Logan, better known as Reverand Rock 'n' Roll, will be singing for Her Majesty. But that's not all. Angela's grandmother, Dame Jordan Logan-Fisher, world traveler and artist extraodinaire, is rumored to be a part of the Royal Entourage! Harley Compton Fitch II, Angela's grandfather (but never actually married to Dame Jordan so far as this reporter could find out!), is a famous American industrialist. Fitch and a party of exclusive jet-setters will be sailing on his new yacht up the Thames to be on hand for the festivites. Watch out, Henley! With Fitch blocking the river, there might not be room for you to hold your regatta. Oh—need we add?— Fitch's yacht has been christened the *Angela*. Yet another feather in the cap of this charming American princess. . . ."

Joseph read these words aloud in a false upper-class accent. Raymond did his part by sticking his index finger down his throat and groaning at intervals. Then Desmond Logan's voice was replaced by the insistent beat of Michael Jackson.

And over it all, the man with the bullhorn exhorted them to be brave, to keep their spirits up. Under the tarp, Raymond and Joseph's eyes met.

Perhaps, Joseph thought, there was another way to demonstrate than to sing, get wet, catch cold, and listen to the same speeches by the same tired man. Maybe the best way is to meet violence with more violence. What, he thought, would a heartless American industrialist do for a "charming American princess" of his own flesh and blood? Perhaps the only way to win peace from killers was by violence.

Raymond, who had been watching his expression, said softly, "Let's stow this place and find a pub. My peter's getting mildew on it." Until closing time, they plotted.

She was frantic. For one of the very first times in her life Angela was in the position of giving a party rather than having it given for her. Her high heels crunched along the gravel path that ran through the side garden of Rhodes House, parallel to that wretched wall, which even now was being dismantled piece by piece to make a hold big enough for the Queen, the Prince, and their entourage to walk through.

Back inside Rhodes House, the furniture in the ground-floor rooms had been packed away and card tables set up. Scores of secretaries, assistants, advisers were sent from Buckingham Palace, and the youngest Rhodes Scholars had been working for weeks. This was to be a party for two thousand people. All scholars were to be given—in theory at least—a chance to stay in their old rooms or in their old college. Men who had made worldwide reputations in medicine, philosophy, and theology had thrown tantrums on the phone and by letter. Eighty percent of them claimed to have stayed in their college's very best corner rooms with fireplaces. Statistics and student records proved that at least fifty percent of the scholars were lying. But how do you tell a member of the intellectual, social, and moral elite of his country that he's just a big fibber?

Now, peering from the path in Rhodes Garden through the hole in the wall at the emerald-green lawns of Wadham Garden, Angela was assaulted once again by the mixed emotions with which she regarded this whole display. Even now workmen were covering the piles of stones with a combination of Astroturf and green canvas. The whole thing looked like a high school setting for a very bad production of *A*

Midsummer Night's Dream. And yet, and yet, how grand it would be . . .

"Quite a spectacle."

Angela looked up to see two young men loitering on the path before her. "Widows and orphans starving," one of them said cheerily, "and the establishment spends money knocking things to pieces like this."

"Ah, but they could be spending money on rockets, couldn't they?" she rejoined. "At least there's no harm being done here."

Both of them beamed at her.

"Do you study here?" she asked.

"We're up from the London School of Economics. We've spent most of the weekend over at the Abingdon vigil."

"I thought of going," she said, "but I've been terribly busy."

"You haven't missed much," the shorter of the two remarked. "The same songs, the same speeches."

"But oh," Angela said, "no matter how limited one's response is, one must do what one can, don't you think?"

"Yes," the tall one said, with a curious intensity. "We *do* think, and we agree with you completely. My name is Joe Simpson and this is Raymond Barnes. I see from your name tag that you're Angela Fitch."

"Oh, this. We have to wear these so that the hospitality committee can get to be on speaking terms. I'd better get used to it. . . ."

When a light summer rain began to fall, she had no hesitation at all about accepting their invitation to tea rather than return to the stuffy reception room at Rhodes House. When she returned to her own room at St. Hilda's, she settled into her books with the satisfying sense of having made two new friends.

In the basement of Rhodes House, the sub-warden and two junior secretaries set up maps on every wall with push pins, time lines, and blinking lights, so that the windowless room looked like a military command post for a very complicated war. All the colleges were represented: Balliol, Merton, St. Hilda's, Trinity, the lot. Each college was covered with tiny colored dots.

"It's simply too much," the sub-warden complained. "There aren't enough rooms to sleep in, and the Randolph

Hotel is full to capacity. I don't know how they'll all eat. The old boys may have forgotten that if they stay in college rooms they'll have to shower in their basements at best. Of course one night they'll dine in their own college halls. And I still have to find a tent that will adequately shelter two thousand people."

His secretaries punctuated his tirade with deferential murmurs.

"*Why* must these colonials insist on returning to this primitive rite? *Why* must they insist on bringing their spouses?"

The two secretaires laughed nervously.

"I can only say I'm pleased," he said, "that we thought of including the morning Thanksgiving service at Christ Church Cathedral on Thursday morning. Half a day of kneeling on hard stone will show them the true stuff of Empire. But have you read the service they've written for it? All they do is thank God for making them of such splendid materials. Ill-bred louts."

The ladies commiserated softly and the sub-warden reverted to the two subjects that had obsessed him for the past six months and would keep him from a sound night's sleep until this reunion was over.

"The tent. And the Queen's garden party. The wall is down now. We've made the dress code clear, *if* those females can find enough gloves to go around. We have to remember to insist that they leave their cameras at home. We can't have a lot of vulgar flashing in the Queen's eyes."

In another basement, miles away in Scotland Yard, a group of security men worried. The entire United Kingdom was in a state of severe unrest. Peace demonstrations here and in continental Europe threatened at any moment to belie their label and turn into riots. Intelligence from Ireland indicated that the IRA planned to take advantage of this wave of unrest with a round of bombings. Princess Di and Prince Charles received death threats. In this long list of possible troubles, the Reunion of Rhodes Scholars up at Oxford was duly noted but given minimal attention.

"You'd have a damned hard time infiltrating that one, sir. A Rhodes Scholar is like an Oxford lawn. You'd have to roll and water a terrorist for a hundred years to get him to look like one of those boyos."

* * *

Matthew sat with Chuen-yup in the back of a taxi. They had come up from Paddington by train. The country so far looked polished, miniature, and domestic. Matthew could not believe these were the streets where he grew from a boy to a man. He glanced sideways at the glossy Chinese politician, whose chubby face looked as smooth as a new porcelain vase. Chuen-yup wore his favorite three-piece suit and the tie that saluted "friendship" in three languages.

"How do you like it so far?" Matthew asked in Chinese.

"This country is very beautiful, but I cannot help but wonder where they keep the jade girls."

"Under the hedgerows," Matthew answered. "They only come out at night. They're as hard to catch as greased pigs. Won't you give up you idea of staying at a hotel and share my old rooms at Merton with me?"

"Absolutely not," Chuen-yup said. "All through the dark nights of the Cultural Revolution I had to listen to your tales of ten-course meals in the restaurant at the Randolph, then drinking in the bar until three, and *then* retiring to your room with shopgirls where you victimized them under the capitalist system until dawn. I look forward to enjoying the spoils of corruption. You can stay in touch with me by telephone."

"I just don't want to bail you out of jail like the last time."

"Me? Deng Xiao-ping sent *me* to watch out for *you*," Chuen-yup answered. "Besides, there is a Chinese saying. 'There are no snowdrifts or vodka in southern England.'"

"Just remember that and don't embarrass me."

When they stopped at the Randolph, Matthew stayed in the cab, but he saw that the lettered sign had not changed, nor the modest porte cochere, nor the great pots of red geraniums that brightened the drab English day. As soon as Chuen-yup disappeared into the hotel, Matthew spoke to the cab driver. "I'll be going on to Merton."

"Right-o, sir. That would be for the reunion, wouldn't it?"

The cab pulled up at the Merton College lodge. Matthew got out with an ache of nostalgia and paid his fare. Only when confronted by the porter was he forced back into the real world. He had yet to pick up his new clothes from the tailors. Though Chuen-yup had dressed for this trip, Matthew preferred to wear the clean but worn work clothes of a fairly properous Shanghai farmer. The porter looked at him askance.

"I'm returning for the reunion," Matthew said. "I've been told I'll have my own rooms."

"And which ones were they, sir?" asked the porter with heavy sarcasm.

"St. Alban's Quad, staircase four, suite three. They were much envied because the fireplace actually drew."

"Indeed."

Matthew announced his name. He might be wearing a patched work shirt, but he was a Nobel Prize winner. Not even Merton College, with its seven hundred years of distinguished history, had more than a couple of these. The porter flushed and asked Matthew to wait while he telephoned the Warden, who scurried out to welcome personally the college's most distinguished son.

Matthew saw that the gray stone walls of Merton had been scoured and sandblasted. Otherwise, all was as he had seen it so many times in his mind's eye. He felt close to tears as he walked up the dark staircase to his old rooms. Someone had put up reproductions of etchings of Chartres Cathedral and set out volumes of John Donne and T. S. Eliot. In those days he had read those pages and thought of Jordan. He sighed. So many years had gone by, so many years.

But here the present offered an inviting prospect. The fire had been laid and was even now being lit. A decanter of sherry and a platter of cheese and fruit awaited him, as well as a tidy stack of telegrams.

Matthew sank into his old easy chair in front of the fire and opened the first of the envelopes. His son, Paul, was staying at the Randolph and wanted to see him.

Chuen-yup begged off, saying that a father and son should dine alone, especially since they were in the habit of seeing each other only once every five years. Matthew's clothes had been delivered that evening, and, dressed in a conservative pinstripe, he entered the lobby of the Randolph. On his way to the dining room, he passed a bar where he saw that Chuen-yup had, with unerring territoriality, found a corner booth and a year's supply of salted nuts. He sat with an oriental gentleman who looked vaguely familiar. Chuen-yup beckoned to Matthew and stood up, crying out in English, "I have found a countryman who is here on business. He is not a Rhodes Scholar, but he says he knows you."

The other man wore three diamonds—one on each little finger, and another, almost as big as a kumquat, stuck into his tie. "Can it be?" Matthew faltered. "Can it be you, H.H.?"

The Chinese man bowed. "You and me, we teraphone many plety girl in nightclub! It's good to see you, Matthew, old scout! We were all so proud when you won the prize. I've been in Hong Kong many times on business and thought of you in Shanghai. I've wanted to visit, but I'm sure of the welcome your government would give me."

Matthew filled in Chuen-yup with a rapid burst of Wu. "This is the worst running dog of capitalism who ever left China."

"Excellent," Chuen-yup said, chuckling. "I'm sure we will have a wonderful evening."

Leaving them, Matthew continued into the restaurant where the famed Osbert Lancaster paintings for Beerbohm's *Zuleika Dobson* decorated the room. Paul waited at a table. Matthew saw with a pang that his son's hair was turning gray. They embraced self-consciously and sat down.

They had seen each other three times in the last fifteen years. Just after Nixon opened China, Paul came and stayed on Matthew's farm for a week. He eagerly took up the disciplined life, working from dawn to dusk in the fields, and at night listened quietly to China's still disenfranchised intellectuals. His work at Yale's Center for Asian Studies allowed him to understand most of what was going on, but he was shy about speaking. Some years later, Paul turned up in Stockholm. But for those few weeks, Matthew had been a celebrity and again Paul stayed in the background.

Matthew ordered a lavish meal: cucumbers *à la reine*, lobster soufflé, rack of lamb, and blackberry fool. The wine steward brought a heavy and comforting cabernet sauvignon. Still Paul said almost nothing. It was against Matthew's grain to make a direct statement and yet, he thought, he was sixty-seven years old now. If his son remained as reticent as he was now, Matthew might go to the grave having never really known what it was to be a father. (It was characteristically Chinese of him that he did not think of his daughter, Joyce, from one year to the next. She did not bear his name and was no longer properly his concern.)

"Are you always this quiet?" Matthew asked.

"When I was young, I never stopped talking. But you changed my life."

"How is that?" asked Matthew suspiciously.

"I was almost dead and you brought me back to life. As I may have told you before, when I left you up in the mountains, it was as though I had a new skin. I made my way down to the base of the Himalayas and found another monastery. At the place where I stayed, all speech was forbidden." He paused appreciatively as the puffed and rosy lobster soufflé was set in front of them. "I stayed in Nepal for several years. At times it seemed I was regaining my health; other times, it seemed I might die. I'd realized from our talks that you were truly devoted to the land, but I didn't feel that way. Many afternoons when I was ill the monks would put me out on a veranda. I had nowhere to look but up. I began to see that the sky is deep and full of spirits. Don't laugh."

"I'm not," Matthew said. He took a bite of soufflé together with a sip of the red wine and felt the mixture of texture and tastes on his tongue. Could it be that he was more of a sensualist than his own son?

As if Paul followed his train of thought, he said, "It's a good thing you didn't know me when I was young. If a body was alive, sooner or later I'd find myself making love to it. If a drug existed, I'd ingest it. . . ."

When the rack of lamb came, Matthew risked one more question. "Have you ever been in love?"

"The right answer should be, 'Only with God,' but yes, there was a person once I might have loved."

Matthew sighed. "It's the traditional difference between the Indians and the Chinese. The Indians invoke divine beings while the world around them falls into disarray. The Chinese know that we have only one life. If there's a heaven, it had best be on earth." He ordered champagne to go with the blackberry fool.

The dinner had been genial but somewhat strained. After brandies, Matthew and Paul, father and son, rose sedately, left the restaurant, and went down the hallway of the Randolph. Halfway along their short journey, Matthew heard an all too familiar voice raised in the singsong Chinese vernacular.

"Her vagina held tiny teeth that nibbled me like minnows. I tell you, all this is true. One hundred and forty-seven tiny teeth. I was able to count them during the hour and a half it took me to reach my own climax. . . ."

"Old liar," H. H. Fong answered. "Do you think I am so dull that I do not know you have plagiarized this adventure from *The Tale of a Thousand Peonies*?"

"You question my prowess? Surely then, I must divest myself of these clumsy Western trousers and show you the terror of all Asia!"

"Not again," Matthew groaned. "You can wait here if you want to, Paul."

But son followed father into the Randolph Bar, where perhaps a hundred English men and women watched as two well-dressed Chinese gentlemen began to unbuckle their belts.

"Chuen-yup, I'm writing a report on you," Matthew called in Chinese, "and I'll send it to the Politburo. After they read it, you'll be lucky to be able to spend a weekend at a fourth-class friendship hotel in Canton."

H.H. took Matthew's arm. "Do you remember our nights in arms of beautiful women? We were young then. They would always say yes, because we were handsome and strong. *This* man here must crib his adventures from the pages of our country's pornography. But you and I, Matthew, we slashed our way through England's female flesh with our mighty swords and left them begging for more. Show him, Matthew! Show him!"

"Yes, it's true," Matthew said. "We left them sobbing, but I think it's best if the three of us kept our swords a secret." Diplomatically, he appealed to the motto on Chuen-yup's tie. "Friendship before all, isn't that right? We don't want to cause an international incident."

The bartender went back to making a round of Pimm's Cup for a party of six at the next table. Matthew, feeling utterly exhausted, excused himself, leaving Chuen-yup and H.H. with Paul. He took a cab back to his college. Paul ordered another brandy. Chuen-yup and H.H. departed arm in arm, exclaiming to each other in confidential tones that each of them knew a brothel full of eager shopgirls. Paul relaxed after they had gone and gave himself up to his own solitude in the midst of the bar full of old boys, up for the reunion.

"I spent twenty years in the Arctic," a voice sounded above the melee.

And another: "I eradicated malaria in Southeast Asia almost single-handedly, so they tell me."

At the table for six, a famous economist enumerated his publications and forbade his wife another drink. "I've been to the Galapagos," she said challengingly. "I've seen tortoises a thousand years old. I can have another drink if I want."

Down the bar from him to the left, he heard a woman dressed from head to foot in what must have been a million silver sequins shouting at the bartender, "I flew in with Charles on the Concorde and I'm flying home with Charlie on the Concorde. But I told him, 'Charlie, I'm not learning how to eat with a fork in my left hand for any amount of money and that's final.'"

Paul turned his face away from the strident voice and caught the eye of a man sitting alone, the only one there who had not joined in the chorus of egos, each clamoring for recognition—"I published, I wrote, I eradicated, I traveled." This man had centered his attention on a series of Scotch-and-sodas. Though middle-aged, he was strikingly handsome. His eyes were sunken, his cheekbones stood out startlingly in the half-dark of the room. He looked into a world which only he could see, and Paul knew by the expression on his face that what he saw was a nightmare. Then the man picked up his drink. The light caught his manicured fingernails. His knuckles, the backs of his wasted hands, Paul could see even from this distance, were tan. Later, Paul would marvel that it was by his hands, not his face, that he recognized . . . He got up and made his way through the crowded room to the comparatively quiet corner.

"Andrew, it's me. It's Paul."

The man looked up, and Paul, trained as he was to see through to the essence of things, recognized an undefended look of love so powerful that he recoiled. It was terrible to be loved like that. But then, Andrew's expression changed. His eyes narrowed, his full lips drew back over expensively capped teeth, and he flirtatiously tapped Paul on the forearm.

"Darling!" he said. "It's *you* after all these years. I hoped that you might be somewhere around. It certainly took you long enough! I've been waiting how many years for the phone to ring? I waited for just a letter, even a postcard, but I suppose it must have got lost. It doesn't matter. I've met the most wonderful boys, and all because of you. Why, I might be married now to another heiress, putting two or three brats through school, running the power mower on Sundays for a little fresh air—"

"Andrew, I—"

"I do wish it was another evening, darling. I wish I could take you back to my rooms to meet Phil and Chris and Bob and Don. We all came over on Dad's silly boat. Tonight he's giving a tedious party for a lot of heteros and the boys have all gone off to find . . . well, you know, Paul, what they've gone off to find. What you gave me."

"Andrew," Paul said, "I've thought of you. I've wanted to call you or write you a hundred times, but—"

"Never mind," Andrew said. "It doesn't matter in the slightest. One has one's pleasures to look after." Andrew's voice became increasingly shaky. Then, incredibly, he reached into his pocket, pulled out a compact, flipped it open, and looked at himself in the mirror. "I don't know what it is," he said. "I've been so pale. And you know how it is with a mother like mine, Paul. She never remembered to tell me, when I was growing up, not to leave home without my blush!"

Paul took hold of his friend's hand. "Andrew," he whispered, "please. You don't have to be like this. We can go out, find someplace where we can really talk."

"Talk?" Andrew simpered. "I remember that line. After a talk with you I couldn't sit down for a week."

"Please," Paul said, "let's go."

Andrew's artificial grimace vanished. "I don't believe I've really talked to anyone since you. It's true, we couldn't talk to each other then, or now either, I imagine, without a talk turning to a kiss, and a kiss turning into something else. I don't think we can do that now. I'm sick, Paul."

Paul groped for the right words. "You'll never believe this, Andrew, but I've been living a celibate life."

Andrew laughed. "Aren't you the trendy thing? A real boy of the eighties!"

"I loved you, Andrew."

"But 'our pasts are now complete.' Isn't that what you consciousness-raising types say? Isn't that right? Isn't it?"

"Yes," Paul said heavily. "Yes, that's right."

"I know what I'm going to do now," Andrew said. "I'm going to go back to the boat and get drunk."

The next morning, the day before the formal reunion started, the harried sub-warden of Rhodes House was interviewed by a reporter from the American daily periodical USA Today. Karen Heller had traveled the world. She had interviewed world-famous novelists at Michael's in Los Angeles. She had written incisively and knowingly about the "Washington Man" for Gentleman's Quarterly. But the intricacies of the English system of so-called public education left her totally at sea. She was, the sub-warden had decided, quite incapable of grasping the most elementary facts of English university education. She was also incapable of keeping her short and narrow skirt pulled down over her pretty knees.

"I don't get it," she repeated. "I'm sorry, but I just don't get it. Run it past me one more time."

"My dear young woman, as I have already explained to you, the University of Oxford is made up of thirty-one colleges, but in order to be enrolled as a member of a particular college, you must have already been accepted as a member of the university."

"But didn't you just say before that," Karen Heller asked brightly, "that in order to be a member of the university you had to be accepted as a member of a college?"

"Quite."

"Well, I'm sorry, but I just don't see how it works."

"Miss Heller, it has worked very well for over seven hundred years."

It was the second day of the reunion. Tonight each college would hold a formal dinner. So far, wives and women friends trod softly, foreigners to this university and this way of life. Husbands, dignified personages in their own country, had been catapulted back in time to schoolboys in terror that the women with them might prove a source of embarrassment.

But this afternoon would be a different story. This was the day of the Queen's Garden Party. The dress code had been severely and precisely prescribed: afternoon-length dresses, garden hats, and elbowlength gloves. From all over Oxford, from hotels and boardinghouses, from college rooms, crowds of men dressed in three-piece suits—almost every one of them accompanied by a pretty woman in flowered chiffon holding on to a wide-brimmed hat with a carefully gloved hand—converged on Wadham Garden. Some of them came into the lawn from the sidewalk, but more walked down the gravel path along the south wall of the garden of Rhodes House so that they might see once again the place that had been the agent of their move from drab provincial worlds to the centers of power.

Then they stood in the wide expanse of Wadham Garden. Under a canopy a liveried band played national favorites— "The British Grenadier," "Under the Maple Tree," and "Rule Britannia." The women looked to see how their counterparts were dressed while their husbands examined each other closely for signs of age.

Within the rectangular garden two concentric circles of rope had been placed. The circle itself was big enough that it would take royalty precisely an hour and a half to walk through it. The guests jockeyed for position to see the Queen.

Her Majesty and Prince Philip would start out from the breach in the wall. They would walk slowly in opposite directions, each with an entourage, each with a royal umbrella in case it might rain. At precisely forty-five minutes into this ceremonial walk, the Queen and her consort would cross at the far end of the circle and proceed, each in his or her same direction, back to where they started. Their duty done, they would be spirited away to a private reception.

It was Jordan's task, and not by any means an easy one, to walk backward at a distance of about twenty feet in front of the Queen. She accompanied Lady Blake, wife of Lord Blake, Chairman of the Rhodes Trust, and another lady-in-waiting, the Duchess of Dorset. The three of them should never appear to hurry. When the Queen stopped to shake hands and engage in charming bits of small talk to a star-struck Australian, so, too, should Jordan and Lady Blake and the Duchess stop, look out into the sea of scholars, and ask politely, "Have you traveled far?" or "Isn't it a shame the sun hasn't seen fit to shine on our party today?"

As she walked, Jordan marveled at the presence of the Queen. What a tiny little thing she was. Today she wore an exceptionally dowdy outfit—a chartreuse coat-dress made from a synthetic fabric with bumps in it—matched by a pancake hat of the same preposterous material. And yet, the Queen drew all eyes to her, and that was that.

Except—except, Jordan felt the hairs rising on the back of her neck. Her palms within her white kid gloves began to sweat. She looked across the rope to a nervous young wife and said, "Have you, uh, have you . . ." and could not remember the rest of her sentence. Jordan knew that one pair of eyes here was not on the Queen. It took all of her control to maintain her calm, to remember that whatever had happened in the past, she was now a Dame of the Order of the British Empire. She silently thanked her mother for every lesson she had learned in self-control. And Jordan reminded herself, as she straightened her spine and refrained from touching the wisps of hair at the back of her neck, that to be British and of the upper class was to maintain absolute control.

It took a full ten minutes after her first realization to back up to, draw even with, and then serenely look into the eyes of a man who five years ago had won a Nobel Prize.

"It's Matthew, isn't it?" she said, extending a hand. "Isn't it a shame the sun hasn't seen fit to shine on our party today?"

The royal party completed its progress and disappeared into Rhodes House. At last Angela could put down her clipboard. There had been no awkward interruptions, not even a plane flying overhead. She looked at the scholars flocking now to the striped marquees where they and their companions helped themselves to sandwiches, squares of cake, and cups of weak tea. Angela took one last tour through the tables. In a moment she would be going on to the private reception where she would see Grandpa Harley and Grandmother Jordan. It would be interesting, she thought, to see those two in the same room together.

Two men came toward her. They wore name tags, but Angela knew that they were not invited guests. Gate crashers, of all the nerve! she thought, recognizing Joe and Ray.

"How did you . . ." she began.

"Angela, you've got to come with us right away. Just outside the gate there's something you must see."

As Joe took her elbow, Angela wondered what could have gone wrong. The only thing she could think of was that someone's inconsiderate wife had fainted. Perhaps they could carry her in and look after her behind one of the marquees. They reached the gate and stepped out onto the public sidewalk. Before she knew what was happening, Joe threw both his arms around her, held her close, and kissed her on the mouth. As he pulled away, he said, "Darling, I've missed you so much." Then, adroitly taking a clean white handkerchief out of his pocket, he pressed it to her nose and mouth.

No one on the street saw two men hurry a beautiful young girl into the backseat of a waiting car.

He had the most terrible hangover he could remember. At three this morning he had wakened to vomit into his gold-plated toilet. After that he was unable to sleep, except for a few moments caught between fits of retching as he laid his feverish cheek on the marble floor. His servant had found him this morning and, with a disgust he did not try to conceal, stripped off Andrew's clothes and pushed him under a hot shower.

Andrew sat now in a deck chair with a breakfast tray beside him. Dry toast, beef tea, and a mug of iced vodka. Andrew knew from other horrible days like this that if he judiciously combined these ingredients, he would be able by six o'clock to restore himself in time for another night of drinking.

With anguish and clarity, he recalled what had happened the night before. He had seen Chuen-yup, his childhood torturer, who didn't recognize him. Why should he remember the "albino lizard"? After that, he had talked to Paul, touched Paul. . . .

Now, shivering under the overcast sky, he knew that he was failing his daughter in one of the few things she'd ever asked of him. This was the very hour he was supposed to attend a private reception for the Queen at Oxford. His mother—how he still hated the bitch—would be there, and his daughter too. His father, his stepfather, and most likely Matthew would be there. God knows, the Queen would be there. But Andrew was on a tasteless yacht, tied up at Henley, drenched in sweat, assailed by waves of nausea, and unable to get the mugs to his mouth because of his shaking hands. He had to lean over to sip from each cup under the sardonic eyes of the skeleton crew.

He lay back and closed his eyes, feeling every cell of his body rebel against the hundred-proof vodka and then accept it.

He heard footsteps and voices on the deck. How dare they, he thought irritably. They know I'm sick. Then he felt an altogether impossible sensation and for a short time thought he must be dreaming. Almost immediately he came to a worse conclusion: this must be the DTs. Cold metal about the size of a quarter pressed against his temple and a voice asked, "Do you want to die or do you want to get up and do as we say?"

He opened his eyes and was jerked out of his chair. "What is this? Who are you?" Someone pinned his arms behind his back and cuffed his wrists.

"Which one is your room?" the voice asked.

"Aft, belowdecks."

He was hustled through the passageways of his father's yacht and pitched into his room. It took him at least five minutes to get to his feet. By that time, the door to his cabin opened again and a girl—bound and gagged—was flung face-down onto his bed. He staggered over to her and put his head down to the pillow, trying to get a look at her face.

"Who are you?" he asked. His voice sounded frail. The girl, apparently heavily drugged, did not move. Afraid that she might suffocate, he nuzzled at her head with his own until her face turned toward him.

"My God!" he exclaimed. "Angela!"

Usually the only thing more tedious than moving down a reception line was standing in the line itself. But for once, what was ordinarily a more than dull experience had Jordan's knees shaking. She surprised herself by confiding to the Duchess of Dorset a few details about her previous liaison with Matthew Granger. The Duchess giggled in a most unladylike manner, and eagerly waited to meet the Nobel Prize winner.

Matthew appeared, slouching, almost at the very end of the line. Jordan placed a gloved hand on the Duchess's forearm. "There he is," she whispered.

"My dear, he's so very handsome!" the Duchess said. "But who can that exotically piratical chap behind him be?"

"*My father's testicles!*" Jordan muttered in the Wu dialect. "How much can one woman stand?"

Then she was extending her hand to Matthew, not even condescending to speak a direct word to him, but simply introducing him to the lady-in-waiting. "Duchess, allow me to present my old friend and sometime fiancé, whose considerable intelligence has not yet extended to mastery of the telephone. And I believe I know his companion."

Keeping as straight a face as was possible under the circumstances, Jordan went on, "Duchess, let me present Nyi Chuen-yup. If I'm still up on my Chinese politics, now Minister of International Relations. For seven short years we lived as husband and wife with the army of Mao Tse-tung in his wartime stronghold."

The Duchess pushed back her carefully curled hair with a perfectly manicured hand, then batted her eyelashes at the stocky Chinese.

"Such adventures you must have had," she said. "I'm absolutely eaten up with envy."

Chuen-yup, whose mission English flowered on this sort of occasion, leaned forward confidentially and declaimed, "A dull tale becomes an adventure only when it finds a home in the ears of a beautiful woman."

The dignitaries behind Matthew and Chuen-yup, like

impatient customers in a cafeteria, began to circle around the foursome in order to reach the Queen. In a few minutes the line broke up. Matthew kept his eyes squarely on the floor. He seemed equally unable to speak to Jordan or to move away. Chuen-yup and the Duchess plunged into what sounded like a mutually fascinating exchange.

"Matthew, I . . ." Jordan glanced past the man on whom she had lavished so many fantasies and dreams. The lanky muscular form of Prince Philip caught her eye. She heard that the Prince had been inveigled into coming to this reception only on the condition that he bring some of his own cronies. Jordan had already met some of them. A jolly if light-headed lot, they lived only to chat in grunts about their yachts, the hunt, and polo ponies. She could see the Prince was involved in conversation with a burly man standing next to a petite, elegantly dressed woman. The woman was the movie star Tailing. Her escort must be, she realized in horror, the brute who had raped her some forty years ago—Harley Compton Fitch.

Following her eyes, Matthew looked across the room and saw his old rival.

"I see the two of you are still together," he said.

"Don't make me puke!" she said savagely. As he widened his eyes, she continued, "And don't stand there looking like a sheep, Matthew!" She was on the point of going on when a uniformed man came in with a message for the Queen. He leaned in and whispered to Her Majesty, who shot a look across the room at Jordan. What could it be now? By this time the Queen was at Jordan's side and touched her elbow. "Dame Jordan, will you please accompany me?"

The Queen led her into an anteroom, and Jordan saw that the Prince was following with Harley, who grinned at her in the same taunting way that he had as a youth. As Jordan searched for a devastating comment, the Queen said, "Colonel Napier, my personal security chief, has come to me with some rather distressing news. We've just received word that your granddaughter has been kidnapped."

As Jordan tried to absorb this, the Prince said to Harley, "At least we know where they are, old man. They've holed up on your yacht."

Jordan heard Harley say, "I believe our son is aboard as well."

But the man who had always remained a brute in her mind stood now pale and shaken. Before Jordan could fully grasp what was happening, the door to the anteroom opened and the Queen's messenger came in with Matthew Granger, Nyi Chuen-yup, and Tai-ling.

Harley buried his head in his hands, and choked out the words that perhaps only Jordan and Matthew fully understood. "It should have been me," he said. "They took the wrong one. It should have been me."

Jordan heard a sigh. Matthew, too, hid his face from the eyes of the group. Instinctively, Jordan started for him, even as the delicate figure of Tai-ling moved to comfort Harley. Colonel Napier's voice cut in with muted urgency, "There are many things about this that should reassure you. These kidnappers, so far as we know, are neither foreigners nor terrorists of any kind, but young people motivated by ideal- ism, however misdirected. That is not to say that they are unarmed or that they have ruled out violence. Their demands are simply stated, even if they may not be easily met. They have said that they will not release Angela Fitch until her grandfather signs over to them controlling shares in Compton Fitch Enterprises and a million pounds sterling."

Harley's eyes narrowed and his face turned blotchy as he asked through gritted teeth, "Is my son involved in this?"

"No, sir. Your son has been taken prisoner, as we understand it." Now Colonel Napier turned his attention to a hastily scrawled paper in the palm of his hand. "The kidnap- pers have also demanded that their message of peace be communicated to the entire world. They've asked to speak in person with Matthew Granger and the Bishop of Oxford. They've asked as well that we send for Dame Jordan and her son." Here the colonel looked bewildered. "Reverend Rock 'n' Roll?"

On the stage outside Abingdon Air Base, Desmond Logan felt that he had sung for a full two hours—all of his old favorites—until the crowd, exhausted and dispirited from the long days and nights of their fruitless demonstration, took heart again. He knew the way to end the concert was with the words of John Lennon, and he exulted in the thrilling response of fifty thousand voices singing out, "All we are saying is, give peace a chance!"

Then he was finished. He staggered down the steep wooden steps with his head and shoulders wrapped in a rough towel, depleted. The towel was rudely whipped off and a pinched face peered into his. Desmond felt stark terror. Since Lennon's death every mass-media entertainer had to face thought of assassination. This rodentlike creature, however, was absurdly cheerful as he asked, "How do you feel about the kidnapping of your niece, Rev? What do you think of the peace movement now in the light of this heinous act?"

Desmond blinked. There were far more flashbulbs than usual. "Kidnapping?" he asked.

"Your niece, your niece," the intruder bleated.

Before Desmond could reply, a wedge of Scotland Yard officers, bearing truncheons and canisters of tear gas, pushed through the crowd, surrounded Desmond, and jog-trotted him, with troops on either side, through the shoving crowd to the heavily guarded gates of Abingdon Base. He was whisked to a rain-slick runway on which a small group of people huddled near a Huey helicopter.

Despite his overcoat and scarf, Matthew Granger shivered as he stood under the rotor. Not since his early days at the Kuling American School had he felt so buffeted, so vulnerable, so pummeled by the unexpected. With relentless intensity, his past had come to meet him; in the raucous cries of H. H. Fong at the bar of the Randolph, in his uneasy reunion with his son, Paul, and in the appearance of his nemesis, Harley Fitch. And there was Jordan. When he first saw her, she looked like a woman of middle age, but then during the party, the years slipped away from her face until he was confronted by the enchantress, the woman who enraged him and ensnared him. . . .

When she heard the news about her granddaughter, she turned into a grieving old woman before his eyes. How he longed to put his arms around her. But Matthew's mind rebelled. As long as he did not love a single human being he was safe. As long as he channeled all of his affections out into the larger world, he was rewarded. But to think again of one human being and of that human being's happiness—something in Matthew panicked at the thought. It was too late. He had failed with Valerie. He had certainly failed with Joyce. And Paul's feelings for him were . . . obviously mixed. Matthew knew he loved Jordan. But another part of him, a chilly part, counseled him sourly, get out now while there is still time.

The doors of a military vehicle, parked for a few minutes by the side of the tarmac, opened. A uniformed officer strode toward the group, shielding his face from the sleeting rain. Just behind him a young man followed in a Burberry coat. Jordan drew in a shaky breath.

"Matthew, there's something you don't know . . ." she said.

The man with the trench coat came up to her and said, "Mother, you're not to worry. We'll all do everything we can to make sure Angela is safe." Then he turned to Matthew.

"Colonel Napier has filled me in, sir," the young man said to Matthew. "These are terrible circumstances for us to finally meet. My name is Desmond Logan. And I know you must be Matthew Granger. You're my father, I believe. . . ."

"Your father?" Matthew choked out.

Now that the rescue party was complete, Colonel Napier wasted no time in ordering everyone to board the chopper. Behind him Matthew heard Harley sneer, "You always were too stupid to find your own socks, Matt." Without a word, Desmond guided his mother to the copter. The others tactfully turned away. Matthew stood alone on the tarmac, his face turned up to the rain. His mind, ordinarily so quick, was engaged in the simplest of computations. Nine months plus how many years? From afar he heard the pilot shout to him, "We're waiting for you, sir."

Chuen-yup leaned out of the side door and called, "Come on in, you old goat. Enough posturing for one day. Few men can count the number of their own children."

Matthew fought down the urge to turn and run. It took far more bravery to climb into the copter than it had to cross China behind enemy lines. But he did it for the most cowardly of reasons—so that he would not look like a perfect fool.

He sat down next to Chuen-yup, who muttered to him in Chinese, "Didn't I tell you to stay away from that woman? You put your slippers under her bed and there's another rice bowl on the table. And look at him, Matthew, he could do with a few months of rehabilitation."

Just behind them, Jordan's voice sliced through in Chinese, "The two mangy dogs still cannot resist sniffing about the luscious female, but her puppy shall outrank them both."

The men hunched their shoulders and slouched down in their seats.

The helicopter lurched off the ground. Under cover of the deafening noise, Matthew stole a glance at his son. Why had he not seen the resemblance immediately? That was his father's nose, his mother's long-lashed hazel eyes.

* * *

A half-dozen helicopters hovered over Henley, waiting for troops to clear a landing area. Already, within two hours of the kidnapping, the British armed forces were making a spectacular show. Around the perimeters of this buzzing circle of aircraft, a few smaller media helicopters swarmed impudently, trying for full camera coverage of what promised to be a major news event. The tow path along the north bank marked the beginning of the police barricade where gawkers milled. At the top of the embankment, soldiers stood with their feet apart aiming machine guns at the yacht. The street beyond, which ordinarily separated the life of the river from Henley, marked the last boundary to the real world. The Huey swayed cautiously above the river and the town, and then landed at the top of the embankment just behind the human cordon. Rain continued to fall as a late summer dusk shrouded the town.

Within Henley, a one-block area had been completely sealed off from the public. One side of this block faced on the river. The block included curio shops, boutiques, a haberdashery, and the Regatta Hotel. The English inn, which combined the authenticity of the eighteenth century with a few conveniences of the present, had been designated as the command post. Its guests were evacuated and a maze of telephone lines and electronic communications set up.

It was to the Regatta that Colonel Napier shepherded his group of dignitaries. They were greeted at the door by the stout, reassuring proprietress of the place, who had prepared their rooms and stirred up a big pot of oyster stew. Despite Mrs. Botsford's cordial welcome, the entry hall of the Regatta looked anything but inviting. Extra lights had been strung across the ceiling. Thick cables lay on the floor and went up to the mezzanine. Three technicians behind the reception desk struggled to get the new banks of telephones in working order.

The moment he was inside the front door, Harley Fitch began to take charge. "Give me a phone," he said. "Give it to me now! Get the kidnappers on the phone immediately."

Simpson and Barnes were waiting for his call.

"Yes. We'll do what you want if you return Angela unharmed. The million pounds we can do. But to give you a controlling interest in CFE means that many bankers will have to transfer the stock from New York. It's about seven o'clock now. Give me twelve hours. No—thirteen."

Only as he hung up did Harley realize that he had not even asked to talk to Angela.

Matthew said in a low voice, "Another kidnapping."

"At least *this* time we know what to do," Harley snapped. "Just a few hours and my men will take care of it."

Matthew was stung. "You still think your money and your power can take care of everything, don't you, Harley? The people who have your granddaughter have asked to talk to *me.*"

Harley came out from behind the counter.

Matthew stepped back, jutting his chin in the air, once more the missionary's bratty son. "Oh, I grant you they know your name. Don't you stamp it on every bomb you build?"

Harley's neck swelled against his shirt collar. He lashed out with his right fist, trying to pack sixty years of hatred into one punch. Matthew jumped back and picked up a chair. For all of Harley's complacent belief in having kept fit, he lived a sedentary life. Matthew had spent the last thirty years working days in the fields. He moved as easily as a Chinese tumbler as he glided out of the heavier man's reach. Harley puffed after him like a tired bull lunging at a bright, fresh matador.

Too ashamed merely to stop, Harley slowed down enough to let himself be restrained by Colonel Napier and Tai-ling. Matthew perched on the reception desk and swung his legs.

"I'd like to hit you, Harley," he said. "But gentlemen don't hit. That's the way I was brought up."

Mrs. Botsford said, in the tone of a patient governess, "What you all need is a good pint of stout, I daresay. Come into the pub. Sit down and take off your wet clothes and I'll bring you all a cup of hot stew to ease your feelings."

Colonel Napier, with his own brand of tact, said, "Mr. Fitch, I'd like you to take a look at what we've done in the mezzanine," and led the way for Harley.

Desmond went up to Matthew and burst our laughing. "Once she got up the nerve to tell me who you were, Mother always said you were a sweet talker."

Jordan remarked with a trace of asperity, "Now that you've put on your little show, Matthew, do you think you could pony up for a round of stout?"

Each one taking an arm, Jordan and Desmond escorted Matthew into the hotel pub. Most of the others followed.

* * *

Upstairs, one wall of the Regatta's mezzanine was covered by a detailed map of this section of the Thames, the slips with the Fitch yacht placed at the center.

"We've evacuated all the adjacent boats, Colonel Napier," a lieutenant said deferentially. "All the waterfront buildings have been vacated. We're free to attack when and where you see fit."

"There will be no attack," Harley rapped out. "That's my yacht you're talking about, and my son, and my grand-daughter."

"No one desires the safety of your family more than we do, Mr. Fitch," Colonel Napier said. "We're here only to ensure the general good, and—within reason—we'll make every effort to accede to your wishes."

"I'll need phones up here," Harley said. "I'll need half a dozen phones and two good translators with a knowledge of French, German, and Japanese. The major stockholders of Compton Fitch Enterprises live all over the world and I'm not at all sure how eager they'll be to turn their shares over to my granddaughter's kidnappers. It was a stupid move for them to ask for stock instead of money. It gives us a chance to buy time."

Downstairs, once it had been made clear that no confrontation with the kidnappers would take place until dawn of the following day, a dozen or so of the rescuers settled in the pub with fatigue, relief, and a certain elation.

Chuen-yup had acquired a handful of coins from Mrs. Botsford's cash register and managed to get through to the Queen's entourage, asking that the Duchess of Dorset be put on the phone. "Your friend, Dame Jordan Logan-Fisher," he said, "is sorely in need of a woman's comfort. I am sure your Queen, as kind as she appeared, could arrange for you to be transported here." Then he lowered his voice and spoke sibilantly into the receiver. "The hours have passed so slowly since I have last seen you. Please take an old man's loneliness away." He hung up with a smug nod.

A dozen of Colonel Napier's top security unit—men and women—began to edge into the side booths of the pub. They would remember this night for the rest of their lives, because they would be spending it in the same room as Desmond Logan, Reverend Rock 'n' Roll. One of them came over to Desmond and said, "Two or three of us have a few questions about the meaning of some of your lyrics, Rev. We know you must be tired after your concert this afternoon, but none of us got to hear you, on duty as we were, and it would be a great honor for all of us."

"Of course," Desmond said. "I'd be glad to talk to you." Desmond went with him across the room to where his companions waited.

Alone now, Matthew and Jordan eyed each other warily. "So!" Jordan said. "You've finally managed to best Harley. I should say it's about time!"

Matthew stared at her with as much dignity as he could muster.

"Matthew, you needn't look as if you've bitten into a green persimmon! The last time you looked at me with that expression was in Yenan, when you realized I was going to stay with Chuen-yup!"

"You're an impossible, self-centered woman!"

"And don't you just love it?"

"Your granddaughter is in danger," he said sternly. "Andrew is in danger." Then he blurted, "Why didn't you ever tell me *we* had a son?"

"You wouldn't have believed me. You would have thought Desmond was Harley's son. Don't pretend you wouldn't have, Matthew."

He shook his head.

"Then why didn't you get in touch with me by telephone five years ago when you were in Stockholm picking up your precious prize?"

Matthew looked down at his fingernails. "I was afraid, Jordan. Can you understand that? Some people are born for action, for love, and good times. Some people aren't. Every time I reach out for happiness, it's taken away from me."

"Poppycock! I've known you since we were children, and that self-pitying line doesn't wash with me."

Matthew answered with surprising strength. "Wait a minute! Who are you to grill me? Has your life been such a shining example?"

"You're right, of course. Hardly a day goes by that I don't think of Andrew. I've failed him all my life, and I'm failing him now. And I've failed Chuen-yee as well. But . . . all I can think of at the moment is you." She paused. "Fifty years ago—it was in this month, wasn't it?—we had an engagement party. Isn't that strange?"

"You were so beautiful. I couldn't believe my luck. You were everything that was bright and free in those days." Then he added lightly, "But you look much better now than you did in those caves."

"If things had only turned out the way they should have." The moment hung in the balance. "I suppose we'd be a stodgy couple tending our roses."

"Could I be properly introduced to my son?"

"Of course," she said, and stood. "I'll take you over."

Matthew remained seated. "Can't you bring him over here? He's with all those people."

"Get up, you snail!"

Matthew nervously stood and took her arm. Jordan whispered excitedly up into his face. "He's *absolutely* your son. He has your mother's beautiful eyes."

"I noticed."

"Look at the way he holds the crowd. Doesn't that remind you of how your father used to preach in the mission?"

Now, they stood in front of the booth where Desmond sat talking. Jordan gently waved away the security force and Desmond hesitantly got to his feet.

Matthew took a deep breath. "I'm sorry," he said to Desmond, and his apology extended to Jordan as well. "If I'd only known—but of course I should have known."

Desmond, embarrassed, took refuge in flippancy. "Well, at least I'm not a child of divorce," he said. "And don't worry. It's done wonders for my image to have a missing father."

A girl stuck a coin into a jukebox at the far end of the pub and Matthew cringed at the noise. Desmond said, "That's one of my songs, sir. How do you like it?"

"It's very nice. It's very interesting. But years in China have wrecked my ear for Western tonality and I'm afraid I don't quite get the drift of the lyrics."

"People from the older generation usually say that." Desmond allowed a girl to pull him out onto the pub's tiny dance floor.

Matthew turned back to Jordan. She looked up at him expectantly. "Dancing makes you pregnant," he said. "That's the way I was brought up."

"The story of my life," she said.

Tentatively, he put his arms around her.

Midnight on the mezzanine. Translators had been brought in with computerized print-outs of every stockholder in Compton Fitch Enterprises. Tai-ling's own attorneys, who had flown across the Atlantic on the Concorde, would spend the next two or three hours transferring all her stock in CFE. The translators painstakingly checked off the other shareholders, talking one moment in fluent German, making the next phone call in halting Czech. Harley had been in touch with Andrew's ex-wife, Pamela; his partner in shipping, Horace Westphall; and all of his bankers.

At three in the morning, Tai-ling went to Harley and massaged the back of his neck. "You've done as much as you can. Now it's best if you get some sleep. You'll need all your strength tomorrow morning."

Harley looked at Tai-ling, put his head down on the desk, and said, "I don't know what else I can do. I don't know if this is going to work."

In the hotel pub, a kind of plague mentality had set in, a sense of the fragility of life, a knowledge that no matter what the morrow might bring, tonight was made for love. Napier's security unit had stacked their guns by Mrs. Botsford's cash register and danced. Every girl had a turn to put her arms around Desmond.

Chuen-yup excused himself to make more phone calls to the Duchess. He talked with the press as he waited at the main entrance of the Regatta Hotel.

"It is very exciting here," he said. "All are very brave in the face of imminent disaster. It is a wonderful example of countries working together in international friendship."

Finally his waiting was rewarded as he heard, from the outskirts of the crowd of journalists, an imperious female voice. "Stand back, please. I come with a message from the Queen."

"Is it my coveted plum blossom, that flower as delicate as a spring breeze, yet so strong that she can withstand even the snows of winter?"

"Hardly winter, Mr. Nyi," said the Duchess of Dorset as she joined him. "I should say both of us are scarcely into the fall of our years. Your gallantry, though well meant, is, I fear, misplaced." The Duchess passed him and went into the dark bar. She had dressed for this encounter as if she were a Tolstoyan heroine just in from Siberian snows, trailing a fur neckpiece and wearing a good portion of her jewelry. A fur cap perched on her short curls. "I come with a message from the

Queen. She knows the traditions of England will inspire and uphold you all and she has charged me with bringing this lad here to see his father."

Just behind her, Paul Granger appeared, his hair uncombed, his tie loose. "Dad! I was so afraid I'd never see you again." He crossed the room and put his arms around his father. "If anything had happened to you without my saying . . ."

Matthew said, "I hope you can forgive me. I loved you very much, but—"

"I know, I know."

As Jordan watched all this, seeing Matthew's son, a son who might have been theirs, Chuen-yup came to her and pulled her aside. "Until this moment I have not found an appropriate time to tell you about Chuen-yee."

"I was afraid to ask."

"He is alive and being cared for. That's all you need to know at this time. He will survive. I know it."

"I have missed him, but, knowing you, I have never really feared for his safety."

Jordan turned to greet Paul Granger. "I fell in love with your father before you were born. Then, when I met your father again, in China . . . I never meant your mother any harm."

"My mother is a senator now," Paul said. "She has become an American institution. She would have been deprived of all that if she had stayed with my father or—if my father had stayed with her." He changed the subject. "I've heard that Reverend Rock 'n' roll is here tonight. I've always wanted to meet him."

Mrs. Botsford handed him a drink and he disappeared into the gloom. The Duchess explained to Chuen-yup that there were twelve kinds of Pimm's Cup and he suggested that before the night was over he would like to sample each of them. They staked out a corner booth and began a long, intimate conversation.

Jordan took a deep breath and looked up at Matthew. "I know I should be worried about Angela and Andrew. And I *am*. But right now, just to see you again, Matthew . . ."

"We're in the eye of a storm," Matthew said. "If when we were twenty someone had said that we would meet again after twenty, thirty, forty, almost fifty years, I would have found it impossible to believe."

"Some people are like magnets. They draw others to them. I read an American novel that said there are only two hundred people in the world, and the rest is done with mirrors." Jordan paused. "Matthew, we've always been drawn together. Neither one of us can deny it."

He looked around the room. "It's quite amazing, isn't it, the family you and I have managed to put together in the last fifty years? We've managed to cover the world." He stood. "Come on, Jordan," he said. "Here's my plan. We pry a couple of Pimm's Cups away from Chuen-yup and the Duchess. We'll have one more dance and then find a comfortable booth."

She gave him a look of frosty dignity.

"Just some sleep," he said. "Don't get your hopes up."

"Well!"

Gray light showed in the porthole. Angela was more than grateful for night to be over. Joe and Ray had untied her an hour after taking possession of the yacht. They considered her father too weak to be a threat. Angela and Andrew spent a restless night in the stateroom.

Father and daughter talked and dozed and talked some more. They speculated on what was going on in the outside world and the mental stability of their captors. At one point during the long night hours, Raymond opened the door, leaned in, and said, "Joseph and I want you to be sure to understand that we're doing this only in the cause of world peace." He slammed the door and left.

This was no way to work for peace, Angela thought. This would only provoke violence, and she and her father were the targets. Although she feared for herself, she was desperately worried over Andrew. He was extremely ill. At times during the night he grew incoherent. He suffered an illness that went beyond alcoholism. She'd known for years he was gay and she'd heard rumors (before she had left for England) of a tenacious pneumonia that afflicted a few of her father's friends in San Francisco.

At a little before five in the morning, Joseph brought in a tray of tea and toast. "It won't be long now," he said. "They're meeting our demands. You'll be back with your family soon." He left and locked the door again.

Andrew lay flat on the bed, his face gray and damp.

"Daddy," Angela said, "you've got to eat something. Just sit up and try. . . ."

"It's been a long time since you've called me that. I know I haven't ever been a father to you. You had so much love from everyone else, and I had so little. I was jealous!"

"Daddy, I never had you! And I never knew why."

He smiled up at her tear-stained face. "Don't worry, Angie. I'll find some way to get us out of this. I won't let them hurt you. They can't hurt my little girl."

He closed his eyes, but kept a firm grip on her hand.

At five in the morning, Harley Fitch held a last meeting with Colonel Napier. "Remember," he cautioned the colonel, "there is to be no violence. I don't trust the military and I never have. I've supplied too many munitions to too many hotheads. I know that a mild man who holds an Uzi can turn into a murderer with a flip of the safety."

"Mr. Fitch," the colonel said, "our country owes both you and your corporation a great debt. You have armed us against any and all enemies of the Empire, and we are more grateful than we can say. We've set up a human cordon along the embankment just above the yacht. The men are armed. But you must remember that we are dealing here with a media event that has international implications. We must send a direct signal to terrorists everywhere. They cannot defy the British Empire and expect to be scolded by policemen with billy clubs."

"But . . ."

"It's just a spectacle," the colonel repeated. "It's simply for the cameras. Show the flag and all that." He pulled himself up to a military stance. "Sir, I appreciate all you've done, but perhaps it's time now for you to go on downstairs and get a bite of grub. Have some tea and do shave, sir. You want to look well when you go on the yacht. There'll be cameras everywhere."

The colonel waited until Harley disappeared. Then he picked up a radio phone. "Well, the old bull has finally gone off to graze," he said. "I expect everything will go off without a hitch. But remember, Captain, we cannot appear to be knuckling under before terrorist forces of any kind."

By six in the morning, Mrs. Botsford had combed her hair, put on a fresh apron, and gone into the kitchen to prepare a real English breakfast for everyone in the hotel. She put out heavy skillets filled with sausages and stacked her oven with batches of scones and thirty dishes of shirred eggs.

In the pub's morning light, people appeared to have fallen asleep as in a fairy tale—dozing over drinks along the bar or up against the walls. Desmond lay flat on his back on the floor. His body was covered by sleeping girls snuggled against him like a litter of puppies. Chuen-yup and the Duchess were still awake, still drinking, utterly engrossed. In a corner Matthew sat up straight, his eyes closed. Jordan's head lay on his shoulder.

Harley woke them. Tersely, he told them of the night's progress. With his old disdainful competitiveness, he said, "I suppose it will be just you and me, Matt. We keep Desmond here until we've made our settlement and gotten Angela back. But, remember, there's no real reason for you to go. I'm the one who'll be taking them the money. And, of course, it's my granddaughter they've got."

Matthew could only sigh. "Of course I'm going. Don't be an ass, Harley."

Jordan, wiping the sleep from her eyes like a little girl, said, "And I'm going too."

"You can't go," Harley said.

Matthew nodded his head. "For once he's right."

"How are either of you going to stop me?"

Mrs. Botsford came in, cupping her hands to her mouth, and shouted in tones she hadn't used since she had been an air-raid warden during the Second War, "Breakfast is served and I'm sure you'll all need it. Let's hop to it, boys and girls."

The Thames reflected bright sunlight as the door of the Regatta Hotel opened and three elderly persons stepped out briskly into the deserted High Street. A tiny woman rushed after them, threw her arms around one of the men, who held her tightly and muttered in her ear, "I love you, Tai-ling. I always have. Never forget it." She left him and stood in the hotel's entrance, looking lost and frail as she stood next to a tall gaunt woman who sported a fur cap on top of her curls.

Jordan, Matthew, and Harley crossed the wide street. The human cordon, a group of armed and burly soldiers, each one carrying an Uzi, opened up for them. The trio walked a little stiffly down the embankment to the river and waited as the *Angela*'s gangplank was lowered.

Harley growled under his breath to Matthew, "If anything happens, for God's sake, keep Jordan out of the line of fire."

One by one, they walked up the gangplank and stepped

out onto the quarter deck. Matthew pulled Jordan back by the railing while Harley strode out into the center of the deck and shouted, "Simpson, Barnes, we're here. There's no point in any of us playing games. We have everything you want."

A pair of shuttered doors swung open and four figures emerged. Angela and Andrew stood directly in front of Barnes and Simpson, who held handguns. Matthew saw that these were no more than boys, as young and inexperienced as the confused thugs sent by the warlord to kidnap Harley so many years ago. Harley, with a surge of fury, realized that his own love for Angela must have allowed him to be hoodwinked by these two punks. This was obviously no terrorist group. Jordan took it all in, too, but her glance went directly to her son. Why couldn't Andrew have *done* something? How could he have allowed his own daughter to be victimized like this? In spite of herself, she felt a wave of familiar scorn.

"There's no one else here?" Harley asked, trying to confirm what his own eyes had already told him.

Raymond Barnes, who held Andrew, answered, "That's right, sir. We wanted to make a statement separate from the demonstration, and we thought this would be the best way."

"But remember," Simpson interrupted, "we still have your daughter, and one bullet can blow her away."

Jordan could no longer control her indignation. "And this is your idea of bringing about peace in the world?"

"Let's get on with it," Harley said. "I've brought the shares. And Matthew Granger is here"—his voice dripped with scorn—"'to deplore the world situation.' You'll get your Reverend Rock 'n' Roll as soon as Angela's safe on shore."

Simpson and Barnes looked at each other. The tension rose. Nobody moved. Then Barnes said, finally, "I guess that's it."

"Good. Now, if you'll let Angela—and Andrew—come forward . . ."

As Harley extended his hand with the briefcase, and Simpson loosened his grip on Andrew so that he might take the shares, Andrew suddenly shook himself free and shouted, "Now, Dad!"

"*No!*" Harley bellowed, but Andrew pushed Simpson to the ground, took hold of Angela, and thrust her behind him. It was Andrew who took the bullet from Barnes's gun in the back of the head.

Harley and Matthew acted almost as one: Matthew

knocked Jordan flat to the deck and shielded her with his own body while Harley did the same with Angela. During the next sixty seconds the deck of the *Angela* was raked by on-shore Uzi bullets. In the silence that followed, Matthew called out shakily, "Hold your fire!" He looked down into Jordan's frightened eyes. Then, cautiously, he crawled along the deck past the bodies of Simpson and Barnes to Harley Fitch.

Harley lay across his granddaughter in a widening pool of blood. Matthew heard Angela's hysterical whimpers as he hooked an arm under Harley's shoulders. Using all his strength, he flipped him over. Angela screamed as she pushed her grandfather's steaming intestines from her body.

Matthew lifted Harley's head into the crook of his elbow. "You saved Angela's life."

"Thank God. . . ." Harley's eyes were already glazing over.

"Don't talk," Matthew said. "Help is on its way. You're going to be fine."

"You always were—a bad liar." Harley's body convulsed. He gave Matthew a big, triumphant, bloody grin. "Meet . . . you . . . at . . . 110 Shanghai . . ." His eyes opened wide as the life seeped out of him. With death's last shudder, he stuttered, "T-Tai-ling . . ."

Ten days later, at the center of the curving avenue leading to The Beeches, Tai-ling watched from her limousine as Angela lingered on the steps with her grandmother and Matthew Granger. A discreet touch of her manicured fingernail brought the window down far enough for her to hear what they were saying.

"I'm still not sure I'm ready to do this," Angela said. "Interrupting my studies . . . Is that what Grandpa Harley would have wanted?"

"I knew that man," Jordan said. "The truth is he didn't give a hoot about education. He loved his business because that was the way he could get the best of people. Competition was his life. Remember, those shares that your grandfather were going to sign over to your kidnappers don't strictly belong to anyone right now. This is your chance to take control of the company and do some real good in the world. You'll get the better of all of them, my dear."

Tai-ling allowed herself a slow sad smile. Matthew

Granger was coming down the stairs and across the gravel. He rapped on the window and she rolled it down an inch farther.

"We haven't had a chance to really talk," he said. "I wanted to tell you how brave you were in the old days when you used to help my mother with the orphan children. You were her favorite student. I'll never forget all that and you mustn't either."

She watched his face, which, to her eyes, looked remarkably like his father's when he was in the middle of a long sermon. "In the end, Tai-ling, the past is all we've got."

She laughed in his face. "Don't be so pious, Matthew! And don't idealize the past. The past is when your best friend raped your fiancée! Haven't you ever wondered why? Harley was in a rage that night." With cool satisfaction, she watched his face crease in pain. "Harley and I had been lovers before he found out we had the same father. Otherwise, I'm sure he never would have touched your pale blond friend." Tai-ling continued, "There's no point in mourning a past that robbed you of all your joy. The past is nothing unless you let it be. The future can be everything, if you want it. Perhaps the time has come for you to take what's really yours."

After a last round of embraces, Angela said good-bye, was handed into the backseat of the limousine by Matthew, and pulled a chinchilla lap rug up over her knees. As the limo left the grounds of The Beeches, Tai-ling was ready with a crystal goblet of champagne.

"To the two of us," Tai-ling said. "And to Compton Fitch Enterprises."

The girl drank and cautiously peered over the rim of the glass. Again, Tai-ling smiled. She had loved Harley Fitch for most of her life, and he was gone, but she still had the girl. Harley's blood ran in Angela's veins, but it remained to be seen whether she had Harley's ferocious appetite for dominance. The next decade promised to be interesting.

Jordan and Matthew went back inside The Beeches. In the drawing room, they settled down to a plate of smoked trout and a pitcher of Jordan's martinis.

"What will you do now?" she asked guardedly.

"Whatever decision I make will depend on you."

"No, no, no, no, no! You can't play that game with me anymore. Whatever you do is your decision, not mine."

Matthew set down his drink, and for a moment Jordan regretted her sharp tongue.

"For the last fifty years, you've been conceited, self-centered, rude, and overbearing. And that's just the top of the list!" He took her in his arms and kissed her. Then he said, "Is this the only way to keep your mouth shut?"

"What rot!"

He grinned at her and said, "I've been thinking. I have an extensive farm on the upper banks of the Whangpoo, just a few *li* from the Lungwha Pagoda, where we first fell in love. We're going back there to live out our days together. I've booked us on a slow, a very slow, boat to China. . . ."

"Whatever you say."

"It'll be a long voyage. Rio, Caracas, Athens, Melbourne, Dakar. We'll have many adventures before we get home, my darling."

Jordan sighed. "I've had adventures, Matthew, but it's been so long since I've had a man to love."

But they were too intelligent to base the rest of their lives on mere romance. Matthew Granger was given, as a token of the Chinese Government's esteem, a town house in Shanghai—the former home of the British distributor of the reparation funds from the Boxer Rebellion. Jordan Logan-Fisher's artistic reputation in the People's Republic was officially rehabilitated. She was extended a separate invitation to return to China so that she might continue to record the pictorial history of the most populous country in the world. Chuen-yup, when he found that Jordan would be coming home, made arrangements for Chuen-yee's release. He also began a long courtship by correspondence with the Duchess of Dorset so that Jordan might not lack either family or friends in the sunset of her life—or so he told himself. Paul and Desmond promised to visit once a year. The machinations of Compton Fitch Enterprises remained half a world away. Whoever won in that clash of Amazons, it would be of little consequence to the new, elite, foreign colony of Shanghai.

Six months later, the *Heavenly Peace* took advantage of the evening tide as it chugged slowly upriver into the mouth of the Whangpoo. The captain's eyes rested on a middle-aged couple who, arm in arm, scanned the Chinese horizon for the first twinkling lights of the pulsing, thriving—but always mysterious—metropolis of Shanghai.

Acknowledgments

For overall general information as well as specific details, the author is indebted to *The White-Boned Demon*, by Ross Terrill; *Son of the Revolution*, by Liang Heng and Judith Shapiro; *Red China Today*, by Edgar Snow; *Chen Village*, by Anita Chan, Richard Madsen, and Jonathan Unger; *China Winter*, by Eduarda Mansi; *Battle Hymn of China*, by Agnes Smedley; *The Soong Dynasty*, by Sterling Seagrave; *Unfinished Business in China*, by Mary Ellen Saunders; *Chinese Secrets and the U.S. Presidency*, by Dragon Chu; *Quotations from Chairman Mao Tse-tung*; and *Who Killed Joe McCarthy?* by William Bragg Ewald, Jr.

The author wishes to thank Clara Sturak for her enduring patience; Elaine Markson, who guided this craft upriver; and Daniel Weaver, who became through his editing an Old China Hand.

M.H.

Notes

Prologue

Although the standard Wade-Giles system of romanization of Chinese forms the base of this book's transliterations, it is frequently departed from in the interest of making words more easily pronounced by Western readers. Thus, some names combine sound elements common to Cantonese with others drawn from the Shanghai dialect and Mandarin. In a few instances the unpublished notes of Terrence Laughlin on the Wu (Shanghai) dialect have been drawn upon, but the basic reference work is the Reverend F. L. Hawks Pott's *Lessons in the Shanghai Dialect* (Revised Edition, 1934). However, for certain names of later dates, the Pinyin modernization has been adopted, as in Madame Mao's name—Jiang Qing.

Liberties have been taken in the personal names of the warlord Nyi Chuen-yao's family. Instead of using different praenomina to distinguish between generations, Chuen has been used for each in order to avoid confusion.

Street and waterfront urchins in Shanghai used to taunt foreigners with a singsong chant that ran:

Ih, nien, san, se, sze wan, tloo, tlee, foh,
Hoo lung seh sze sut teem boh,
Wan Sze-jing sze com pla doh,
Mei koh nyung sze dam fo loh.

Put into more standard English this reads:

One, two, three, four is one, two, three, four
Hoo lung seh is a steamboat,
Wang Sze-jing is a comprador,
Americans are damn fools.

Wang Sze-jing was indeed one of Shanghai's leading compradors, used by a variety of Caucasian as well as Chinese families.

Book I

Out of deference to the feminist movement, "single women" has been used to designate the unmarried missionaries, though in actual usage of the time they were called "single ladies." In urban Shanghai, *radees* referred to respectable Western females; *oomung* were those who sold their favors for a fee.

The explanation for the name of the Boxers given in the text reflects an error held for many years in which the word *chuan* of the organization's name was misinterpreted as meaning "fist" rather than "group" or "society."

Book III

Herbert Yardley, self-styled cryptographer and *bon vivant*, suffered greatly from bronchitis and alcohol poisoning during his World War II stay in Chungking, where he complained equally of the foot-long rats and the fact that Chiang Kai-shek gave him nothing of importance to decode.

Book IV

The restoration of the Summer Palace was one of the Empress Dowager's pet projects. She is reported to have appropriated a large sum of money intended by the Foreign Office for the strengthening of the Chinese Navy and used it to construct a white marble boat for her own entertainment in the waters of the lake on which the main structures front.

Book V

For more information on the great San Francisco oil slick and the bird "hospital" that was set up on the shore beside the

Cliffhouse, see Carolyn See's "The Veterinarian," part of a longer series on "Work in America" that appeared in *The Atlantic Monthly* and received a Sidney Hillman award in 1971.

The two girls who followed Mick Jagger across the nation, pledged to sleep with him together or not at all, were noted in the popular press of the day. They coined the phrase, "He was great, but he wasn't Mick Jagger," and, of course, applied it to Mr. Jagger when the time came.

The author of *The Art of T. S. Eliot* and editor of Donne's devotional poems, the first woman to hold the Merton Professorship of English Literature at Oxford, Helen Louise Gardner, was created Dame of the Order of the British Empire in 1967.

Book VI

Madame Mao's brutal art criticism is quoted directly from Chen-jicai's *Chrysanthemums*, a collection of stories depicting daily life in the Cultural Revolution (1966–77). Chen-jicai was—by his own account—so threatened by Jiang Qing's reign of terror that he would write a page, read it, then throw it directly into the fire. These stories alone survive that period.

The public rooms of the Randolph Hotel at Oxford are actually decorated by Osbert Lancaster's illustrations of Max Beerbohm's classic *Zuleika Dobson*.

The wall between Rhodes House and Wadham College was indeed breached on the occasion of the Rhodes Reunion. The scenes involving members of the Royal Family are, of course, entirely fictitious beyond the garden party itself. And the Thames Conservancy Board has yet to explain how the *Angela* was able to sail as far upstream as Henley.

As to the larger matters of fiction, I have taken several liberties with precise historical events, both as to date and content in such matters as Senator McCarthy's role in his investigations, and Mme Chiang's exact wording in her Hollywood Bowl address. The same is true in relationship to the American government's role in our recent cultural history, as well as the scheduled hours of particular television shows—and their sponsorship.

SPECTACULAR ENTERTAINMENT ALL SUMMER LONG!
SUMMER SPECTACULAR FREQUENT READERS SWEEPSTAKES
WIN *A 1988 Cadillac Cimarron* Automobile or
12 other Fabulous Prizes

IT'S EASY TO ENTER. HERE'S HOW IT WORKS:

1. Enter *one* individual book sweepstakes, by completing and submitting the Official Entry form found in the back of that Summer Spectacular book, and you qualify for that book's prize drawing.

2. Enter *two* individual book sweepstakes, by completing and submitting two Official Entry Forms found in the back of those two Summer Spectacular books, and you qualify for the prize drawings for those two individual books.

3. Enter *three or more* individual book sweepstakes, by completing and submitting—in one envelope—three or more Official Entry forms found in the back of three or more individual Summer Spectacular books, and you qualify not only for those three or more individual books but also for THE BONUS PRIZE of a brand new Cadillac Cimarron Automobile!

Be sure to fill in the Bantam bookseller where you learned about this Sweepstakes . . . because if you win one of the twelve Sweepstakes prizes . . . your bookseller wins too!

SEE OFFICIAL RULES BELOW FOR DETAILS including alternate means of entry.

No Purchase Necessary.

Here are the Summer Spectacular Sweepstakes Books and Prizes!

BOOK TITLE	PRIZE
On Sale May 20, 1987	
ACT OF WILL	A luxurious weekend for two (3 days/2 nights) at first class hotel, MAP meals—(transportation not included) Approximate value: $750.00
MEN WHO HATE WOMEN & THE WOMEN WHO LOVE THEM	Gourmet food of the month for 6 months N.Y. Gourmet Co. Approximate value: $750.00
VENDETTA	Schrade Collector's Knife set Approximate value: $750.00
On Sale June 17, 1987	
LAST OF THE BREED	Sharp Video Camera and VCR Approximate value: $1,600.00

WHITE DOVE (available in US only) THE MOTH (available in Canada only)	Lenox China white coffee service Approximate value: $750.00
THE BE (HAPPY) ATTITUDES	Set of DP workout equipment Approximate value: $1,000.00

On Sale July 15, 1987

THE UNWANTED	Bug Zapper and Samsonite Chairs— Table—Umbrella—Outdoor Furniture Approximate value: $1,300.00
A GRAND PASSION	Cake of the month plan Approximate value: $800.00
110 SHANGHAI ROAD	$1,000 American Express Gift Certificates Value: $1,000.00

On Sale August 12, 1987

HIS WAY	Disc Player with library of Sinatra discs Approximate value: $1,000.00
SUSPECTS	Home Security System Approximate value: $1,000.00
PORTRAIT OF A MARRIED WOMAN	Minolta Auto-Focus Camera Kit Approximate value: $750.00

OFFICIAL RULES

1. There are twelve individual sweepstakes, each with its own prize award. There will be twelve separate sweepstakes drawings. You will be entered into the drawing for the prize corresponding to the book(s) from which you have obtained your entry blank, any one or up to all twelve. Submit your completed entry on the Official Entry Form found in this book and any of the other participating books ... mail one or up to all twelve completed sweepstakes entries *in one envelope* to:

Frequent Readers Sweepstakes
PO Box 43 New York, New York 10046

2. NO PURCHASE NECESSARY TO ENTER OR WIN A PRIZE: Residents of Ohio and those wishing to obtain an Official Entry Form (covering all 12 sweepstakes) and the Official Rules send a self-addressed stamped envelope to: Frequent Reader Sweepstakes, P.O. Box 549, Sayreville, NJ 08872. One Official Entry Form per request. Requests must be received by August 14, 1987. Residents of Washington and Vermont need not include return postage.

3. Winners for each of the 12 sweepstakes will be selected in a random drawing to be conducted on or about October 19, 1987, from all completed entries received, under the supervision of Marden-Kane, Inc. an independent judging organization. If any of the 12 consumer winners selected have included completed Official Entry Forms from three or more books, or have included completed Official Entry Forms from three or more books, or have entered 3 or more sweepstakes on the Alternate Mail-In Official Entry Form (See Rule #2) they are qualified to participate in a separate BONUS DRAWING to be conducted on or about Oct. 19, 1987 for a 1988 Cadillac Cimarron. In the event that none of the twelve individual sweepstake prize winners qualify for the BONUS PRIZE, the bonus prize will be selected from all completed sweepstakes entries received. No mechanically reproduced entries accepted. All entries must be received by September 30, 1987 to be eligible. Not responsible for late, lost or misdirected mail or printing errors.

4. By entering this Sweepstakes, each entrant accepts and agrees to be bound by these rules and the decision of the judges which shall be final. Winners will be notified by mail and may be required to execute an Affidavit of Eligibility and Release which must be returned within 14 days of receipt. In the event of non-compliance within this time period, alternate winners will be selected. Winner(s) consent to the use of his/her name and/or photograph for advertising and publicity purposes without additional compensation. No substitution or transfer of prizes allowed (vacation prize subject to availability, and must be taken within one year of notification). Taxes, License and Title Fees are the sole responsibility of the prize winners. One prize (except for Bonus Prize) per family or household. Retailer named on winning twelve blanks will win duplicate sweepstakes prize. (Retailers are not eligible for bonus prize.)

5. Sweepstakes open to residents of the United States and Canada except employees and their families of Bantam Books, its affiliates and subsidiaries, advertising and production agencies and Marden-Kane, Inc. Void in the Province of Quebec and wherever else prohibited or restricted by law. Canadian residents will be required to answer a skill testing question in order to be eligible to receive a prize. All federal, state and local laws apply. Odds of winning a prize in each sweepstake depend upon the total number of completed entries received for that sweepstake. (All prizes will be awarded)

6. For a list of major prize winners, send a stamped, self-addressed envelope to: Frequent Readers Sweepstakes, c/o Marden-Kane, Inc., P.O. Box 711, Sayreville, NJ 08872.

---

110 SHANGHAI ROAD
OFFICIAL ENTRY FORM

Please complete by entering all the information requested and
Mail to: Frequent Readers Sweepstakes
P.O. Box 43
New York, N.Y. 10046

NAME _____

ADDRESS _____

CITY _____ STATE _____ ZIP _____

BANTAM BOOK RETAILER WHERE YOU LEARNED ABOUT THIS SWEEPSTAKES

NAME _____

ADDRESS _____

CITY _____ STATE _____ ZIP _____

Completed entries must be received by September 30, 1987 in order to be eligible.

ISBN-0553-26572-5